# RECOVERY

# RECOVERY

## John Martin

iUniverse, Inc.
New York   Bloomington

# RECOVERY

Copyright © 2010 by John Martin

iUniverse books may be ordered through booksellers or by contacting:

iUniverse
1663 Liberty Drive
Bloomington, IN 47403
www.iuniverse.com
1-800-Authors (1-800-288-4677)

Because of the dynamic nature of the Internet, any Web addresses or links contained in this book may have changed since publication and may no longer be valid. This is a work of fiction. All of the characters, names, incidents, organizations, and dialogue in this novel are either the products of the author's imagination or are used fictitiously.

ISBN: 978-1-4502-0555-9 (pbk)
ISBN: 978-1-4502-0556-6 (ebk)

Printed in the United States of America

iUniverse rev. date: 1/18/2010

•

Other books by John F. Martin

Deployment

*To my family, who puts up with me and my writing.*

*And remember*

*Everyday young American men and women volunteer to stand on the ramparts, so the rest of us don't have to.*

# PROLOGUE

There wasn't any more movement on the road. The mechanical ambush, claymore mines spaced out the length of the killing zone, had done its job well. The added automatic weapons fire from both sides of the pass had convinced anyone left alive that there was no profit in firing back, unless they were determined to collect on the promise of virgins in paradise. It was time to grab Sharp and head to the pick up point. The rest of the convoy should be well on its way to the border and the cover of the French gun ships.

He could make out Sharps position in the light of the burning trucks. His last radio call wasn't good. He had been hit, but Grant didn't know how badly. Sharp had already picked up a hole in his leg before, in the raid on Al Fashir. They had taken heavy casualties on that run, but they had rescued the American congressmen and their party. It hadn't been a fair trade. Dillinghouse, the senior congressman, had been about as self centered as a politician could get. He even complained about having the bodies of the soldiers who died saving his ass on the same plane that flew him out of Africa. At least a camera crew had caught it on tape.

Sharp was slumped against a boulder, barely conscious. It was quicker for Grant to hoist him over his shoulder and head for the medics than to try to strip his body armor and gear and poke around in the dark. Grant hadn't gone far when he ran into the stretcher team. Elko, the medic, had them drop Sharp on the litter and stripped off his armor. She asked where he was hit, then used a penlight to illuminate the wound. A wadded up bandage was jammed against the hole. Sharp got a shot of morphine, and an IV was started. She would replace fluids for the couple of hundred yard run to the trucks. Once there, she could get some more light and try to stabilize him. The French had agreed to a medevac mission a few miles further on. If she could stabilize him until then, the French doctors could probably keep him alive.

Grant wanted to know if everyone was accounted for.

"We've got everybody. You two are the last," First Sergeant Harrison responded.

"Casualties?"

"We lost three more dead, a couple more wounded. Sharp's the worst. You OK?"

"Yeah, I'm fine. Let's get out of here. See if we can't get the French to meet us closer to the border. Sharp won't make it much further than that."

Harrison got his men loaded. He was the First Sergeant, that was his job. Grant slumped down in the back of the truck, watching the medics work on Sharp. The medics had his bleeding under control, and they were trying to force fluids into him to replace his blood loss. He was in critical shape.

The truck started moving, all available weapons pointed out, just in case. Grant slid out and walked over to Harrison's vehicle, pulled off to the side watching the convoy pass.

"What happened to the Arabs?" Harrison asked.

"I don't know. When that last group came through, there was one hanging back. After we tripped the claymores, he turned around and headed back to the barn. Nobody else came down the road." He looked at Harrison in the faint glow of the medic's lights. He didn't look good. "How about you, Ralph? How are you holding up?"

The First Sergeant just shook his head. It looked like that simple move took some effort. "I'm starting to run out of steam." He took out a small brown vial and popped a pill. "And maybe a touch of angina. Sorry, Luke."

Grant reached over and squeezed his arm. "If we get a bird for Sharp, you get on it too. You've done enough for me this trip."

Ali Alawa Sharif's vehicle stopped in front of Hakim Mousada. In the east, the sun was just starting to rise. The camp was filling up as the word spread that the infidels had slipped by to the north. The ambush positions were being abandoned. Hakim Mousada wanted to know what happened. Sharif would not answer. Word would spread soon enough that he had ordered his driver to flee the ambush rather than share the fate of his fighters. The road to the north was littered with Arab dead, and all the Americans had escaped. He could only guess how they would judge him, but he knew it would not be merciful.

Hakim Mousada was giving orders. The government had agreed to more peace talks, and the African Union was sponsoring them in a neutral country. It was only a matter of days before African peacekeepers started to return.

Sharif was unconvinced. "This plan will fail like the rest of them. We will see to it. Darfur will be Arab, as will all of Sudan, then all of Africa. It is the will of Allah."

"Maybe so, Ali Alawa, but no one is interested in more fighting right now. These Americans were fierce, and they killed many fighters."

"They were also bled. That is something they are unprepared to accept. This will be like Somalia. I doubt we will see them again."

# CHAPTER 1

"Welcome home, Sergeant Sharp"

Sharp looked around the Sergeant Major's office. It wasn't much, just a desk and a few ratty chairs. "Not what I'd expect to find you in. I've seen better quarters in a boneyard."

Lucas Grant could only smile at the reference. They had once spent a couple of days in Central America in a hide at the edge of a cemetery. There was a mausoleum just off to the side. They had used it to cache their extra equipment. "Dave, the 289th has indeed fallen on hard times. This is not the hard charging National Guard we went to Africa with. There are some powerful people who have decided that we're an embarrassment, and they don't like us anymore. I'm sure you've been following the story."

Sharp had. Hell, a blind moron would have been able to follow the story of the American soldiers who had managed to destabilize Sudan and ruin all of the United Nation efforts to bring relief to the refugees. There had been a massive campaign in the Arab world to advertise the "slaughter" of the Janjaweed freedom fighters. There had been little or no mention of the extermination of the refugee camp by the Janjaweed poison gas attack, poison gas provided by the mullahs in Teheran. Instead, every story seemed to lead off with a burning American vehicle on the streets of Al Fashir, complete with charred bodies inside, and dead Africans scattered around it. That had been Major Halvorson's Hummer, knocked out by a direct RPG hit. The bodies had been planted after the fact. Grant's men had taken more casualties making sure no American bodies had been left behind, a point that had even been ignored in the US.

Both soldiers knew why they were taking so much bad press. It could be traced back to Congressman Walter Dillinghouse, the idiot so many Americans had died trying to rescue. His behavior had been less than heroic, or even politically correct. He had argued with Halvorson about leaving his bags behind (containing a hefty quantity of blood diamonds, courtesy of the Janjaweed), sobbed and soiled himself on the ride out of Al Fashir, then tried to have the American bodies and wounded removed from his evacuation plane. It had all been captured on video, but Dillinghouse had managed to get most of the footage confiscated or classified so it couldn't be shown. He was planning hearings to orchestrate getting his version of events into the public eye. To do it, he was planning to offer up the 289th as war criminals to whoever wanted them.

He was being well paid for his efforts, and the Janjaweed had arranged for his diamonds to be replaced by the Sudanese delegation at the UN.

Even the United Nations was screaming for American blood. The local High Commissioner for Refugees had been snubbed in his efforts to get American engineers to do extensive work on his properties in the Darfur region. Once the Sudanese Liberation Army rolled into town, the Americans had also refused to help him evacuate his assets, including a very expensive Mercedes Benz. His report was only slightly more negative about the 289th than Dillinghouse.

"That would explain why none of the kids have gotten any recognition for this fiasco yet."

"Yeah, we're the hot potato. The Pentagon is waffling about the 'Combat Zone' status of Sudan. Dillinghouse got to somebody over there. In the meantime, we don't know whose chain of command we're in. Central Command say that now we're in Europe, we belong to USAREUR (US Army, Europe) USAREUR tried to shift us back to the National Guard Bureau, but they claimed once we're federalized they have no control, so USAREUR pushed us over to NATO. NATO said no way, they had no interest in African operations, and since we didn't have any equipment or a NATO mission, we couldn't be a NATO asset."

"So who owns us?"

"Right now, we defaulted to Corps. They aren't thrilled, but there's nobody left to hand us off to. We're getting used as post engineers and detail people. And they won't take our award recommendations. They keep coming back with the comment 'No Authority to Approve.' You may have come back to a hard luck outfit. Maybe you should have taken the discharge."

That was an offer the Army had made to all the wounded soldiers while they were recovering. A few had accepted the offer. Sharp had considered it for a while, but the reality of his life smacked him in the face. "C'mon, Luke. What the hell did I have to get out for? Where was I when you found me for this? I was a fucking drunk who couldn't even keep a bimbo interested in me. At least here you keep me dried out and in shape. I even get to hold on to some self respect."

"I keep getting you shot up. That's not much to look forward to."

"Beat's the alternative." Sharp stared at him for a moment. Then broke out into a grin. "You guys are the only family I need or want. Now show me where my bunk is and tell me who else is back."

"Grab your gear. I'll take you there."

First Sergeant Ralph Harrison had been in and out of Army units for 20 years, but he had never seen one that could get disorganized as fast as the 289th Engineer Support Command. He had only been in the hospital recovering from his latest heart attack for a few weeks, and his temporary replacement, Master Sergeant Winder, had managed to completely fuck up everything. As the senior uninjured NCO, Winder was tapped to fill the slot. Unfortunately for the unit, Winder used the excuse of doing two jobs to do neither, and abuse his authority in both. Casualties had caused a lot of shuffling of positions, and instead of trying to help sort out the confusion, Winder contributed to it and used it as an alibi.

The first and most important problem Harrison had to correct was the manning chart and strength report. Up until the moment he had been loaded on a Medevac chopper, Harrison had been meticulous in accounting for his soldiers. Winder had ignored his notes, and pretty much ignored everything else. He hadn't kept track of where casualties were being treated, or their status. They weren't accounted for when they were discharged from the Army, or returned to the unit. He had no accurate listing of replacements that had been provided by the

National Guard home station, and had no idea where the active unit supplements, the Intelligence section, Water Treatment and Satellite Commo were. It was worse than when he had first taken over from the old First Sergeant, Perrone. He had been useless, but at least he could count heads.

He was lucky that he had a good working relationship with the Personnel NCO, Staff Sergeant Sheila Gordon. It was also fortunate that, for any personal foibles she might have had, she kept good records, and, if she didn't have the records, she kept the loose documents that might come in handy later. He would have preferred to work with the S-1 herself, Captain Bonneville, but the section had staggered their post-Sudan leave time, and Bonneville had been the last to go. Her leave coincided with Harrison's return.

He was surprised Bonneville had gone and CSM Grant had stayed behind. Their relationship in the desert seemed to indicate that they would have gone on leave to the States together. It was only after he had spoken to Gordon that he realized that a unit in the field could get away with more than one under scrutiny in garrison, and their relationship had suffered. They were still friends, but distant. Harrison felt bad for his long time comrade. He knew Grant needed more around than him, Sharp and Price. He needed a good woman to anchor him.

Almost as bad as the strength reports were the duty rosters. Extra duties, such as KP, guard, CQ and Staff Duty need to be doled out fairly and equally. Nothing is worse for a young soldier's morale and attitude than to realize that his name comes up more often than anyone else in his squad or section does. It's also a mark of a poor NCO who lets that happen to his soldiers, and the 289th still had it's share of poor NCOs. Combine them with a lazy Senior NCO like Winder, and abuses ran wild. Instead of maintaining accurate rosters,

Winder would parcel out details according to his likes and dislikes. If an NCO had worked well with Grant and Sharp in the desert, he got the bulk of the lousy details. Even the NCO's who Winder blessed with the good details passed them off primarily to the young soldiers who had borne the bulk of the risks in Sudan. Having done a good job was it's own reward under the Winder regime. He had even let it be known that if anyone thought about going to the Sergeant Major, his Evaluation Report, and future promotion opportunities, would suffer. There was a collective sigh of relief when Harrison rebuilt the duty rosters, eliminated some unnecessary jobs and combined others. There wasn't much he could do about past inequities, but the soldiers knew they'd be treated fairly from now on. One thing Harrison could do was arrange for the poorly performing NCOs to pick up some subtle, extra duties and training, most of it after regular duty hours. Even the slow ones started getting the message and made efforts to improve.

Training schedules were out of whack, but there was little he could do about it. There was a lot of input from Corps that ate up their training time, plus demands from the local post commander who took delight in using the National Guard as his personal day labor pool. One Army, my ass, Harrison thought. There are still people out there who look at it as 'light green/dark green', meaning reserve/regular components.

Harrison was a professional. And he was exceedingly good at his job. He had long since realized that he couldn't get everything done at once, and if he concentrated on one particular chore, other things tended to get worse. His method was selective prioritization. A First Sergeant who's done his job long enough realizes that there are little aspects of a lot of seemingly unimportant or mundane tasks that are interrelated. If they can be properly identified and sorted out, you can create a real domino effect towards getting it all done. In this case, a proper roster was the key. A correct strength report, with accurate ranks and status, defined all the other issues. From there the duty rosters gelled, the rating plan for the NCOs laid itself out, and he knew who he had for instructors for the training schedule. Once those basics were taken care of, he could count on being able to delegate a lot of the mundane tasks back to where they belonged. In any organization there are certain people who excel in upward delegation. They can be so good at it, supervisors don't realize until too late that they're doing the work they pay other people for. Ralph Harrison wasn't one of those supervisors, and the NCOs soon realized it.

He also knew that information was power, and he made it a point to visit as many of the unit activities each day to see what was going on. A key to morale was the soldier had to be kept busy at meaningful tasks. They had to know that their supervisors were interested and involved in their duties, and that they had someone who would listen to them and give appropriate feedback. Right now, Harrison knew that his unit morale was crap. Being used as permanent duty troops was wearing thin on soldiers who had just been through some intensive combat. Not getting any of the recognition for it hurt too. The 289th had a lot of soldiers who were due awards for Sudan, and the Army playing with them like a political football was a betrayal.

First stop was the Sergeant Major. Harrison hadn't had much time to socialize with his old friend since his return, but now that the paperwork shuffle was ending, the hours would be shorter and they could try to catch up. Harrison would still be, in his wife's words, "a fat retired slug" if not for Grant calling him back in. His wife was being kind in her description. Harrison was settling into boredom and apathy. While his wife was active in local politics, and a pretty good financial planner, Ralph Harrison couldn't find anything exciting enough to get him out of the house. Willa didn't like the idea of him being back in the Army, especially with Grant, but she knew it was best for him.

"What's the word, Sergeant Major?"

Grant looked up from his desk to see Harrison leaning against the doorframe. "The word, my friend, is fucked up. Our beloved Corps commander and his loyal CSM have seen fit to swamp me in enough made-up paperwork to choke a horse."

Harrison looked over at the pile and raised his eyebrows. Grant continued. "Now the son of a bitch has me doing an after action report on every piece of equipment we lost."

"How hard can that be, Luke? We lost two Hummers and a Deuce and a half coming out of Al Fashir, a dozer and flat bed in the air strike, and we dumped one more deuce coming out. Where's the problem?"

Grant just shrugged. "After all the after action reports were collated, and the CID spooks swarmed everybody, it seems like I was identified as the 'combat leader' of our little expedition. Ergo, I get to explain a lot. He's got the maintenance section and the Engineer Equipment Officer doing the same thing. Every time I ask why I get a lecture about the responsibilities of a Command Sergeant Major. Seems like our beloved commander managed to wash his hands of what happened and pinned the blame on 'poor execution' by his junior officers and senior NCOs." He paused and took a sip of his coffee. It was cold. "Well, he is an ambitious Lieutenant Colonel who wants to be a full Colonel, not to mention National Guard. You really don't think the National Guard Bureau or the Governor is going to let one of their precious assets get beaten up when there's a genuine Regular Army hero to blame, do you?"

Grant wadded up a sheet of paper and tossed it at a wastebasket in the corner. Harrison looked over and saw that it was the latest in a pile of rejected sheets. "Combat losses I can account for. The motor pool kept pretty good records. What I can't explain, and what they keep hammering me on, is the shit we couldn't bring with us."

That was a problem. In the hurry to evacuate from Chad, they had to leave most of their equipment behind. The two C-5As and the C-141 pulled their light vehicles and cargo trucks, and, probably because they were active Army assets rather than National Guard, they grabbed the satellite truck and trailer and all the water section vehicles. That left over two dozen pieces of equipment behind.

"After the State Department nixed the idea of leaving our equipment behind as reparations to Sudan, I thought they were picking that stuff up on a space available basis?" Harrison asked.

"They are, but the French are running the stuff into the ground and stealing everything they can. They should have left a rear party to watch the stuff, but the French were hot to have us out, and everybody caved." He pulled out another sheet. "And all the maintenance is being charged off to our budget. The S-4 is going nuts. There's one 5 ton down there that's had 11 tires replaced already, and it still hasn't been moved. What they have managed to move is scattered from Diego Garcia to South Dakota. The Air Force is off loading it the first chance they get."

"Too bad they didn't do that with the B-17."

The B-17, the Wicked Witch, had been a side project. The bomber was found crashed in the Sudanese desert, left over from WW2. They had recovered it as a morale building exercise, and for shits and giggles they had arranged to have it shipped back to the States. It went out on the plane with the dead, wounded and congressmen. It had been a thorn in Harrison's side ever since. It was the first time Grant had thought about the plane, with its provocative nose art, in weeks.

"How is that a problem?"

Harrison sat down. "The manifest got lost. By the time the plane got to Andrews nobody could find anything on it. The base commander went ballistic when he saw it hauled off and dumped on his flight line. Guess who's name the crew chief could remember?"

"Yours?"

"You got it. They did some fast checking and came up with my home address. The Air Force sent me a bill for $13,527 for hauling it. I guess they charged me by the pound."

"Willa must have been thrilled."

"She was. Your name kept coming up. I don't think she likes you anymore."

"Did she ever?"

"Probably not, but it's a good thing it's a money market account she has us all in, or you'd be heavily invested in Enron." Years ago Harrison's wife had set up some investment plans for Ralph and his 'soldier friends' as she called them. She had been getting above average returns on their money, and Grant was probably the wealthiest Sergeant Major in the Army.

Grant asked, "What are you doing about it?"

"Willa checked around and found out what a B-17 carcass in any condition is worth. Seems that it's a pretty good return on the money. She whipped off a quick check, and as soon as the Air Force cashed it she turned her lawyer loose on them. She seems to think that if I'm getting billed to move it, it must be mine."

"The down side?"

"I'm sure Willa will let me know." He waved his hand, as if brushing it off. "Now, do you want to hear some good news?"

Grant just nodded. Good news was few and far between, and even the best news lately was usually all bad.

"Only four sets of boots out of the fold: the CO, the new XO, the S-1, and Price. Colonel Perkins and Major Carstairs are in DC for the hearings, Captain Bonneville is due back off leave in a few days, and Price is due out of the hospital in a day or so. If he takes leave he should be back in about three weeks." He paused. "How are things with you and the good Captain?"

Things hadn't been that good. When they got back from Africa Colonel Perkins had pulled them aside to 'counsel' them about their relationship and how it would be frowned on in Germany. Some one, and Grant suspected Master Sergeant Winder, had informed the Inspector General about the relationship. There had been a low-key investigation, but the people who really knew said nothing, and the people who didn't know only had rumors. It had blown over, but there was still some simmering under the surface. Harrison was aware of Winder and his back channel dealings. He had seen the mess he had made of the company in a few short weeks. "We have to get rid of Winder. He's really a parasite." He told his friend.

Grant agreed, but he knew he had been wrong to get involved in the first place. "Yeah, Ralph, but it's my own fault for thinking with the little head instead of the big one. When I decided not to take any leave that really iced it."

"Sorry, Luke. She was good for you. Now you'll probably just go out and get yourself shot at some more." He paused. "Oh wait. You were still doing that anyway. I guess the only difference is you'll come home to an empty sleeping bag and a cold MRE. Just like the rest of us peasants."

"You done busting my nuts?"

"Yeah, for now. Listen, I'm out making my rounds. Stop by my quarters after chow. We'll get some of the guys together and take Sharp out for a welcome home beer."

# CHAPTER 2

Staff Sergeant Jonah Price had taken a severe wound to his shoulder, among other places, in the ride out of Al Fashir. He had been one of the first casualties loaded on the evacuation bird. After some quick repairs at the French hospital in Abeche, Chad, he was transferred to Landstuhl in Germany, then on to Walter Reed. When he was allowed to wake up and decide on his own if he wanted his medication he made two discoveries. The first was that his arm hurt like hell, and the second was that as bad as it felt, when he started to twitch and flex his muscles, it wasn't as damaged as it looked. Unfortunately, he had developed a serious infection that kicked his ass and slowed his recovery.

The hospital stay was the longest he had experienced in his career, and he had had a bunch of them. This wound would earn him his 7th Purple Heart Medal, if the Army ever got around to issuing it. The delay was puzzling, both to him and the medical staff. Combat casualties normally got their awards on an expedited basis. There was an edge to knowing your peers recognized what you had been through, and that little boost was a big help in recovery. There was no question in anyone's mind that Price had been wounded in hostile action, but his paperwork kept coming back. It hadn't been denied, there just wasn't any action taken on it. The cover letter stated it had been 'deferred' for later review. No one had ever seen that comment before. Price didn't really care. It was just one more oak leaf cluster in an already crowded splash of color on his uniform, and being a bullet magnet wasn't a qualification he wanted to advertise. What he did care about was that he heard that the other wounded from Sudan were getting similar treatment. Price already had a Combat Infantry Badge, so not getting a Combat Action Badge, the new award for soldiers who weren't infantry who were getting shot at, didn't bother him. But the raid on Al Fashir was one hell of a cherry popping experience for troops who were normally involved in construction support. It took him a few days to find out who was screwing whom over.

He still had contacts in odd places, and one of them, who should have known better than to talk about it, let him know that there had been an effort to have Sudan declared a non-combat area, and an investigation was pending as to whether the 289th had 'grossly over-reacted' to the situation. The prime mover behind it was Congressman Walter Dillinghouse, who was now insisting that he and his party were never in any danger in Al Fashir. Dillinghouse was circulating the story that he had been making great inroads into solving the humanitarian crisis and ending sectarian violence in Darfur. His favorite quote, and one that cost him quite a few dollars to have written for him, was "The precipitous actions of a rogue band of soldiers have jeopardized the chances for a peaceful solution, and have condemned countless innocents to privation and slow death." He was getting a lot of face time repeating that story.

Price knew better. Lying on the floor of the medevac coming out of Sudan, he looked more dead than alive, but he was never fully unconscious. Dillinghouse, ignoring the casualty at his feet, engaged in a twenty-minute conversation with an assistant that he didn't think would be overheard or ever repeated. Price went over the conversation repeatedly in his head, and as soon as he could write legibly he committed it to paper.

There was also the videotape. Cynthia Maddox, the reporter, had given it to Price before he was loaded on the plane. There was something urgent about it, and she said someone would get it from him in Abeche. She made a quick gesture that she said only the person getting the tape would know about. He was fuzzy about who picked it up, but they knew what to say to get it from him. Shortly after he got to a more rational state of mind at Walter Reed, an unmarked package arrived for him. It was an edited copy of the tape, and some additional raw footage. The only message with it was a short post-it note that said, "When the time comes. C". It was still in the bedstand drawer. He had watched it once. The raw footage was a remarkable piece of film. From the angle of the shot you could tell it was taken either by a hidden camera, or by a cell phone left on a table. Unlike most film of this type it was crystal clear. All parties were easily identifiable, and, thanks to an amazing sound quality, you could hear them frequently referring to each other by their names and titles. Even more amazing were the contents of the red bag that they were discussing. It changed hands at the end of the meeting, and Dillinghouse slipped it into his briefcase before leaving the room. The last person to leave, someone who hadn't been on screen, walked over to where the camera sat, and, never showing his face, turned it off. Price knew what he had was powerful and dangerous. And he knew how to use it.

Checking out of Walter Reed was rather easy. The only hard part came when they were trying to cut his new orders. Price had no intention of taking a couple of weeks leave. The doctors had intended for him to go home, take it easy for a few weeks, and do follow up outpatient care at a local VA hospital. Then he was going to be assigned to a local National Guard unit and let them figure out what to do with him. Price didn't see it that way. Arguing with the personnel people got him nowhere, so he took matters into his own hands. The tape cassette was valuable negotiating currency.

The driver who picked him up asked how he was.

"There's been a complication. I need something else from you"

The driver put the transmission back into park. "Price, you're the one who came to us. We made our deal with you, it's too late to change."

Price was unconvinced. "It's never too late. How bad do you want this guy?"

"What do you want? Maybe we can work it out."

Price told him.

An hour later, after he had been suitably wired, he found himself in the lobby of the Congressional Offices. A receptionist, who Price immediately sized up as having spent way too long in the anti-war movement, was refusing to admit him to Dillinghouse's office. The little prick was refusing to even call the secretary. "I have a complete list of all the scheduled appointments. You aren't one of them."

"I have an appointment. It was made an hour ago, check again."

A sympathetic staffer was going by and heard part of the exchange. He came over and asked what the problem was. Price told him. The staffer nodded and told the receptionist to make the call.

"He doesn't have an appointment."

"You aren't listening to me. I said make the call."

The receptionist, a very partisan political wanna-be, didn't like to be told anything by 'those people' from the other party. He stood his ground.

"Fine," the staffer said. "Come with me."

"You can't do that! He doesn't have an appointment!"

The staffer just smiled. "Go fuck yourself." And walked by with Price in tow.

"Thanks" Price started. "I had planned for everything except that little prick. Why'd you do it?"

"The problem with this place is everybody owes their job to some politician or other, and they don't think they have to listen to anybody. I'll guarantee he's wrong about that. He won't be sitting there when you come out. Besides, I spent seven years in the Navy and I've never seen anybody with a silver oak leaf cluster on his Purple Heart." The silver oak leaf was the equivalent of five bronze clusters.

"Thanks, but this is nothing. I've got a buddy with two of them, plus he's due another bronze cluster." When he saw the staffers eyes go wide he added, "I come from a very accident prone group of guys."

The staffer brought him in Dillinghouse's office and introduced him to the secretary. "Sergeant Price here has an appointment with your boss."

The secretary rifled through some papers. She looked up at Price and smiled, "I told you on the phone that the Congressman was very busy today, He won't be able to see you. Maybe I can fit you in next week."

Price wasn't going to budge. "Next week I could be back in the Sudan." The mention of the Sudan got everyone's attention. His new friend looked at him and asked, "Were you one of those guys?"

"Yeah, I was." Turning back to the secretary he reached into his pocket and pulled out a small red bag. "Tell Dillinghouse I've got this. When I leave it goes with me."

Another staffer, hearing the word 'Sudan' and seeing the red bag came over. Price recognized him as the guy Dillinghouse was talking to on the plane. He reached out and tried to grab the bag. "Let me help you with that."

Price pulled it back and returned it to his pocket. His escort looked confused. "Sergeant Price, is there anything I can do for you?"

"You don't want any part of this. I don't think you even want to be in the room now."

The staffer shook his hand and walked out. As soon as the door was closed he turned back to Dillinghouse's staffer. "I've got a DVD to go with this. I walk out it goes straight to a reporter, somebody ambitious, with an axe to grind. Am I getting through to you?"

He was. The staffer motioned for him to follow. The secretary immediately got on the phone for the Capitol Police.

Dillinghouse was sitting behind his desk when Price and the staffer walked in. He made no effort to greet Price. He just started in. "You think you have something?" Price threw a DVD on his desk. "Stick that in your computer and watch a few minutes." Dillinghouse did, and after he had seen the meeting in Sudan from another angle he looked up at Price. "I don't suppose this is the only copy?"

"Just because I look stupid doesn't mean I am. You want this back?" He held out the red bag.

"So, while your Major was getting me on the truck, you were ransacking my room and taking my diamonds. Is that it?" Actually, it wasn't. A member of the Sudanese delegation to the UN had gotten caught in a drug sting in New York He tried to make a deal to get his cocaine back. Once the FBI had gotten the red bag, the Sudanese was locked away for safekeeping. It was irregular, but they thought it was worth the diplomatic protest. Price was happy to go along with what Dillinghouse thought, but he didn't answer him.

"So what do you want? Money? A promotion? A discharge? What?"

"I want you to back off."

"Back off? Back off of what?"

"My unit. Let them get on with their jobs and find a new whipping boy. Let the Army process their awards. Stop trying to make them out to be the bad guys."

Dillinghouse smiled. He pointed to the bag and the DVD. "You think you have something? Let me tell you, son, you have nothing. When you walk out of here you'll just be some bitter soldier who got caught with his hand in the cookie jar. I can explain away the DVD as a setup, and I never saw those stones. Later on, I'll just call my boy at the Sudanese embassy and they'll send over some more. I'll have mine, and you're company will just be a bunch of incompetents who screwed up a humanitarian mission. It'll be like Katrina relief, only on an international level." The phone on his desk rang.

Dillinghouse answered it and listened for a moment. "Send them on in." He turned back to Price. "You got anything else? Make it quick, because the cops are here. You can think about what just happened in the guardhouse."

The door opened and four men walked in. Only one was in uniform. "Take him away, boys. I've got work to do"

One of the men spoke. "Congressman, are you in session right now?"

Dillinghouse shook his head. "No, we went into recess yesterday. Why?"

The agent smiled at him, then at Price. "Thanks, Sergeant. We can handle it from here." He put out his hand to shake Prices'. "By the way, your orders are in the car. You're going home." As he was closing the door behind him he heard the FBI agent speak. "Constitutionally, I can't arrest you when Congress is in session. Now you're fair game."

As they were walking out of the building another FBI agent intercepted Price. "I want to thank you for that, Sergeant. I don't recall when I've enjoyed anything as much."

"How about my orders?"

The agent reached into his jacket pocket and pulled out a sheaf of papers. "Read these and make sure they're what you wanted. I won't be able to change them." Price scanned down the orders until he got to the assignment line. He was going back to the 289th, and he had to report to the transportation section at Andrews AFB. "These will be just fine."

"This guy and his buddy will probably make a deal with the prosecutor, but we need to make sure we can find you if we need you to testify."

"Like I'm going to be hard to find." He paused for a minute. "What kind of a deal would you guys let him make?"

"It wouldn't be us, but you never know what his politician friends might try to do. Funding, and all that. You'd be surprised how many of them have their hands in the cookie jar."

"Maybe I should have just grabbed those rocks and went on my way?"

The FBI agent just laughed. "Nah. Being a dishonest politician may be a bipartisan activity, but it's a closed club. Nobody would have pardoned you."


Colonel Perkins and Major Carstairs were just ordering dessert when Carstairs cell phone rang. As he pulled it out to answer, Perkins gave him a quick dressing down. "That's in incredibly bad taste to have your phone on in a restaurant. Do you really think you're that important?" Carstairs would not have been Perkins first choice for Executive Officer. He had been an adequate operations officer, but just barely. His biggest asset before activation was his political connections.

Now that Perkins could see his career crumbling, thanks to the Al Fashir fiasco, he was barely tolerant of him.

Carstairs recognized the tone. He knew what Perkins thought of his abilities. What was more sobering was that Carstairs knew it was an accurate assessment. He had never pretended to be the next reincarnation of George Patton, and had always been ready to exploit any political or family connection to stay competitive. They were only dining together because they had been forbidden to wander while awaiting the hearings to begin tomorrow, and they were also forbidden from discussing, even casually, the events that brought them here.

"The legal guy in the Congressional Office gave me this phone and told me to never turn it off." He couldn't resist one little dig. "I guess orders outweigh anybody's concept of good taste." He spoke into the phone in a low voice, conscious that other diners were looking at him. Perkins strained to hear what he was saying, but the conversation seem to consist of a series of "Yes, Sir!" answers. He'd have to wait to find out who was so impatient that he had to interrupt his dinner.

This was the real Chet Perkins. He had begun to learn some humility in Sudan, especially when his people were in real danger and he had no control over events. At the time he realized he had been fortunate that General Price, the State Adjutant General, had forced Sergeant Major Grant and his retreads on him. He passage of time, however, with the realization that he wasn't getting any credit for any of the combat glory, but he was going to be responsible to congress and the world for all the faults of the operation, brought his old bitterness to the surface. He had been a very average officer, who had peaked in his career, when he managed to parlay a little political influence into a shot at General stars. It was a good bet that he would never see that now. Most of his former patrons and allies avoided having any public contact with him, but he hoped they were still working behind the scenes.

Carstairs finally terminated the call.

"Well?"

"That was the Judge Advocate. He wants us in the Congressional Liaison Office ten minutes ago." The CLO was in another wing of the Pentagon. They were dining in a small restaurant off of the Pentagon Mall. It would take about fifteen minutes to walk there.

"They'll just have to wait. They've inconvenienced me enough this past week. I intend to finish my desert. Will you be having any?"

Carstairs was in a tight spot. He had taken the call, so he knew what the exact wording of the order was. Knowing Perkins as he did, he was certain that he would be blamed for any tardiness, no matter what he said. It would be best to distance himself.

"I think I'll head on up there. If at least one of us shows up, I can make excuses for you." Excuses my ass, he thought. I'll just tell them he was finishing his cheesecake. Let him take it from there. Perkins saw through it immediately. He had realized his XO wasn't as loyal as another candidate might have been. "Hold on. I'll come with you."

Even after they hurried to the CLO, they still had to cool their heels for another 20 minutes while a parade of officers, most of lesser rank than Perkins, streamed in and out of the office. Perkins kept up a constant stream of grumbling under his breath, but managed a smile for every officer who acknowledged him sitting there. Finally, after what seemed like an entire West Point graduating class had come and gone they were called in.

The CLO, a full colonel, didn't waste time with small talk. "The hearings are off. You two are booked on a return flight out of Andrews tomorrow morning."

Perkins was surprised at this. The hearings had been scheduled to begin the next morning. "May I ask what happened, Sir? We've been getting prepped for this for a week now. I'd hate to have to leave now, just to get called back after my unit has been given an assignment."

"You don't know what happened? Either of you?" They both had blank looks. I'm sure you're familiar with one of your soldiers, a Staff Sergeant Price?"

Price? Of course. If there were a problem it would have to be because of one of Grant's people. "Yes, Sir. Sergeant Price is recovering from wounds at Walter Reed. I didn't realize he was involved in these matters."

"Well, he wasn't, but somehow he got a video of Congressman Dillinghouse taking a bribe in Khartoum. He gave it to the FBI, and they arrested him this afternoon."

"Price or Dillinghouse?" Carstairs asked.

"Dillinghouse! Don't act stupid. Now the people on his side of the aisle are up in arms. They're saying it was a set up by our CID. You sure you don't know about this?"

"This is a big surprise to us, Colonel. I haven't seen Price since he was evacuated."

The CLO had his suspicions about Perkins before, but this confirmed it. He had been here a week and hadn't taken the time to visit one of his wounded soldiers. This guy was a politician, but he was most likely telling the truth. He wasn't imaginative enough for something like this. Perkins was still talking. "I hope now that this is over I can take a few days to handle some personal affairs back home. This deployment has been hard on my business and family."

"Your business? Your file says you were a government employee. Nice try, Perkins. These deployments are hard on everyone, but your request is denied. We want you out of the country. Be on that plane tomorrow. And police up Sergeant Price. He's a transient somewhere over at Andrews. Take him with you before he pulls a *coup d'état.*"


Price was wandering through the transient lounge. There were several hundred service people there, all waiting for a ride somewhere. Those of them without priority orders were put on a waiting list, and as space became available they were manifested on a flight. The experienced travelers could estimate how long their wait would be. They didn't hang around in the lounge. Price was somewhere in the high 400's on the standby list, so he knew he be there a couple of days. He had staked out a couch in a far corner, piled what little gear he had on it, and made himself comfortable. His shoulder was still acting up, but Price had never been one for too many pain pills. Instead, he had stopped at a surplus store before reporting in and picked up a backpack hydration system. He needed one anyway, because his last one was shredded by the same RPG hit that shredded his shoulder. He had also dumped two liters of vodka in it. Vodka wasn't his choice of drinks, but he didn't want to be advertising his semi-inebriated condition. He was walking back to his couch when he noticed her. She was sitting by herself, about as far from everyone as you could get and still be in the building. She's a good-looking woman, he thought to himself. Grant did OK when he hooked up with her. He gave a quick look around to see if the Sergeant Major was with her. He didn't think he would be, because he couldn't picture Grant, a CSM and a Medal of Honor recipient, sitting in a transient lounge. Grant would have a priority. Besides, if Grant had been in the country, he would have stopped by the hospital.

Price didn't know if he should go over. Everything about the way she was sitting said she wanted to be alone, but something didn't look right, and he couldn't figure out what it was. He decided he should at least go over and let her know he was here. If she wanted company, she'd let him know. If not, he could go back to his own corner.

Her Class A jacket was laid over the back of the chair next to her. As Price got closer he thought she was sitting in a shadow. Then he realized it wasn't a shadow. Her arm was bruised. He walked in front of her and saw both arms had bruising, mostly above the elbow, extending under her short sleeve shirt. It looked like someone had been grabbing her pretty roughly. Grant? Couldn't be. Grant might shoot a woman if he had to, but he wouldn't slap one around. The man didn't have it in him. He called out her name and she looked up. There was another bruise on her face. This one was older and starting to fade, but it looked like a hand print. Price forgot his military courtesy.

"What the fuck happened to you?"

"Hello, Sergeant Price. I'm glad you're out of the hospital."

He sat down next to her. Whether she wanted company or not, she was going to have some. "Yes Ma'am, thank you. Now who's been working you over."

"Let it go. I just had an accident. It's nothing."

It had been something, but nothing she wanted to talk about. After she had gotten home and spent a few days with her kids, the ex-husband started coming around. He seemed to have changed, and she was mad enough at Lucas Grant for not coming with her to accept a dinner invitation. He had been the charmer that she remembered from when they had first married. Not at all like the abusive thug he turned into. She had been charmed enough to get romantically involved with him again, to the point where she agreed to go away with him for a couple of days.

All was well the first night. She had been missing Grant, and sex with her ex turned her on like he had never seen before. The next morning he started working on her in earnest. He wanted the kids; he wanted to get back together. She was receptive to a point, but then he started hinting around at joint finances. She remembered him from before. He couldn't be trusted with a buck. He had spent them deeply into debt, then had left her with the bills. It had taken a few years to work out of it, and in the meantime her military security clearance had even been in jeopardy because of indebtedness. She also remembered that it had been one of her credit cards that this whole little tryst was being charged to. She made the mistake of telling him as much.

He sulked for the next few days, and started drinking heavily while she was around. She was starting to fear the old person that she remembered, when he snapped on her. He had a signature card from the bank. He wanted to fill out her account information and put him on the account. She said no. She was making decent money from the Army, and her civilian job was still paying her. She was putting away a good chunk every month and she didn't want to see it pissed away again.

He had been drinking all along. He was good at it, and managed to hide the fact of how much from her. Until now. It wasn't the answer he wanted to hear. He had grabbed her arms and shook her like a rag doll before she could get away from him. That's where the bruising came from. Her mother called the police, and while they were taking him out of the house he lunged at her and gave her an open handed slap across the face. He spent the night in lock-up.

He called the next day, pleading with her to take him back. When she wouldn't budge he grew angry again, and made more threats. Her mother told her to get a restraining order, but she knew those never stopped him before. She decided to return to Germany a few days early. At least she could get away from him. The kids would be safe with her mother.

"Is the Sergeant Major here?"

She got a far away look, like a pleasant thought had just crossed her mind. "No, he didn't come home. He decided to stay in Germany with the company." Price could tell she didn't want to talk about it, so he invited her over to where his gear was. "It's better than waiting alone, and I promise not to bother you with small talk. Plus," he held up a six pack of mixer, "vodka tonic. Something to take the edge off." He picked up her duffel bag and led her to his corner. We make a hell of a pair, he thought. Two beat up people with no place to go and nothing to do. She asked if he knew anything about the upcoming hearings. They were going to be waiting for a while, so Price gave her the long version.

"Do you remember when I got hit in Al Fashir? "

LTC Perkins was in a bad mood when he woke up. The thought of being summarily dismissed and ordered out of the country had not sat well with him. Unfortunately, word of the suspension of the hearings hadn't circulated yet, so his political friends were still avoiding him.

The only positive thing that had happened so far was a message from the Chief of Staff when he returned to his room. He found out that the 289th was being alerted for a move, and they would be getting a construction mission. That was the limit of the message. Perkins had tried to find out more, but all he could learn was that it would not be in the Theater of Operations, meaning it wouldn't be in the Gulf region. That was fine with him. The Sudan and taught him that he wasn't particularly suited for a combat command. Something more benign suited him just fine.

Carstairs didn't want to bring any more wrath on himself, so he was quiet for the ride to Andrews, only speaking when it was absolutely necessary. They checked in at the flight desk, and Perkins reminded him about Price. Carstairs asked if he was checked in. The Airman looked at his computer, and verified he was, and that he was still 426 on the standby list. Perkins pointed out that his priority read "...and party" and directed Price be included. Then he asked him to be paged.

Carstairs tried to caution him. "If he's that far down the list, he may not even be in the terminal."

"Even better. If he isn't here when they call the flight, he's missing a movement. He'll be AWOL and out of my hair."

"That's not fair to him, Colonel."

"After all that son of a bitch has put me through, do you think I really care what's fair to him or not? You really don't understand what just happened, do you, Carstairs?"

And then he noticed Price standing in front of him. He could tell by the look on his face that Price had heard most of the exchange. He had been making his way back to Captain Bonneville with the morning coffee when he saw Perkins come in the building. He was going to ask if the Colonel could help him and Bonneville get higher up on the list when he heard the page.

"It's nice to know I'm loved, Colonel."

"Watch your mouth, Sergeant. Get your gear together. You'll be on my flight."

"Yes, Sir. How about Captain Bonneville?"

"Is she here? Wonderful. Airman, add her to my roster. Get her over here, Sergeant. We're scheduled for wheels up in an hour." Without taking a pause he turned to Carstairs. "XO, see if you can't get the Unit on the phone and give them a heads up. Tell them we'll need transportation for four."

# CHAPTER 3

Harrison and Sharp waited for the last of the company to finish the morning run. In the weeks the First Sergeant was recovering from his latest heart attack, morning PT had become a sham under Master Sergeant Winder. Even the troops who normally looked forward to the morning workout had been avoiding what they considered a waste of their time. Winder was in the habit of assigning Physical Training to those who had displeased him, or that he just plain didn't like. Many mornings he wouldn't even fall out in PT gear with the troops, just stand on the sidelines and call out encouragement, or insults to the soldiers who had let their conditioning run down. The CSM, usually an active participant in what he considered an important morning ritual, had his own wounds to recover from. LTC Perkins, a supporter of Winder, ordered him to avoid the morning sessions so as not to undercut Winders authority. Grants own daily workouts usually took him past at a distance, far enough away to avoid being noticed, but close enough to see the shambles it had become. As soon as Harrison was back PT had returned to a more rigorous standard, something that was not universally popular, especially with the Winder faction who had enjoyed the lower standards and lax attendance reporting.

That first morning reveille was a shock on many levels. Harrison had personally walked through the barracks in his PT uniform rousting the troops. Then he did the same thing with the NCOs. The icing on the cake was when he had the troops formed and, instead of beginning the morning routine, he started a roll call. Each time he got to a name that was not officially excused, he sent a runner for that person, delaying the start until everyone was present. After leading a brief session of stretches, pushups and sit-ups, basics of the Physical Fitness Test that he could see some were having difficulty with, he led them on an easy run through the area. Watching the performances during the stationary exercises, he wasn't surprised at the number of dropouts. He did make everyone finish, even if they walked the two miles. To add to the embarrassment of not finishing the run, Harrison held the formation until everyone had completed it. Winder and the Supply Sergeant, Harte, were the last two in. Most of the troops understood what was going in and enjoyed the little spectacle. They enjoyed it even more when he announced that, beginning the next morning, anyone not completing the run with the group would participate in remedial PT in the afternoon, after regular duty hours. He also announced the date of the next PT test for record. The number of stragglers decreased every day. Now there was just a small group, every one of them had failed the new PT test, Winder among them. Harrison had changed the stakes in the game.

NCOs are evaluated annually or sooner if their rater changes. With Carstairs moving up to XO, Winder was getting a new rater, and Carstairs had just completed his last act as S-3. Major Carstairs, not wanting to be bothered by an out of cycle evaluation, basically glossed over the past few months. There are certain 'buzz' words that promotion boards look for. Some are good, and some are recognized as bullshit, to fill out a mediocre report. Carstairs used all the bullshit phrases, then gave it to Harrison to forward. The First Sergeant reviewed it, and caught the fact that the PT scores and his height and weight hadn't been added to the remarks section. Officially, while a copy might slip by a local review board, a promotion board would consider it incomplete and not recognize the period it covered, not really the end of the world for a routine promotion opportunity that a soldier was otherwise qualified for. Harrison grabbed his rosters so he could add in the PT test scores, and Winders height and weight.

As well as failing the PT test, Winder was overweight. Somehow, he had managed to pack on the pounds from beer and *wurst* during the few weeks they had been in Germany.

Everybody signed off on the EER before it had been given to Harrison, including Winder. Before Harrison could forward the report, he had to include a cover letter from the company commander outlining remedial action to be taken for the failure to achieve standards by a senior NCO. That included putting Winder in a formal remedial PT program, and on a diet. Harrison was about to break the news to him.

Sharp watched as Harrison called Winder over. "I'd love to stay and watch this."

"Well, you can't. As much as I'd like to humiliate the bastard, I have to do this one on one. I'll see you at breakfast."

Sharp shook his head and walked over to where Price was waiting for him. Price pointed over to Harrison and Winder and asked, "What's that all about?"

"Winder's about to get screwed, and he did it all to himself."

"Are we getting rid of him?"

"No."

"Then I don't care. The problem with where we went and where we're going is people like him. The less I have to do with him, the better my day goes."

They went through the serving line, both taking small portions. It was their habit when not in the field to watch their diet generally. Beer and pizza after hours could be good, but the slower pace of operations when they were out of the field tended to pack the pounds on. Price was concerned that his enforced idleness had cost him some muscle tone and added a roll of fat to his midsection. He was working extra on his own to get back in shape. They hadn't been sitting long when Harrison joined them. Sharp looked around for Winder. ""Where's your buddy?"

"He found a sudden need to go find someone to complain to. Won't do him any good. The staff is holed up getting ready for the briefing. There's some Russian Major in there with them "

Sharp asked how he knew he was Russian. "I spoke to him and that's how he answered me. Those guys don't like talking to the enlisted swine."

Price grunted. "Get back to Winder. You give the asshole some bad news?"

"That's all I'm going to say about it. You need to let it go."

"Let it go my ass." Sharp said. "I need to get out of that fucking headquarters section. I spend every fucking day on the other side of a five foot partition listening to that piece of shit babble on about how good he is and how he knows what's best for the Company. He's got most of those idiot Lieutenants and half the enlisted kids listening to him. He ain't shit and we need to get rid of him before we start getting shot at again and he gets someone killed."

"Relax, Pricey. Don't blame the First Shirt. You need to do what I do. Get out of there during the day."

"Menklin doesn't like 'his' section out of his sight. Especially me. He keeps complaining he never saw me in Africa, and he'll be damned if I'm going to be part of Grants private army again." Menklin was the Intelligence Officer.

"Top, you better tell him, or he's gonna be a pain in the ass all day."

"Tell me what."

Harrison smiled. "I've got a deal for you. You promise to keep your head out of your ass, and I'll talk to the new CO about you moving into a platoon." Price reached up, grabbed both his ear lobes and pulled down. "This good enough? What are you going to give me, a construction squad?"

"No, you little prick. I've got something better. Horizontal Platoon doesn't have any heavy equipment left. Until they get some, nobody wants to be in charge of them. I've asked all the squad leaders, and none of them want to step up."

"What about Angeles?" Angeles was the Platoon Sergeant.

"Sergeant Angeles hip put him out of the Army." Angeles had been nailed by a sniper on the airstrip in Sudan. His Platoon Leader, Lieutenant Harnell, was killed trying to help him. "I need a Platoon Sergeant, and if you keep yourself from self destructing, you might even make the next promotion cycle."

The Russian Major was arguing with his aide, a Russian Lieutenant about something rather important. Grant could tell by the way the Majors' finger kept poking into his subordinate's chest. There was something else going on. Every so often the junior officer made a reference to a colonel, and he didn't think they were referring to Perkins.

The Russians had been going through a stack of maps, charts, tables and photos of the new project the 289th had just inherited. Grant thought of it as an inheritance, because as he could see it, they would be the fourth group to be awarded this road improvement contract. The Russians had begun it, almost 20 years ago. Then came the fall of communism, and the ex-reds ran out of money. Then the Ukrainians tried, but Moldova was to be an autonomous region, and they didn't want the Ukrainians in their borders. There had to be another reason why Moldova didn't want free construction help on a road, but every time that came up it was diplomatically skirted. Lastly, the Moldovans tried, but they claimed lack of expertise and cash flow. Something was starting to stink about this project. He needed Price in here. The amateur linguist could eavesdrop and see if there was any more information he could pick up. Grant asked Perkins if he could send over to the Mess Hall for another jug of coffee. Then he got on the phone to Harrison.

"Tell Price to get his ass over to the chow hall and pick up a big pot of coffee and bring it here. Tell him I need him to play dumb and watch the Russians."

"Problems?"

"I don't know yet. That's why I want him."

When he hung up Bonneville was by his side. "Sergeant Major."

"Ma'am."

That had been the scope of their conversations since she had returned from leave. Their relationship had been cooling before she left, and now that she was back it was ice cold. Fuck it, he thought. Easy come, easy go. Then he smiled at himself for the subconscious pun. She saw his brief smile. "A penny for your thoughts."

"Nothing worth a penny. I was just playing a word game with myself."

She looked away, then down. "I need a favor. The Colonel wants me to go up to Corps and pick up the awards packets this afternoon. Are you still hand carrying those equipment reports to Corps?"

"Almost every other day. Why? Need a ride?"

"Well, yes, I do. I was hoping I could go with you."

"All right. I'll be going over later this afternoon."

He looked at her. In the past, riding alone with her had always been sexually dangerous. They had a lot of history. Then again, this'll be in broad daylight, they both have places to be and things to do. What could possibly happen? Besides, his driver, who talked non-stop for the entire trip, would double as a chaperone. She squeezed his forearm and walked away. Now what the hell was that all about? If she had decided

41

to go back to the formal military relationship, he had pretty much already figured that out. He didn't need two hours of her in a 'look but don't touch ever again' mode to get the message.

Price came in with the coffee. He had one of the Robinson twins with him, carrying cups, creamers and sugar. He waved them over. "Robinson, whatever you see or hear keep it to yourself." He jerked his thumb in the direction of the Russians. They were still arguing. "Bring those guys some fresh coffee and set up next to them. And make nice. I want to know what's going on."

Price and Robinson did as they were told. The Russians, wondering why this personalized service was so long in coming, stopped talking long enough to accept fresh cups. The younger one, the Lieutenant, made a few attempts to trick Price into letting on that he could speak Russian. Price, however, was an old hand at playing dumb. He never responded to anyone in a foreign language unless he had been the one to initiate the conversation. That way, he always had a few seconds to process what he had heard and could respond with either a blank look, a dumb 'huh', or make no response at all. It always worked.

Briefing prep was almost complete, and Perkins laid out the order the staff would go to present their piece of it. In deference to the Russians, who had a real enlisted phobia, Grant had been the only NCO present, and he had only been grudgingly accepted. He had managed to listen in on enough critical information to give his own briefing to key NCOs later on. He'd get whatever Price picked up later on.

He could hear Harrison calling the formation outside the hall. There were a few minutes of commands and organization, and then the doors flew open and the troops filed in. This wasn't the detailed brief. Instead, they would get an overview of the scope of the mission, training, travel and logistics information, personnel changes and any individual duty assignments. The detailed planning would happen at the staff level, then filter down to the platoons for refinement and execution. This was a dog and pony show to impress the Russians as much as the junior enlisted. What nobody on the stage realized was that the Russians weren't impressed, and neither were the troops.

LTC Perkins opened the briefing. Behind him was a covered easel, as he began his presentation it remained covered, his idea of building excitement.

"Our assignment is going to be a movement by rail to our project area. Once there, we will co-locate at a host nation military base and commence construction operations approximately 20 kilometers away. We will be building an all weather, gravel surfaced road approximately 50 kilometers in length. There are no extreme terrain challenges involved, but there are several streams and one fair sized ravine that will require upgraded bridging. This will give the construction platoons their own missions ahead of the heavy equipment, and at times will require some remote basing."

Sharp and Harrison were sitting together. Harrison was making notes. Plans like this always required security plans, messing operations, bivouac layouts, resupply operations and a wide variety of other support that somehow never make it into the master plan. Sooner or later, they'd be on the ground with everything they brought with them, and some bright light would look around and ask, "Hey, what about...?" and all eyes would turn to the First Sergeant, and he would have to make it happen. Unlike Africa, where he wasn't involved in the planning, this time he would have what was needed when they hit the ground. Since he would not be allocated any extra shipping space, he would have to find places on everyone else's loads to carry his supplies.

Sharp was likewise making notes, but his were all mental. His job would be less well defined, depending on the scope of operations, terrain layout and tactical situation. Briefings like this usually painted a rosier picture than what actually existed, so he would wait until the question and answer period to ask for specifics, then work off of plans, orders and maps. His primary thought was how to get a large-scale map and arrange to either be on a reconnaissance or arrange to be on the advance party.

"You going to take any notes, David?" Harrison asked.

"Right now I just want to hear where this will be. What we're doing is up to somebody else to worry about right now. The only one who doesn't have a smug look on their face is the Sergeant Major. He's worried about something."

And Grant was. Price had been hanging close to the Russians picking up bits of information. Every so often he would shoot Grant a concerned look, but he never had the opportunity to explain what he had been hearing. The Russians had contented looks. They had done their jobs well convincing the Americans the situation was other what existed.

Perkins was still speaking, caught up in his own excitement. "Those of you who remember, we went into a high threat area in Africa that required constant vigilance and some extraordinary effort on the part of many of you. I'm pleased to tell you that some of the awards we recommended have been approved, and we'll have that ceremony later this week. More importantly, I'm sure you'll all be glad to know that we will be going into a no threat environment where our primary security concern will be pilferage and petty theft." He paused for effect. "Our destination this time. . ." and Captain Bonneville pulled the cover off the easel, "will be the Republic of Moldova!"

A ripple went through the audience as soldiers turned to one another asking if anyone knew where the hell that was. Perkins let them buzz for a moment, then called out "At ease!"

He continued, "Moldova, or Moldava, depending on where you see it spelled, is a small country sandwiched between Romania and the Ukraine." He had Bonneville put up a map of Europe. He picked up a pointer and smacked it sharply against the map. "Here." He gave everyone a moment to let that register. "When you write home to tell the folks, don't confuse it with Moldavia," the pointer smacked again, this time in the area of Czechoslovakia. "It's a totally different country." He had Bonneville take down the European map and he continued with the smaller, Moldovan map. "Our area of Operations will be here, a little to the north of the city, or town, I'm not sure how large it is, of Kipercheny. It's not too far from the Dnestr River, which I'm told is very scenic. I'll let the S-3 take the next portion."

Captain Blackman, until recently the Headquarters Company Commander, gave an adequate, if sketchy explanation of the project. He walked the audience through the terrain they would be following, a continuation of an existing road leading to a small rail junction called Lashtyg. "The existing road is in poor condition, but it continues to be used as a market road by small villages along the way. We will undoubtedly encounter civilian traffic on a regular basis, so there will be a need to construct bypasses at regular intervals. The route has been surveyed and marked, but we will be using our own surveyors to verify the route and make sure the markings conform to our system. I'm going to be followed by the S-4. Hold your questions until the end."

The supply officer went through a list of support agencies that would be responsible for rations, fuel and other amenities. The answer that everyone was waiting for was how were they going to do road construction when none of their heavy equipment had been returned to them? Captain Gaston explained.

"Later today, we begin drawing replacement equipment. There are POMCUS stocks left over from the old REFORGER exercises that we can draw on."

That caused a murmur to run through the audience. Most of the younger soldiers were unfamiliar with acronyms left over from the Cold War days. Gaston was pleased with himself by coming up with a bit of arcane data, LTC Perkins wasn't amused. "Gaston, you better explain that to the troops and stop trying to confuse them."

Gaston was taken back by the rebuke. "Yes, Sir. POMCUS stands for Prepositioned Operational Material Configured to Unit Sets. Essentially what that means is the Army used to stockpile complete sets of equipment for specific units. That way, if an armored battalion or a transportation company was sent over for the REFORGER exercises, they would only have to send the troops, who would draw everything they need in a kind of one-stop shopping. REFORGER stood for Return of Forces to Germany. It was an annual exercise the Army used to run." Hoping that he had satisfied the Commander (and maybe impressed him a little too) Gaston continued. "The Engineer Equipment Maintenance Officer will organize that pick-up separately from this briefing. He'll be getting together with the Platoon Leaders and Platoon Sergeants immediately after we adjourn." Almost as an after thought, "I know that the Horizontal Platoon has taken some serious hits lately. The S-1 will address those in her portion."

The S-2, Intelligence, was next. He hadn't had time to research any of the country conditions, so he briefed from information the Russians had provided. He painted a rosy picture of Moldova and it's economic and political health. "The country has enjoyed a long period of stability since it gained independence. Politically, it used to be a part of the Ukraine under the old Soviet Union, but the changeover to independence was peaceful. There is a minority area well to the south of our operations area, mainly Turkish in origin, but they are pretty well integrated in the political fabric, so there's no conflict. There is some organized crime in the larger cities, but it should be of no concern to us until we institute some kind of leave or pass program. Now I will pass the rostrum to Captain Bonneville."

From the end of the stage CSM Grant looked at Bonneville as she took he position in front of the easel. It was hard for a woman to look attractive in the Army Combat Uniform. With long sleeves, baggy trousers and bulging pockets, there weren't many ways to look feminine. Somehow, Bonneville always did. Grant thought he might be partial to how she looked, given their past relationship, but mentally comparing her to other women in the unit, he decided he was right. He tried to remember how she had looked naked, when they were making love in that run down building in Sudan. The memory caused a stirring in his groin that he quickly shook off. Not the time or the place, he thought. He wondered what she wanted to talk to him about on the ride to Corps.

Bonneville's briefing didn't rely on information from the Russian brief. She had already been working on personnel assignments and augmentations prior to the news of the new mission. Her talk was concise and to the point.

"First, I know you're all concerned about our casualties. Unfortunately, there will not be any more returning. Several have opted for the early discharge the Army offered, and others had wounds that were serious enough to disable them. If anyone is interested in particulars, stop by my office and I'll give you what information I can." She let the murmuring subside before she continued. "As Colonel Perkins stated earlier, most of our awards have been approved. Some have been downgraded, but there are still quite a few to be presented. Unless there are any other changes, we will have an awards formation on Saturday morning. I'll have list of who is getting what available later in the week." She paused again. "Now, let me address the situation with the heavy equipment section. Lieutenant Stanley will move over from the S-3 shop to take over the platoon." Grace Stanley was a female Lieutenant with a degree in engineering, but no practical experience. She had performed adequately but unremarkably in Sudan, but was the only qualified officer of the appropriate rank for the position. Her job would have been easier if one of the squad leaders had stepped up to handle the platoon. They hadn't, and the platoon was in a state of disarray. The stabilizing influences were the few soldiers left who had been used as infantry in Africa.

Bonneville continued. It had already been decided that the equipment section would be augmented, and she explained how those people were already in the system and should be arriving in the next few days. There was a tentative list, but she wouldn't know the final numbers until they were on the plane and enroute. "Next, we have to fill the Platoon Sergeant vacancy. That will go to Staff Sergeant Price." She turned and looked at him as the group broke out into applause and whistles. "Congratulations, Sergeant."

"Thank you, Ma'am." Behind him Price could hear the Russian Major comment "They put a waiter in charge of construction."

Bonneville waved the audience back into order. "Other position changes you already know about. That concludes my part of the briefing. Colonel Perkins?"

Perkins returned to center stage. "Thank you, Captain. We'll be on the road in two weeks. That concludes the briefing. The maps and blueprints will stay up for a while, and the staff sections will be here to answer any questions. The first of the equipment draws begin this afternoon. Sergeant Price, I suggest you organize your drivers and mechanics. First up will be heavy equipment."

After the troops were dismissed a bunch from the equipment section crowded around Price to congratulate him and welcome him to the section. Grant moved in closer to get his attention. "Hey, rock star. Enjoy your moment in the sun, then come see me."

Price nodded then continued shaking hands. Harrison and Sharp walked over. "What did you need Price for?"

Grant shrugged. "I don't know yet. Those two Russians were yakking up a storm, and I don't think they were talking about the same things they told Perkins. I'm hoping Price was able to pick up a few things. Give him a few more minutes up there, and then bring him over to my office. I want to talk to him before I head up to Corps."

"Corps? Again?" Sharp was amazed. "For Christ sake you've practically been living up there. What more do they want to know about wrecked equipment?"

"This time it's boiled down to Halvorson's Hummer. Everyone says I gave the order to abandon it. Corps still wants to know why I didn't try to salvage it."

"Do they think RPGs and machine gun fire might have something to do with it?"

"They're just fucking with me. I know it and they know it. Perkins said this would be my last trip. If they aren't satisfied, he'll step in."

"I don't know why the bastard hasn't done something before this."

"He's still playing politics. Remember, any shit that we stir up splashes on him, and he still wants to be a general someday. Get Price over to me. I have to leave pretty soon."

Bonneville was gathering up her papers when she saw Grant with his two NCOs. Great, she thought. Just like old times. Every time I need some time alone with Lucas, those two show up. She went over to the First Sergeant as Sharp was bringing Price over.

"Is the Sergeant Major still going to Corps this afternoon?"

"Yes, Ma'am, right after he talks to our new Platoon Sergeant here."

She looked at Price. He could see a little pleading in her eyes. "Remember that I need to ride with him, so don't keep him too long."

Price took her arm and walked her a few feet away. "You haven't told him yet, have you?"

"No."

"Are you going to?"

She shrugged her shoulders. "I don't know yet." And she walked away.

Sharp had watched the exchange. "What was that all about?"

"Can't say. I promised not to."

"Bullshit!"

"Maybe so, but I did promise."


Ali Alawa Sharif was still looking over his shoulder as he got on the plane.

After his failure to destroy the Americans in the ambush by the border, he had been summoned to Khartoum to explain why. His failure, after the elaborate and expensive plans that had been made, did not sit well with either the Mullahs in Tehran or the Muslim Brotherhood. He had not been worried about the meeting, since his organization only counted on the occasional success. But he had been detecting a shift in attitudes once he was on the road to Khartoum. As he passed through each district and his escort changed, their treatment of him became brusquer, and not at all what he expected as a leader of the Janjaweed. He decided that at his first opportunity he would shake his escorts and make his own way.

His chance came just outside the capitol. His escorts stopped for a midday meal in a small bazaar. Sharif took the opportunity to excuse himself to go to the toilet. His guards had not expected any trouble, so they had been lax in their duties. As soon as Sharif was out of sight of the guards, he searched out an almost derelict taxi. With the traditional bargaining half-heartedly done on his part, he agreed to an exorbitant sum for a quick ride into the city. He insisted the driver fill his gas tank before they left. He did not want to be caught on the road after giving his escorts the slip.

Once inside the city, Sharif directed his driver to take him to the diplomatic quarter. His first thought was the Libyan Embassy. He had the driver take him by. There appeared to be an excessive police presence in front, as if they were waiting on someone. Sharif knew that someone must be him. There had been ample time for the guards to alert the city that he had fled. He grunted at the driver to continue driving. Sharif needed a few moments to plan. Almost by accident, his gaze fell on the Algerian flag fluttering up ahead. He had only minor contacts with the Algerians in the past, but they were always fruitful for both sides. They were also very low key, hopefully low enough that no one would expect him to try to hide there. He told the driver to stop.


The Algerians had been polite, but distant. Rumors of Ali Alawa Sharif's failure had circulated throughout the diplomatic quarter. It had taken the intervention of the resident intelligence officer to arrange his transport out of the country. After dark he had been disguised as one of the uniformed sentries from the embassy. He was placed in the front seat of an embassy limousine as a member of a security detail and driven to the airport. There had been a regular courier flight from Oran that night, and Sharif would have a seat on it. It would be the first leg of his self imposed and very precarious exile.

The flight to Oran was unremarkable. There were a few Algerians with him; most appeared to be routine passengers, going about some embassy business. There was one, however, who was almost certainly a security agent, detailed to keep an eye on him. What the hell did they expect him to do, hijack the plane? Algerian security must have been planning for him before he got to Khartoum.

Fifty years earlier, Algeria had been the last jewel in the French overseas crown. The Indo-China war had ended badly for them, but the lessons they had learned enabled them to ruthlessly suppress an Algerian Nationalist movement. Captured documents had revealed the extent of the French success. The Algerian Liberation Front had been so devastated they had decided to give up their armed struggle for the foreseeable future. That made the French decision to sever colonial ties with Algeria all the more unpalatable. French Algerians, *pied noirs*, or black feet, had felt betrayed. Parts of the Army went into revolt, and the terror campaign spilled over into metropolitan France. But the revolt had relied on publicity as well as terror, and the leaders became well known. The revolt eventually collapsed, and Algeria was given its independence. No one was more surprised at the victory than the Algerian Nationalists.

Oran was still a spectacular city. The French had blended the old and the new to give it a uniquely cosmopolitan look. Ali Alawa Sharif was not interested in sight seeing. His 'escort' had brusquely ordered him into a waiting car and he was being sped to only Allah knew where. The Algerians had no axe to grind with him. They were barely on the periphery of the Islamic movement, his presence as a hostage would not serve them any useful purpose. And as far as intelligence value went, he knew a lot, and would be happy to share it. There were no secrets he wished to keep at the expense of personal pain or discomfort. He could not fathom any need Algerian intelligence had for him. He had simply been looking for asylum.

He was taken to a non-descript building on the edge of the city. There were sentries in the inner courtyard, but no sign of what made this building important. Signs were in a combination of French and Arabic, but they gave no clues. The office he was taken to was rather barren of decoration. All the expense had been placed into useful equipment. The man behind the desk was fat. That was the only word to describe him. There was no humor in the mans eyes, and it seemed he had little time to waste on Ali Alawa Sharif. He got right to the point.

"The Janjaweed has discarded you. There is a use for you with us."

"If I'm not interested?"

"Say so now. I dislike wasting my time."

Unspoken was the threat of a quick death if he was not willing to work for the Algerians. "I am currently without a purpose in life. Perhaps your needs will suit me."

The fat man was not amused with his glibness. "We have a need for your talents in Marseilles. You have no doubt heard of the unrest in France. We need someone to help organize a greater message to the French."

"And someone like me cannot be traced back to you?"

"You have a quick grasp of the situation. The Janjaweed and the Sudanese are looking for you. They believe you have gone to ground in one of the Arab countries. In France you can be anonymous and relatively safe. With a new identity and a clean face no one will recognize you. Avoid the religious fanatics and you can have a comfortable life. Choose now."

Sharif had made up his mind before the fat man had finished speaking. A comfortable, anonymous life in France while he did the Algerians bidding suited him. It would give him a chance to rebuild his life, and perhaps redeem himself enough to regain his stature in the Brotherhood. "I will be happy to serve."

"Good." He spoke a few words, in French, into an intercom box on his desk. He heard the door open behind him. "Go with this man. You will be furnished with new identity papers and briefed on your assets in Marseilles."

As Sharif neared the door he heard the fat mans last warning. "Do not stray from our path, Ali Alawa. We can be far more creative than your former associates."

Sharif had spent a week in Algeria. There had been injections to change the shape of his eyebrows and cheeks. He had been drilled in a very basic identity, enough to get him through a cursory interrogation, but nothing more. The 'assets' the fat man had spoken of consisted of a number of small, anonymous bank accounts, and a very short list of contacts. One of them would be his new 'employer' who would provide him with a legitimate income and a cover as a day laborer to move about freely. There were few specifics as to his mission to incite unrest. It was explained to him that French intelligence screened all immigrants initially, or at least it was believed they did. Sharif would live his cover for a few weeks until it was thought he was no longer a person of interest. Then, and only then, would he be given more information.

He had been taken to a bus stop in a rattle trap taxi, with directions on how to get to the harbor. The Algerians were severing their connection with Sharif as early as possible. The French still had a pervasive influence in their former colony, and the Algerians were certain that many of their people were known. Sharif was not to have any association that could be traced back to them, just in case.

The ferry trip was an agony for a desert dweller. The weather had deteriorated soon after they passed the mole in Oran harbor. Most of the passengers were reduced to seasickness for the trip. The weather only abated shortly before they arrived in Marseilles, but there was little improvement. Marseilles had a dirty harbor smell to it that filled the Arab quarter. Sharif found himself staying in a small hotel, sharing a small room with other recent immigrants. The personal hygiene of many of them left much to be desired. He found it distasteful that Muslims could be so unclean. He had to suffer through it for several days until he was able to arrange his first contact.

Once he had begun working under his new identity as a painter, he had been able to move to a small apartment and commence a relatively normal life. His new job, which was all too obvious as a do nothing position, had him painting the interior of a building that seemed to have already been freshly painted. The cover must have been the crazy woman who constantly complained about the color and quality of the work. Still, for a few hours labor he made a more than adequate wage and had the freedom to explore his new surroundings. He discovered that living in his new surroundings forced him to learn a new language, and he was surprised at how quickly he learned enough to get by. He was even learning enough to be able to understand parts of the newspaper. He began to rely on French papers, because the local Arabic ones were sorely lacking in accuracy. He was beginning to assimilate into his new surroundings. He began to look forward to whatever assignment the Algerians had in mind for him.

# CHAPTER 4

Price hadn't been able to pick up much from the Russians. They were mostly swapping insults about the Americans and commenting on various members of the briefing team. Captain Bonneville came in for more than her share of salacious comments, as did several of the other female officers who were present. The Russians still hadn't figured out they were only one or two steps removed from being classified as a third world country. There were only two phrases that kept being repeated without any context to explain them. They referred to 'Trans-Dnestr' several times, almost like it was a bad thing, and 'heavy stocks' like it was good. Price couldn't tell if they were talking about their investments, which he doubted, or something more mundane. He would leave that up to others to figure out for now. He was in a hurry to get his people together and go draw equipment.

Grant was equally as puzzled by the two phrases. He trusted Sharp and Harrison to do some research on the area. Moldova wasn't a place that made the papers very often, if at all. It would require an effort to tap into some outside sources. Sharp suggested letting the S-2 handle it. Captain Menklin was supposed to be a qualified Intelligence officer. He even wore the collar insignia, but so far hadn't displayed any great insights into any situation they had found themselves in. Price had worked for him in Africa, at least on paper. His opinion was the guy would get the weather report wrong if he was standing out in the rain. Not much of a recommendation, but like most of the officers, he was there because of who he knew, not what.

"We've got less than two weeks. Start collecting information. At some point we'll have to bring in the staff officers, so let's make sure we have enough to show them something."

Sharp wasn't convinced of the need. "It's a NATO gig. Won't they have all the info we need?"

Grant shook his head. "Sudan was a Central Command assignment, and look what happened." They had effectively gotten their asses handed to them, then got thrown out of the country. "No, something isn't right here. Where we're going is sandwiched between Romania and Ukraine. How come the Russians are briefing us? And why didn't the NATO packet say anything about that?" He continued. "This might just be something to get us as far under the radar as possible until Dillinghouse and Darfur die down, and maybe it isn't. Let's just make sure that if this is a simple road job, we're not putting it over a cliff. That clear?"

Everyone nodded agreement. There was a knock on the office door. It was Specialist Nelson, the Sergeant Major's driver. "What is it, Nelson?"

"Sergeant Major, We're all ready to go, but I've got a problem with vehicles."

"That's two things, Specialist. What's wrong with the vehicle, and who is 'we'?"

"Oh, I couldn't get a Hummer for the trip. Seems like all the staff has some place to go, so Sergeant Mitchell fixed me up with an old Blazer," The blazer had been a transitional vehicle between the Jeep and adoption of the Hummer. "And the 'we' is me and the S-1. She says you know about her going."

"OK, Nelson. I know about the Captain. I'll be right out."

Harrison was chuckling. "A Blazer? I thought they were all in the bone yard! The Army hasn't bought any of those in 20 years. Bring a cell phone. I'll arrange a pick-up after you break down."


Harrison was right. The Army hadn't bought any of the Chevy Blazers since the mid 80s. They had served their purpose as a bridge between the Jeep and the HUMMV, but would have a zero percent survival rate if they had to go into the same areas as the Hummer. As they were phased out, those that weren't sold as scrap or returned to the States to be sold off as surplus ended up in NATO support units, or loaned to the UN for service in the Balkans. As those agencies were able to upgrade, the Blazers trickled back into the US system. Because of the need for Hummers in Iraq and Afghanistan, the Blazers were reconditioned as best as possible and put into service. Breakdowns that couldn't be 'economically repaired' were consigned to bone yards to be cannibalized to keep others running. That's where this particular vehicle came from. Mitchell had pulled it out of a scrap pile and salvaged enough parts from various sources to keep it on the road as an extra set of wheels. It looked worse than it was. The motor pool had completely rebuilt the engine, and everything else worked. They had also become adept at swapping parts from better examples they found unattended.

Grant took a quick walk around. Fuck it, he thought. Better than walking. Captain Bonneville was already in back. "Nelson, what do you normally do when you aren't running my errands?"

"I'm an equipment operator, Sergeant Major. I usually run a loader."

"Why don't you go see Sergeant Price and help draw equipment? If there's a choice of equipment, maybe you can help pick out the best one."

"You sure, Sergeant Major?"

"Go ahead, I've made the trip often enough. I won't get lost."

He got behind the wheel and started the truck up. He looked over his shoulder at the Captain. "Are you going to sit back there for the whole trip, or come up here and keep me company?"


The trip up to Corps was uneventful. They made small talk, Grant not wanting to press any uncomfortable issues, Bonneville not volunteering any more information than necessary. There were long periods of strained silence until just before they reached the turnoff for Corps. As they waited in a line of vehicles going through an MP checkpoint, she finally turned and spoke. "I really need to talk to you about what's going on between us."

"As far as I can tell, right now there's nothing going on between us."

They were interrupted by the MP at the gate, checking IDs and the vehicle dispatch. "I don't get to see many of these, Sergeant Major."

"You know how us old soldiers are, Son. We tend to go back to the good old days. Maybe next time I'll have a jeep."

The MP laughed and waved them through. Grant continued with his previous chain of thought. "You changed when we got back from Africa. I don't know if it was the Perkin's warning about being close to the flag pole, or you just getting nervous because we were back around the real Army, but you started to act different. I thought giving you your space would help, but it didn't. You were another person when you came back from leave."

"I wish you had come home on leave with me."

"That wouldn't have worked, and you know it. You have your family and kids. My brother's family is nice, but you with your family, I would have had to spend time with mine. That's never a good idea."

"I thought you got along with them."

"I do, because we don't spend a lot of time together. If it wasn't for the fact he gets to live in my house for free and take care of it while I'm gone, we probably wouldn't even speak to each other."

"What would that have to do with us?"

"I get cranky. You wouldn't like that."

She thought about that for a few minutes. "My ex started coming around while I was home."

"How'd that work for you?"

"He was only interested in two things, getting laid and getting his hands on my pay and benefits. When he couldn't get them both he went back to his old ways."

Grant could figure out which one he did get. Oh, well, it was good while it lasted. She was still talking. "I'm sorry."

"Sorry for what? We were an item. Now we're not. I'm not like your ex. You have your own life to live." He pulled into a visitor's spot in front of the Headquarters building. "I'm not going to try to run it for you, and I'm not going to blame you for living it."

"I just wish it could be like it was before."

"Is that what you really want?"

"Yes. Can we try? Please?"

He looked at her. If this conversation continued, one of them was going to start crying. He reached over and squeezed her knee. "Let's continue this later."

The Corps Commanders secretary directed Grant to the Chief of Staff. This was something new. He had always gone to the commander's office for his weekly ass chewing. He must be trying to spread the wealth. After Grant reported, the CoS directed him to sit. The CoS came around his desk to join him. He held his hand out for the equipment report.

"You've wasted a lot of time on this, Sergeant Major. I will say that you've kept better track of equipment across two continents than most commanders do in their own motor pools." Grant didn't respond. The

CoS went on. "Well, this is over. This isn't something you should have been doing. Once CENTCOM got wind of it they put a stop to it."

Grant still didn't respond. He knew he had been wasting his time. He didn't need to be reminded of it over and over. "Ever wonder why, Sergeant Major?"

"I've been on somebody's shit list for a long time. This was just part of it."

"You've been on quite a few of those lists. Those two contractors had some influential relatives." He was talking about the two contractors he was supposed to watch in Iraq. "Getting them killed wasn't the best career move."

That did it for Grant. Those two ass holes had gone out and gotten themselves whacked. He was tired of taking the blame. "Maybe it's time those influential relatives knew why those two are dead. I'm sure they were never told they were totally unqualified to be there, had no idea what they were doing, and practically walked around with a neon sign that said 'Stupid – Kill Us' in downtown Baghdad."

"That's enough. We don't have to go there."

"Well yes we do. My last posting would have been Sergeant Major of the Army. Instead, because those two wanted to go out and see if Baghdad was like Saigon in the 60's, I've got rag heads in Africa trying to kill me."

"Sergeant Major. . ."

"No! Before we killed his 'translator' he bragged about the infidels who were looking for Iraqi women to defile. Those boys spent most of their time looking for women. They were about to be charged with attempted rape on a little Air Force girl they cornered outside her quarters. Get that report declassified, and get off my back. The Army was ready to sacrifice me so some politician wouldn't be embarrassed by his worthless nephew or whatever the hell he was."

"He's still an important man, and important to the Army."

"And I'm still important to me, and I still have a copy of the CID investigation on those two. My last official act might just be to wait for somebody to run for reelection and hold my own press conference. After what happened to Dillinghouse I wouldn't have any trouble getting air time."

"That's a dangerous attitude, Sergeant Major. I hope you don't repeat it. I know you've been fucked over. My job here was to tell you it's done. I can't do anything about the rest of your career. I just want you to know this Headquarters won't be interfering with it any more."

Grant was sitting in his vehicle, still stewing about his meeting with the Chief of Staff, when he saw Bonneville coming out of the main entrance. There was a soldier following her. They both had their arms full of boxes. Grant got out and took her load. The soldier put his in the back of the Blazer and said he'd be right back with the rest. They were still arranging the load when he came out with another soldier, similarly loaded.

"What the hell is all this?"

The two soldiers helped put the larger boxes in the back seat. "These are from the Corps G-2, Sergeant Major. Maps. There's some classified documents, too, but those will be going down by courier in the morning."

Bonneville climbed into her seat and wiped her forehead with her beret. She looked over her shoulder at the pile. "They loaded me up with everything! Orders, citations, medal sets, commendations, badges. You name it, I've got it back there." She pulled a fat manila envelope of the top of the pile. These are the rosters of everything. I have to go over them before the end of the week to make sure everything is correct."

He smiled at her. "That should keep you tied up for the rest of the week."

"It will, but not tonight. Can we go someplace? Away from the Army? I need to get some things off my chest."

That comment gave him a mental image, and his smile must have given it away. She noticed it and returned it. "That's an evil look, Sergeant Major." She fastened her seat belt. "I like it."

Congressman Walter Dillinghouse came out of the courtroom stunned. He couldn't believe that after his lawyer had made such a piss poor motion to have the evidence of his malfeasance, the diamonds and the video tape, suppressed, the US Attorney had made such a feeble objection to object to it. The judge said he would rule in a few days. It had to be more than just coincidence. Could the Sudanese, his sponsors, have gotten to the Justice Department? He doubted it, but he would do some checking with the few sources he still had left.

Once he was back in his office, which was still showing the signs of repeated FBI searches, he sat in the semi-darkness of his office. He still couldn't believe how his fate was turning. A secretary, one he hadn't remembered seeing before, knocked on his door, and announced "The Speaker would like to see you right away." Before she could leave he asked who she was. "I'm new. I was just hired a few days ago."

"What happened to the other girls?"

"Most of them have left. For one reason or another."

Dillinghouse wasn't satisfied. "And you decided that this was the job you had to have?"

"No, Sir. I decided that this was the job that was going to pay my mortgage and give my kids some medical insurance for a while. As long as you don't resign or get voted out, I'll be here."

"Purely mercenary, eh?"

"Just like you, Sir. I'm in it for the money."

Well, he thought. I guess that's going to be what I can expect until somebody else steps on his dick a little harder. At least she had big boobs to look at. He grabbed his cell phone and headed out to the Speaker's office. There was a time, not all that long ago, when the Speaker of the House of Representatives would have been a little more polite in asking him to come up. Instead of 'right away' it would have been more like 'at your convenience' or some other solicitous plea. He didn't like this new tone.

There were only a few staffers in the outer office. The receptionist made a quick call and sent him right in. At least I don't have to cool my heels like the freshmen (or the other side of the aisle).

The speaker was an older woman. In spite of efforts at hair color, surgery and botox, she still showed her mileage. And it was a lot of miles. She got right to the point.

"I've had to call in a lot of favors for you. I don't like to do that, especially now."

'Now' was her way of saying it interfered with her claim to be running a scandal free party. Ethics were the hot button topic, and she spent a lot of time and effort making sure her party didn't get the same scrutiny as the other guys. Dillinghouse smiled inwardly at that thought. Both parties had their share of shady characters. It was all a matter of not getting caught. Dillinghouse went on the defensive. "I appreciate what you've done, but I think someone else may be greasing some skids for me. You should have seen what happened in court a little while ago."

"I know what happened in court! Who do you think made it happen, the tooth fairy?"

"I didn't know."

"That's the idea. You think I'm going to advertise I have a US Attorney for the District of Columbia in my pocket? Or a Federal Judge?"

This was a surprise. Many judges were politically compromised for one reason or another, but it was rare that anyone in government would actually admit to owning one. "You have the judge, too?"

She shook her head. No wonder this idiot got caught, and by a soldier, of all people. "One is no good without the other, but you still have a price to pay for this largesse."

Dillinghouse was on familiar grounds now. This he could deal with. "There's always a price, Amanda. What's yours?"

She walked to the window and looked out towards the White House. "I plan to be in there in a few years. That'll cost two things: influence and money. Influence can't get the money, but money certainly will get the influence. I expect you will help with the cost."

"Of course. How much support would you like me to arrange?"

"I need ten million pledged to my exploratory committee in the next 72 hours."

Dillinghouse choked. "Ten million! In 72 hours? That's insane!"

She smiled at him. "Walter, I know you have the contacts. If you can't get the pledges before the judge rules, I'm afraid you'll have to look at a short trial and a long sentence." She sat back down. "Oh, one more thing. If the judge rules against you, I'm afraid we'll have to vote to remove you. It wouldn't do to have someone as ethically challenged as you reminding everyone who's party you belong to."

With that she took his arm and walked him to the door. "I hope to hear from you soon, Walter, at least in the next couple of days."

Drawing equipment from a consolidation site is a lot different from having it issued to a unit to keep. When it's issued, the unit can inspect for deficiencies, make note of problems, and not get hammered on its maintenance budget, because repair parts can be written off as part of the initial issue. On the other hand, the ECS equipment is a matter of what you sign for is what you get. The site expects the equipment back in the same or better condition than what it was issued, and they aren't the pickiest people in the world when it comes to issue condition. It's up to the unit to inspect what they're drawing and decide whether to accept the equipment with annotated deficiencies, or try another piece. Many a unit has found out the hard way that if they didn't note a problem at the start, it's their dollar that repairs it before the ECS people have to take it back, and the inspection is very detailed during the return inspection.

SSG Price was aware of this, having drawn equipment many times in the past. He never drew stuff this big before, but he knew the same rules applied, and stayed on his operators and mechanics to be thorough. Lieutenant Stanley had never gone through anything like this. She was impatient to take possession of the equipment for her first command. Price had to constantly intercede, trying to keep the process on track and give his new Platoon Leader an education at the same time. He finally got his point across when they were about to sign for a front-end loader. Price noticed some corrosion on a hydraulic fitting. Stanley was willing to ignore it, but Price insisted the operator put a little stress on the system by trying to lift the front end by it's own bucket. The strain was enough to blow the fitting.

Stanley got the message. She let her NCOs do what they did best, and she paid attention to what they did. Price encouraged her to ask questions. "I don't care how stupid it may sound to you, ask it. Three months from now, some general's going to come along and ask the same question. That's not the time to plead ignorance. The last thing you'll hear is the general telling his aide to get your name."

The next surprise was a big one. As soon as they finished drawing equipment, they were directed to another holding area. A transportation outfit was waiting for them. They were to immediately start processing the equipment for rail shipment. The transportation people were only there as instructors. The 289th would have to learn to rail load and unload their own equipment, and they only had a week to do it in. Their equipment was scheduled to leave before the main body with only a small detachment as escorts. They would hook up with an advance party at Kipercheny. Price started making plans to get as many of his people as possible on the advance.

Bonneville's plans for the evening were dashed as soon as they returned. Perkins had scheduled a staff call for the evening, right after dinner. He told them to expect to be there until the wee hours, as he wanted to finalize all their plans, rosters and operations orders. She pointed out that there would be a classified courier coming down in the morning with classified material. Perkins just brushed her off. "Anything he brings down can be put into the annexes. They'll just be maps, signal instructions and re-supply information. It'll be easy to plug it into our plans." She hid her disappointment and went looking for the Sergeant Major. Grant was in the First Sergeant's office, getting an update from Harrison and Price. Price relayed what he had learned from eavesdropping on the Russians. It wasn't much, and it raised a bunch more questions.

"Why the Russians? They aren't anywhere near where we're going to be. I don't understand why there weren't some locals briefing us."

Sharp interrupted. He had just returned from his own intelligence gathering mission. "I still have friends over in 7th Group. They had quite a bit on Moldova and faxed me a bunch of it. Some of the stuff is classified, so we'll probably never know, but there'll be more here in a few days."

Harrison was interested and asked first. "What'cha got for us?"

"I think Uncle Ivan is trying to fuck with us. Seems like the locals don't want any roadwork done in that area. It's not for them. The Russians still have 'detachments' scattered all over the area, plus more across the river."

Grant picked up on that. "The river? Is that what they meant by the 'Trans-Dnestr'?"

"Exactly. Seems like the Russians still have a shit load of gear in storage in the country. The US has been trying to pressure them into pulling out, and it looks like the road is part of the pressure."

"How so?"

"Ivan says the road net sucks, and he can't back haul his stuff out securely. That's the key word: Securely. The Trans-Dnestr is a breakaway republic. They pretty much ignore the Moldovan government. They even have their own currency. Moldova used to be part of Romania. The Trans-Dnestr used to be part of Ukraine. It's like the Balkans. Nobody is where they want to be. At least these people aren't shooting at each other. There's no ethnic or religious differences to speak of, just some Turks, but they have their own region far to the south."

"So how is this new 'Republic' hanging on?" That was Harrison.

"Just barely. Right now the two sides are content to ignore one another, but the Russians, Ukrainians and Romanians are all trying to stir things up. Not having too much success, though. I think part of it is the national product. These people specialize in wines and brandy. Something about civil war having a tendency to fuck up the grape vines."

Bonneville spoke up. "That still doesn't make any sense. Why are we getting involved?"

Harrison agreed. "The good Captain has a point. Why are we getting involved?"

Sharp answered them. "European Union playing geopolitics. Lucky us. We get to be pawns again."

"EU?" This was from Price. "What the hell is the European Union doing involved in this?"

"Come on, Pricey. You been living under a rock? NATO was cold war, when everyone here was worried about the big, bad USSR. They all wanted the US to be the bad guy and take the heat. Now the Soviets are gone, and the Russian Federation isn't considered much of a threat, so the Europeans came out from under their rock. They're flexing some muscle when it comes to shit that doesn't require much, and using NATO for all the really crappy jobs, like Kosovo and Afghanistan."

"What's that got to do with us?"

Sharp sighed. "My buddies at 7th Group told me that there isn't any Islamic threat in that part of the world right now. They're hoping we'll be a magnet for it. Then they can point out how bad US leadership is, minimize NATO and roll the assets up into the EU. Oh, yeah, and still keep the American money."

The Sergeant Major put the cap on it. "As soon as we get the rest of the info from 7th Group we'll meet again. In the meantime, start planning on how to stash extra gear on the equipment train." He didn't have to specify what he meant by 'extra gear'. They all knew what he meant.

In the hallway Bonneville told him about the staff meeting. Grant hadn't heard about it yet. "So much for getting away from the Army for the night."

"Is there anything we can do?"

"It's about two hours until the meeting. If you don't mind skipping supper, I've got solid walls and a lock on my door."

She smiled at him. "Give me ten minutes before you come up. I want to get ready for you."

She had been waiting for him, kneeling on his bed, her hair loose, wearing a sultry smile, an oversized T-shirt and, from what he could see, nothing else. He crossed to the bed. "I can see that the wicked witch has been reincarnated." The Wicked Witch had been the name of the crashed B-17 bomber they had recovered in Africa. The nose art, a naked witch, was popular throughout the company, with both the males and females.

"Come here and let me show you how wicked!" Grant slid off his shirt as her hands unfastened his belt and opened his trousers. The thought of what she was going to do had him instantly aroused. Grant had never met a woman who enjoyed sex, both giving and receiving, as much as Linda Bonneville did. She was enthusiastic, imaginative and talented. She enveloped him like a warm cloud. His hands reached down and cupped her breasts. Her nipples were like pencil erasers, and she liked to have them played with. She lay back, pulling him after her. She was still shuddering as she pulled his face to hers, her hands guiding him. "I want to feel you inside me again." They both climaxed together.

She didn't let him rest long. She 'ooh'd and aah'd as she moved up and down, her head thrown back. Her hands held his on her breasts, squeezing his fingers into her firm skin. She stifled a moan as another shudder overtook her. Then she slumped down and lay atop Grant, still using her muscles to squeeze him.

Finally, they just lay together, her head on his chest. As she cupped and squeezed him, he stroked her hair with one hand while teasing a nipple with the other.

"I've missed that," she said.

"So have I. Nobody does the things you do to me."

"I'm glad."

They were quiet for a few minutes. Then she spoke. "I'm sorry I got involved with my ex-husband when I was on leave. All he ever wants is sex and my money."

Grant grunted. "That's all most men want, but you can spare me the details."

"You're not mad?"

"About what? You make your own decisions. If I get included, that's great. I'm too old to be throwing tantrums like a teenager. It would only bother me if you were doing us both at the same time."

She gave him a squeeze that made him wince. He could feel himself stirring again. "You better cut that out, Linda. It's almost time for Perkins and his meeting."

"Fuck him," she giggled. "No, on second thought, I'd rather fuck you." She thought for a moment. "You said most guys. Does that include you?"

"Nope. I've got my own money." Then he pushed her back down. "We need to get going."

She stood up naked in front of him. She leaned over and kissed him hard on the mouth, and moved away as he tried to grab her again. "OK," she laughed, "but now you owe me one, and I'm going to collect later." She dressed quickly, opened his door a crack to peek out, then was gone. Grant could still smell her on himself. He decided he better take a quick shower. He hoped she had the same idea, or after a few hours in the conference room, everybody would know what had just happened.

# CHAPTER 5

The equipment train was loaded and ready to go. There were a few last minute additions to the cargo in one freight car that the NCOs had collectively decided they would need. Most of it was 'off the books' supplies, such as extra ammo they had scrounged up, spare parts, and comfort items. There were also two passenger cars attached for the troops. It was not the advance party Grant or Price wanted, but Colonel Perkins and his staff had drawn up a list that reflected what they would have ordinarily sent to Annual Training, not for a deployment to a foreign country. The lessons of Sudan were already fading from his memory.

Price was still grumbling about the makeup. Both Grant and Sharp were trying to calm him down.

"Pricey, this is where you always shoot yourself in the foot. This is what it is, make the best of it." Sharp was worried his friend would do something to end his career yet again. "You aren't in charge. Those people are. Just do your part, and try not to let whatever they fuck up splash onto you."

"God damn it, you know it isn't right! Luke, Bonneville may be your honey, but she's in over her head here. Between that asshole Winder and Gaston the S-4, there's not enough experience to know when they're in trouble. What happens when we get there and we find out it ain't as rosy as the Russians said? Then what? We've got no extra fuel, damn little in the way of food and water, and the weapons are all locked up. These jokers didn't even bother with a map until I pointed out they might need one."

Price was right about a lot of things. Bonneville wasn't supposed to go with the advance. It was supposed to be the XO. Carstairs had begged off, saying he was still trying to get the new S-3 set up, and that the Adjutant was the person responsible for an administrative move like this. Perkins had accepted the arguments and assigned Bonneville at the last minute. Grant had little time to bring her up to speed, and he was counting on Price to keep her out of trouble. He knew he could rely on his old friend, he just had to get through the verbal barrage before Price's professionalism kicked in and he started acting like the NCO he was. The 7th Special Forces Group had provided most of the information they were working with, and it had all been provided unofficially. In spite of Grant's best efforts, Perkins preferred to use the information that came down from Corps as gospel. Grant had had an opportunity to compare both sets of data. The Corps packet provided a lot of good information if you were a tourist, or if you were a businessman looking to set up shop. What it lacked was the nitty-gritty info like attitudes towards foreign military, interest groups, minorities and extremists. 7th Group had included that type of information, but it was still sketchy. Boiled down to the lowest common denominator, the threat potential could be summed up as 'you probably won't have a problem, but..." Not the most reassuring assessment in the world, but you could say that about most countries in the world, or even a lot of major cities in the US. The NCOs had done their best to prepare the Advance Party. They could only do so much. Price had about a dozen soldiers he could count on, and that's where he concentrated his efforts. He counted himself lucky that Sergeant Elko, the most experienced of the medics, and a woman with whom he had a mutual understanding, had been assigned. She would be someone he could bounce ideas off, and hopefully an ally for Bonneville when Gaston and Winder started ganging up on her. She was the nominal commander of the Advance, but Price knew those two would be obstacles.

CSM Grant was trying to be practical. "Pricey, stick to your orders. Hold your ground and back Bonneville up. You establish a base camp, prepare the equipment, and wait for the main body. Nobody needs to be a tourist, and I don't want any heroes. That clear?"

It was clear to Price.

The signal was given to load up. Grant had already said his good-byes to Bonneville the night before. There wouldn't be any public displays of affection. They were both all business. She came over to say god bye one last time. Grant gave her a formal military salute, and as she returned it, he winked. It took the edge off the parting for both of them. "I'll see you in Moldova, Captain."

"You too, Sergeant Major. Don't keep us waiting. We have a lot to do."

"Yes, we do, Ma'am, Yes we do."

Then she turned and climbed into the coach as the train started moving. Grant stood and watched it until it made the curve out of the rail yard. There was another line of cars waiting to be loaded. This one was shorter, with no flat cars for motor vehicles. Those were all on the first train. Just box cars for organic equipment and carriages for personnel. They would be leaving in three days.

It would be a long three days. The emphasis had been on preparing the advance party. Very little had been done for the main body. The old adage that the troops do well what the commander inspects was proving accurate. Most of the sections had still not packed or inventoried equipment. With each section sending some personnel, some section NCOs took advantage of the opportunity to go with the advance, leaving subordinates, in many cases inexperienced subordinates, to try and figure out how to execute load plans. Grant knew the line platoons would figure it out quickly. The staff sections he wasn't so sure about. It was still a case of lessons learned being forgotten quickly. Grant decided to work with one section at a time, then move on. If they paid attention, they would be fine. If not, it would take them a long time to reorganize at the end of the trip.

Sometimes you get lucky. Grant found that was true when he checked in with the Personnel section, S-1. Bonneville had left her section in good shape and ready to go. All the orders had been cut and signed, rosters were made up, loading assignments done, and the payroll changes submitted. Sheila Gordon, the personnel NCO, was in the process of updating records as she packed them, and had her computer updates loaded on a lap top so she could keep working on the train ride. NCO and Officer evaluations were up to date, and suspense dates for future promotion boards were already posted.

Grant had not expected SSG Gordon to return after her leave time. There had been rumors about her involvement with the civilian reporter, Cynthia Maddox, in Sudan. There were more rumors that Gordon was going to shop her story around to the tabloids. That evidently proved itself false, because here she was, and there hadn't been any uproar in the press about it. He was glad she was back. Gordon was a hard worker and knew her stuff. She seemed to be a loyal subordinate, and his NCOs, especially Sharp, had faith in her abilities. Grant could give a rats' ass less about anybody's sexual orientation. As long as they did their job and didn't bother anyone, a standard he held for everyone, he was satisfied.

The S-2 section was less organized, but, at this stage of the game, no matter what Captain Menklin could have done wouldn't have made a difference. He had the information Corps and NATO had provided on Moldova, sparse and, sometimes, inaccurate as it was. He had been fed the information 7th Group had provided in small increments, so as not to overwhelm him. Unfortunately, Menklin was an unimaginative type who could thrive in the political atmosphere of the 289th at home station. Once he got into the field he had no clue as to how to interpret raw data. He would be lost now that Price had been reassigned to a line platoon. Grant made a mental note to keep an eye out for one of the more intellectual types out in the line platoons. Maybe he could convince one of them to transfer. At least there was a stripe attached to the position.

The Operations Section had a mixed blessing with the absence of Master Sergeant Winder. Winder stifled creativity because he had a need to take credit for everything. The troops responded by doing as little as possible, and only when directed. Sharp was starting to break them of that habit, but he had spent so little time actually working in the section, that he was still considered an outsider. The upside was that in Winder's absence Sharp had been a little more forthcoming in praise and encouragement, and some of the soldiers were taking the initiative. A few of them had been around long enough to know exactly what needed to be done and were slowly starting to share that knowledge.

S-3 had been given the sketchiest of plans. They had maps. The blueprints of the job were adequate, although all the information hadn't been translated into English. The section surveyors would be working overtime to re-shoot all the data and draw up new prints. Unfortunately, no one could have been convinced that they needed to be on the advance so they could start work. It would cause delays on site. Lieutenant Stanley and SSG Price would probably have to take the heat for that.

The S-4 was, in Grant's opinion, a disaster. Captain Gaston, like Winder, had abandoned his section. All they could do was process deliveries that were expected, but Gaston had taken some key documents with him. He should have never been allowed to go on the advance. His argument that he needed to verify contracts and suppliers on sight was just an excuse to avoid responsibility. His assistant and the rest of the S-4 section would pay the price for any shortfalls, while Grant was certain Gaston would take credit for things that went right that he had no influence over. He was another one that thrived in a political atmosphere, but was worthless on his own.

Civil Affairs, the S-5, was easy. 1LT Sage had been reduced to ineffectiveness by the turn of events in Sudan. As a result, he had been overlooked in the planning for Moldova. He had nothing to do, and once his office supplies had been boxed up for shipping, he had remained largely out of sight. Grant anticipated that he could be problematic in the future. There was nothing worse than an officer who has been marginalized who still thinks he's important. All it could mean was that Sage would be doing something both stupid and dangerous. Grant just hoped it wouldn't be as bad as the Chaplain had been in Sudan. Lieutenant Moraine had managed to get so deeply involved in Arab affairs that he went bad and got himself killed, very slowly and very painfully.

Grant decided he needed a break for himself. His packing had long been completed. If he wasn't wearing it, it was in his rucksack or duffel bag. His new best friend was a laptop computer that the S-1 was taking care of for him. Any comfort items were long since gone on the train. Price had a whole platoon and plenty of vehicles to use in arranging a civilized lifestyle. He and Sharp would take care of them at the far end. Grant just went to the closet sized office that was left to him and put his feet up on the desk for a few minutes. A nap was out of the question, besides, he only indulged in them when he was on the go in 24 hour cycles. He found that if he was getting 6 or 7 hours sleep at night he had plenty of reserves for the rest of the day. He just needed some 'alone' time, and maybe a cup of coffee. He decided to go looking for one in the Mess Hall. It would give him a chance to see how SFC Moura was doing with his packing.

Price was in his element in the confusion of the equipment unload. Since there were only a few soldiers who had paid attention at the briefings, most didn't know what was going on. Winder was one of them, so instead of trying to find out what the plan was, he grabbed one of the first vehicles off-loaded that he could drive (most of the larger trucks were beyond his abilities) and disappeared toward what he believed would be their new quarters. Elko was with Price watching him. "Where's he going? I thought our buildings were over to the left."

Captain Bonneville joined them. "Where's he going?"

Price was slow to respond. "I'm not quite sure, Ma'am. I think he loaded up all his personal gear and went looking for quarters." That was the best explanation. Winder was the type who would grab the best quarters for himself, then padlock the door so nobody could inspect them for appropriateness.

"I thought our buildings were over there." She pointed to the left.

"They are."

Bonneville looked at Price. "Should we send somebody after him? He took Captain Gaston with him. It wouldn't be good if they got lost."

Price chuckled. "Think they're smart enough to turn around once they hit the fence? No, let them go. At least we'll have a few minutes to get things done while they're gone." Then he had a thought. "I've got an idea." He called the Gold Dust twins over. The Robinson brothers weren't that hard to tell apart anymore. One of them had picked up a scar on his forehead, among other places, in Africa. "What are you two doing?" They were both still assigned to the S-4. At least on paper, but they took every opportunity to work with either Price or Sharp. They had both volunteered for the advance, and they were both still trying to work their way into a transfer to Price's new platoon. They preferred soldiering to the 'make work and waste time' attitude of the headquarters section.

"Ma'am, why don't you give these two NCO's that box of padlocks and hasps? They can scoot over to where we're supposed to be and start securing the building."

Bonneville caught on to what Price wanted. She had spent considerable time on the train with building plans, assigning quarters and office spaces based on hierarchy and needs, not personal whims. Price had figured out what Gaston and Winder were doing. She handed over a rolled up floor plan to the headquarters building and what would be the Officer and Senior NCO quarters. "There's a box of signs and stencils in the back of my truck. How long will it take?" Edwin, the one with the scar, looked at the plans quickly. "Give us one more helper and we'll be back in an hour."

Price nodded. He looked over to a group of soldiers who were waiting for a forklift to free up so they could start unloading a freight car. "Johnson! Go with Robinson here."

Gaston and Winder parked in front of what they believed was their building at the far end of the parade ground. Gaston looked around and had his doubts. "Winder, are you sure this is where we belong? I thought we were at the other end of the compound." Winder looked at a sketch he had made. He had drawn the end of the parade ground and the four primary buildings they were to be in. In his typical haphazard fashion, he had failed to note any reference points or directions on the sketch. He had started looking at it upside down, and that was the image he had fashioned in his brain. "This is the place. Emile. The best rooms are on the second floor at either end. They're the farthest from the entrances. dayroom and showers. All the first floor rooms are smaller. They'll be good for the junior officers and NCOs. Grab your stuff."

They lugged their duffel bags up the stairs, and made more trips for cots and other gear they had brought. Winder picked out what he thought was a superior room. It even had a private bath, which would be a real luxury. Once the door was secured, no one could get into it to see what he had. After everyone was moved in it would be too late. He was proud of himself as he went looking for a broom to sweep up with. Gaston had found a similar room, although his didn't have a bath. He was pleased with it. He too went looking for cleaning gear. He was just finishing up when Winder came to his door. "I've got some hasps here so we can get padlocks up. Don't put your name on the door until after everyone's moved in."

Gaston looked out his window. He could look down and see the rail siding at the far end of the field. "How come nobody else is coming this way?"

"Don't worry about it. That idiot Price is probably getting everything off the train before he lets anybody start looking for creature comforts, and Bonneville is dumb enough to let him take charge. She's lucky she looks good in a sweaty T-shirt, or I don't think Perkins would keep her around."

Gaston laughed. He had been one of the officers who had spent time trying to get in her pants when she was first assigned. She had pretty much shot everyone down, some more rudely than others. The married officers got the worst treatment when they tried to hit on her, and since she had access to all the personnel files, she knew who the married ones were. Gaston was married, but he still resented the rejection. Since that day she had berated him in front of several fellow officers he had made it a point to give her as little cooperation as he could get away with. He knew Winder was wrong about Perkins keeping her around for her looks. She was a good S-1 and adjutant, one of the few competent officers Perkins had chosen for staff positions. Still, Gaston thought, she would have been a better team player if she had put out a little. The Army was a lot like Vegas: What happened in the field, stayed in the field.

Gaston waited for Winder to finish wandering around the building, poking into all the rooms. He scavenged up some furniture for their rooms and found one of the crappiest rooms on the first floor. He added to the mess by breaking out a window and kicking a hole in the bottom of the door. Then he took out a marking pen, and in big block letters assigned the room to CSM Grant.

The room detail came back in less than an hour, their work complete. It was a change from when CSM Grant had first met them. It had been at home station and they were working on inventorying office space and equipment. They had been incredibly slow when it came to counting chairs and desks, and were in the habit of taking long lunches when they were unsupervised. Grant had timed them at four hours his first day on the job.

They were good soldiers at heart though, and all they needed was supervision and leadership. They responded well to both and had subsequently earned promotions. They finished all their assignments quickly, and were always available for more. They handed Bonneville a key roster and her floor plan. She noticed they had made some pencil changes and asked why. Robinson told her about some of the rooms they had looked at. The plans didn't show it, but there were three rooms on the second floor with private baths. They had taken the liberty of assigning them to the CO, XO and her. She saw her room was no longer next to the Sergeant Major's, but having her own shower might be a good trade off. The headquarters building had also been secured and labeled. The platoons would each get a floor in the other two buildings. Those would be up to the platoon sergeants to assign. For now, the advance party would be consolidated into one building.

A group of Moldovan officers had come over to watch what was going on. In spite of the language barrier, Bonneville tried to be friendly and show them around the equipment. Price watched her struggle for a while, then offered to translate. As it happened, as soon as he began to speak Russian, two of the officers developed an amazing gift for English. Price let them handle the translations and went back to his own work.

Bonneville was surprised to learn that, in spite of the government reluctance to have foreign soldiers in their country, the Moldovan officers looked forward to working with the Americans. In spite of the 'ugly American' label, most foreign armies realized that working with Americans was always beneficial. US soldiers were friendly, readily shared their rations and personal possessions, and were eager to demonstrate their equipment. They also usually found time and resources to do projects on the side that would benefit the host nation and its people in some way. Americans could also be counted on to arrange future contacts, which usually included trips to the US that were fully paid for. It was hard to ignore such largesse.

The Moldovans spent time examining the heavy equipment as it came off the flat cars. When it was time to leave they invited Bonneville, and all of 'her' officers, to join them at their Mess for the evening meal. A woman in charge of all this equipment was an oddity in Moldova, and they wanted to learn more. Being an attractive woman didn't hurt either.

The Moldovans were leaving as Gaston and Winder were driving up. They stopped near where Price was getting the last dozer off.

The unloading had gone remarkably quickly. When the Russians designed this base they had planned for rapid loading and unloading of heavy main battle tanks. The loading docks were wide enough to accommodate their heaviest equipment, and were built level with the flat and freight cars. It was also long enough to accommodate four cars at a time, with ramps at either end. It made the process easy for the limited numbers of equipment operators Price was able to bring with him.

Price could see that they were pleased with themselves. Obviously, they had helped themselves to the best quarters available. He had to stifle an involuntary chuckle. The Robinson's had told him they had also 'reassigned' Gaston and Winder to a couple of the smaller rooms, both overlooking a dumpster at the end of the building. Winder, it seemed, created bad blood with every subordinate he met.

"Hey, Price!" Winder was yelling over the noise, "when are you going to start moving gear to the motor pool?" Price just ignored him. Winder came closer and repeated himself, and when Price continued to ignore him he made the mistake of grabbing his arm. Price took the fingers and twisted Winder to the ground. He was still squeezing the fingers rather painfully as he feigned surprise at seeing Winder on the ground. "Damn, Master Sergeant, I thought you were an Arab sneaking up on me." He let go of the fingers, but didn't offer to help him up. "Are you OK?"

Winder picked himself up and brushed off. His hand was burning from the pain of the takedown, but he tried not to show it to Price. It didn't work. Price could see Winder was in pain, and let a small grin slip. "Arab my ass. You could hear me talking to you!"

Price stepped closer. Winder involuntarily backed up. He may have the rank, but he also knew he was afraid of Price physically. "Well, I guess that'll be between me, you and my physical profile. I can either claim bad ears or posttraumatic stress. But feel free to complain to someone. I'm sure the troops would like to hear you whine about how easy it was to put you down."

Winder backed up another step. He knew Price was challenging him, hoping he would throw a punch. Winder also knew he would lose, just like he lost when he tried to take on Sharp in Sudan. He knew the only edge he had over these men was his rank. They were professional enough to respect it, but they thought very little of the man behind the stripes. ""Your day's gonna come, Price. I just hope I'm there to see it."

Price smiled even wider. "When I get mine, Winder, you won't have the balls to be anywhere near that situation. And if you are there, your eyes will be closed, and you'll be hiding."

Gaston had let this go on long enough. It was to the point now that if there were punches thrown, it would be his ass for letting these two bicker back and forth. He stepped between the two. "Break it up. You two act like NCOs in front of the troops!" A few of the soldiers had seen what was going on and had stopped working to watch. One had whipped out his cell phone and snapped a picture of Winder on the ground. It would look good hanging on a bulletin board.

Gaston ordered the men back to work. "Sergeant Price, let me ask. When is the equipment going to start moving to the motor pool? Isn't it a wasted effort to stage it over there just to have to move it again?"

Price smiled again. He was starting to enjoy himself. These two clowns would get lost in front of a urinal. "The equipment's not being staged, Sir. That's our motor park."

"Why is it so far from our barracks?" He looked over his shoulder, then back at Price with a puzzled look on his face. "This doesn't make sense. Let me look at the site map again." The 'again' was for the benefit of soldiers who were working as slow as possible behind them. They knew what was going on and didn't want to miss any of it. The stories would be passed around with the beer for many nights to come. Price passed over the map. "This isn't right. Sergeant Winder, let me see your strip map." As soon as he compared the two pieces of paper, Gaston started feeling foolish. He was trying to come up with something to say so he wouldn't look foolish when Price ended all chance of that. "You two didn't put your gear over in those buildings, did you?" The troops were laughing now. Winders face was red from embarrassment. Gaston took his arm and started to lead him to the truck. A voice stopped them. "Is that the missing truck? We need that vehicle to move these tool boxes to the maintenance shed." Captain Bonneville was standing in the door to the freight cat. "I want all the equipment secured before dark." Price plucked the keys out of Winders hand. "If you want to wait, I'll have a detail help you retrieve your stuff later."

There was a new face walking down the hallway. Ordinarily he wouldn't have attracted any attention, but this guy was walking in civilian clothes, with a full duffel bag on one shoulder and a B-4 bag in tow. All baggage had already been loaded for the morning departure. Who was this guy?

Dave Sharp was making his way down the hall with a fresh case of beer. He came up behind the stranger and called to him. "Hey buddy, what are you doing with that luggage? It should have been loaded hours ago." The new man just turned and looked at him. His eyes drifted down to the case of beer, then back up. "I'm just signing in. Where would I find the S-1?"

"The S-1?" He pointed off to his left. "About a couple of hundred miles that way. She's already deployed. How about the Personnel NCO? Will she do for ya?"

He nodded, and Sharp motioned for him to follow. He entered a room with a hand-lettered sign on the door that read 'Orderly Room – Moving Sale' and called out. "Enjoy it while it lasts, this is the last case available." The stranger saw there was a mixed crowd in the room. An older face was sitting behind a desk, staring at him as if trying to identify him. That must have been the First Sergeant. "Are you the First Shirt?" A voice over his shoulder answered.

"That would be me."

He looked at the NCO. He was sitting in a half circle of chairs. He had a beer in his hand, as did most of the other men and women. "What can we do for you?"

Sharp answered for him. "I found him lost in the hallway. He says he's joining the rest of us orphans. I guess he needs to see you, Sheila." He turned back to the stranger. "This is Staff Sergeant Gordon, Personnel NCO and all around humanitarian. Anything you can do with him tonight, Sheila?"

Gordon put down her beer and stood up. "I can get his paperwork and get him added to the manifests. Come on with me. It'll only take a few minutes. What's your name?"

"Morgan."

"That first or last?"

"Last."

Harrison stood up. "Well, hell, son. There a front end to that name?"

"Daniel."

"Good. Daniel, you come back here after the Sergeant is done and we'll find you a place to sleep. We've got an early call for loading tomorrow."

Morgan didn't say another word to them. He picked up his bags and followed Gordon down the hall. Sharp was the first to speak. "Not the most sociable person I ever met. What do you think, Sergeant Major?"

Grant sipped from a glass of amber liquid. Most people who knew him knew he preferred tequila. "Intelligence. Maybe CID, but definitely an officer."

"How do you know that?"

"His bag. Other than me and the First Sergeant over there, how many enlisted men do you know who lug around a B-4 bag?"

Sharp finished his beer and reached for another one. "He didn't look too happy about his reception. I guess he never saw NCOs drinking together after duty hours."

"Officers and NCOs!"

"Lieutenant Robles, I stand corrected. My apologies to you too, Major Carson. Think he'll tell the Colonel?"

Grant finished his drink. "I don't much care. If new guy is upset about his greeting, he should have either reported in uniform during duty hours, or introduced himself. As long as what we do doesn't cross any line, off duty is just that."

Gordon pulled out a briefcase that she had labeled 'Last Minute'. In it were a few folders, some computer disks and a laptop. She fired up the computer, slipped in a disk and called up a file. "OK, Daniel, give me your orders and I'll get you loaded on the system."

Morgan handed over his orders and Gordon quickly scanned down them. "OK, Daniel, I just have to put in . . . Oh crap!" She had read the line with his identifying data. It seemed that Morgan, Daniel, new guy was actually, Morgan, Daniel, Major, US Army and the new Operations officer. "I'm sorry, Sir. You should have said something!"

"Don't worry about it."

"Let me get this entered and I'll get you on your way. Colonel Perkins would probably like to meet you."

"Take your time."

Gordon entered all the information, routed it to all the places it had to be, then hit the 'Send' button to get Corps and the backup files updated. She put everything away and led him down the corridor to where Perkins was having a last minute staff meeting. There was nothing new or important to discuss, but Perkins believed that if a meeting had been scheduled it should be held. It didn't matter that he had two categories of meetings, one for full staff and one for inner circle. Meetings would be held, and he didn't like interruptions.

"What is it, Sergeant Gordon?"

"New officer, Sir. I thought you should meet him right away."

The last thing Perkins wanted to do was greet a new Second Lieutenant. That was something his exec could do in the morning. "Not now. Have him report to Major Carstairs in the morning. Make sure he knows where to get on the train." Perkins had arranged for a private seating car for officers.

Gordon looked over he shoulder at Morgan, not knowing what to do. "Thank you, Sergeant Gordon. I'll take it from here." He walked into the office and sat at the first empty chair he came to. Morgan could see that military courtesy was not a strong suite of this unit, either up or down the chain of command. Perkins was visibly annoyed by this. "You don't need to be here, Lieutenant. I thought I was clear about that."

"It's not Lieutenant. It's Major. I'm Daniel Morgan, your new S-3. I'm pretty sure you'd want me at your staff meetings."

Gordon hurried back to the NCOs to let them know who the new guy was. She told them how Perkins had greeted him, and that caused a round of laughter in the room. The two officers joined in. It may have been inappropriate to laugh at their commander, but Perkins considered them women first and officers second, and as such were usually excluded from his circle. Harrison commented that it seemed Grant was right again.

"New guy seems like a charmer. Think he's a plant?"

Grant did. "Yeah, if he's here to keep tabs on us we must have impressed the hell out of him tonight."

"Think we should call it a night?"

"What else could happen? I'm having another drink"

Major Carson moved her chair over to the desk and sat beside the Sergeant Major. "Good idea, Sergeant Major, pour me one too."

"Here you go, Major." And he poured until she signaled him to stop. He also felt her hand on his leg. This couldn't be good.

She looked at him with half a smile on her lips. She spoke in a low voice, almost a whisper that no one else in the room could hear. "This 'Major, Sergeant Major' business is going to take up a lot of time. How about for tonight it just be Luke and Sylvia?" He looked back in her eyes as her hand slid a little further up. "You know," he said, "I'm going to hell."

"I hope so."

"But I don't think I'm going there tonight."

"We'll see."


Command Sergeant Major Grant stood off to the side of the formation as First Sergeant Harrison called the roll. Despite there having been a number of last night drinking parties, everyone was present and in proper uniform, if not fully sober yet. They would have the better part of three days on the train to get over it. He looked over to where the staff was lined up. Major Carson was nursing a monumental hangover. You would think a doctor would know better than to try to keep up when she wasn't used to hard liquor. He had gotten Lieutenant Robles to put her to bed, even after Carson had repeatedly asked Grant to do it for her. He had dodged that bullet. It was better this way. Major Carson was probably just feeling the effects of the booze. There had been a rumor that she had found out her husband had been stepping out on her while she had been in Sudan and had ended it while she was on leave. Grant had always heard that revenge sex was the best, but he had never been able to master the skill of balancing two relationships at the same time. Hell, he had trouble with one. Still, he remembered what the good Major had looked like in her too tight T-shirt, and how she felt when she kept brushing against his arm. Yeah, he thought to himself, someday I'm going to hell.

The formation was called to attention. Perkins had a short, unmemorable speech prepared, then returned the formation to Lieutenant Fuller. He in turn gave it to the First Sergeant, who marched the company to the train. As soon as all hands were aboard, they left for Moldova.

# CHAPTER 6

Dillinghouse was sitting in his office, alone. In spite of the Speaker getting his ass out of a huge jam, he was still a virtual pariah in the House. Former allies paid lip service to his previous power and influence, but they still kept their distance. His fortunes were about as rock bottom as they could get.

One of his aides came to the door. Since the scandal had been made public, staffers who had no idea of who they were working for had left. The long termers, the ones who had been with him from the start, knew who and what he was, and had profited right along with him. They had no where else to go now, so they stuck it out with their boss to the bitter end. This one was holding on to a half sheet of paper. He had a puzzled look on his face. This is interesting, Dillinghouse thought. He usually has the inside track on everything that comes into the office.

"What is it, Joseph? You look lost."

Joseph was. He came closer. "This e-mail just came in, addressed to you, but on the office server. It's kind of cryptic, but I think it refers to that National Guard bunch you're having so much trouble with."

That interested the congressman. He held his hand out. "Let me see it!"

Dillinghouse scanned the short message. The return address was from a private e-mail account, but he could see it had been routed through the military network. 'Sidewinder289@Argus.com should be a fairly easy person to identify. As he read down, it became easier. There was an electronic signature.

"Joseph, see what you can find out about this Master Sergeant Charles Winder. He seems to be baiting me with some dirt on the Guardsmen."

"Are you going to answer him?"

"No. If there's any contact, keep me out of it. Use the office server, but no names. This could be our friends at the FBI making a feeble effort to entrap me. Let me know what you find out about Winder."

The train ride had been nothing but boring. After the first few hours of watching the scenery roll by, the novelty wore off and the troops slipped into a three day fog of personal music players, hand held video games, books and long naps. There was a little excitement when it was announced that they would be rolling through the Transylvania region of Romania at night, but even the speculation over the existence of vampires only lasted a few hours. A set of night vision goggles had been broken out to check for the flying undead coming out of the Carpathian Mountains, though it seemed as Dracula and his clan hadn't been warned about the train load of fresh American throats ripe for the biting.

The arrival at their new base was almost a disappointment. Compared to the countryside they had been through, this place looked bland. The countryside rolled out in all directions, not quite flat, yet flat enough to be monotonous. In the distance there were some low hills all around, but there were no distinguishing terrain features. Price had corrected their first impression though. Ravines and gullies, some gentle and others rather steep chopped the ground up. It was not wise to go racing around cross-country unless you aware of your route. It was even more dangerous after dark.

Price had arranged a detail to handle some of the senior NCO baggage while he took them on a quick walking tour of the area. Harrison begged off for now. His main interest was getting his soldiers situated. There was plenty of time for tourist shit later. So Price led Grant and Sharp around. Once they were far enough away he went into his real briefing.

"This isn't much of a road we're building. I've been up and down it twice. It's two-lane and gravel surface. My guys tell me it just needs some resurfacing. The roadbed is solid enough for what it's getting used for. Half a dozen culverts need to be replaced, and there are a couple of bridges we'll need to reinforce to get our equipment over, but no big problems."

Sharp looked skeptical about the road and the situation as a whole. "They stuck us out here for a reason. What are we? Bait?"

"That's the problem. I don't know. I've been talking to the locals" he meant the local garrison, "and there ain't squat happening around here. We're the most excitement they've had since the Russians didn't go away."

Grant didn't understand that. "What do you mean, 'didn't go away'?"

"Just that. They've got a small compound about ten miles to the southeast. About a half mile square, double fenced, 15 to 20 buildings."

"What's in it?"

"Even the locals don't know. Seems like the only Russians there are actual Russians, no Ukrainians, Georgians or any others. Just full blooded Russians. They don't mix much with the locals, all their supplies are flown in, and they seem to have a pretty regular rotation policy."

Sharp picked up on the 'flown' part. "Where's the air strip? That wasn't briefed."

"They have a dirt strip about halfway between us and them. For some reason, all the photos and maps started just to the north and west of it. It looks like they were trying to keep us in the dark. I've been on it, but I haven't seen any birds on it. Looks like it'll take an Antonov 124, nothing much bigger."

Grant considered the possibilities. "Have you seen the Russian place?"

"Not yet. They've got a couple of checkpoints on the access road. I haven't had the time or energy to go cross-country yet. I figured I'd save that for you two. You're gonna have plenty of free time on your hands."

Grant nodded. "Dave, he's right about that. We need to get your new boss interested in all this. If he can schedule up some training for us 'unemployable' types, we'll have a reason to go look. Anything else?"

"Just reports of what they call 'bandit activity' further on up the road. The locals think it's just the local gangsters collecting tolls from the farmers, but so far they haven't been able to get the local police to do anything about it, or let them do something."

"That'll have to change once we're out there. If they're just bandits, we don't want to get mixed up in local law enforcement. If it's something else, I'd rather the military take care of it. I'm sure they'll be sensitive to us swinging loaded weapons around and shooting up locals, even if they are thugs."

"Sharp's got a new boss? I've only been gone a week. What did you do to Stanley?" Stanley Fisher had moved up from assistant after the S-3 became the XO. Price thought he looked like Stan Laurel.

"I didn't do anything. They sent a new Major in for the job. And this guy is a real tight ass. I haven't heard him use more than three words at a time since he's been here. I don't think this was his first choice on his wish list."

" He'll probably get along good with Winder."

"Master Sergeant Winder! There's a name I've missed hearing. Where is the ass hole?"

Price told Sharp about their first few days. After the side trip to the wrong building, Gaston and Winder had spent the time since whining about their room assignments. With the new officer there'd have to be another shuffle. There weren't any more rooms on the officer and senior NCO floor, and Winder was the junior of the seniors. He'd have to move.

As they walked back to the buildings Sharp pointed out the new Major walking their way. Price squinted at him. "I know that guy!"

Suddenly, Winder walked out of the building with SFC Harte, the supply NCO. They turned towards Major Morgan, and as they passed the two NCOs rendered a hand salute. Hartes was more or less a proper salute. Winders wasn't. Winder didn't like to salute anyone but the Group Commander, and he believed his rank should have exempted him from saluting any lower ranking officers. Since he couldn't get away with not saluting, he resorted to using a 'Hollywood' salute, or one of it's many variations. His position as a friend of Perkins usually gave him the license to get away with it with the Group officers. This time he used the version that kept his elbow at his side, with his hand curled around his thumb. The hand went casually to the middle of his beret, then snapped away like he was swatting a fly. He didn't even bother making eye contact with the Major, or interrupt his conversation with Harte. Major Morgan was not a regular Group officer. He still expected a formal salute.

"Stop right there, Sergeant!"

Winder stopped and turned a contemptuous look on his face. "Are you talking to me?" Harte gave a little chuckle. This officer didn't know what he was in for.

"Put a 'Sir' after that, Sergeant, or have you lost any concept of military courtesy."

No one spoke to Master Sergeant Winder like that. Well, almost no one. The CSM and his friends still hadn't learned their lesson. This guy would have to learn quickly.

"Yeah, OK, Sir," it came out as a sneer. "I saluted you. What else did you need?"

Morgan stepped up and into Winders face. Through clenched teeth he spoke. "Get at the position of attention when you speak to me." Winder was so off guard, he assumed the position. Who was this guy? Morgan immediately launched into a lecture about the proper position of attention. There was enough quiet menace in his voice that Harte found himself standing next to Winder, following the same instructions. Once Morgan was satisfied with that lesson, he launched into another on the proper rendering of the hand salute. "The salute, gentlemen, is not a personal statement of style. It's a military courtesy that has a long and proud history, so let's get this right, shall we?"

He ran them through a series of salutes, critiquing and correcting until he was satisfied with their performance. It was only then that he returned their held salute and walked away. As he passed Grant and company, the CSM called his group to attention and they all delivered salutes with drill team precision. Grant acknowledged Morgan, Morgan returned the salute and went on his way. Winder and Harte were still rooted to their spot, watching Morgan walk away. Sharp spoke first. "I see you made a good impression on the new S-3."

"That guy? Where the fuck did he come from?"

"I don't know, but the first time I met him, I was carrying a case of beer and I didn't offer him one, but I think you just managed to top that."

The Sergeant Major had to add, "Good way to make a first impression, Winder. I hope you have the –3 shop set up the way he likes it. You might be in for a long day."

As they walked away Price stopped and called over his shoulder. "By the way, I think he'll be taking your room, too."


Ali Alawa Sharif watched the glow of the fires from the roof of his apartment building. It was the fourth night in a row that the Muslim youths had been rampaging through the streets of Marseilles, burning buses and police cars. It was all carefully coordinated. They began in the same area every night, and as soon as there were enough police and riot control troops committed to the scene, new disturbances would break out in another district. It had been a very effective tactic so far, and the French government was deploying more assets every night to try to stay ahead of the disorder. In a few more nights, Sharif estimated they would be at the tipping point. There would be little or no reserves left for the government. At that point there would be more disturbances at points far removed from here. His plan was to drag all of France to the point of anarchy, and just as quickly pull back. There would be concessions from the government, but not enough to satisfy the young Muslims, and then the troubles would begin again. Sharif was pleased with his handiwork. This was not unlike waging Jihad. All you had to do was find the right audience for your message and cultivate a few disciples. Then you could point out the inequities of life and plant your ideas. Soon, they would think it was their own movement and raise their own followers.

His one regret was that none of these Muslims were yet committed enough to embrace martyrdom, but that would come. All it would take was one or two police over reactions, a few Muslim youths injured severely, or, even better, killed. Then there would be volunteers aplenty to strap on explosive vests. It was his plan. If the police did not cooperate he had some Corsican thugs lined up who would be more than willing to shoot a few while disguised as riot police. Sharif smiled at the thought. Never leave an atrocity to chance.

He was suddenly conscious of others on the roof with him. In the dark he could not make them out. Probably neighbors who were concerned about the riots. He turned to one on his left to speak.

"It's shocking..." There was a gun pointed at his face.

"Good evening, Ali Alawa Sharif. How are you this fine, clear night?"

Sharif was momentarily shaken. No one but a few Algerians knew his true identity, and this man was not an Arab. "You must mistake me for someone else, monsieur, my name is. . ."

"Yes, yes, yes, Ali Alawa, we know the name your new masters in Algeria have given you. We have other things to discuss, come with me."

It wasn't an invitation. He was taken from behind and shackled. He was quickly and efficiently searched and relieved of his knife. Then he was roughly hauled downstairs. He was surprised to be taken to the room next to his. Inside there was a good deal of surveillance equipment. They had evidently been watching him for a while. He hadn't realized French counter-intelligence had been this close to him. Still, he decided to practice denial. Perhaps he could bluff it out and only suffer the indignity of a beating and maybe a few days in jail. His cover was vague enough to be believable, and he was certain the Algerians had prepared his back-story.

His inquisitor spoke first. "Please, spare me your denials or any fairy tales about being a poor Algerian immigrant." He opened a dossier. "You are Ali Alawa Sharif, born in Syria of Druze parents. An interesting beginning for an Islamic fascist."

Sharif began to protest, but a nod from the stranger brought a blow to the base of his skull that caused an intense pain to flow across his head. "Thank you, Leon. Now, no more interruptions, Ali Alawa. My time tonight is rather limited. As you can see, there is a great deal of equipment we have to move. Now, where was I? Oh yes, Druze parents. You were educated in Egypt and Jordan and joined Hezbollah at a rather young age." He looked over his glasses at Sharif and smiled. "They must have seen something in you. They didn't send you in to blow up a Jewish bus.

"From there you moved into Al Qaeda, I see you helped blow up the American Embassy in Khartoum then moved on to roadside bombs in Iraq. You are talented. You, above all others, were trained in the use of Sarin gas in Syria. An honor no doubt."

Sharif interrupted, but the stranger held up his hand. "Please, don't make Leon hit you again. We have discovered the hard way that several such blows can cause temporary blindness. That would affect the outcome of our little discussion." He spoke a few words to the man behind Sharif. Russian? What was going on?

"I'm almost finished. You were seconded to Ibn Mousa al Saif." He paused and smiled again. "He must have been a disappointment to the Brotherhood. Anyway, you planned and executed the Sarin massacre on the Jbala'a refugee camp. Then you conducted that brilliant counter attack on the Sudanese Liberation Army at Al Fashir. I must say, it was a masterpiece. You must be proud. Then events seemed to have outpaced you." He paused and read to himself. He took off his glasses and sighed. "Such a fiasco after such successes. And it was all your fault. Leon you may strike him again." There was another blow, and again the pain. This time there was a bright light that filled his eyes. It took several moments to subside. "Your poor performance deserved that. You assassinated al Saif and bungled placing the blame on the Israelis. Then you bungled the attack on the American camp. I see that was costly. And finally, a simple ambush in the dark and the Americans not only avoided it, but they ambushed your ambushers." Another pause. This one a little longer. Sharif braced himself for the blow that didn't come.

"This last, Ali Alawa. To be seen running away after your Jihadists are wiped out! You didn't embrace martyrdom?" He looked at Sharif again. "No, you aren't the martyr type, are you? You don't seem to be the type to gamble on imaginary virgins in the afterlife. You may speak now."

"Are you going to kill me?"

"Ali Alawa! I'm surprised at you! It's only in American movies that the villain talks his captive to death. I have nothing so diabolical in mind. If I were going to kill you, it would have happened on the roof before you knew I was there. No. I have plans, and I need you for them."

"Plans? What do you want me to do?"

"I want you to avenge yourself on your enemies. I want you to make them suffer as you have."

"I'm doing that now!" Sharif was puzzled. Didn't this fool realize he was behind this unrest in France?

"No, no. Not this piddling little temper tantrum. The Algerians are wasting your talents. The American engineers that embarrassed you are still vulnerable. Are you interested?"

Sharif was. Martyrdom was not something he relished, but if he could take revenge on those Americans, it would be better than all the virgins in paradise. "I'm listening."

"Good. But that's all you need to know for now. Here is money and a train ticket. You can travel on your Algerian passport. You will be met in Bucharest. Leon needs to take a photo, your fingerprints, a writing sample and a DNA sample. We will create a new identity and give it to you there."

Leon had set up his camera equipment. It only took a few moments to snap the pictures. He had Sharif write out a few sentences in both Arabic and script. There was a slight prick as he took a blood sample, and for good measure snipped off some hair.

"How do you know I won't go underground again?"

"Ali Alawa, look at reality. Al Qaeda wants you dead, as do the Syrians, Iranians, Sudanese and the Janjaweed. The Muslim Brotherhood has issued a fatwa for your head. There is no place for you to go. The Algerians would disavow you, the United Nations wants you for the genocide at Jbala'a, and the Americans have their global war on terror."

Leon had completed packing up equipment. There were more anonymous faces coming and going, emptying the room. The stranger stood back with his arms folded, watching the activity. He had more to say. "Ali Alawa, we found you by accident, based on a rumor, nothing more. What if we had been looking for you? Now, look at all the parts of your being Leon has collected." He quickly listed them. "It would be a small matter for us to provide it to the French and Interpol in a gesture of international cooperation." He turned to leave the room. Almost casually he continued. "And if we do have to find you again, we will do much worse than kill you."

"How do you know where the Americans are?"

The stranger laughed. "I have my ways."

Construction season was in full swing. The Moldovan officers had agreed to show the engineers where they could establish a gravel pit, and had arranged for their soldiers to work with the Americans installing culverts and doing basic traffic control. The road was in fairly constant use by the local farmers. Lieutenant Sage had also been working out contracts to get local stone masons involved in the rebuilding and expansion of the bridges on the route. Prices main concern was getting his equipment to and from the job site. There would come a point, and it would come soon, where it would not be economical from a fuel or time standpoint to be shuttling equipment back and forth from the base to the road. He would have to be on the lookout for staging areas, and figure out ways to get the equipment secured and protected in them. It would require more cooperation from the Moldovans, or the 'locals,' as he preferred to call them.

LTC Perkins had been making the rounds of the Moldovan officers, ingratiating himself to them by committing his manpower and equipment to doing repair and utility jobs on the Moldovan end of the base. The jobs had all been small so far, the Moldovans not wanting to scare off the Americans with the amount of work they wanted done, but they could see that Perkins was eager to please, and their to do list was getting longer. It still wasn't having an effect on the heavy equipment section, but one platoon of vertical construction people was now exclusively working on base.

Grant had other concerns to keep himself busy. He had been lobbying Perkins to let him start a full schedule of tactical training. The Group was still earmarked for deployment to Iraq, and despite all the detours, there was still a strong possibility they could end up there. The combat lessons from Sudan were still fresh in everyone's minds, but many skills are perishable, meaning that unless they are practiced with some frequency, the nuances of what makes them effective fades. Grant was worried that the fading had already begun. He could see it on the job sites every day. The regular drills of checking the roads for Improvised Explosive Devices, or IEDs, and checking the area to make sure it was secure were now only being halfheartedly done. Even Price was getting lax in sending out scouting parties to check the area around where they were working. And what he considered to be a potentially fatal flaw, Price had allowed the Moldovan soldiers to take over traffic control almost completely. They weren't even paying attention to the trucks and carts coming through anymore.

The Moldovan Senior Sergeant, on the other hand, had been impressed with the quality of the NCOs the Americans had. In their infrequent meetings, Grant was told how the Moldovans, following the Russian example, had place heavy reliance on the officer corps, and had placed little or no responsibility in the NCOs. Senior Sergeant Yvegniy Kosavich had a good grasp of the English language, and claimed to have read extensively of US military history. In one meeting, he spoke admiringly of the NCO ethic.

"In all your histories, I read of great things your junior leaders have done. Not just your Lieutenants, but your Sergeants as well. You have many heroes from your enlisted ranks that I read about. In the old Soviet Union, and even now, there are but a handful of enlisted men that are spoken about. Kalashnikov the rifle builder, and Zaitsev the sniper. And even Kalashnikov became an officer and retired as a general." He looked off at Price having a quick meeting with his squad leaders. There were no officers present on site at the time.

"Something like that could not happen in my army. If all the officers left, all work would stop. There is no initiative and no reason for it. I like your Army."

The Moldovan had another intent in this conversation. Grant could tell he was building up the flattery to ask for something. "I understand that you have your medal from your congress for bravery. Is that true?"

Grant knew what he meant, and said it was.

"Is it also true that many of your sergeants have many medals for bravery also?"

Grant admitted that was true.

"My soldiers should know such men. If I arrange it, could you perform a series of lectures to teach my soldiers how to lead?"

Grant saw an opening and decided to take it. "Senior Sergeant, how about I go one better than that?" He could see the Moldovan was interested. "What if we did some joint training, your soldiers and mine? We have all this space, and all this time, and there is so little to do at night."

Kosavich thought for a moment. "How could we do such a thing?"

Grant was ready. "Talk to your commander. I'll talk to mine. They meet each other frequently, and if we both plant the seed, perhaps something will grow. And if they think it was their idea, the seed will grow faster."

Grant had been right. He had spoken to Perkins, and Kosavich spoke to his Colonel about how it would be good if the two armies could perform some exercises together. The Moldovan mentioned it casually to Perkins one day at lunch, who immediately replied that he had been thinking of the same thing. The die was cast. Although the Moldovans had little in the way of training resources, they would be happy to provide soldiers and translators and guides to the area. Perkins agreed that he would have his staff work up some training exercises. That evening, Perkins passed the assignment down to Major Morgan, who was less than excited about the prospect of having to baby-sit the Moldovan army. The next morning he called an impromptu meeting of the S-3 staff and laid out the assignment.

Morgan called for suggestions from his staff, and was disappointed with what he heard. The suggestions ranged from cross training on equipment, to social exchanges, to classroom lectures. He looked over at Sergeant Sharp, who, although he was in on Grants plans, wanted to see which way it was going.

"Sharp, you're pretty quiet over there. What do you think?"

"All good ideas if you're getting together with a third world militia, but these guys are supposed to be trained infantry. They might be up for a little more."

"What would you suggest?"

"How about weapons quals, then move right into some tactical training, map and compass, GPS, night operations, patrolling, all the stuff that infantry does. I'll bet the locals don't like sitting in classrooms any more than I do."

Morgan liked the ideas and turned to Winder. "Master Sergeant, what could you put together, and how long would it take?" He watched the panic look in Winders eyes as he groped for an answer. "Never mind, Winder. You don't have a clue, do you?" He turned to Sharp. "OK, it's your baby. Give me a training schedule for the next couple of weeks by the close of business today. You're relieved of any other duties in the section. From now on you'll be my joint training NCO. Winder, you'll have to start doing your own work now."

That had been weeks ago. The training had been developing to the point where there was some joint training going on every day, and a couple of nights a week. Grant and Sharp had been using it as a cover to do some off the books training. They had been scouting the airfield, using the surveyors working with the locals as a cover. It appeared to be long enough to handle a small US cargo plane, and Grant was still puzzling over how to get that to happen. Morgan was about to help.

Grant had been sitting at the edge of the field. A Russian bird had just left when Morgan drove up and saw him sitting there. "What's up, CSM?" Morgan wasn't such a stickler for military courtesy when they were alone. He rode Winder hard for it, but he was one of the many who didn't like Winder, and could see he was a poor excuse for a senior NCO. Grant just pointed at the field. "We need to use this."

"Why?"

"I want to know what the Russians are doing. I need some recon before I go in on the ground."

Morgan didn't seem surprised at the statement. "Before you go in? Isn't that kind of presumptuous of you? How do you know I want you to go in there?"

"Oh, you want me in there." He looked at Morgan. "And you want to go with me."

"Why, CSM, why would you presume such a thing?"

"Couple of reasons. One, you spend almost as much time as I do out here."

"And two?"

"Price remembers you. You wore a lot more junk on the left side," Grant was referring to qualification badges, "way back when."

"Why didn't you say something before?"

"I stay out of your business, you stay out of mine. It's worked well so far, but now we need each other. I need pictures."

"And I need to get in there. I'll get you a plane, but I already have the pictures."

Grant just nodded. "I should have known." The two of them just sat there, staring at the field. Morgan got up to leave. "Let's get together later, CSM, and make some plans."

"Can I bring friends?"

"No. I think it's best if it's just the two of us for now. After all, we will be conspiring to break a few international laws. It's best if we keep that quiet for now."

Ali Alawa Sharif thought fondly of his notoriety when he was a rising star in the Brotherhood. In those days, and they weren't so long ago, he had access to the finer things in life, and could enjoy them in the security of the Brotherhood envelope. It was a convenient excuse in Islam, that you could avoid many strictures if it was in the furtherance of the cause, or to protect yourself in the presence of your enemies. Easy women, drink and fine foods were his to enjoy. Sharif wasn't like the fanatics. Then again, many of his fellows weren't. Jihad just gave many an excuse for excess.

His current condition was far from ideal, but, as he thought, it was far better than what it could have been. It was not easy being an outcast from the Brotherhood, always hiding, depending on pigs like the Algerians and the Russians to help and protect him. He was eager for whatever 'errands' these Russians had planned for him. Perhaps then he could get back into the good graces of the Imams. The thought of his enemies, the people who were the cause of his woeful existence, the Americans, were only a few miles away. He had seen them working on the road from the cargo plane he had flown in on. So near, yet so far.

The Russians had kept him hidden and isolated here, wherever 'here' was. They had taken him off the plane like a piece of baggage, hidden in a cardboard box. His meals were all delivered to him in this room, spacious, but still a detention cell as far as he was concerned. His one small window looked out over another dull building. He could see Russian soldiers training, at least he thought they were Russians. Several times he thought he could hear Arabic voices, but when he questioned his handlers they just laughed, and continued his briefings.

The briefings! Could anything be so boring as a Russian explaining a country he was totally unfamiliar with? On several occasions, the briefers had contradicted themselves with their meaningless babble. Only a few things were clear to him, and these were the important facts. The Trans-Dnestr region was ripe for open revolt, an attitude he was to inflame. And there was a small, vocal Muslim presence in Kipercheny, a presence that he might be able to lose himself in if he were careful. He was still in possession of his Algerian papers, and the Russians had told him that his exploits as a rabble-rouser in Marseilles had spread to the mosque. They didn't say how, but it was obvious they had a man inside it.

Today's briefing was different. There was another Arab present. Sharif hadn't traded names with him, that was forbidden, but he thought the man might be a Yemeni. Man was a generous term. This was only a boy, barely out of his teens. And he was constantly smiling. But it was proof that there were other Arabs here.

The good news was his departure was announced. He had been furnished with a mixture of the local currencies, Moldovan *Leu*, American dollars, and Euros. All three were freely circulated, and he was surprised to hear that the dollar was preferred. There was a safe house, to be shared with the man who would pick him up. This, he was sure, would be the Russian agent. He was to establish himself as quickly as possible, present his *bona fides* as an Algerian Jihadist, and start selecting targets to stir up resentment towards the separatists. It was simple enough, except for the Yemeni. What the hell was his part in all this?

"His name is Yusef Sa'alam. He is a martyr."

Son of a bitch, Sharif thought. They're going to saddle me with a nut case that is looking to die. He began to protest, but was cut short. The Yemeni was told to leave the room.

"Yusef has trained long and hard for his martyrdom. He is not to be wasted on buses or restaurants. Those are best left to the unsuspecting," he was told. And that was true. It was easier to give a disguised bomb to a patsy. They would act naturally and raise less suspicion. And they would be as surprised as everyone else when the cell phone detonator rang just before the blast. The Russian continued. "As you must have guessed, there are other 'students ' here. This one" meaning Yusef, " is more anxious than most of the others. His value is very short term, so we give him to you to use. Find a valuable target, and don't squander him."

These Russians were the worst kind of infidels, but they understood how to spread terror. A suicide bomber who didn't know he or she was going to die, who belonged to no organized cell, was virtually unstoppable.

There was more. "As your own projects develop, you may find you need some trained assistance. When you do, contact us through your handler." Ali Alawa hated to think he was under the control of a 'handler'. He would do his best to break free of that constraint. "There are students here who are very talented in various fields. They may be made available to you. Just remember that they are not expendable. Each has been selected and trained for their own purposes. An opportunity for them to practice their new trade will help us assess their effectiveness." What went unsaid was that they were largely imaginary assets.

Grant had a chance meeting with Senior Sergeant Kosavich, and decided to ask him what he knew about the Russian base. Kosavich invited him back to his Sergeants Mess, where he offered Grant a local beer before telling his story. "Why do you want to know about the Russians?"

"Could we call it professional curiosity and leave it at that?"

The Moldovan NCO thought about that for a moment and agreed. "For the moment, professional curiosity, as you call it. Could I give you the history of both these places?"

Grant accepted the offer. He was getting something for nothing, so he could live with the frills.

"When the fascists, you call them Nazis, invaded in 1941, they saw this valley and liked it. That landing strip was originally for the Luftwaffe, but that first year, they moved so fast, they only had time to build the field, then it was too far in the rear to be of use. They left a small signal detachment there. It would have been forgotten about, if not for Stalingrad." He stopped to sip his beer. His eyes had a far away look, as if he were remembering a happy memory. "My father told me about them. In the beginning, we were like the Ukrainians. We hated the Soviets, Stalin, and everything Russian. The fascists were liberators. They were our friends. That didn't last long. After the combat troops moved on, the SS and Gestapo came. These were to be work camps, for the Jews from Romania and Moldova. They built this all with local labor. It is all very good construction

"The builders were very good, but too slow for the SS. They executed a few stone masons as an example, and work slowed even more. My father was one of the workers. The SS made them live here, so they made sure the buildings would be sound for themselves in the winter. The construction took so long here, and at the other camp, that they were never to send Jews here. One day a Panzer General came through, some say it was Guderian, and he saw the rail lines and the good buildings, and decided to have it taken over by the *Panzertruppen* as a repair and refit facility." He paused again. "As you may know, the fascists were very good about recovering their battle damage. If it could move, it went back to battle. Eventually, the other camp became a rest camp and a sniper school. The fascists used this until the Russians crossed the Dnestr in 1944. For some reason, they didn't destroy this, but they took almost everything with them. There are a few tanks they left behind. The Russians had some prisoners fix them. They were going to put them in a museum in Moscow, but they lost interest and they are still here."

That got Grants attention. "You have German Panzers from the war?"

"Yes, a few, with some other things. I will show you some day. The warehouse they are in is full of junk. Where was I?"

"The museum in Moscow."

"Oh, yes. They lost interest. The Russians were going to turn this into a tank school, but the Warsaw pact came along and gave this area a different purpose. It was a school for their specialists. We never knew what. The Russians like their vodka more than our wines, so there was never much mixing. Our women didn't like to mix with them, either.

"Then your Ronald Reagan, God bless the man, he tore down the Berlin Wall. When the Russians started to leave they gave us this camp, but they kept the other. We wanted them to leave, but they wouldn't. They tried to keep using the rail line, but we wouldn't let them, so they started to use the landing strip for their planes. Now, we never see the Russians."

Grant thought about this for a bit. "Is there anyone else there?"

"At one time, there were a lot of foreigners. I think they were Egyptians."

"Why Egyptians?"

"I don't know. They came into the city once or twice. We have a little mosque, but they didn't like it, so they stopped coming."

"Why didn't they like it?"

"My friend, I'll tell you a secret. The Moslems" he used the old term, "they don't really like everybody. They have a pecking order. They are worse than the Hindus. They have their different types of Arabs, then their different types of Islam. After that, you are like the fascist *untermensch*. It is all very ugly."

"You said 'we'. Are you a Muslim?"

The soldier shook his head. "I was speaking as a Moldovan, not a Muslim. Remember that we have had many decades of socialism. It is hard to break the habit of thinking of all property as ours."

"Are any of your soldiers Muslim?"

Kosavich thought for a moment. Grant could see he was mentally running the numbers in his head. "I think there are three. No, I'm wrong. There are four. At least they say they are. I think two of them just do it to get the extra time off they claim for prayers." He laughed. "But they are young soldiers, conscripts. You would have the same problem if yours were not patriotic and voluntary."

Grant filed that away as an interesting piece of information, then tried to steer him back on track. "What about the base now?"

Kosavich grunted. "Almost empty now. Maybe 100, 200 soldiers. We watch it from time to time, especially after the plane comes. The security goes up for a while, then it gets slack again. It probably means something to the Russians, but we haven't been able to guess why. Soon they'll all be gone and we can have it back." He laughed. "I don't know what we'll do with it. My army is so small. Maybe we can rent it to the Americans. You seem to like it here."

"We do, but we're not here forever. We're just building a road, and then leaving." Grant hoped that was true. He also hoped the story about the security was true, and that they were in a down cycle now.

Two nights later, Morgan and Grant were laying in the deep grass on a small rise a quarter mile south of the Russian base. Their vehicle was parked off the airstrip, a camouflage net thrown over it. A trip wire that they couldn't identify stopped them. The resolution in the night vision sets wasn't good enough. Morgan resolved to come back in daylight for a better look. Grant had a better idea.

"Stun gun. Short it out and see what happens."

"Where we going to get a stun gun?"

"Same place everybody else does. The Internet."

Morgan just grunted. It was probably a better idea than he had, but would take longer. He focused his binoculars on the compound, noting any activity. He was using a special set that detected infra red, but so far he had seen nothing. There were only four watchtowers, one at each corner. They were high enough over the fence lighting to not have any details washed out. Morgan hadn't been able to detect any cameras. The sentries had the bored posture of men who had been watching and not seeing anything for a long time. He slid back down into the pocket formed by the rise. Grant was scanning the area around them, just in case. He had told Morgan what he had learned about the security arrangements. They seemed to be slipping down to the low side.

"What do you think, Major? Other than the wire, I can't see anything out of the way here. What are we looking for?"

"I don't know. When I got exiled here this place was an after thought, one of those 'by the way, if you have time' directives that isn't an order, but definitely more than a suggestion."

"Are 'they' pissed at you enough to get in trouble over nothing?"

"How do you know they're pissed at me?"

"You're here."

They discussed their options. There wasn't much more they could do with the equipment on hand. They could head back the way they had come and make a wide circle around the compound, out of sight, but a trip of several extra miles. It seemed like a waste of time. Grant suggested they circumnavigate the compound, meeting up on the far side. They could get a look at the entire perimeter and see if the trip wire had any breaks or equipment hook ups. Grant had a set of digital camera binoculars. He could zoom in on any signs or markings and get a snap shot. Morgan agreed to the plan, and headed off to the left. He wanted to cover the front of the compound himself.

Grant crawled carefully but quickly, taking advantage of the terrain to stand and move quicker when he could, all the while checking the ground for signs of activity and the compound for anything of interest. He didn't see anything until he hit the backside of the compound. Whoever had laid the wire had gotten lazy on the backside, and it was only strung about 150 yards from the main fence line. He came to what appeared to be a break in the wire, then he saw where it followed the support rod down and disappeared into the ground. The return line, maybe? A few feet further on he found the footpath they had crossed further out from the compound on their approach. He hadn't realized at the time that it ran all the way in here. The wire crossed under it. Someone on the security detail had gotten real lazy. Instead of having to follow any elaborate procedures to cross the line, they had simply put it in a conduit and run it under the path. There must have been a considerable amount of traffic to take that shortcut. He tried to make out where the path led, but it curved a few yards from where he lay. Funny, he thought. This didn't show up on the photos. He fit the camera to the eyepiece of his NVGs and took a couple of pictures. He decided to chance exploring a few yards down the path.

He looked back towards the compound. The lights back here were angled differently, just enough to keep the glow off the path. He decided to take a chance and get a closer look. Halfway to the gate he detected movement. There was a foot patrol outside the fence. He dropped to one knee on the side of the road and drew his side arm. At that moment he decided to take Sharp up on his offer of a home built suppressor for his Argentine .45. The guard walked up to the path, then turned and opened a gate and went inside. He spoke to someone inside one of the darkened buildings, and a light went on. It looked like this was a guard shack, and the relief was being roused for their shift. Grant made note of the time and backed away. Shift change would be a good chance to get away. The guards would be more interested in looking for their reliefs than watching an area that nothing has happened in for months or years. He went back out into the dark and made his way to the rendezvous point.

Morgan wasn't there yet, but that didn't surprise him. He had the main road to cross. He waited another fifteen minutes before the Major appeared.

"Any problems, Major?"

"No. They were changing the guard on the checkpoint. I had to wait for the traffic to die down. There's a lot of security for a place this small. How about you?"

"I'm not sure yet. I need to look at the photos again. Let's get out of here."

They pulled into their own compound as the dining facility opened for breakfast. Dining facility was a fancy name for their mess hall. There weren't any kitchen facilities for them to use in this section of the base, so they had appropriated one of the maintenance buildings for the purpose. The Moldovans had a lot of lumber stacked around, strange, since there were so few trees, and it was used to build American style picnic tables. Morgan and Lucas took over one away from the morning flow of soldiers. They had added some quick detail to the photos of the Russian site they had each carried at the airstrip. Now they passed the pictures back and forth, comparing each other's memory for detail.

Colonel Perkins came by to check on them. "You two disappeared early last night. What are you up to?" If he noticed the pictures he didn't comment on them.

Morgan was the first to answer. "We went out to check a few training sites. One of them was farther out than we had planned."

"Well, you two are the ones that insisted no one go anywhere without keeping in contact with the duty officer. I expect in the future you two will do the same thing." With that he walked off to his own table. Perkins had the kitchen crew set aside an area for him and his staff. It was his intent to use it for working lunches or informal conferences during meal times. Usually, he was joined by his XO. Sometimes other officers would eat with them, but it looked more to Grant that they were just putting in an occasional appearance to keep the Colonel happy.

Price had walked up on them also. He looked down at the pictures on the table and gave out a little chuckle. "The Russians, huh? Why didn't you say something? I could probably help with some of your questions."

Grant shook his head as he turned the pictures over. "Not now, Pricey. You don't need to get involved in this."

"Have it your way, but wandering around in the dark is the hard way. See you later."

Morgan watched him walk away, a puzzled look on his face. "The hard way? What did he mean by that?" He watched Price sit down with SFC Sharp. There was a short conversation, with Price gesturing over his shoulder at Morgan and Grant, followed by the two of them laughing. "I don't know," Grant said, "but I have the feeling those two are ahead of us already! Come on."

They picked up their trays and joined the two NCOs. They both kept their heads down, but it was easy to see they were both having trouble stifling their laughter. Grant took the lead. "All right. What do you know?"

"Geez, Luke," Sharp got out with some difficulty, "I thought you just told Pricey not to get involved. You changing your mind?"

Morgan was getting angry. "Cut the crap! If you two know something, spill it! I don't have time for this shit!"

Price and Sharp stiffened up. Grant knew his two friends had information he needed. He also knew he wasn't going to get it with Morgan around. Price had his contrite tone, a tone that sounded sincere, but Grant knew was about as phony as it could get. "We didn't mean nothing, Major. We were just having some sport with the CSM."

"Save your sport for some other time. Sergeant Major, why don't you get some sleep, and I'll see you after lunch." He stood up and walked away. Sharp watched him dump his tray and leave the building. "You know, Luke, if you're going to be making new friends you should really be more picky. That boy's got a bad attitude and he's going to get you in trouble."

"Yeah," Price added. "And when he does, you're going to need to call somebody for bail money."

"All right. Lay off. He's the S-3, and he doesn't want anyone else involved in this."

Price and Sharp looked at each other, a hurt look. Price slipped into his contrite tone again. "Gee, Sergeant Major, we're good enough to hang out with when you want somebody to get his ass shot off, but not moonlit walks in the countryside?"

Sharp had his own complaint. "Yeah, and what happens when you need someone shot from 600 yards? Your old eyes can't do it, and he wears contacts."

Grant was getting pissed. "You two assholes have been there, haven't you?"

"Us?"

"Yeah, you two. Are you going to tell me about it?"

Price and Sharp both pulled out digital cameras. "Do you want us to tell you, or would you rather see the slide show?"

Grant looked puzzled.

"Yeah, slide show. We've been there twice with the Moldovans. They go there once a week to play soccer against the Russians. We've got team pictures, background shots, security routines, and most of the buildings identified. It's some kind of school. They claim for engineers, but I doubt it. No heavy equipment and no half assed construction sites."

"They just let two Americans walk around?"

"Who's American? Price speaks Russian, and they tell them I'm Spanish, so I have to speak English to be understood. It must be crazy enough to work."

Grant looked at the information they were laying on the table in front of him. "And why were you collecting all this?"

Price adopted an 'Aw shucks' posture. "We knew you were interested. You spend enough time out by that airstrip. You think we didn't know you were going out last night? Who do you think was your security team? Us and a few more. We've been running some night training in that area, just to see if the Russians were doing the same and watching us."

"Are they?"

"Nope. They don't seem to be the least bit interested in anything we do except build that road. They drive out every couple of days and watch us from the hills."

Grant stood up and gathered the papers. "Give me the memory cards. I have to go make peace with Morgan now."

# CHAPTER 7

Price was pointing off towards the hills. "There's the Russians. They're a little early today." Morgan lifted his camera binoculars and snapped a picture of them. It was too far away for good resolution, but he'd rather have a bad picture than none at all. Even a grainy, out of focus shot could tell the photo interpreters something. He continued to scan the hills to the north, then stopped short.

"Who's that?" he asked as he pushed the shutter button.

Price followed his gaze until he could barely make out another figure on the hills. He picked up his field glasses and looked. It was a solitary figure. He was standing there with his own binoculars, watching them. The fact that he had been seen didn't seem to bother him. He even waved at Price.

"Cocky bastard, whoever he is."

"Can you make out any details?"

"No. He's even got a bandanna covering his face. Probably one of the 'bandits' the locals keep talking about. He's probably trying to see what he could steal."

Morgan put down his binoculars and motioned Price to follow him. He walked over to where the stone bridge was being rebuilt by the Moldovan soldiers, augmented by some civilian laborers. Morgan didn't like the idea of the civilians working so close to the Americans, but Perkins had over ruled him. The locals had the skills, and the salaries the US was paying them went a long way towards international goodwill. Lieutenant Sage, the Civil Affairs officer, was even trying to arrange extra rations so they could be fed at the end of the day. Morgan had protested that one so strongly that even Perkins had backed down a little, but he still told Sage to explore the possibility of one meal, on Friday evenings, at the end of their workweek. The Americans were still working six days a week, with occasional Sundays. Until the 'cultural tours' were established, there was little else to do.

"Sergeant Price, are you checking the site before you start work?" Morgan was worried that all the attention they were getting from the hills boded ill. He didn't want to be surprised some morning by an IED in the middle of the work site.

"Every morning, Major. I have a team come out a half hour ahead of the main body to poke around."

"Why earlier?"

Price snorted. "The Colonel says if the locals see us poking around like we didn't trust them, it would hurt their feelings."

Morgan walked away shaking his head. Up and down the chain of command, the inept and the incompetent boxed him in. His commander was inept, and Winder, his key NCO, was flat out incompetent. The situation in the S-3 shop had devolved to the point where Winder was in charge of only what could be termed 'minimally invasive' responsibilities. That is, as long as it didn't affect operations or time sensitive material, he was in charge of it, but still had one of the specialists checking his work. His only strong subordinate, was SFC Sharp, and he was so wrapped up in joint training with the Moldovans and extra-curricular training of the Americans, he only saw him every couple of days for a quick update. The extra-curricular stuff was starting to worry Morgan. He had little or no control over it, but it seemed to be some of the most popular training around. The young soldiers, men and women, willingly gave up their nights and days off to Sharp, and sometimes Price and Grant, with no expectation of having any time off from their regular duties. The only answer he could get out of the soldiers when he asked why they were willing to give up so much was "Well, they were right last time" meaning Sudan.

He checked his watch and went looking for Perkins. The Commander had decided today would be a good day to get out of the office and get a tour of the work projects and training areas. He had also decided that it would be a good day for his S-1 and Surgeon to see the sights, so he brought them along too. The 'ladies' as he referred to them, were busy getting on the equipment and taking each others picture. Morgan hated 'get out of the office' day.

The Colonel was back at the Hummer with the two female officers. He was looking at his watch, as if he was concerned about the time. "Morgan, Major Carson and Captain Bonneville have duties in the rear. Have the Sergeant Major take the ladies back while we go out and observe the training."

Grant wasn't heading right back, and let the two women know that if they were in a hurry he could make other arrangements for them. Major Carson gave a flip of her hand. "I don't care how long it takes to get back, Sergeant Major. I couldn't handle another two hours of Colonel Perkins' travelogue, and I'm sure Captain Bonneville would agree."

Bonneville did, but she when she told Perkins she had to get back, she was hoping for a nice afternoon alone with Grant, roaming the countryside. She hadn't counted on the doctor picking up on the idea too. Carson was too curious about her relationship with Grant. She had the feeling that Sylvia Carson was a potential rival.

About a mile down the road Grant handed a pair of binoculars back to Bonneville and told her to look for the signs of anyone watching them from the ridge. She did as she was asked, but wondered about whom would be watching them. When she told Grant there was nothing in sight, he veered off the road and began going cross-country towards the hill line. The two women looked at each other, wondering where they were going. Bonneville, used to these route deviations, but still uncomfortable with them, asked if she should have brought a weapon.

"No' Grant answered. "I have mine."

Carson's eyes went wide at that. She hadn't realized anyone in the unit was habitually traveling armed. As they crested the hill they found a dirt road running parallel to the crest, just back from it. There was a vehicle moving off to the south. Carson pointed it out to Grant. "Is that what you're looking for?"

Grant followed her arm and stared at the Russian Gaz. He lifted his binoculars for a closer look and shook his head. He swung around to the north and looked for a moment, then shut off the engine. Bonneville was the first to ask, "Why are we stopping here?"

Grant was silent for a moment, then restarted the vehicle. "We aren't. I was listening for another engine." He turned onto the road and headed back north. Carson asked if he was looking for the man on the motorcycle.

"How did you know about him?"

"The soldiers were talking about him watching them just about every day. They were speculating on who he was." There was a pause. "Who is he?" Carson noticed that he had taken out his weapon and had checked to make sure there was a round in the chamber. She also noticed that it wasn't an issue 9mm.

"I don't know yet, but I hope to find out."

Grant saw a motorcycle approaching and stopped in the middle of the road. He handed Carson a digital camera and told her to start snapping pictures as soon as the rider got close, and not stop until he had passed. Then he got out of the vehicle and stood by the front end, holding his pistol behind his back. Bonneville got out and stood behind him. "What's going on?"

Grant was silent as the bike slowed to pass them on the shoulder. The rider glanced at the Sergeant Major, then the glance became a stare as he slowed even more. Bonneville could hear Grant mutter "Son of a bitch" under his breath. The motorcyclist said something out loud that Bonneville couldn't understand, but sounded like Arabic. The two men had recognized each other. Grant was bringing his weapon up as the rider twisted his throttle and sped off. Grant spun around and bumped into Bonneville. By the time they had disentangled the motorcycle was hidden in a cloud of dust. He was still standing at the back of the Hummer with his .45 raised when Carson came around from the other side "I think I got some good pictures of him when he slowed up." Then she noticed the gun in Grant's outstretched arm. "Oh, shit!' And back stepped around the vehicle. Grant lowered the hammer and holstered his weapon. This was bad, he thought. He should have set himself up better for a clear shot, but he didn't want to alarm the women. He hoped somebody else wouldn't have to pay for his mistake.

He got back in the vehicle and turned it around. Both women were asking him what was going on. He tried to pass it off as nothing, just an encounter with a bandit, but Bonneville wasn't buying that. "You knew we were going to meet someone back there! You had that planned!"

He stopped the vehicle and turned to both women. Militarily, he was outranked, but neither one of them had a need to know what just happened yet. "He's been watching the road. I wanted to know why, that's all. It just happened quicker than I had planned."

Carson spoke. "And you were supposed to be alone when you met him. We weren't supposed to be here." She stated it like a fact. Grant could only agree with her. "No, Ma'am. You weren't supposed to be here." He looked at Linda Bonneville. "Either one of you."

All she could do was look at him and snap "You son of a bitch! And you just had to do that anyway! What if he had started shooting at us first?"

"I wasn't going to let that happen."

"Yeah, I could see you were in control of the situation. You want to go get yourself killed, you go do it on your own!"

Carson looked back and forth between them. This was interesting. She had thought there was something from the way they acted together. Now she was sure. This shooting stuff aside, she saw a second chance for what she wanted back in Germany.

Harrison and Grant were in the First Sergeants' office, nursing a couple of beers.

After the Colonel had returned from looking for Sharp (he never found him), he was in a bad mood. He dismissed Grant's claim of seeing the Arab from Africa with a wave of his hand. "You're crazy, Sergeant Major. What would he be doing this far away from home? The news reports have the Janjaweed killing people faster than ever. Think he has time to come up here and watch us build a road?"

Grant was adamant, but Major Carson had mishandled the camera, and all she got were shots of a tire and the back of someone's head. Without proof, Perkins was not inclined to give him the benefit of the doubt. "Sergeant Major, all you saw was a beard under a helmet and goggles. I can't even pick out my own son when he's dressed like that. I don't want you wandering around loose waving illegal pistols at civilians. You turn that thing into the arms room. And from now on, you let me know when you're leaving the compound, and you better have someone with you. That 'lone wolf' stuff may have worked for you in Sudan, but we're in a no threat environment here."

Grant wanted to argue, but Perkins cut him off and dismissed him. Morgan was waiting outside.

"If it's any consolation, I believe you, but you should have waited."

Grant looked into Morgan's eyes. "You knew who he was." It wasn't a question.

"I had my suspicions."

"Then why the fuck aren't you in there telling Perkins I'm not a whack job? You know what that rag head is capable of. Are you going to wait until we're filling body bags again before you say anything?"

"Sergeant Major, I can't tell Perkins. Once I do, he's gonna wonder how a guy who wasn't in Africa with you knows about this guy. He may be an ass, but you have to have more than a GED to become a Lieutenant Colonel, and he'll figure out I'm not what my orders say I am. What's going on is too important to have him making noises up the chain of command. Give me a couple of days."

"Tell me what you know about this guy."

"Not now. I have to get ready to go out."

"Go out where?"

"Your buddies, Sharp and Price, have been in the Russian base twice during soccer games. Somehow, they've managed to get in twice after dark, too. They agreed to take me back in tonight. I have some surveillance gear I want to leave behind."

Grant grunted. "I'm coming with you!"

"No, Sergeant Major. You're not. Perkins doesn't like me wandering around too much at night either. He knows we have some 'night training' tonight, and being the prick he is, as soon as we go out the gate he'll probably be looking for you. He's just ass hole enough to go out looking for us, and God only knows where he'll end up with his navigation skills. I don't need that. We'll talk tomorrow."

Both conversations had left a bad taste in Grant's mouth. He was hoping the beer would wash it out, but so far it hadn't worked. He had to admit, though, Morgan was right. When Sharp had led his phony training class out the gate, Perkins was right there counting noses. As soon as they were clear he sent for Grant, just to make sure he wasn't hiding in one of the vehicles. He had asked Grant some make-work bullshit question about NCO evaluations, something he never seemed to worry about, then dismissed him again. He told Harrison about it.

"Between a Major and a Lieutenant Colonel, I've been 'dismissed'" he held up his hands with his fingers curled over, "twice. Do you know how long it's been since that's happened to me, especially by a field grade?"

Harrison was trying to calm his friend down. He had been on edge since he had gotten back, and really wouldn't tell him why. All he was able to do was keep feeding him beer. "Luke, if you aren't going to tell me why you're wound up like a cheap watch over this I can't help. Who was that guy?"

Grant drained his beer and tossed the empty into a waste can. He reached over for another one and looked for the bottle opener. "When are these damn third world countries going to learn about twist tops?" He got the bottle and took a long drink. "Remember right after the air strike, those two Arabs came to the gate?"

"I remember. That oily politician that did all the talking and his driver?"

"Yeah, those two. Only now I think the driver may have been the brains of the operation. He was really cool with guns pointed at him. The politician was ready to piss his pants."

"What about them, Luke?"

"That was the driver today."

Harrison put down his beer and was silent for a minute. "You sure?"

"I'm sure. And Morgan knows something about him, and he doesn't seem too worried about it."

"That's not good, Luke. Are we bait for something?"

"I don't know." He finished his beer. "This isn't working for me. I've got a bottle of Mexican fire water in my room."

"If it'll calm you down, why not? As long as that *pistola* the CO's upset about is put away."

"Yeah, that one is in the arms room."

"That one?" Harrison took another pull at his beer. "Of course you'd have more than one."

Grant smiled. "I've got too many points on my license to just have one. I may be going to hell when I die, but it doesn't mean I'm going to cooperate."

"Want me to see if the good Captain Bonneville would like to join us?"

Grant shook his head. "Don't bother. She was quiet all the way back after she dressed me down out there, probably because Carson was with us. When we got back she really let me have it. I really didn't think she was capable of using that vocabulary so smoothly. She's really pissed I was out looking to kill that guy and brought her along for the ride. I tried to talk to her after supper, and she just told me to get the fuck away from her. She's probably right. Sometimes," he looked at his friend, "now more than ever, I start to think I should just give this up and let retirement take me. I could probably convince her it could be a good life. Neither one of us needs the Army." He looked at Harrison, who was laughing. "What's so funny?"

"I've read this book before. There's something the two of you haven't figured out about each other yet. It might even be something you two haven't figured out about yourselves."

"And you have?"

"Hey," he pointed to the tag on his desk. "That says 'First Sergeant' for a reason. When we stop being good at being first, the Army makes us Sergeant Majors, but I digress. She may not like what you do, but that's what attracts her to you. When we were in Germany, away from all the shit, you two could have been like a couple of rabbits. Instead, you almost started to avoid each other."

"That was the different. In the rear an officer and an NCO can't be close."

"Bullshit. You know how to work the system. You know how to avoid the system. As soon as we got back out here you two managed to find time. She likes you for the danger of you. Take that away, my friend, and you're just another old man looking to get laid."

"That can't be all of it."

"No. Part of it is who she is. She likes you stray dogs who might just bite. Look at her ex-husband. Why do you think she hooked up with him while she was on leave?"

"Lonely?"

"No! You weren't around. No danger, no challenge. No one she knew she couldn't change but could try to anyway. She likes that middle ground, not too safe, but not too dangerous. As soon as you get to either extreme, she'll push."

Grant wasn't buying it. "It's gotta be more than that."

"Sure it does. Let some moron put a mortar round into the motor pool. She'll be hiding in your sleeping bag waiting for you to protect her."

"That's cold."

"Luke, have you figured out yet that you're a bullet magnet? Every place we've ever been, you manage to find someone who wants to kill you. That's not exactly something that'll endear you to a woman in the long run."

"You said we have to figure out something about each other. What am I doing?"

"You, my friend, need someone to protect. It can be her, or one of these young kids. The thing about her is, she always seems vulnerable. The kids manage to learn how to take care of themselves."

"I'm not a bullet magnet!"

"You're not? For Christ's sake, Luke. All you have to do is show up and people start shooting. I'm surprised the Moldovans haven't declared war on us yet.'

"What about you? Willa seems to put up with it." Willa was Harrison's wife.

"Willa knows two things about me. The first is that I don't go looking for trouble."

"And the second?"

"If I find it, it's your fault. And speaking of Willa, she sent me some papers I have to go over with you, Sharp and Price. We'll do it next time everybody's reasonably sober."

"What kind of papers?"

"Willa started a non-profit for the B-17. Seems like there are a lot of people who are interested in getting the old bird flying, and they're willing to donate time, money and spare parts. The non-profit keeps me from paying a sack full of taxes."

"You mean that wreck is going to fly someday?"

"Fly? Hell, I've got a pilot's license. When we get back I'm going to work on my multi-engine rating."

After dinner, Bonneville had gone to her room. All she wanted to do was be alone and work out her anger. She had reached her limit with Grant over this latest adventure. All she wanted out of a relationship was stability, and she kept making bad choices. Her ex-husband was a prime example. It was bad enough she had stayed with him long enough to have two kids, putting up with the drinking, the abuse and the financial instability. She didn't want anymore of that. Seeing him when she was on leave was a bad idea, one that she made worse by having sex with him. She should have known that as soon as he started drinking and she started saying no to him about her money, his old ways would come back. They did, and it would have been a worse beating if they hadn't been in public.

Grant would probably be a different man than once he was out of the Army, but there was no way he'd get out of his own free will. And, being the man he was, he'd probably find something equally stupid

141

to get involved in. She took off a boot and threw it across the room. Almost at the same time, there was a knock on the door. Bonneville thought at first it might be Grant coming by to apologize, something he wasn't too experienced at, but managed from time to time. Then she realized that the knock had been rather weak, not at all the type of battering the Sergeant Major would have given her door.

She limped over, one boot on, one boot off, and pulled the door open, ready to snap at someone. She was surprised to see her Personnel NCO, Sheila Gordon, standing there with a bottle and two glasses. She stopped short of snapping at her. Instead, she tried a polite dismissal. "This might not be the best time, Sheila. I'm in a really rotten mood."

Gordon slipped past her and put the bottle down on the little table by the bed. "Everybody has heard how you ripped up Sergeant Major Grant this afternoon. I figured you'd be mad enough to want to be alone, but you should have a drink and a little company." Bonneville closed the door and dragged her booted foot back to the bed. She dropped heavily onto it and laid her head back on the pillow. "A drink sounds good, but I'm not going to be much company." She sat up and mocked pulling at her hair. "That man is so frustrating! I don't know what I'm going to do!" and she lay back down.

Gordon clucked her tongue, like one would expect their mother to do just before a scolding. She poured two glasses of wine and handed Bonneville one. She pushed herself up on her elbows and took the glass. "Is this some of that local Chardonnay I've been hearing about?"

Gordon knelt down and picked up the booted foot. As she started to unlace it she answered, "I don't know what kind it is. I can't read the label, but some of the girls bought a case, and it's pretty good." She pulled the boot off and looked for its mate. She saw it on the floor and threw the other one at it. Then she started rolling off the wool, cushioned sole combat boot sock. Bonneville thought about stopping her, but decided against it. *She's trying to be nice*, went through her mind. *She's a good friend, and I need a good friend right now.*

"God, Linda, unclench your toes! You're as tight as a drum. Here," she was saying as she stood up. "Unclip your belt and roll over. I'm going to work some of the kinks out of your back."

Bonneville did as she was told. Gordon had a knack for massage, and she knew how to hit all the right nerve endings to make the experience extremely satisfying. Bonneville had enjoyed her touch before, even if it did sometimes get carried away.

"Why don't I lock the door before somebody else barges in. I don't want you half-relaxed, then have to start over. Bonneville giggled at the idea. While Gordon was at the door she finished her glass and poured another. She had that half finished when she felt Gordon climb over her and straddle her back. She felt her shirt being pulled up and her bra being unclasped. She finished pulling off her shirt, then slipped the bra out from underneath her. The rough texture of the GI wool blanket on her bed felt good rubbing against her nipples. She let out a little sigh and wiggled her hips deeper into the bed.

"That's better," she heard Gordon say. "Just relax and let me take care of you. I'll have you feeling better in no time." Bonneville enjoyed a few minutes of the gentle rubbing. When she felt the other girl move off her she started to turn. Gordon reassured her. "Just lay still, I'm moving your trousers so I can work on your lower back." She felt the heavier texture of her camouflaged pants sliding down her leg. The flow of cool air on her skin made her tingle. She gave an involuntary shudder, then ground her hips and her chest into the blanket. The rough scrapping made her groan. She heard Gordon say "That's better. You're getting into the mood now." Bonneville also heard some more rustling of clothes. She took another sip of her wine as she peeked over her shoulder. Gordon had taken off her uniform, too. She felt a sudden flush, and then she felt her nipples hardening. She suddenly felt wet between her legs. She put her glass down and slid her hands under her breasts, cupping and squeezing them. Gordon resumed her position, straddling her. She could feel the other woman's skin against her. Then Gordon lay on top of her. Linda felt her breasts against her back, the nipples hard, like hers. Gordon put her arms around her, sliding her hands underneath, between Linda's hands and her breasts. The other girl started gently rubbing them. She whispered in Linda's ear, "Would you like me to take care of that for you?"

"Oh, yes!" and twisted around so she was facing the girl on top of her. She wrapped her arms around Gordon and closed her eyes as she felt another tongue exploring her mouth.

Ali Alawa Sharif sat in his room in the dark. He didn't think the American recognized him on the road, he was too busy rubbing up against his whore. He must have interrupted them as they were getting ready to defile each other. He had noticed the other whore still in the truck, fumbling with something. Had he no shame? Two women, in broad daylight, by the side of the road?

He knew that big American. That was the one who had stopped him at the airfield in Sudan. He was pretty sure that it was the same one who had ambushed his fighters on the road, spoiling his attack on the retreating Americans. The woman he was with, that must have been the white whore that Ibn Mousa al Saif wanted so badly. Poor Ibn

Mousa. If the man hadn't spent so much time thinking with his penis, he might still be alive

Sharif smiled at the thought of Ibn Mousa al Saif on his last helicopter ride. He enjoyed killing him.

Yusef was in the next room, praying again. The boy was getting on Sharif's nerves. He was a praying fool. He did his regular prayers five times a day. When he wasn't in the apartment, he was praying in the mosque. And when he wasn't working on his explosive vest, he was praying some more. Sharif had never seen anyone so eager to die. He was continually asking what his target would be. What was potentially worse, his status as a 'martyr' was becoming known. If the congregation knew that he was already resigned to die or if he had planned to travel to Iraq or Israel was unknown. Sharif hoped that, if pressed by anyone, he could explain it away as the ramblings of a youth that had spent too much time praying.

Still, it was a useful sideshow to his recruitment for Jihad. The local Muslim youths were undereducated, unemployed, bored and easily led. Some of them were following Yusef as one would a western rock star. Some of them could be made into useful dupes. The local Imam, not one who could be considered a deep thinker, was content to let his congregation babble on about the Jihad, as long as he didn't have to risk incurring the wrath of the local secret police. They were still in the pay of the Russians, but the locals didn't know that. Sharif had spent time, and a little cold, hard cash, convincing the Imam to include the standard 'Death to Israel, Death to America' chants in his prayers and sermons. Even Sharif puzzled at how quickly hatred could take over a prayer service. Puzzled, but glad it did. It made his recruitment efforts easier.

The Russian agent was becoming a problem. He had a list of ideas for attacking the Americans that he kept dragging out, pointing out the benefits of blowing up this stretch of road or another. He seemed to be blissfully unaware, in his revolutionary fervor, that Sharif had already abandoned the Russian plan and was developing his own. The Russians were thinking locally, while Sharif was planning globally. That and the Russians were cheap when it came to payment. Sharif had decided that his handler was as eager as the boy for martyrdom, only he didn't know it yet. Sharif planned to kill him in a memorable fashion. The Russians didn't understand terror for terrors sake. They had grown weak since their empire had crumbled. Everything was secrecy, deniability and blame shifting. Everything had to have a political meaning, with long, convoluted rationales. They missed the point of Jihad. Subdue, convert, and kill. God demands it. When you cut a throat, God is great. A long political excuse just bores the killer and the victim.

Ali Alawa Sharif wasn't political. He wasn't religious. He enjoyed what he did, and Allah made it respectable. Everything else was bombast.

He had watched the Americans long enough to formulate a plan. The Moldovan workers had given him the key, and his plan was set. Yusef would be pleased. He was going to get his virgins soon.

"Yusef! Come in here! I have some good news for you. The day you have prayed for will soon be upon us. And I may have employment for some of your friends."


Morgan watched the door as Sharp and Price gathered intelligence. Their main target, a building in the middle of the compound, they had not been able to access. The doors were all gated steel, and the

146

windows were too. There was an oversized shed attached to one end, it looked like an after thought to the construction. From the vents and the airflow, Morgan guessed that it was an air-handling unit. He looked for a spot to hide one of the little instruments he had brought. They were about the same size as an Ipod, and just as easy to hide.

They had zeroed in on what appeared to be the main administration and classroom building. In a departure from what they had expected, there were no locks on the door. Hell, except for that one building they couldn't get in, there hadn't been locks on anything they had looked at so far.

Morgan had noticed that all the interior signs were in a combination of Cyrillic and Arabic. The Moldovans had insisted that all the staff here were ethnic Russians. These signs said otherwise. He looked around to see if the other two were finishing up.

Both Sharp and Price were carrying empty rucksacks. They were careful not to take anything that would be missed, but it still left a gold mine of information. There were stacks of mimeographed material, as well as boxes of slim manuals in both Arabic and Russian. They had even found some material in English. Anything they thought might be missed was photographed.

The rest of the team was either securing the vehicle hide or watching the outside perimeter at the point of entry. What appeared to be formidable security was actually a sham. The guards were inattentive, they were careless with perimeter gates, and even the duty sergeant in the guard shack was sleeping when they peeked in. They didn't seem concerned that their sworn enemies of the last sixty years were just a few miles up the road. They were really taking the end of the cold war to heart.

Price finally found a door that was locked. He took a few minutes to examine it, then went to work on the tumblers. Sharp came up behind him and asked what he was doing. When Price told him, Sharp reached up and took a key off a nail in the doorframe.

"Try this."

The room was packed with boxes of explosives. Price translated the Cyrillic markings as Sharp snapped pictures. "You better get the Major in here. He should see this."

Sharp went out and took over Morgan's position. Morgan came in and let out a low whistle. "Son of a bitch! What the hell is all this doing here?"

"Major, as far as I can tell, this is a bomb making school. They've got posters on wiring up cell phones and a stack of vests loaded with pockets."

"A school? Where do they test this stuff?"

Price shook his head. "They probably don't. I'm not sure of all the markings, but I think this one means 'inert'."

Morgan slipped a lid and took a brick out. "Maybe they won't notice this is gone. We need to get it tested. You got a GPS unit?" Price did. "Get a coordinate, right here. We may need it later."

There was a rattle at the door. Price snapped off his light and turned to see what it was. They needed the radios they had in Sudan. What they had brought here was totally unsuited for this 'sneaky pete' type stuff. The door opened and a hand reached in, searching for a light switch. Morgan was moving as fast as he could to get behind the door. The overhead lights went on in a blaze and Price lost what little night vision he had. Whoever it was stepped into the room, and

Morgan delivered a blow to the back of the head that stunned the new arrival and dropped him to his knees. Morgan kneeled besides him and grabbed the back of his head. He knocked the mans arms out from under him and drove his forehead into the floor. There was a sharp crack and blood started flowing from the nose. Price came up besides them and snapped the light off. He glanced out into the hall and closed the door.

"This isn't going to look good when they find him!"

Morgan was looking around the room. "Shut up and help me find something to make this look like an accident!"

Price looked up at the ceiling. "Give me that chair." Morgan slid it over and Price climbed up. He used his knife to pry open a link on the chain of an overhead light fixture.

"Watch out! It's coming down." The light swung just low enough to hit an average sized man in the back of the head.

Morgan looked at Price. "Think that'll fool anyone? That light isn't very heavy."

"You should have thought of that before you whacked the guy! All it has to do is get them wondering. A little doubt goes a long way."


Forty-five minutes later they were all back at the vehicles. Sharp did a head count and gave Morgan thumbs up. Price was sitting in the back of a Hummer with him, watching him examine his block of phony plastic explosives. "I'm trying to figure you out, Major."

"What do you mean, Sergeant?"

"Back inside there, when you looked at all the shit in the closet, you sounded surprised. What I'm not sure of, is whether you were surprised it was there, or surprised you were right."

"Does it matter?"

Price turned away. "I think it does. This whole thing stinks. I think we're being set up for something." He paused, then continued. "What were those things you were dropping all over the place?"

"I didn't drop them 'all over the place', I only left two. I hope you remembered where they went, because you might have to recover them later."

Morgan looked back at the brick of explosives he had taken. "But you are right. Somebody's being set up, Sergeant, but I'm not really sure if it's us or them."

"Yeah, that's been the story since I joined this chicken shit outfit. Somebody always seems to leave the important stuff out of the briefings."

Grant was headed back to his room with better than half a bottle of tequila left. Harrison had decided to call it a night and chased his friend off. "Go get some sleep. I don't want to find out you spent the night finishing that bottle off alone." Grant knew his friend was right. This wasn't the first time he had been in hack with his commander, and probably wouldn't be the last. In some sense, his latest restriction might even be a good thing for him. Morgan was an operator. He was obviously working for another command, and could probably tap into assets the 289th didn't have access to. It would be better to let him take the lead in all the other dark work they were doing. Grant could clear his plate and concentrate on the Arab.

The hallway was quiet. He looked at his watch and was surprised to see how late it was. The entry team would be back from the Russian compound in a few hours. He debated waiting up for them. Fuck it, he thought. Leave that one for Morgan. Price and Sharp would keep him advised on what was happening and what they found, and if they needed Grant to get involved they would ask. Grant made a quick turn into the latrine. Might as well get rid of the excess booze now, then he wouldn't have to bother getting dressed again later. That was one of the down sides to living in a mixed gender barracks. Propriety was always an issue now. Years ago it would have been one set of quarters for the men, and a separate one for the women. Nobody gave a rat's ass if you wandered down the hall in your skivvies.

When he came back into the hall he saw Major Carson in her robe, coming out of the women's shower. She was still toweling off her hair as she walked towards Grant.

"You're up late, Major. Busy night in the dispensary?"

She draped her towel around her neck. "One of the mechanics was trying to get a repair done. He slipped with a wrench and sliced his thumb open pretty good. I had to stitch him up." She looked down at the bottle in his hand. "Looks like you're having a busy night tonight too." She reached over and took the bottle out of his hand. "After that little road trip you gave me today, I could use some of this. Do you mind?"

Before he could stop, he heard himself answer her. "Do you think we should be standing in the hallway swilling booze straight from the bottle?"

She smiled. "You're right. Bad example. I have glasses in my room," and she turned and walked back towards it. Grant hesitated a moment. Carson looked over her shoulder and saw he was still standing there. "Coming?"

I'm definitely going to hell, he thought to himself, then walked after her. "I hope so!"

Carson's room was a little bigger than Grant's, and had a little bit more in the way of creature comforts. From somewhere she had managed to get a dresser with a good-sized mirror and an overstuffed chair. She even had a field desk in one corner with a laptop set up on it. "You've managed to make yourself comfortable here, Major." He looked around the room, and decided that the safest place for him would be in the big chair. He remembered when she had groped his leg, but she had been drinking quite a bit that night. It might just have been the booze and a momentary slip, nothing more. In all the time since there had been nothing to indicate anything but, and she never gave a hint of anything but a proper officer-enlisted relationship. Still, there was a story going around that she had started legal work to divorce her husband. He parked his ass in the overstuffed chair. Better to be safe than sorry.

She picked up a pair of glasses from the dresser and filled them both halfway. She handed one to Grant, then sat down on the edge of her bed. When she crossed her legs the robe fell open to about mid thigh. Funny, Grant thought. I see more skin when she falls out in her PT uniform, but this is turning me on. He concentrated on his drink.

"What was all that about on the road today? You looked like you wanted to kill that man."

"I did. And make no mistake, I will." Damn, I shouldn't have said that.

Her expression didn't change. "Who was he?"

Grant considered whether he should tell her. He tried to figure out if it was the booze or if she really had a need or a right to know. He figured she did. "He was one of the Arabs from Sudan, the ones who told us to get out of town." That got her attention. Her eyes widened a little, and she gave an involuntary gasp. Then she regained her composure. "Are you sure? What is he doing here?"

"I don't know, but I don't want to wait to find out. Too bad the Colonel doesn't agree. He thinks I'm imagining things."

"Are you?"

"No way in hell, Major. I know who he is."

She shifted her legs, and her robe fell open a little more. She took the towel off her shoulders and tossed it onto the dresser. Grants eyes followed a line from her knees, to her thighs, then up across the tops of her breasts showing over her robe, then he looked at her face. She had a hint of a smile. She put her glass on the night table by the bed and stood up. Grant took a chance and asked. "What now, Major?"

She walked over to him and paused, looking down on him. Then she sat in his lap. "I remember telling you once that all this 'Major – Sergeant Major' business wasted a lot of time." The she kissed him, forcing his lips open with her tongue and exploring his mouth with it. When he responded she picked up his hand and pushed it inside her robe. Grant felt her breasts were firm and her nipples were already hard. He slipped his hand out to unfasten the belt of her robe. He pushed the fabric aside so he could see her body. He wasn't disappointed. Her breasts were round, with hardly any sag. They were tipped with big, round and brown circles, he didn't know what they were called, and two of the biggest nipples he had ever seen. He took one in his mouth as his hand wandered down to explore her wet spot. She stood up and took his hand, and guided him over to her bed.

Yeah, definitely, he thought. I'm going to hell.

She dropped her robe on the floor. Grant was surprised she had been in the hall wearing nothing under the robe but skin. Her hands went to his waistband and slipped in. He could feel her skin against his, squeezing him. He slid his pants over his hips, and stepped out of them. She pushed him down on the bed and threw one leg over him, her backside facing him. She bent over him and he could feel the warm wetness of her mouth. Grant grabbed her hips and pulled them back to his face. He could smell her musky wetness, then the rush of moisture as his tongue made contact. Her first orgasm was quick and powerful. She lay still for a moment to catch her breath, shuddering, then lifted herself up and reversed her position. She expertly guided Grant deep inside her and rested her hands on his chest as she began rocking, slowly at first, then a more frantic motion. He could feel her fingers dig into his skin as another wave of pleasure rolled over her. She collapsed on top of him as he thought, my god, she has a quick trigger.

She only rested, quietly, for a few moments. "Thank God, I needed that," she gasped out. Then she rolled over besides Grant and pulled him with her. Again she guided him to where she wanted him. He could feel her muscles close around him. "I want this one slow. I've been waiting for it a long time!"

When she was asleep he slipped out of her room and returned to his own. On the way he passed Sergeant Gordon in the hall. Neither one had seen where the other one was coming from. The Sergeant Major gave a cursory nod and wondered why she was up so early. Gordon wondered the same thing about the Sergeant Major, but passed it off quickly, still enjoying the thought of the night she had just spent.

The green light of Grants clock told him it was almost time to get up again, so he grabbed his towel and headed for the shower. Once he had washed the scent of a woman off his body, he'd go for a run. It had been a long time since he took one of his pre-dawn runs. He remembered that they always seemed to invigorate him, no matter how tired he was feeling.

Four miles later, he was feeling like a new man. I may be an old man going to hell, he thought, but I'll be going there with a smile on my face.

# CHAPTER 8

Winder was standing at LTC Perkins office door, folder in hand, anxious to speak. He had not enjoyed his stay in Moldova so far. He had anticipated a return to his former swaggering stature once the 289th returned to a straight construction mission. Captain Fisher being named the new S-3 just before the movement made it even sweeter. He had always been able to manipulate Fisher, a notoriously weak officer who would certainly be passed over for Major unless he could find some way to complete his staff schooling. And Winder had found a way to make that happen. Instructors at the State run course came and went, but the curriculum stayed the same. Winder had found it easy to get into the course content and remove some of the more heavy-duty assignments that were given out. All he had to do was make sure that the current instructor didn't previously assign the papers passed in. He had been feeding Fisher copies of someone else's work as his own research. Fisher wasn't any the wiser, and Winder was cementing another supporter in his quest for State Command Sergeant Major.

As events developed, Fisher was on track to graduate from his course and possibly get selected for promotion on the next go around. Performance as a Group Operations Officer could only help at the board. Then, thanks to Grant and his toady Harrison, he was axed from getting a slot at the Sergeant Major Academy, just because of that damn PT test. In the old Guard, that wouldn't have been a problem. The First Sergeant would have taken care of the score card and he would have passed with a comfortable score, maybe even a PT badge, depending on how stiff the competition was for the school slot.

Then this Major Morgan showed up. What a prick! First, he dressed him down because of a casual salute. Where the hell did this guy come from? Nobody treated a Master Sergeant like that. Then he started nit-picking his work. Hell, it was stuff he used to pass on to the lower ranks then just endorse. Morgan was making him do it himself. The man didn't realize Winder was a *supervisor*, not a *doer*. That's what the rest of the section was for. Now, Morgan had taken away all his support and assigned him all the crap work, and nit-picked that, too. He had made Sharp his teachers pet and had given him the juicy training assignments with almost no supervision.

Winder may have been down, but he wasn't out. He was still the senior enlisted man in the section, and he could still get access to what was going on. He knew Morgan and Sharp were up to something. They spent way too much time out in the field, especially at night, when there was no training scheduled. Then he found the pictures in the safe. At first, he didn't have any idea of what they were. It took him a while to figure out that he could compare the coordinates on the photos to a local map. He realized it was the Russian place down the road. A bit later, he saw that the file was getting fatter. They were spending a lot of time watching what the Russians were doing.

A couple of days ago, while everyone was out of the office, something that was happening more and more, leaving Winder behind with his crap jobs, he discovered they had been going into the compound. Not just the daylight visits posing as soccer players, but at night, too, and even going into the buildings.

The best part? Colonel Perkins didn't seem to have any idea of what was going on. Winder saw his chance to use this to get rid of all these people, put them in their places and become the top dog again. He just had to wait until the moment was right, and he could have his revenge on all of them. The moment had come.

Major Morgan had been trying to arrange an aircraft to come in and use the strip. He had checked with the Moldovans and learned that, although the Russians had built it and claimed it, it was essentially Moldovan property, and they had no qualms with the Americans doing their test. The Air Force was willing to try, but they first wanted some ground data on the condition of the strip. Morgan had provided a full set of survey plans, and had the soils section do an analysis. Once he added some video of a Russian AN-124 cargo plane both landing and taking off, the Air Force consented.

The plane they sent was a C-27J Spartan. It was an all weather cargo carrier that had been designed to go anywhere. According to the hype, it didn't even need a runway. Once the USAF announced plans for sending the plane, the straphangers and the tourists decided to get in on the act. Perkins had been notified to expect "a large party of dignitaries and media, including the CENTCOM Commander (or his representative) and a film crew." They would land mid-morning and leave at dusk. A full schedule of activities was anticipated.

Winder planned to use this visit as the perfect time to expose what was going on. He started to photocopy what he could, when he could, and try to eavesdrop on as many conversations as he could. The exit briefing would be the perfect time. After all the handshakes and pictures were taken, there was usually a small reception for the senior people and visitors. He would have everything with him and present it to whoever the ranking man was. He'd be the man of the hour.

The party had landed on time, and it was smaller than anticipated. General Manuel Ramirez, CinC, CENTCOM, had decided against a dog and pony show. He had quickly pared down the passenger list, bringing only his immediate staff, a public information team, and, against his better judgment, a civilian news crew. As long as the PIO could keep her distracted, he could find out what he needed to hear. He hoped having her as a smoke screen would help.

As the party came down the ramp, a small convoy of vehicles pulled up to carry everyone to the base. Ramirez looked around for Morgan, but couldn't find him in the crowd. He exchanged pleasantries with Perkins, introduced everyone, and impatiently waited for Cynthia Maddox to do her greetings of everyone who she remembered from her last time with the 289th. She had been particularly interested in two NCOs in particular, but Ramirez could attach no importance to them at first. Then he realized it was probably SSG Price who had gotten the video that the FBI used to snag Dillinghouse. He had been at Walter Reed Army Hospital recovering from wounds received in Sudan. Maddox must have gotten the films to him there. The other was the Personnel NCO. He couldn't remember her name off hand, but the two women walked off arm in arm. *I must have meant something.*

"Shall we get this circus on the road?" he announced in his best command voice. Ramirez had just gotten his fourth star and liked to remind people he had once been a small unit leader, just so they wouldn't think he had forgotten his roots. He was also anxious to get through the formalities of the tour. He wanted to know what was going on here, and why Morgan wanted a classified courier. Morgan had been assigned here because he was the one insisting the Russians were up to no good, but he thought it had been illegal bio testing. That would explain the security and the regular flights into the middle of nowhere. He was also convinced that the Russians being the moving force behind the 289th coming here for the road project was just another smoke screen. Ramirez had gotten tired of Morgan's repeated memos, and sent him to the 289th as operations officer just to get rid of him for a while. Could he have found something out?

In any event, his intelligence chief did have some news for them. He had discovered quite by accident that the Janjaweed terrorist they had dealt with in Sudan had fallen out of favor, and had most likely been killed by his own people. Ramirez though it would be a nice little nugget of information to share with the soldiers. After the casualties they had suffered, their hasty retreat through the desert, and the continuing slide of Darfur to anarchy, it was at least some proof that their mission there had made a difference. That would be part of the exit briefing. He might even let the civilian press hear that story.

On the ride to the bridge site Ramirez had to endure Perkins rambling about his mission and how well they were interfacing with the Moldovan Army. He carried on about tons of gravel moved, miles of road, and the amount of stone the masons had placed. Everything was phrased in terms that reflected on him as an individual. He never mentioned any subordinates by name or shared any credit. Noticeably absent was any reference to his own units' training or morale. Ramirez regretted not riding with Grant or Morgan.

He had to admit that they were doing a first class job on the road. The paved section had ended just past the main base area, and the transition to gravel was barely felt. He wondered how it would hold up under the strain of winter. Not that he really cared. They would be long gone by then, and Moldova was not high on anyone's list of strategic allies. He had seen the all the reports. There was little to offer in the way of natural resources and religious minorities were kept in check. Other then in the breakaway Trans-Dnestr region, the old Soviet methods were still used to control dissent. Once the Ukraine got control of that the problems would go away. Except for wine and brandy, this place had nothing to offer. The Russians were welcome to it.

They stopped at the bridge. Ramirez could see where a temporary bridge had been opened downstream to get equipment across. The road was just as finished on the other side. It looked like the bridge was the only thing holding them up. The estimate was that they would be done in a month. Recovery would be a simple matter; they would use the same rail lines to back haul the equipment. The problem was what to do with the 289th. They were a NATO asset here, and once back in Germany they would be an orphan again. Nobody really wanted them.

Ramirez walked the road for a bit with his staff, asking questions of soldiers and having his picture taken. Maddox, the reporter, had her crew set up and she was shooting interviews with young soldiers. That surprised Ramirez. Cynthia Maddox always had a reputation for not liking soldiers. Something about the 289th must have changed her mind. That was fine with him. A little extra publicity for the younger soldiers always paid dividends. The female Sergeant that had greeted her back at the airstrip seemed to be hovering close to her. Well, that was only normal. Here was a very successful and powerful woman who was showing the young girls they could do it too. He didn't pay any attention when she had her crew continue to film background shots of the road while the two women walked off up the streambed. Probably looking for a quiet place to do an interview, Ramirez thought,

Price had gotten him up on a bulldozer and showed him how to backfill some material around the bridge abutments. "Sergeant Price, I didn't know you had any experience with this equipment. You are a constant source of amazement."

"Yes, Sir. And who would have thought a four-star would catch on so fast? I still remember when you were a full bird in Saudi Arabia, trying to figure out where the jack was in your Hummer."

"I still think that was a setup."

"Maybe it was, but I got the hour I needed."

Price had been part of a point element during Desert Storm. He had been charged with clearing a fixed position before the armored forces crossed the border. Ramirez had laid out a plan that Price was certain would cause more casualties than necessary. He planned to take it out before the scheduled start time without alerting the rest of the Iraqi Republican Guard units in the area. Ramirez had refused permission, so Price arranged for his accident. As it turned out, Price was right. Ramirez' plan had them advancing through a minefield covered by heavy machine guns. Price had looped around and took them from the rear. The Iraqis never knew what hit them. It took Ramirez a long time to let it go.

Ramirez hopped off the dozer and returned Price's salute. "Have the motor pool add this to your license, General. It'll look good next to the helicopter." Ramirez just waved his hand over his head without looking back. His eyes traveled up to the hill line some distance away.

He could see a vehicle parked up there, but couldn't make out any details. From his briefings he knew those were the Russians, keeping an eye on progress. They were the ones who wanted this road. When he got to the parking area he saw Morgan and Grant scanning the hills through binoculars. He could see they were looking in the wrong direction. He tried to point out the Russians to them. Grant shrugged him off. "They aren't our problem." He passed the glasses to Ramirez and pointed further off to the left. Ramirez looked, and could see a lone figure standing by a motorcycle, watching them through his own glasses. "Who is that?"

Morgan answered. "We don't know for certain, but the Sergeant Major thinks he's the Janjaweed leader from Sudan."

"What? Are you certain?"

Morgan and Grant both looked at him. "The Sergeant Major's pretty sure, General."

"Well, That'll make Colonel Schaeffer happy. We'll talk about this later." He signaled that his visit here was at an end. He ordered Colonel Schaeffer, his intelligence chief, to commandeer a vehicle so they could talk privately on the return trip. He told Morgan and Grant to get in with them. "And somebody find that reporter. There'll be hell to pay if we lose her out here."


Sharif had seen the plane making its approach and had ridden to the edge of the hills to watch it land. An opportunity, he thought, and used his cell phone to call Yusef. This would be where some of his admirers could be of use. He explained what he wanted and continued towards his usual observation point. Since his meeting on the road with the Americans, he had taken to carrying a small pistol. He considered it ample if he got close enough for a kill shot, but small enough that he could dispose of it if needed. He actually hoped he would run in to the big American again under the same circumstances, on that stretch of road, far from the eyes of his fellow soldiers, and, with the two women. There were many uses for the infidel whores, including the one Ibn Mousa al Saif had in mind. He had listened to him describe what he would do often enough. Having two of them could be immensely satisfying.

He got to his position before the convoy arrived. He watched idly as the usual routine played out, then the line of vehicles arrived. There seemed to be an important visitor here, with all the saluting he could see going on. There was one man who everyone seemed to defer to, guiding him around and making a big show of what was going on. He got so interested in the spectacle that he almost missed the two men who were watching him. One was a stranger to him, but the other was the big American. He looked around quickly, but saw no sign of the whores he had been with. They must be back at the base. No matter. Having them would be a bonus. He wasn't going to make the same mistakes as Saif and make them the priority.

Another man had joined them. It was the visitor. There was a reflection from the insignia on his hat, but Sharif couldn't make it out. He must be important, the way everyone was paying attention to him. Sharif was tempted to wave at them, but he controlled himself. This was not the time to heighten their curiosity. Let them wonder about him, and perhaps think he was just a curious villager keeping an eye on the foreigners. There was no need to make them think anything else. He would give them enough to worry about soon enough, and then, they would have no more worries in this world.

He swung his glasses to the south. It looked like the Russians had had enough of this and were leaving. That was good. On the days the Russians hung around, Sharif had a long detour to make to avoid them. He had been leaving the Americans alone. It hadn't been part of the Russian plan, but the longer the Americans were able to operate unmolested, the more lax their security became. His handler was increasingly adamant he do something, so he had decided to make a demonstration. As long as the Russians were providing money and supplies, he wanted them to think he was a dutiful servant. There were plans for the Russians, too. Sharif regarded his treatment from them as less than he deserved. They were exploiting a temporary advantage the Americans had gotten on him. Some of them would have to suffer too.

He waited until he thought it would be safe. The Russians usually headed right back to their base after watching for a while, probably in a hurry for more vodka. He kick started his bike and headed off, following the ridgeline as long as possible, just to make certain the Americans were aware he was going. It didn't take long until he was roughly opposite where the Americans had landed their plane. Yusef's friends should be somewhere close, waiting for him. Their instructions were to stay out of sight until he arrived. It wouldn't do for the Russians to see them carrying one of their precious RPG launchers. He parked his bike and walked towards the crest. In a small ravine off to the side he could see the back end of a Trabant, a small East German made car that was very under powered and spewed clouds of black exhaust. It was hard to believe that the same people who perfected the Mercedes Benz and the BMW made this. The socialist influence definitely stifled their creativity. The two occupants recognized Sharif and got out to meet him.

"Leave the weapons in the car and come with me" he told them. "We don't want anyone to see you before we are ready." He led them to the edge of the crest and had them get on their bellies and crawl forward with him. He used his binoculars to scan the valley, looking for security outposts that would interfere with a stealthy approach. The Americans appeared confident of their safety, with the flat plains stretching out around them. It was probably a little over a mile to where the plane was parked, and Sharif was carefully plotting a route to a good firing position. The beauty of the RPG was the gunner did not need to watch the missile in flight once it had been launched. Depending on the range and his own skills, he could have the launcher reloaded and ready to fire before the first missile impacted. Sharif didn't believe these two had such skills, but, in any confusion they could stir up with an RPG and an AK-47 burst, they should be able to get off one or two more rockets before they were located and killed. Two more martyrs for Jihad, only these two actually thought they were talented enough to get away.

Sharif passed the glasses to the one he considered the more intelligent looking. He gave him a guided tour of a concealed approach, then had him repeat it back to him. The other youth was likewise instructed. He was surprisingly quick, with good eyes. He had been able to follow the first description, and once he had seen it through the lenses he could pick out even more detail that would help them sneak in. Appearances are deceiving, Sharif thought. The dumb looking one is actually the smart one. It was another wonder of Allah. He thought on that for a moment. He found himself crediting Allah with more and more. It must be all of Yusef praying rubbing off on him. He was starting to find God.

He gave the pair their final instructions. They were to take their time closing in, and wait until the plane had its engines running at full throttle for take off before they fired. That's when all the passengers would be on board and they would be trapped on the rolling plane. Nothing could save them from the wrath of Allah. The two nodded in excited agreement, pushing each others shoulders as if they had been given a great prize.

"In the confusion of the flames, you will have no difficulty in getting away. I will see you at the mosque when you return. There will be a feast waiting."

Sharif watched for a few minutes as the two began their long crawl towards the plane. Once he saw a head come up above the grass, as if checking their direction. Then he lost them from view. He was satisfied this would be successful, and he returned to his motorcycle.

Colonel Schaeffer took the picture back from Grant. "Are you certain this is the man you saw?"

"Absolutely certain. The man in this picture, the man on the hill, and the rag head in Sudan are all one and the same."

Schaeffer pulled some more documents out of a folder and scanned them quickly. "This isn't good, General, but it does explain a few other things I've been wondering about." Ramirez had confidence in Intelligence chief. It was one of the positions on his staff that he insisted be filled by something other than a General Officer. He had a theory that once a man was given the star, he immediately got an entourage. No matter how hard he tried, he would always have someone, or several someone's, following him around to take care of his needs. He would also be a middleman in the food chain, no longer a provider. He would get information from sources he was unfamiliar with, be kept out of the loop by subordinates who weren't sure of their information, and as a result, whatever information he gave would be based on a second guess of a second guess. No the most reassuring type of intelligence.

Generals also came with a built in publicity machine. It was called Congress. They approved all General Officer promotions, and published their lists and any back ground information they desired in the *Congressional Record*, and made it a point to send out news releases if the new officer happened to be a constituent. Foreign embassies in Washington, and at the UN, were avid subscribers to the *Record* as a good source of intelligence, and new Generals automatically generated a dossier and were placed on watch lists. A Colonel, on the other hand, was still relatively anonymous. The good ones, and there were some who weren't that good, put out a pretty outstanding product until they got the nomination for his own flag. Schaeffer was one of the good ones, and would be for about another four months.

Schaeffer continued. "When we got the word that this man, Ali Alawa Sharif, had been killed by his own people, we knew it was potentially massive, because of his ties to so many of the parties in and around Iraq. We know he was responsible for the gas attacks against the refuge camp and also the Sudanese Liberation Army in al Fashir. He was also the one who assassinated this Ibn Mousa al Saif. Sergeant Major Grant came close to killing him during the ex-fil from Darfur." Grant hadn't been aware of that. Schaeffer went on. "He was in the last vehicle of that convoy you ambushed. He was the only one to get out unscathed."

He walked across the room to get a drink of water, then continued. "The Janjaweed and the government were so put out by the loss of resources, he was ordered killed. This is where the stories diverged.

Some sources had him escaping before the hit could be made, but a friendly Algerian source, one who has been pretty reliable, confirmed Sharif was dead, and even provided a grainy video of his car being blown up. We were content with that."

Ramirez picked up from here. "That's the problem with not having our own sources in some of those countries. We depend on the kindness of strangers. That brings us to the next question. Colonel?"

"Right. The French, in a rare moment of candor, admitted that there had been some outside agitation for the recent troubles in the south. They had been following an Algerian national who they said was responsible. We have a poor picture of the side of his head. Not quite enough to match him to our boy."

Grant asked, "Why didn't the French do something?"

"Good question. The French said they were about to pick him up when he disappeared. They leaned on another source that said the Russians had spirited him away. He was traced to Bucharest, where the Russians stuck him on a plane. That was the last we knew. It seems now the picture is coming together. With your information about the bomb making school, and the personnel transfers they do by air, I think we just found our confluence of events."

Schaeffer looked at Ramirez. The General knew that his intelligence chief had more he wanted to say, but he didn't want Perkins to hear it. It was time to get rid of him.

"Colonel Perkins?" Ramirez began, "now you're up to speed. I'm sorry you had to be kept in the dark, but I'm sure you understand why." Perkins didn't. He was pissed he hadn't been informed while his unit was conducting covert operations all over the country, but he couldn't say that. Instead, he attempted to get back in control of things. "I understand fully, General. I only hope now I can be kept in the loop so I can coordinate things better. Seems like these gentlemen spent some time at cross purposes." It was a card he felt was well played, but Ramirez trumped him. "Ordinarily I would agree, Perkins, but for now, let's leave it in Morgan's hands. He can coordinate things and keep you up to speed on what you need to know." Perkins winced at the phrase 'need to know'. That gave Morgan the power to pick and choose what he would be told. Ramirez was still talking. "He can also let you know what he needs for support. I'm sure you can see how important cooperation is going to be?"

"Yes, Sir. Absolutely."

"Good. Now, if you don't mind, Morgan and Grant are the prodigal sons every father hopes he never has. I think this would be as good a time as any for me to give them a little four star ass chewing."

Perkins beamed. "I think that's a marvelous idea, Sir. It never hurts to remind subordinates what their place in the scheme of the universe is."

When they were alone Ramirez shook his head. "I had the feeling that guy wasn't wrapped too tight when I met him in Africa. Is it my imagination, or has he gotten worse?"

Grant answered. "He's worse. We just have to try harder to work around him."

"Well, I probably can't do much to help you there. What you're doing here is totally out of my hands. I want Schaeffer to finish briefing you on what he thinks is going on."

Schaeffer unrolled a small map of Europe and stuck it on the wall. "I'll try to be brief. For some time, we've been watching the Russians move materials out of storage in Eastern Europe. After the Cold War ended, they left a lot of stuff in place. With their economy in the toilet, they can't afford to keep it outside their borders, but they don't want anyone to know what it is."

"What kind of stuff?"

"Well, up in the Baltic, in Latvia and Estonia, there were a lot of naval nukes. Down this way there were some Scuds, but the important stuff is in Albania.

"We've suspected for a while they were moving chemical stockpiles out of storage in Tirana. We just had trouble tracking it once it left the country. We never paid much attention to Moldova until you got here. That airstrip and the Russians using it, ties into what we've been thinking. This is their transshipment point."

Morgan interrupted. "Why fly it here? Once it's in the air, just keep going to Mother Russia."

"That's the other part of the puzzle. We don't know where the stockpile is in Russia. The Russians don't want us finding out, so they're hiding it here. We've been able to learn that your road is part of the deception plan. Once it's finished, they'll use that as an excuse to break down their outpost here and road everything back. No one would suspect a low priority road trip if over a thousand miles."

"They're willing to risk taking it across Moldova and Ukraine? Aren't they worried about accidents or nosy customs agents?"

"Not at all. Moldova wants them out. They just don't have the muscle to force them. Ukraine is still somewhat under their influence. Transshipment won't be a problem."

Grant had a question. "What's our part in all this?"

"For now, just watch them until we can figure out what to do about it. If it looks like they're going to move before we're ready, we may need you to try to stop them, or at least slow them up."

"And how are we going to do that?"

"You're both bright boys. I'm hoping you can figure something out."

They were packing up to leave when Colonel Perkins came back in with Master Sergeant Winder. "If I could have a moment of the General's time? You need to hear what this man has to say."

Ramirez looked around the room to see if anyone had any idea of what this was about. Nobody did. "OK, Master Sergeant. I can give you a few minutes."

"Well, General, once I get started, I may need a little more time." Winder launched into his presentation. As he droned on about what he had heard and what he knew, he started passing out photocopies he had stolen. He was so involved in his own voice he didn't notice the wide eyes and dropped jaws. Colonel Schaeffer finally stopped him as he was talking about the man he believed Morgan had killed. "Where did you get all this information, Sergeant?"

"I try to keep my finger on what's going on around here, Sir."

"Nice try. Now, one more time. Where did you get this information?" Schaeffer held up a sheaf of documents.

"They came right out of the files, Sir."

Morgan interrupted. "Those files are kept locked. There are only two keys. I have them both."

Winder gave a broad grin. "I have a spare set of keys to everything in the S-3 shop! You guys just think you were pulling a fast one!"

Ramirez spoke with Schaeffer for a moment. Winder still had a smile on his face. He knew he had just cut the legs out of the people who were making his life miserable. His smile got wider as Ramirez began to speak to Perkins. "Colonel Perkins, right now I'd rather this stay at your unit level. We have a serious case of espionage, and possibly treason if any of this has left the immediate unit. Sergeant Winder, have you spoken of this with anyone else?"

"No, Sir! Colonel Perkins was the first person I told."

Schaeffer asked, "Do you have any more documents or anything that's not here right now?"

"No, Sir. That's all of it."

"In that case, Colonel Schaeffer, why don't you take the Master Sergeant here someplace private and explain his options to him. I'll let Colonel Perkins make any determination as to what kind of disciplinary proceedings to pursue. If one word gets out of this, I'll recommend federal charges. Is that clear?"

Winder was waiting for Morgan's response. This was all going far better than he could have hoped. He had never met general who could make a decision that fast.

Schaeffer took his arm and led him down the hall. He ducked into the first empty room he came to. He slipped back into his 'good cop' persona and started to question Winder. He was hoping to find out what this asshole thought he was accomplishing by stealing files of things he had no business knowing about. Winder droned on about slights, real and imagined, and Morgan and Grant, not to mention the rest of them, marginalizing him.

"Do you think you would have been better qualified to dig out this information?"

"Colonel, I think I could have found it out without breaking any laws."

That was more than Schaeffer was willing to listen to. He launched into a tirade that seared Winders ears. Winder made several attempts to defend himself, each time sounding more foolish than the last. Schaeffer finally gave him his options.

"Sergeant, what you've done goes above and beyond stupidity. If you don't want to agree to these terms, I can have you removed somewhere and held incommunicado until this business is conclude." Schaeffer paused for effect. "Now, one more time! Is that clear?"

Winder seemed to shrivel up on himself. He gave a meek response agreeing to the terms, and stood mute after Schaeffer led him back to the COs office. Ramirez looked back and forth between the two, and Schaeffer just gave a slight nod. "Well, Gentlemen, I guess that concludes our business. A few words with Morgan and Grant here, and we'll be out of your hair." Winder stood stock still as everyone filed out around him. The last to pass was Grant. Winder felt his hand heavy on his shoulder. "Go to your room, Winder, and stay there. I'm sure the Colonel will want to talk to you later."

Winder didn't say anything. He had played this hand and lost, and lost big. He still has his contact in Dillinghouse's' office, but did he dare leak classified material? He would have to think about it.

As they were loading the vehicles, Ramirez had one more question for the group. "What's going on?"

Morgan responded. "What do you mean?"

"Isn't it obvious to you? There's a disconnect here. The Russians have their own problems with the Chechens just a couple of hundred miles from here. Chechens. Islamic radicals. Bomb throwers. Why would Ivan be running a bomb school for Arabs when he's having problems with them, and piling up chemical weapons?"

Schaeffer was the most sanguine about it. "There probably isn't a good reason. They're too compartmentalized. Why else would they be helping Iran with a nuke program? The enemy of my enemy is my friend."

Ramirez wasn't convinced. "This area is a lot more volatile than everyone thinks. When we get back I'll try to convince the NSC that we need more assets here, but until then, you two are on your own. Don't disappoint me."

"Not a problem, General," Morgan answered. "By the way, General, that reporter has asked if she could spend a day or two here, then get picked up."

"Picked up? She think this is a taxi service? Tell her to get her ass loaded or she'll have to walk out."

Cynthia Maddox was disappointed she couldn't spend a few days with her friend. She remembered the night she had spent with Sheila Gordon in Darfur, and it had been a night to remember. That was one girl who knew how to make love to a woman, and who definitely enjoyed it. She resisted the urge to stay anyway. There would be all kinds of problems with the local immigration people if she tried to get out commercially, probably more problems than could be smoothed over by a couple of explosive orgasms. She gave Gordon a hug and a promise to meet her in Germany when this deployment was over, then she gathered her crew and got into Price's Hummer. At least they had had a few minutes together in the grass not too far from the bridge.

Price was still grateful for the help she had indirectly given him to get back to the 289th. He told her so.

"That was my pleasure, Sergeant. But you know he had his charges dropped?"

"Yeah. We get Global News here. But at least I got to meet the twins again" and he pointed towards her chest.

"I am delighted you remember, Sergeant Price! I didn't think you were in any kind of condition to think about that. If you had mentioned it earlier, I might have given them another chance to say hello."

"That's my luck. They didn't name me Jonah for nothing."

They were pulling out as the commo sergeant ran up to Grant's vehicle with a box of trash bags. "What are these for?"

"Sergeant Sharp asked for them."

Grant got out of the vehicle and pulled the commo NCO aside. "What did he say, exactly?" The NCO repeated the story to the best of his recollection. Grant understood immediately. The rest of the convoy was already far ahead of him. He would have to try to get a moment with Morgan and the General alone before they boarded the plane.

Whatever Sharp did, it would be better if Ramirez and Schaeffer knew about it before they took off.

Sharp was sitting on the runway trying to talk Ramirez' security detail out of any extra gear he could get. He missed all the bells and whistles he had been able to score to take into Darfur, unfortunately, these guys weren't budging. He had to be content letting them show him what they had. His small security detail looked like paupers in comparison. He was sweeping the distant hill line with an oversized pair of binoculars when he spotted a head looking down into a gully. He scanned up and down until he saw a movement, then two figures emerged. They seemed to be making a half hearted effort to stay under cover, but they weren't very good at it. Sharp could also see one of them carrying a Kalashnikov. The other seemed to have an RPG launcher. He whispered a curse out loud. "Fuck! This can't be good!"

One of the security detail heard him and asked what he had seen.

"There's two gomers in the grass trying to sneak up on us." The other man took the binoculars and looked towards where Sharp was pointing. "I don't see nothin'."

"Yeah, that probably has something to do with them being in the grass. Hey, Robinson!"

The twin had been lounging on a stack of equipment, watching one of the crew fiddling around under an engine cowling. There had been a slight leak, and he was tightening up a fitting. Robinson had been feeling as useless as Sharp. He hoped the call would be for them to go home. He'd rather waste his time in his own rack. He ambled over to Sharp. "What is it, Sarge? Time for us to go home?"

"Grab your rifle. We're going hunting."

Robinson raised his eyebrows, then went to pick up his rifle and throw on his load bearing equipment, thinking to himself that he could always count on Sergeant Sharp to liven up a boring day. Sharp led him over to the edge of the strip and slid into a drainage ditch. He laid out what he had seen, and what his plan was. Robinson listened, then moved off to do what he was told.

Sharp had him head to the north to begin circling around to intercept whoever these two visitors were. He doubted they were the Moldovans, playing their own Sneaky Pete games, but he'd rather find out as far from the plane as he could instead of just shooting one of them for a bad idea gone even worse. He had Robinson angling to a dried creek bed that was about halfway to the hill line. He was fairly certain they could be there before the other two.

Every fifty yards or so he lifted his head up slowly to scan ahead. He was amazed to see his quarry. They were walking hunched over, their heads up, watching the plane. If this was their best effort at stealth, they couldn't possibly be a serious threat. He started to think the Moldovans were just fucking with him. He heard Robinson's voice in his earpiece. "I think they're already in the creek".

"OK. Start angling into the center so we're between them and the plane. Something ain't right with these gomers."

As Sharp got closer, he could hear the voices of the men talking to one another. He wasn't sure, but it sounded like Arabic. Who the fuck are these guys? He crawled to his right to hit the creek bed high of where they were. He hit the bank at a bend where he could look down on the two a little distance away. They were having a cigarette break. He whispered into his radio. "See if you can get a position below them.

When you do, I'm going to spook them to see what they do. If they run your way, stop them."

"Stop 'em dead?"

"Try yelling at them first. Don't shoot unless it looks like they will." Sharp settled into a comfortable shooting position. Who are these guys?

"Yasim, slow down. My back hurts. I need a rest."

"You always need a rest. Let's go just a little farther, then we can stop." Yasim moved a few yards farther and came to the creek bed. "Sullah, there is a place here you can rest."

The two Arabs dropped into the bed. They both stood erect, their heads just above the surrounding grass. "We'll rest here a few moments."

Sullah reached into his fanny pack and pulled out a pack of cigarettes. He offered one to his friend, who gladly accepted. "Do you have any water?"

"I left the bottle in the car."

"No matter. We'll be back there soon enough." He took another look towards the plane, then they both sat down. "This is easier than I thought it would be. The Americans don't seem to be paying much attention."

"Why would they? They don't expect to be attacked here. The next time will probably be harder." He took a deep drag on his cigarette. "But we will be known as the ones who were first."

The pilot of the C-27J looked out the cockpit window over to the wing where his crew chief was working. There was no way this bird should be having problems. It had just come out of maintenance. "You find the problem yet, Chief?"

"Just a second. It looks like the hanger apes didn't plug the oil sensor in all the way. The bail is the only thing holding it on. It's vibrated most of the way off, that's why you've been getting the intermittent fault. Give me a minute to button it up and you can run her up."

The chief checked his toolbox to make certain he had everything. Then he gave the engine access bay another look to see that it was clear. He buttoned the hatch up and walked back over the wing to his ladder and dropped to the ground. He walked to the back of the plane and stood on the ramp, plugging his headset into the intercom system. "You're clear, Sir. Bring it up slow, then put some boost to it to see if the pressure holds."

The pilot went over his start-up sheet, then hit the starter. It whined sharply as it spun, then gave a puff of black exhaust and ran on it's own. All the dials indicated it was running normally. "OK, Chief, get ready, I'm going to run this sucker up!" He watched the engine turn for a moment, then put his hand on the throttle and turned his attention to the instrument panel. He slowly started building up his RPMs.

The two Arabs looked at each other as the sound of the engine reached them. They threw down their cigarettes and stood to look at the plane. They could see the one engine running, and they heard it getting louder as it picked up speed. They thought their opportunity was slipping away from them.

"Yasim, try to shoot the pilot! I have to load!"

Sullah pulled a rocket out of the pack, removed the packing caps and slid the rocket into the launcher as Yasim climbed on the bank and raised his rifle to fire. He pulled the trigger, and nothing happened. He hadn't put a round in the chamber. He worked the bolt handle and brought the rifle up again.

The sound of the engine had caught Sharp off guard too. He looked around to see what was happening. When he looked back at the Arabs, one of them was standing on the bank, working his bolt. Sharp snapped his safety off to 'semi' and took a quick aim. He squeezed the trigger twice and smiled as he saw his target flail its arms out and fall onto the other Arab. He raised up to one knee to get a better sight line on the second man, who was partially obscured now by his partner falling on him, switched his rifle to 'full'. He could hear Robinson yelling at him, partly in his earpiece and partly in his other ear, "I'm not in position yet, I'm not in position!"

Sullah heard two shots. They sounded as if they were farther away than just over his head. Then he felt his friend falling on him. He thought he must have slipped off the bank in his excitement. "Shoot the plane, you idiot! Shoot the plane!"

He pushed Yasim off him and lifted the launcher to his shoulder. Many things were happening at once, too many things for him to understand without stopping to consider them all. First, there was somebody yelling at him over to his right. He didn't understand who it could be. Could Ali Alawa have followed them, and was yelling at them for their circus like behavior?

Then there was some movement to his left. He tried to make out what it was, but if it was a person he was all hunched over, something black in his hands. Lastly, he glanced down at his friend. He was lying with his back against the embankment. His eyes were wide in shock. Sullah saw the red stain spreading under his chin, where Sharps rounds had exited his chest. It slowly began to dawn on him that their plans were coming apart. He lifted the RPG and tried to get a sight picture on the plane, just like he had seen in the instruction book at the mosque.

At the plane the sound of the engine drowned out the sound of the gunfire. One of the security detail thought he heard a popping sound, and started walking towards the crew chief to let him know. The chief waved him away as the pilot spoke to him over his head set. "It looks and sounds good, Chief. I'm shutting her down."

Sullah stepped up on the banking to get a better shot. His foot slipped as he was lifting himself up he tumbled back down on top of Yasim. As he was falling he heard a burst of shooting to his left. He looked and saw a figure in camouflage clothes stepping into the streambed, that black thing in his hands pointing at him. He tried to swing the RPG around to fire at him.

Sharp saw the shooter slip under his sights just as he fired. The shooter went down into a heap on top of the other one. Sharp swore to himself and stepped into the creek bed. He could still hear Robinson yelling, a lot closer now. He also noticed the sound of the engine fading away. Then there was the figure on the ground. He was trying to bring the RPG around at him. He squeezed the trigger and sprayed the area.

The security detail heard the full auto burst as the engine wound down. They went on alert and scanned the area for the source. One of them spotted Robinson running through the grass, some distance away. They could barely hear him shouting something. Then they saw another head in front of him. The second head looked over to them and they could see him wave. "Looks like those two yahoos went rabbit hunting!"

"Well, you think they would have let us know they were going to do something like that before they started shooting. They could have started something!"

It's a well-known principle that the best and the brightest on a detail watch the people. The rest get to watch the things. They both went back to what they were doing, ignoring Sharp and Robinson.

Sharp was bending over the bodies, stripping them of gear and going through pockets. "Keep an eye out for the rest of those guys. I don't need them wandering over here wondering what we're doing." He turned back to the first body. "And get on the radio. Tell commo that I need the Sergeant Major to bring out some trash bags. Tell them we ran into a litter problem."

"A litter problem?"

"Word for word. Grant will know what I mean."

Sharp finished with one body at a time, keeping any documents or other intelligence items separate from the other guy. He pulled out his digital camera and took a lot of pictures as he went. It could be evidence, in his defense, at some point.

These two gomers were definitely not trained terrorists, nor were they suicide types. One had keys to a car in his pocket. The other had a trolley transfer. They had all the items you would expect to find with someone who stepped out to run a few errands, then planned to get on with his life. Could this be something they tried on a dare, or were they trying to make their bones with someone? From what Sharp had seen of their weapon handling, they sure weren't experience handling two pretty simple weapons. The RPG and the AK-47 were designed for uneducated peasants, no advanced degrees required. Did that mean these guys barely qualified as uneducated peasants?

They waited with the bodies for a bit, then Sharp heard the convoy approaching. He left Robinson with the bodies while he went to make his report to Grant and get the body bags. He knew Grant would have cued in on his message. He was surprised when he got to the plane and Grant handed him a box of extra large black trash bags. "What the hell is this?"

"I got your message as we were pulling out. The commo guy handed this to me. It'll have to do." Ramirez was in the middle of his good-byes when he noticed Grant and Sharp passing a box of bags back and forth. He instantly knew what they were for, and grabbed Schaeffer and Morgan and told them to come with him. He brought them over to where the two NCOs were standing and got right to the point. "What did you do now, Sharp?"

Sharp gave him a quick brief on what had happened, and what he had found on the bodies. Ramirez asked his Intel chief what he thought. "Well, I'm surprised you did all that and nobody here noticed."

Ramirez agreed. "I'm surprised too. When we get back, start looking at replacing whoever was on duty here. They aren't getting it." He turned back to Sharp. "Do you need any help getting rid of the bodies?"

Sharp screwed up his face. "We're engineers. They'll find Hoffa first."

Schaeffer asked that any and all information be copied and sent to him at his secure e-mail address. Morgan promised he'd get it, then Ramirez ended the conversation. "This was supposed to be a simple road building, out of sight, out of mind. What else is going to happen to fuck up this part of the world?"


Cynthia Maddox watched the huddle from a distance. Her cameraman saw her and sidled up to ask what was going on.

"I don't know, but Ramirez looks agitated. They did something he doesn't want the rest of us to know about. See if you can find out anything from the crew. They must have seen something."

"I already asked. They said he went out hunting with another soldier. That's him standing out there in the field" he pointed off in the distance. "Whatever it was, they shot something."

Maddox shielded her eyes and tried to look closer. "Whatever it was, when we take off, you be on whatever side of the plane that flies over him. Have a long lens ready."

# CHAPTER 9

Sergeant First Class Price (Ramirez had brought his promotion orders) was detailed to dispose of the bodies. He considered it a perverse play on his 'wetting down' ceremony for his new stripes. He had a few conditions to go with it.

"If I have to drag a back hoe out to some god forsaken site and fuck up the rest of my day, at least you can have these assholes" pointing at Sharp and Robinson, "wrap them up and give me a hand."

Sharp acted irritated. "What do you mean me? I already did my part."

The bickering was starting to escalate. Morgan stepped forward to stop them, but Grant put out his hand and pulled him back. He just shook his head 'no'. He knew these two would carry on like this as long as there was an audience. As soon as everyone left, they'd get down to work. Grant had seen this act many times before. It was their way of getting psyched up for a distasteful job. Grant also knew that once it was done, it wouldn't be spoken of again. He was relying on the two old pros to instill the same ethic in Robinson. Morgan wasn't so sure. He wanted to micromanage the disposal. Grant had to dissuade him.

"You don't really think this is the first time we've hide a body somewhere, do you?" It was, but Morgan didn't need to know that. "The task has been delegated. As leaders, all we need to do is a follow-up check. You need to have confidence in your subordinates."

Morgan didn't like getting lectured like a Second Lieutenant, but he knew the Sergeant Major was right. He also knew that the less he knew about what they were going to do, the less he would either have to explain away or outright lie about. He had never been a very good liar, and he couldn't think of how to explain this as anything other than what it was, and no one in his or her right mind would believe that. He let the matter drop.

Colonel Perkins, on the other hand, was another matter. He was already upset with this group for what they had been doing behind his back. If he even suspected what had happened out here, Morgan was certain he would blow the whistle on the whole operation and tell the Moldovans. That would lead to arrests, questions, publicity and, he was sure, some local unrest. None of the above was desirable. He had explained his staying behind as his way of making certain the area was policed up and nothing was left behind of any intelligence value. It was a plausible explanation, and, more to the point, it was at least the truth. He wanted to back track with Grant and see if there was anything else these two 'martyrs' had left behind. Nothing they were carrying indicated that they had planned to die here. Morgan pocketed the car keys. They left the burial detail and walked towards the hill line.

The back trail was easy to follow. The two had no sense of field craft. Their line from the where they had come down the gully to where their adventure had ended was almost as straight a line as could be imagined. At the top of the gully it was easy to pick up their trail to where they had watched from the bluffs. Grant pointed out where there had been a third figure lying in the dirt.

"Think it was your friend from Sudan?"

"Who else?"

They tracked back from the bluff and found the Trabant. There were also marks from a motorcycle. That confirmed Sharif's presence for Grant. Morgan cleaned the car out of anything that might identify the occupants. He looked around for a hiding place for it, but there was no place where it wouldn't be found by the first person coming by, and it seemed like this area had enough traffic to make it a problem. They would have to move it.

Grant used his radio to call down to have Robinson bring up one of the vehicles. Then he changed his mind and told him to have the 'trash' brought up, along with all the vehicles, when they were done their police call.

Morgan was intrigued. "What's your plan, Sergeant Major?" Grant told him his idea. As soon as it was dark, they could take the car and the bodies a few miles towards the city. At a suitably isolated spot they could stage the car off the road, load the bodies and torch it. Morgan thought it sounded crude.

"Unload the AK and leave it on the back seat. They have a bandit problem around here, remember? The only one who'll know they don't belong where we dump them will be Sharif, and he may not be able to figure it out in a hurry. It looks like all of Sharp's bullets were through and through. No ballistics to point towards us."

Morgan still wasn't convinced, but he couldn't see any other way. This was the only combination of car-bodies-location that didn't raise more questions than it answered. He sat on a fender to wait for the rest.

The disposal had gone smoother than Morgan expected. They found a turn-off that seemed to lead nowhere. The map confirmed it likely faded out to a gravel pit a few miles further on. There was a good-sized drainage ditch on one side. The car was flipped in with the gas tank on the low side. The cap was cracked enough to allow the tank to drain, and five-gallon can of diesel was poured on the bodies for good measure. Sharp rigged a time fuse out of one of their cigarettes and a book of matches. They were well on their way back down the main road when they saw the flash in the distance. There was no other traffic on the road. Now, all they had to do was get back and explain to Perkins why they were coming in so late. Morgan was determined not to let Perkins interfere with whatever they had to do here. It was clear that the Russians were running some kind of a school here, and its students seemed to be exclusively Middle Eastern types. The chemical weapons were something else. What the hell were they doing with them here?

There was a problem with these two though. The car was registered to one of them, and they had addresses in the city. All the trash and papers they were carrying screamed that they were two local idiots who got involved in something way over their head. As Sharp described them, one of them wasn't even familiar with how to load an AK-47.

Either the terrorists were scrapping the bottom of the talent barrel, which wasn't likely, or the Russians had gotten very sophisticated in creating local covers for their students, which was even less likely. Everything pointed to these two being random elements added to the equation. Someone had to be stirring it up.

There was no getting around it. Somehow they would have to visit the addresses these two were linked to.

Perkins was waiting for them when they returned. He had the XO and MSG Winder in his office with him. He had already dealt with the issue of Winders 'indiscretions' as he called them. There would be a Letter of Reprimand entered into his record, which would conveniently disappear after it had served its purpose. Perkins didn't say that the purpose was to make it look like he actually took some disciplinary action if the matter ever came up again.

He lined everyone up in front of his desk. He had seen Clark Gable do this in a movie, once, and he like the way it worked out. And Gable never was more than a Captain during the big war, holding down a Sergeants' slot as an aerial gunner.

"This has got to end" he started. "I can't have my senior people not on the same sheet of music."

Morgan tried to interrupt. "It's not a matter of us all being on the same page, Colonel. It's a matter of who needs to know."

"Goddam it, Major. Everybody in this room needs to know what's going on! You're using our resources, our time and our people to raise hell out there, and I have my ass hanging out a mile, and I don't even know it, waiting for you to screw up. That's all going to change."

Grant glanced over at Winder. The son of a bitch had a smile on his face. Perkins was about to try to fuck them all.

"From now on, gentlemen, all of your operations get run through this office, and Major Carstairs and Master Sergeant Winder will have full access to all your intelligence. Is that clear?"

"Colonel, I don't think including Winder in the mix is a good idea." Morgan didn't want what they had going any further. He didn't think Winder could be trusted.

"I don't care what you think, Major. You have junior NCOs going out every night. Then you have these two loose cannons," he pointed at Sharp and Price, "working like a private army! No more! Do I make myself clear?"

Morgan said it was. Then Perkins went down the line and had each man in turn acknowledge what was just said. It went down hard, but there was no choice. As incompetent as Perkins may be, he was still the commander. After he had given the orders, anything less would be a court martial offense. Perkins dismissed them with the instruction that Carstairs and Winder be briefed and brought up to date on everything immediately. Morgan saluted and acknowledged. As they left the room he told the three NCOs they were finished for the night. He would take care of the briefing.

Grant saw the look in his eye and understood. He cut off any argument from Sharp and Price and led them to his room.

"What the hell did you let him do that for? There's no way I want him telling those two monkeys anything!" Sharp was beside himself. He had seen Winder and Carstairs at work for too long. He was convinced they would either get him killed or put into a foreign jail for a long time. Price wasn't easy to calm either. It was his ass on the line every time he went out. Winder and Carstairs were barely familiar with where the front gate was, let alone what happened beyond it. Grant worked to calm them down.

"Smarten up. This is for the best. Morgan is the best one to tell them what he wants them to know. All we'd do is fuck it up. When he's done with them, he'll tell us, and that'll be the official story. That'll be all you ever repeat."

There was a knock on the door and Morgan came in. Grant was surprised. "That was fast. What did you tell them?"

"Nothing. Between the two of them, they were convinced they knew everything from the files they saw. All they wanted to do was let me know how they wanted the information passed on."

"So," Sharp asked, "where do we stand in all this?"

"They don't want to talk to you. Especially Winder. Seems they're afraid you'll just lie to them."

"And you won't?"

"It's that officer and gentleman thing, you wouldn't understand. From now on, you pass on whatever you get to me, and I'll brief them. You'll get a copy of what I give them, just in case one of them gets clever and decides to try to trip me up."

Grant was satisfied, to a point. Price wasn't so sure. "Winder's an idiot. There's no way he'll keep his mouth shut. He's probably already telling his buddy the supply geek how he's got it over us now."

"You'll have to live with it, Pricey. At least until we can figure out what's going on, and what we can do about it."

Price was silent. He didn't like it, but for now, there was nothing he could do but keep an eye on Winder. At least he didn't have to worry about him going into the field with them.

When he was alone, Grant pulled a beer out of his Styrofoam cooler. The ice had melted, but the water was still cool. It didn't make much different. Warm or cold, beer is beer, and he had had his share of some pretty lousy brews all over the world. The only thing ice did was make some of the really bad ones taste better, and there were some that actually tasted better warm. Some East African beers came to mind, as well as a few Central American.

After he finished one he grabbed a second. There were also times when beer was better in pairs. This was one of them. He finished it and started stripping down. He put on his running shorts, found his sneakers under the bed, and headed out for a run. The fresh air and the exercise would work out some of the kinks. His shoulder was acting up, too. It had started bothering him while he was in the hospital for a few days after Sudan. A doctor had diagnosed it as nothing serious, and gave him a cortisone shot to loosen it up. The damn shot hurt worse than the shoulder, and that took a few days to wear off, but it took away the pain. Now it was coming back. Not full bore yet, but it was there. Maybe he could talk to Major Carson about another shot.

There was something about his relationship with her that was comfortably casual. When she wanted to see him, she said so. If he could, that was fine and the sex was great. If he couldn't, he'd just tell her. There were never any rolled eyes or hand wringing. She didn't waste time at their next meeting berating him for not giving her enough time. It was an arrangement that worked for both of them, and she understood Grant had things to do without prying.

Bonneville, on the other hand, had been avoiding him ever since the incident on the road. He had tried to talk to her a couple of times, but she was cold. He let it go. If there was going to be anything, he would let her decide. In the meantime, there was Major Carson, and it was probably for the best that he wasn't trying to juggle the two of them.

There was a regular running path worn in to the outside perimeter of the compound. It was almost two miles exactly, and the layout made it easy to lengthen or shorten your run, depending on your ability or needs. There were some soldiers out here everyday, cranking out the miles. Others were only occasional runners, although everyone was encouraged to exercise regularly. Organized PT was only held twice a week. Not really enough to carve any hard bodies, but enough to keep you in shape. Grant was on his second lap when he heard another set of feet behind him. Grant was a solitary runner. He didn't look for company, and he knew others who didn't either. He kept up his pace, not slowing or turning. Whoever it was would overtake him soon enough.

It was one of the local soldiers. Grant had seen him before on his runs. The man usually came up from behind after Grant had finished a lap or two, passed him, then disappeared. It happened at different times, although Grant never attached anything to the coincidence. It was probably just another guy who got his run in when he could. Grant watched the other runner turn a corner ahead of him. When he looked down the row of buildings, the runner was gone. Grant continued on for another lap, not thinking about what happened.

The runner, on the other hand, a casual Muslim whose name was Grigori, was very aware of what was going on. He had been following the same routine for several weeks, watching for the big American to begin his routine. The man was maddening. He followed no set schedule. There were days when he would start early, before the Americans had their group exercise. Some days, he would wait and join them. There were days when the Americans had no group exercise, in which case he would have to wait to see if Grant would come out anyway, or wait until later in the evening. There were even days when he didn't run at all. The only constant was that he ran alone, most of the time. Not much of a constant, but it was all he could reasonably count on.

He had no real idea why he was watching this man, noting his routine. Obviously it was for some evil purpose. The man Yusef had introduced him to seemed sinister, even in a casual setting. Although the man professed to be a Muslim, they had never met at the mosque, always in a coffee shop in the neighborhood. After the second meeting, he had been given a cell phone. It came with strict instructions. The airtime was limited, and he was not to try to purchase more. When the time was used up, it was to be disposed of. Another would be provided in its place.

At first, it seemed that the Americans routine was to be mapped to plan some outrage against him, but his erratic behavior ruled that out. Next, the instructions were for him to locate and report on the Americans quarters. That was more difficult. He could not be followed into his building. All that could be hoped for was that when the exercise was finished, he would go directly to his room. It took several days, from several vantage points, to see what light went on. It took a few more days to verify that it was indeed his room, but even then he could not be certain, but it was narrowed down to two choices. Both had been reported. Yusefs friend seemed to be satisfied. He had directed that the American continued to be watched for any little piece of information.

Grigori had nothing against the Americans. He had come to enjoy the training they were providing, and even enjoyed the brotherhood they showed for one another, even among men of different ranks. The women in their military did not bother him at first, until some of them had started to give orders. His nascent religious beliefs caused him to ask the Imam at the mosque about it. The Imam, not the greatest of scholars, had recently added a political content to his religious teachings. He directed Grigori to Yusef, a young man, about his own age, who seemed to have found a purpose in life and was content with it, although he did not share it. Yusefs passion and sincerity was showing Grigori the error of the Americans and their lifestyle, how they were infidels who were defiling Islam by their presence in the holy places and polluting the sanctity of womanhood by allowing their women to prance around as they did. It had not taken Grigori long to be convinced that whatever he was doing was the right thing to do, for Allah's sake.

He took a shortcut over to where he could watch the Americans building from the shadows. After a few moments he saw the big American pass and disappear towards the front entrance. Grigori looked at his watch and mentally followed Grant as he entered the building, climbed the stairs and walked to his room. It was easy to do. There were similar floor plans in his area, and he had been able to make the same trip while checking his watch. If he were correct, the light should go on . . . now! He looked up from his watch and saw the window illuminate. None of the others had changed. He was certain he had the correct room now. He slipped out the cell phone and pressed the speed dial button. His call was answered after the first ring. There was a one word greeting: "Yes?" and nothing else. Grigori knew he would hear nothing else until the stranger thanked him for his information and terminated the call. This time was different. There were additional instructions. He was told to draw an exact map, and the word exact was stressed several times, and to bring it to the coffee shop after prayers. Grigori said he would, but found himself talking into a dead connection.

Somebody had noticed Grigori though. Edwin Robinson had been preparing for another night exercise. He was to give a class to the Moldovans, through a translator, on the American Night Vision Goggles. It had been his luck that his twin brother had been getting most of the field time with the senior NCOs. Usually, they would swap off, but Edwin's old wounds had been bothering him a bit. He had taken a couple of good hits in Darfur and had been evacuated ahead of the company. His brother had gone on the counter ambush patrol with the Sergeant Major, and had gotten himself a few more rag head kills. Major Carson told him he had probably stopped his physical therapy too early, and had put him on a regimen of free weights and power walking. She had also told him that if he didn't improve, she would consider ordering him out of the field. That was not something he looked forward to, so he followed his workout schedule regularly, and tried to get as much of the training as possible. Eventually, he hoped, they would deploy to Iraq like they were originally activated for, and he didn't want to be one of the staff pukes who never got to go outside the wire.

He was laying out the course he would follow with the Moldovans when he noticed a figure walk between the buildings across from him and step into the shadows. Robinson slipped on his NVGs and looked for the figure. He found him, and watched as the lurker kept looking at his wrist, probably at a watch, then up at the Headquarters barracks. He seemed especially interested when on light went on, and Robinson could see him counting windows, as if to verify. Robinson also took note of the window, then looked back as there was a flash of light. The NVGs magnified the light from the cell phone screen, making the figure clearly visible. I know that guy, he thought. He had seen him in some of the joint classes. Why, he asked himself, is he watching our building? And who is he calling?

He watched as the call was completed and the lurker walked away. Robinson walked over to where the man had been standing and looked up at the lighted window. He counted down, trying to figure out whose room it was. He guessed it might be one of the female officers, and this guy was just another pervert trying to sneak a peek. This would make a funny story to tell his buddies over beers, one of the locals getting his jollies after dark. He'd have to try to find out which lady was putting on a show for the locals. It would make the story better.

There was a movement going by the window, but he couldn't make out who it was. The green distortion from the goggles made it too hard to pick out details. He took them off to try to get a better look, but no luck. When he looked back, the figure was gone. Either he had gotten an eyeful, or he had seen Robinson watching him. Whichever it was, Robinson knew he had to let the First Sergeant know, so he could tell the ladies to keep their curtains drawn.

It was not a PT morning, so Robinson had decided to sleep in and get breakfast late. He could always take his workout later. By the time he got to the mess hall it was practically deserted, and the cooks were already breaking down the line. Well, that was the chance you took when you slept in. He managed to snag a few leftover pancakes and grabbed a cup of coffee. He looked around for someone to sit with, and noticed that the pickings were mighty slim. He had his choice between Winders, who seemed to be having a good time telling Sergeant Harte from supply some story, or Sharp and Price sitting on the opposite side of the room. There were very few people who would choose to dine with Winder. Most of the younger troops though he was an asshole, and the line platoon NCOs had no use for him. Robinson carried his tray over to Sharp and Price.

"Eddie, welcome and sit down. How are you doing?" Price called both him and his brother 'Eddie'. They were identical twins, but his wounds had caused him to lose some weight. The difference between the brothers was obvious now, but Price never treated them any different.

"I'm doing good, Sergeant Price. I'll be back up to speed pretty soon." He picked at his pancakes, then looked around the room again. "Has the First Sergeant already gone yet?"

"Now there's a brave trooper, looking for Top first thing in the morning. You got an urge to volunteer for something?" asked Sharp.

Robinson shook his head. "No, I just saw something last night I think he should know about. I saw one of the locals hanging around outside the barracks last night. He seemed awfully interested in one of the rooms I think one of the officers might have been getting scoped out. The guy even had a phone with him. He was probably taking pictures."

Sharp swung around and got close to his face. "And what did you do about it?"

"When I tried to see what he was looking at, I lost sight of him for a minute and he took off. I didn't see where he went."

"But you saw what he was looking at." It was a statement, not a question.

"No, it was on the second floor, and I was too far away." He felt like Sharp was accusing him of being a peeper, so he tried to defend himself. "If I knew who it was I'd tell you. That's why I'm looking for the Top, so he can warn the ladies!"

Sharp put his hand on Robinson's shoulder. "Relax, I'm just screwing with you, Kid. The women will be glad you picked up on it. Finish your breakfast. The First Sergeant should be in his office when you get done. You should let him know before first formation."


First Sergeant Harrison put out the word at first formation that he would like to have a moment with all the female officers after the formation. He figured it would be best to give the word to the officers and let them pass the word to the enlisted women. It wasn't a matter of chauvinism. He had learned through long years of service that there is a right way and a wrong way to pass information and warnings to women. Personal matters were best left on a woman to woman basis. The lady officers could pass the warning down the chain of command.

The women were instantly concerned, and asked for more information. When did this happen, where was the pervert, how did he find out and what happened to the peeper. Harrison didn't have anywhere near the information they were asking for, so he called Robinson over. After the session with Sharp he was dreading having to face the officers about this, but he sucked it up and walked over. Harrison didn't seem upset. He just told him that he should have gotten more information from him, and asked that he relay the stories to the ladies. After he felt his cheeks turn red and he got over an initial bout of stammering, he told them exactly what he had seen the night before. After they had asked him a few more questions, several of them stated that it couldn't have been them, because they were on the other side of the building. The rest wanted to know what window it had been. When he told them, they all shook their heads. Captain Bonneville seemed to be doing a mental map exercise, then decided who lived there. "I'm pretty sure that's the Sergeant Majors room!" She was more than sure. Before their falling out she had spent more than a few hours there. Major Carson agreed. "I think you're right." She had also spent time there. The two women gave each other a wondering glance, then passed it off. Some of the officers laughed, or giggled, to be more precise. "Maybe the Sergeant Major should learn to keep his shades drawn. I don't think the Moldovans practice 'Don't ask, don't tell' like we do."

After Harrison thanked them for their time and they were walking away, CSM Grant walked over to see what was going on. Several of the ladies giggled as they returned his salute.

"What was that all about, Ralph?"

"You, my slightly graying and gracefully aging friend, seem to have a midnight admirer."

"And you all felt a need to talk about it out here on the parade field?"

"Don't get paranoid on me, Luke. Young Sergeant Robinson saw someone watching you last night." He repeated the story he had gotten from Robinson.

"Really?"

"That's the story, Luke. He may have even been snapping pictures with a camera phone."

Grant thought for a minute. "I don't like the sound of this. If it was a pervert, why me? Why not one of the women, or even one of the young guys if he's a queer? Watching me doesn't make any sense."

"What are you thinking?"

"I'm thinking we need to grab this guy and find out why. I've gotta spend the day with Perkins and Morgan. Can you get Sharp to set something up, and let me know about it when I get back this evening?"


Perkins was huddled with Lieutenant Stanley, getting an update on the progress of her road project. The locally hired stonemasons had been moving right along, completing the rebuilding of the bridge ahead of schedule. The local inspectors had insisted that the bridge retain its original, weathered, hand built appearance. Lieutenant Stanley had planned carefully with her NCOs on the design. Military bridge building is a straightforward process. There are tables and graphs that lay out exactly what dimensions are needed for any given weight class the bridge is intended to carry. Here, the modern underpinnings were designed to be hidden by the hand laid stonework, giving it the rustic character everyone wanted, while giving it the strength to support Stanley's heavy equipment. The masons were putting the finishing touches on now. She estimated that they could close the fords in a few days. Once they were done with the blade work and the fill, they were going to place some sod cut from other areas to fill it in. One or two growing seasons and all traces of the approaches would disappear.

Perkins was pleased. The road was their only reason for being in the country. This bridge had been the major item of reconstruction, and, as a result, a combination choke point and headache. The ford had been a splendid idea, allowing work to continue farther on, instead of having all that heavy equipment laid up idle, waiting to cross.

The cooperation from the Moldovans had been excellent. Perkins credited his own political savvy for that, but in truth, it had been his NCOs willingness to work with the local soldiers, train them on the use of the equipment, and do little side projects for them that remained off the books. There were a number of large jobs the farmers and peasants put off because they didn't have the manpower for, that a bulldozer or backhoe could knock out in a few hours for them. "Hearts and minds," Price kept repeating. "No politics, no bullshit, no guns. The little fellas will remember that long after we're gone." It also took some of the sting out of the extra duties the Moldovans were pulling. As the remote equipment dump was established, there was a need for security. Once the Moldovans learned that the Americans who pulled it with them would be giving instruction, and, more important, practical experience on the equipment, there were always more soldiers than requested. It also helped push the project along a little bit more every night.

Lieutenant Sage was eager to do his part. He wanted to throw a party for the workers when the project was finished. He thought a deluxe meal in the mess hall for them on the last day would be just the thing. He didn't know that the operators had already planned a small blowout at a farm not far from the bridge. There would be a pig roast, beer and wine, all paid for by the Americans. Sage almost soured the proposal when the Colonel agreed to it. Price just decided to fudge his progress reports a little to give them an extra day on the project, and on the payroll. The stonemasons could come to work on their last day, finish up, then head back to the barn for Sage's party. They could come back the next day back to finish up whatever cleanup they had to do, then have the pig roast. More bang for the buck.

Morgan and Grant kept away from Perkins at the stops as much as possible. He was always asking, probing, seeing if they had given Winder and Carstairs the same information he was getting from them directly. Grant knew exactly what Morgan had been briefing, so consistency wasn't a problem. The soldiers who accompanied them on any nocturnal missions were told to respond to any questions that they had been posted as security, and hadn't participated in any of the actual intelligence gathering. The only exceptions to that rule were the soldiers who were detailed to the observation posts established around the airstrip. They were now keeping it under observation at night, after a series of AN-124 flights had come in after dark. From the tail numbers they had recorded, it was always the same two planes that were making regular trips in. The cargo was always on a trailer, covered to protect it from prying eyes. A small Russian truck would back up the ramp, hook on, and haul it off. Then a steam cleaner was rolled up and the interior was hosed out. They hadn't determined the purpose of that yet, but as soon as it was done, personnel would be loaded and the plane took off for parts unknown. They had requested assistance, through NATO and Centcom, to learn where the origination and destination of the flights were, but, so far, they had not gotten any answers.

Grant was watching the hill line, something he always did. Price had reported that whoever had been watching them, either the Russians or the Arab, wasn't coming every day anymore. Grant was certain the Arab had probably just changed his vantage point. He believed the two they had killed at the airstrip had been sent by Sharif. Sharif had experience with American snipers in Darfur. He was probably afraid they would be tracking him, now that the shooting had started. Grant had wanted to try to ambush the Arab further on down the road, catch him on his approach, but Morgan had nixed that. There was no guarantee they could do it without setting up every day in the hopes he'd pass that spot. Then there was the problem of bringing more people into the plan. They had been very fortunate that the tale of the two dead Moldovans had been restricted to five people. The same five couldn't be involved in any ambush. They all had other places to be. That would mean more participants, more explanations, and more opportunities for the story to leak out. Grant would have to be patient, until a better plan could be hatched.

Ali Alawa Sharif had stopped going out to the road, and for the reason Grant suspected. Now that the shooting had started, he feared an ambush. Yasim and Sullah, the two idiots he had sent to shoot down the plane, had failed miserable. Not only had they missed the target, they had disappeared. Sharif thought they were hiding from him, as well they should. He had given them a precious AK-47 and an even more precious RPG. This wasn't the Middle East. There were no neighborhood arms bazaars he could go shopping at. Every weapon had to be begged from the Russians, and they were only to be used for their mission. They were only interested in destabilization of the Moldovan – Trans-Dnestr situation, and, it seemed, they wanted it to be destabilized by an Arab. He assumed that it was to give the appearance that the Chechens were broadening their war against the Russians, and give any countermeasures more legitimacy.

Sharif had made his own plans. He was going to kill Americans, a lot of Americans. It would be his only way of getting back into the good graces of the brotherhood. American bodies displayed on the world press would be his atonement for failure in Darfur, especially if they were the bodies of the same ones who had thwarted him in the desert. It would be enough to have the *fatwa* against him lifted. Then he could regain his old position of respect.

Yusef was to be his weapon against the Americans. The boy was eager to die for Allah. Sharif had already told him what his target was be, and it had pleased him. He had asked for another bomber, but the Russians had told him there were none available. Sharif believed they were holding back until he had delivered on the first one. No matter. The second bomber was to be targeted at the Russians themselves. He would have to find another sacrificial lamb. Perhaps his handler could be his unwitting dupe. He made enough trips out to the Russians. Maybe his motorbike could be rigged with an extra present for his Russian masters. It would be poetic.

Yusef came in from his prayers at the mosque. Sharif could see he was upset. "What is wrong today, Yusef? Have the Jews invaded?"

"Sullah and Yasim have been found! They have been killed in an accident!"

"An accident?" That concerned Sharif. These idiots had his weapons. They failed their mission, then died in an accident? Allah could be cruel in his humor. "How did they die?"

"Their car was found by the side of the road. They had run into a ditch and the car burned."

Strange, Sharif wondered, where could they have been going? "Tell me, Yusef, when did this happen?"

"It would seem several nights ago. They were on a little used road going to a gravel pit. They had a weapon. The police think they were going to test it."

"A weapon? Do you know what kind?"

"I think it was a Kalash," he replied, using the popular term for the AK.

"Are you certain it was a Kalash? There was nothing said about an RPG?"

"No, just the Kalash. Why?"

"In a moment."

Sharif pulled out a map and looked for the gravel pit Yusef was talking about. He located it halfway between where he had left them and the city. He could think of no reason for them to be there. If they accomplished their mission they would have returned to the city. If they had failed their mission, the Americans would have killed them and hid the bodies. The car would still be on the ridge. If they had turned cowardly, the RPG would have been in the car, and the flames would have detonated the warhead. Sharif ran every possibility through his mind, then tried different combinations. None of them worked. The only explanation could be that the Americans had killed them and dumped their bodies on a little used side road. If Sullah or Yasim had been captured, he doubted either of them would have resisted even a cursory interrogation. They would have given him up.

He needed to calm Yusef. The death of his friends in an accident on the way to do the work of Allah could shake his faith. Sharif didn't want him doubting the will of Allah. He needed to be reassured. "Yusef, it's time you learned how they really died. Did you know I had sent them against the Americans?"

By the time Sharif was done explaining, Yusef had regained his faith, and was eager to join his friends in paradise.

Sharp was passing by the dayroom on his way to the shower. The commo section had rigged a satellite dish, and they were bootlegging TV programs from all over the globe. Major Morgan had run a line over to the Tactical Operations Center, the TOC, but kept the channel set to cable news. Winder kept switching to sports channels, until he had to give a direct order that the set be left on the news. Morgan knew that while he was out his orders were being routinely disobeyed by Winder, and had resolved to remove the set. He had sent it over to the Motor Pool. At least those guys knew how to work while the South Pakistan Cricket World Championships were on. Winder, predictably, had whined about it to Perkins. The Colonel had been hinting to Morgan that his section morale had been suffering, and a TV set would be just the ticket to bring it back up. The S-3 had so far ignored the 'hints' and left the set in the Motor Pool. Winder could whine and sulk all he wanted. The boy was getting increasingly useless.

One of the soldiers in the dayroom called out to Sharp, "Whooeey, Sarge, you gotta look at this!" Sharp wandered in, expecting some third world beauty pageant. Instead, the channel was turned to a news station. The screen was full of flames. Every few seconds the camera shifted to the fire fighters. They were wearing protective suits. That was interesting.

The captions across the bottom of the screen were in some language Sharp didn't recognize. The next shot came from overhead. Sharp assumed there was a news helicopter on the scene. It zoomed in on the flames, then widened to show that this was a plane crash, probably somewhere in Eastern Europe, from the look of the scrolling caption. The scene shifted again, this time to zoom in on the tail surfaces, which had separated from the main fuselage. Centered in the picture were the blue, white and red horizontal stripes of the Russian Federation flag. Now his interest was piqued. He still considered the Russians to be the bad guys, cold war or no cold war. If one of their planes went down, it couldn't be a bad thing.

"Mike, go see if you can find Sergeant Price. He's probably in his room. Tell him I need him to try to translate what's going on here."

The soldier disappeared down the hall. Sharp took over his chair and flicked the remote to run up the volume. There was something about the announcer's voice. He could hear a definite waver, almost as if he were in a panic and didn't want to be there. Then the camera zoomed in on a container that was on its side at the very edge of the flames. Sharp couldn't be certain in the bad light and grainy contrast, but he thought he could see the universal symbol for *biohazards*. The camera didn't linger long enough for him to kneel closer to the screen. The scene shifted back to the tail section. It lingered long enough for Sharp to make out the tail numbers. He looked around for something to write on, but there was nothing available. He read the number out loud, and repeated it. "74-85127, 74-85127, 74-85127..."

"What the hell are you doing?" Price walked into the room behind him. Sharp turned to look at him. When he turned back to the screen the tail was gone. He asked Price for a pen to write the numbers down. Price told him not to bother.

"I know the number."

"You didn't even see it." Sharp replied.

"I didn't have to. I can recognize when somebody is shouting my cell phone number out loud. What's the big deal?"

Sharp stepped out of the way so Price could see the screen. Price made his *you interrupted my toenail clipping for this?* Face and looked at the screen. There was a gaggle of troops coming into the room to see what was going on. Price swore at them to shut up while he sat down and leaned into the TV. He made a motion with his hand for the remote, and raised the volume even more. He listened for a moment, then ran it back down, Sharp asked, "Do you know what they're saying?"

"No" he replied, "but I think it's either Croat or Albanian." He was studying the screen intently. "I'm not 100% certain, but I think that's in Albania. I'm pretty sure they flashed 'Tirana' on the screen there a minute ago."

"Tirana?"

"Yeah, the capital of Albania." He looked over his shoulder at the growing crowd. "Didn't any of you take geography in grammar school?" He stood up and walked through the crowd, grabbing Sharps arm as he passed through. "C'mon. We've got better things to do than sit around here. Let's go find the Sergeant Major and see if he's got any local beer."

Mike, the soldier Sharp had sent for Price, spoke up, "I've got some here, Sergeant."

"Well, thank you for the offer, but if I drink the Sergeant Major's, I don't feel like I'm obligated to pay him back." He pulled Sharp after him.

"Christ, Pricey! Let go already! What's your fucking hurry?"

Price looked over his shoulder again to make sure there wasn't anybody close enough to hear. He lowered his voice. "We gotta find Luke, and then Morgan. We have a problem. A major fucking problem."

Sharp looked at him with squinted eyes. "That was one of our planes, wasn't it?"

Grant was nowhere to be found, so they went directly to Morgan. They found him coming out of the shower. He wasn't in much of a mood. He considered a day on the road with Perkins to be worse than a day asleep. Perkins always insisted on a briefing before he went out. That involved prep time, because Perkins liked big flip charts. Winder, who should have been doing the prep work, was next to useless, because since Perkins had made him his official go between with the S-3 (a really useless idea) Winder had taken less and less interest in what was supposed to be one of his jobs. That put the burden on Sharp, who had been spending half his time training Moldovans, and the other half watching the Russians, was out of the loop on the projects, and had to begin almost from scratch. Morgan always pitched in to help, so it took the both of them away from what they were doing.

On the road, Perkins was easily distracted. He liked to make side trips, usually on a whim, which took them miles away from where they should have been. Perkins also had a tendency to get lost. He relied heavily on his GPS unit, but it was of little use because he had trouble translating the information to a paper map. Morgan always had to help him out, but first they went through the ballet of Perkins insisting he knew what he was doing.

Ten hours later, all Morgan had to show for his day was a headache and a layer of dust. As soon as they got back Grant had excused himself to meet with Senior Sergeant Yevigny Kosavich. The Moldovan NCO had promised to show him the warehouse where the German equipment had been stored. Grant figured that after a day being fruitlessly unemployed, as he liked to refer to his days with Perkins as, he deserved a bit of relaxation.

Grant had parted company with the CO as soon as they had returned. There was no point in talking to Morgan about the day, he had been sullen since before noon, upset with what he perceived, accurately, as a waste of time. The Major would need some time to regain his perspectives and get back to normal. In the meantime, Grant headed for the billets to get some of the road dust rinsed off his skin, then head on out to meet with Senior Sergeant Kosavich.

Kosavich, for an infantryman, preferred to use his status as a senior NCO to pursue more cerebral tasks. His administrative duties took precedent over tedious field exercises, for he considered himself more as an advisor to his subordinates than a field leader. He had spent his time on maneuvers, and now considered them to be a young man's activity. He had heard an expression used by some of the Americans, 'I got a GO on being miserable," and thought it was appropriate. He had adopted it as his own. His younger soldiers didn't seem to mind his absences from the field training. They knew their Senior Sergeant made sure they were paid on time, had their leave request processed in a timely fashion, and got hot chow to them as often as he could when they were out in the field. Today, Kosavich would be showing the American Sergeant Major around what he considered to be his pride and joy, as well as his personal retreat: the equipment storage shed.

After the Great Patriotic War, which was how the USSR had called World War 2, a great deal of German equipment had been captured. Some of it was destined to be used as static displays at war memorials. Still more of it would go into museums that would trumpet the great victory of the Soviet system over the fascists. Even more would be doled out to client states outside of the Soviet bloc, to be used as non-traceable military aid.

The Russians turned out to be every bit as efficient as the Germans in storage, documentation and record keeping. Unfortunately, their system was so vast, and the amount of paper so enormous, much of what was filed or stockpiled was never to ever again to see the light of day. What was in their storage room here was an example of that. When the Russians had left this little military base to the Moldovans after the fall of the Iron Curtain, this building hadn't even been mentioned. The windows had been boarded up and heavy padlocks left on the doors. Even the Moldovans ignored it for several months before curiosity overcame them and the cut the locks. What they found was interesting, but not considered useful or valuable as anything but museum displays. The inventory was offered to cultural institutions around the country, but even they had little interest.

Soon, it was all forgotten again by everyone except the soldiers who were posted here. The building had been re-secured, and again was ignored, until Senior Sergeant Yevigny Kosavich arrived. He realized there was a historical value to what they had stored and began making efforts to clean and rehabilitate what was there. Soldiers in the Moldovan Defense Forces found themselves with time on their hands, and Kosavich knew how to fill it. He had details assigned to clean every piece of equipment in storage. Boxes of spares and repair parts were catalogued and organized, then mechanics began the arduous task of making sense out of German manuals and labels, and began restoring everything to working order, as best they could.

There was also some Lend Lease equipment stored here. Soviet xenophobia had relegated it to storage as soon as they had enough of their own equipment on line. They realized that the propaganda image of the mighty Soviet Army would be diminished if it was known that foreign equipment played a part in their victory. Some of this equipment, Kosavich believed, would be of great interest to his American counterpart.

Grant was looking forward to his tour of the equipment shed. Kosavich had invited him during one of their first meetings, but events had never cooperated. After he had learned he would be spending the day uselessly with Perkins, he decided to make time for his own relaxation. After a quick freshening up he was on his way out the building when he saw Major Carson. She was headed towards him.

His relationship with the Major had settled into an interesting pattern. She was always business like in dealing with him. There was never any hint of familiarity one would expect considering their off duty relationship. And it was strictly an off duty relationship. She was always the initiator of any 'meetings' they would have, and she only made the arrangements after duty hours, and when she wasn't wearing her uniform. More importantly, she was never pushy about it. If Grant had other things on his plate at the time he would tell her, and she accepted it. She never brought it up in a pouty way later on. As she had told him, she was doing it for the sex, not for a long-term relationship. That was fine with Grant. He had gotten way too involved with, and attached to, Linda Bonneville. Since her blow up after meeting the Arab on the road, she had been distant, only dealing with Grant on official business. She had been energetic and imaginative, and Grant missed that, but Sylvia Carson had some talents of her own.

She looked beat, and Grant mentioned that as he rendered a salute. She returned it and smiled. "We ran a Medical Civic Action Program, a MEDCAP, at one of the schools on the outskirts of Lashtyg. They must have been importing kids from all over the country for us to see. It was nonstop!" She shifted her bag from one shoulder to the other. It was an oversized medic bag, complete with an oxygen bottle. Grant offered to take it for her. He hadn't expected her to give it up, and she didn't. ""Why, thank you, Sergeant Major. Lugging that O2 bottle around all day wasn't my best idea. But you look like a man going someplace. Am I holding you up?"

"No problem, Ma'am. I've got a meeting with one of the local NCOs. He's going to show me around a little museum they have set up in one of the warehouses." He didn't know why, but before he could stop himself he asked if she'd like to come along. She thought about it for several seconds, then, to his surprise, she accepted. "Do you have time to wait for me to throw this in my room and wash my face? I really feel grimy."

Grant said he'd wait, and watched as she bounded up the stairs. She didn't seem as tired as when he first spoke to her. It only took a few minutes for her to do whatever she had to. Grant noticed she hadn't refreshed her makeup after she washed her face. He made a mental note that she was a fine looking woman even without the enhancements. It was a long walk to the other side of the compound where Kosavich said to meet him. Major Carson was in officer mode all the way, asking him questions about his duties and troop morale, interspersing the conversation with anecdotes about her day on the MEDCAP. He pointed out Kosavich to her when they got close. He was standing alone by a side door to one of the larger warehouses on the compound. He waved when he saw them, and as they got closer, he recognized the Major and rendered a salute.

"I see my friend brought a guest. That's good. I'm very proud of my little display here, and I like to show it off when I can." He pulled a ring of keys from a cargo pocket and opened the door. Just inside he opened a panel and threw a few switches. The interior was bathed in light. Grant caught his breath when he saw what was there.

Kosavich smiled. "I knew you would be amazed at what we have," and he led them around the room, keeping up a constant narrative. There was a description and a story to every piece of equipment. He touched everything they passed, as if making a connection with an old friend. Grant and Carson were encouraged to climb on and into the equipment. The Major demurred, but Grant took advantage of the offer. He was amazed that everything was clean, and, according to Kosavich, operational. He told Grant that if the Americans could provide some diesel fuel and lubricants, he would arrange a driving demonstration for them. Grant agreed to look into the possibility.

At the back of the room were racks and racks of weapons, all in pristine condition. There were hundreds of K98K rifles, racks of MG42 machine guns and crates of MP40 submachine guns. There were also boxes of Lugers and P-38 pistols. Kosavich again encouraged Grant to handle them. Each weapon he touched was clean and functional, ready for issue. Kosavich motioned to a steel door on the far corner of the room. "We have ammunition for all of this back there. Maybe you would like a firing demonstration sometime also? My soldiers don't care for these weapons, but perhaps yours would like to try them?" Grant assured them they would.

Kosavich then led them to a large double door in the back of the room. He once again pulled out his key ring and worked the locks. "I have saved the best for last. I think you will be amazed and delighted with what I have back here!" He pulled the doors open and reached around to throw a light switch. Kosavich was right. Grant was amazed.

Sitting in front of him were four M-3 General Stuart light tanks. Other than the old Soviet Army markings on the sides, they looked like they did when they rolled out of the factory in 1940. The hatches were open and Grant peered inside. Even the ammo racks were fully rigged for combat. Kosavich told Grant to climb in, just as his radio crackled. He carried on a brief conversation, then got a serious look on his face.

"My commander wishes to see me on a matter of some importance. I hate to cut our tour short. Would you like to remain here and look around until I return? It should be about 45 minutes to an hour."

Grant looked at Carson, and she just shrugged. "I don't mind. I find this all very interesting, and I would hate to be the one to break up the Sergeant Major's fun."

Grant smiled at her. "Thank you, Major." Then to Kosavich, "Thank you for your kind offer. I would like to stay for a while. If we have to leave, I'll shut off the lights and lock the front door."

Kosavich gave a wave and left. Grant disappeared back inside the M-3. He was studying the main gun when he heard Major Carson speaking to him through the commander's hatch. "There's not all that much room, is there?"

"No, Ma'am. They sure weren't build for comfort." He looked up and saw she had taken off her blouse. She was wearing one of her too tight t-shirts, and what looked like a thin sports bra. Her nipples were pushing out the material. She smiled down at him. "Move over, I'm coming in. Give me a hand."

She sat on the edge of the hatch and dropped her feet in. Grant reached up and held her legs to guide her in. She slid herself part ways in stopping when her chest was level with Grant's face. Her hands came in and went to either side of his head. "Hmm," he heard her say, "I think I'm going to like close quarters," and she pulled his face against her breasts. Grant found a nipple and bit down on it. She gave a yelp and slid the rest of the way in. Her lips found his, and he could feel her hands working at his trousers. As she freed him from the restraint she interrupted the kiss. "Is there enough room in here, or should we get out?" He sat her on the loaders seat and knelt in front of her. He was wiggling her trousers and panties over her hips before he answered. "I think there's room," then slid her hips toward his. She shuddered then pressed her mouth hard against his as she thrust herself onto him. Her orgasm didn't take long, and it was followed quickly by his. He started to pull back, but her legs came up and held him in place. "I'm not finished yet," she said, and he could feel her muscles squeezing him. She was making small movements with her hips as she continued to squeeze rhythmically. She came again as Grant felt his arousal growing. Now it was his turn to hold her as she started to pull away. She just smiled and closed her eyes, rocking into him until they both exploded again.

They made love again on the floor behind the tank after Carson had worked her magic with her mouth. Grant was totally spent when she was finally satisfied. In what was really an unusual move, she wanted to cuddle for a while after they had dressed.

Grant decided to ask. "Why me?"

"Why you what?"

"You know what I mean. Why me? You could have gone after one of the officers. There wouldn't have been any of this officer/enlisted crap, no sneaking around. Instead you came after me. Why?"

She sat up and thought. "The officers in this unit gossip worse than a bunch of high school girls. If I went with one of them, everyone would know and I'd be getting propositioned by all of them. This is better."

"How?"

"You're discreet, and if you aren't, your friends are. I noticed that in Africa when you were hooking up with Captain Bonneville. It happened, and there wasn't any gloating. If she had been a little more circumspect, nobody would have known or suspected." She thought again. "Have you told anyone about this?"

Grant shook his head. "For the same reason as you: discretion. I don't want the troops thinking that the female officers are fair game. Even if I am rooting around with you, there's still that element I want to preserve. They don't need to know."

"You know I'm going through a divorce?"

"I heard the rumor."

"Want to know why?"

"That's your business. I don't want to know. That way I don't feel like a hypocrite when I tell the troops to mind their own business."

She laughed at him. "Gossip sets a bad example, and this doesn't?"

"Gossip is public. This is private. I'd rather keep it that way. I like to pick and choose what I'm going to hell for."

She still had her head on his chest when they heard Kosavich come back. He came through the door calling out Grant's name. Grant got up to intercept him, giving Carson a moment to put her blouse back on. Her nipples were still erect, not a vision Grant wanted to share with anyone.

"Your people are looking for you. They sent a vehicle!"

Carson came out from the back room. If Kosavich suspected anything, he didn't let on. Carson wanted to know what happened, but Grant could only repeat what Kosavich had said. He could hear the Hummer idling outside.

As they walked out Kosavich grabbed his arm and lowered his voice. "Something bad has happened, my friend. I can't say any more. Perhaps you are being summoned to hear the same news."

"How bad is it Yvegniy?"

"I can't say any more. If your officer has the same information for you, you will know."

# CHAPTER 10

Lieutenant Colonel Perkins was skeptical when Morgan first brought the news to him. The thought that the Russians could be stockpiling chemical weapons a couple of miles away was ridiculous, especially considering how easy it had been for Morgan and company to breach their security. The tail numbers on the plane were either a coincidence, or they were transcribed wrong. Morgan had insisted, to the point where he had sent a soldier off to record the news item the next time it came on. It must have been the biggest story of the day coming out of that part of Europe. All the European news agencies were carrying the story. They finally found one in a language that Price could translate. He had given his quick and dirty version to the Colonel, who, after a few moments reflection, decided to call the entire staff together to discuss the situation.

Morgan tried to dissuade him of that idea. "Colonel, it might be too early to let the entire staff know. We need to develop the intelligence. Too many people know, and before you know it they're telling the folks back home."

"Don't you think they have a right to know?"

"Eventually, they do, Sir. But right now we have to identify the threat and isolate it before Ivan over there finds out we know. We have to be able to isolate him."

"What do you mean 'we'? This is an international matter. It's on Moldovan soil. We have no business in it until we're asked."

"Colonel, once the Russians get asked, they'll deny it. While everyone is trying to figure out some way to get the UN or some other useless group to investigate, they'll be hiking it out of the country. Besides, they have that school going on. All we need is for some rag headed idiot to get his hands on that stuff."

Grant added his thoughts. "He's right. Colonel. Remember what happened when the Janjaweed used the Sarin on the refugee camp. They could have a delivery system over there they could use on us. The rag heads are pretty serious about that 'death to America' stuff."

Perkins was adamant. He wanted his staff involved in any decision making.


It was a contentious meeting, but, in the end, they were no closer to a decision than when they started. In spite of the volumes of information Morgan had collected from the Russian compound, the repeated landings of the plane that had crashed in Albania, and the graphic images of firefighters in protective gear hosing down barrels with HAZMAT markings, Morgan was the sole voice calling for some action to prevent the Russians from moving any stocks they may have had out of the area. The rest of the staff was closer to Perkins in their opinions. None of the NCOs were allowed to participate. In the end, the only action Perkins was willing to take was to report their findings and intelligence up their own chain of command to NATO.

Morgan still wanted more, he asked that at least there be an informational copy be sent to Central Command in Florida. Perkins refused.

"We are not a Central Command asset, Major. I've thought long and hard about General Ramirez and his directions to us, and all I can conclude is that, since he has no authority over us, it was a non-binding order, and I resent the fact they're trying to run my operation outside of the chain of command."

"Then you won't mind if I make an informal report?"

"I will mind, Major Morgan. I want you to consider everything that we've found out to date, and anything we've discussed here as classified. You are not to discuss it with anyone without clearing it through the XO, or me is that clear? We are not going to take any action until there's a decision made by the people in Brussels."

Morgan attempted to argue, but Perkins cut him off. "I'll have no more of your insubordination, Major. If you persist in this arguing I'll have you placed under arrest and confined to quarters, is that clear?"

Morgan was silent. He glanced over at Grant, looked around the room, then lowered his eyes and started writing in his notebook. Perkins, believing he had won his argument and imposed his will on the staff, smiled at the group. He laid out his plan. He intended for all information to be transmitted to Third Corps in Germany for forwarding to NATO. The observation posts that had been established around the airfield would be scaled back to avoid any affront to the Russians, in case the conclusions had been wrong. And, lastly but most importantly, there would be no more intelligence gathering missions or intrusions on the Russian compound. This was to be given over to NATO as their responsibility.

"I can't stress enough that this can't leave this room. Especially the NCO's. You've gotten too close to your Moldovan counterparts. I can't have you broadcasting this to them and causing a panic."

Grant interrupted. "I think it's already too late for that. I think they already know."

"How can you be sure of that?"

Grant repeated his brief conversation with Kosavich. "He was pretty shaken up."

"That may not mean anything. Don't repeat any of this to him unless he brings it up first. Then I want you to report anything he says directly to me." He paused. "One more thing, Sergeant Major. I know you've been using all this combined training as an excuse to circumvent me. Effective immediately, all night training will be cancelled. I don't want you or your pirates out running your own operations anymore."

Sharp stood and waited for Perkins to acknowledge him.

"What is it, Sharp? Do you have a problem with that?"

Sharp tried to be disarming. His night ops had been productive, but he had a major intrusion planned for tonight. He tried to salvage it. "Sir, cutting out the night problems will be fine. I can go back to a normal routine. But there is one small problem."

"What would that be?"

Sharp adopted an 'aw shucks' pose and scrapped his feet on the floor. "I've had a couple of the local platoons on reverse cycle for a couple of days," reverse cycle meant they had been doing all their activities at night and sleeping during the day, "just to get them ready for the last couple of exercises."

"What are those, Sharp? Invading the Ukraine?"

A laugh ripped through the crowd, and quickly subsided when Perkins held up his hand. "What's the problem, Sergeant?"

Sharp looked up. "We have two exercises tonight. One right outside the fence. Sergeant Robinson has been getting ready to run a night navigation course with NVGs for the locals. He's been doing the train up all week."

"What's the other?"

"Night firing."

Perkins huddled with Major Carstairs for a few moments. Carstairs nodded his head a few times and called Winder over. The conversation continued briefly, then Perkins gestured them to back away.

"All right, Sharp. The training for tonight can continue. I'm satisfied the ranges you use are far enough from the Russians to be safe. Just one or two provisos though."

"Yes, Sir?"

"First, all training will be supervised by Major Carstairs and Master Sergeant Winder. Nothing happens, and no one goes anywhere without them knowing about it. That clear?"

"Perfectly, Sir."

"And secondly, the same applies as far as talking about any of this. We start panicking the common soldier here, and only God knows what might happen." Sharp sat down. He glanced over at Grant, then at Price. There was just an imperceptible nod of heads as they made eye contact. They could work around this.


Morgan was silent as he left headquarters with Grant. He knew there were actions they could be taking, if nothing else to disable the airstrip to prevent any planes from coming in. The Moldovans didn't use the field, so there would be no trampling on their sovereignty. It would be a matter between them and the Russians, nothing more. It was a dirt strip, and they had heavy equipment. The job could be finished in a couple of hours, and all the Russians would have is manpower and some hand tools to try to undo any damage.

"What are you thinking, Sergeant Major?"

"Kosavich said it was pretty bad news. I can't imagine what could be worse, unless the Russians had a leak over there. I need to talk to him again."

Morgan nixed the idea. "For now, you better keep this to yourself. If we have to do anything it might be better if the locals didn't know we're as panicky as them."

Grant had already considered some possibilities, but there weren't any he was ready to discuss. "In that case, it's late, I'm tired, and there's nothing we can do tonight."

"I didn't think you'd give up so easy."

"I didn't say anything about giving up. I'm going to find some senior NCOs, have a few drinks, and indulge in some 'sergeant's business' with them. This is where my chain of command starts to work."

Morgan stopped and put his hand on Grant's arm. "What are you going to do?"

"Whatever it is, Major, you don't want to know. I may have some assets you need to be able to deny knowing about."

"Can I join you?"

"Tonight probably wouldn't be a good idea."


"That was quick thinking, Dave, but what do you think you're going to do on short notice?"

"I don't know, Boss. There was just something about being cut off like that. I guess I just wanted to poke a stick in his eye."

"Yeah, I know the feeling. We need to get eyes on the Russians. They'll probably be in an uproar now that their plane went down. They might be looking to cover their tracks and do something with the shit they already have stockpiled here. Let's see if we can get past the babysitters and head south for a few hours. Any ideas?"

Price was the first one to speak. "We can put them out."

Sharp rolled his eyes. "And that's going to help how? You start smacking those two around and we'll never be able to do anything."

"No, you moron. We don't need to touch them. Look, they've been up all day, and now Perkins told them they have to stay up all night. That means coffee, a lot of it."

"How do them having full bladders help us?"

"Jesus Christ! You mean you never heard of spiking somebody's thermos?"

Grant interrupted them. "That's a good idea, but where are we going to get a Mickey for them?"

Price pulled out a bottle of pills. "I've got three kinds of these, and if that's not enough, I can ask around. If push comes to shove, I can probably get something from Elko, or you can get it from Doc Carson."

Grant raised his eyebrows at the mention of Carson's name. Price caught the look and made a brush off sign with his hands. "What? You think we don't know about that? How stupid do you think we are?"

"Drop the subject and leave her out of this." He started on another thought, then stopped himself. "But you might want to check with Elko about what kind of a dose it would take to put them down for a few hours."

"Consider it done."


Sergeant Elko had been a willing conspirator. She offered to get Carstairs to give her a ride out to the training areas. "Will he go for it?"

She smiled. "He spends as much time as he can over at the dispensary. He 's determined to get into somebody's pants, and if it isn't Major Carson, any one of the medics will do. A little extra make-up and a tight T-shirt when I ask him, he'll fall over himself to accommodate me."

She had been right about that. Carstairs and Winder had even gone as far as offering to share their coffee with her. It was so easy she was almost disappointed. At the firing range Sharp had wandered over to where they were parked to see how it was going. Elko gave him the thumbs up from the back seat. He invited them to join him on the firing line, and it was no surprise that they both declined. Winder had been slugging down coffee, and his eyes were already drooping. Carstairs seemed to be alert, but Sharp noticed he had a full cup in his hand. He walked back to the line and Elko caught up with him.

"How long?"

She looked over her shoulder and shrugged. "They way they've been putting it away, I'm surprised they're not out already. I'll check in a few minutes."

"How long will they be out?"

"I don't know. Once they're down I'm going to give them each a shot. It should be good for about five hours."

Sharp looked at his watch. "That'll be about sunrise. Will they suspect anything?"

"No way. They won't feel the injection, and I've got clean coffee to put in their thermos. But you owe me, big time."

"What do you want?" Sharp asked.

"I want to go."

"You don't know what we're doing."

"I don't care. After going through all this, it must be pretty important. I want in."


They were strung out in an arc around one side of the Russian compound. All the Americans had been using NVGs, and they had detected the infrared projectors the Russians were using from the towers. From the activity level, they seemed to be on full alert. Every light inside the compound was on too. They wouldn't be getting in tonight.

Sharp radioed back to Grant to give him the news.

"Leave an OP with a couple of radios and come back in. Make sure the OPs are out of sight."

Sharp called them back to the rally point and counted noses. Everyone was there. Elko had a disappointed look on her face. She had been expecting more excitement. They were crossing the access road headed back to where their vehicles were parked when they spotted lights coming at them from the compound. They took cover as a small convoy passed. When it was gone, Price called out that there had been Arab speakers on one of the trucks.

"Any idea what they were saying?"

"No. Just bits and pieces. I think they're headed to the airstrip."

Indeed they were. The vehicles dropped their passengers, then positioned themselves on both ends and in the middle of the strip to illuminate it with their headlights. Sharp was pleased with himself that he decided to leave his vehicles under netting in the creek bed, instead of just parking at the end of the runway like they normally did. They were obviously expecting a plane. Did they think the one that crashed was still coming? Didn't they know?

Sharp called Price over and pointed him at the group that was milling around in an assembly area. He mimed what he wanted done, and Price understood and headed off. Sharp kept scanning the area, looking for any security the Russians might have posted, but couldn't spot any. Another truck drove up from the compound and parked by the group. He could tell by the glow of the cigarette that there were two people in the cab, but neither made an effort to get out. There was a movement on the back of the truck. He could make out the outline of a head wearing night goggles. Price must have taken a risk and checked the cargo. He heard the driver yell at the group in Russian. There were some return catcalls, then the group moved over to the rear of the truck. The figure jumped down and disappeared in the tall grass. He hadn't been seen. Sharp could make out a bucket brigade line start unloading the truck and piling the contents on the edge of the runway. As the pile grew, he could see Price creep up to it from the blind side. He opened one of the crates and dropped something in, then vanished again.

Price had made his approach from the far side from Sharp. The Arabs were making so much noise that any sound he might have made would have been masked. It emboldened him to get even closer.

He was in the tall grass several yards from the group. There seemed to be general agreement that the Russians were infidels and they deserved to be put to the sword like all the rest. Some of them found it fitting that the very people their brothers in Chechnya were fighting against had trained them. One called out, "It is almost like their false prophet, Marx, said about the capitalists. He said communism would destroy the West with their own money. We will destroy the Russian infidels with their own weapons!" That raised a laugh from the entire group. The speaker must have been a leader of some sorts.

A truck approached from the general direction of the compound. It pulled up to the edge of the apron and stopped. Price could hear the occupants discussing whether or not to back in. Finally, one just cursed and told the driver to stay where he was. "These fucking Arabs can lug this shit if they want it. I won't be sorry to see these bandits gone."

Price crept up to the back of the truck and lifted the tarp. He could just barely make out the yellow Cyrillic markings on the crates. He climbed up and opened one of the boxes to be certain. Then he made a quick check of the others, and opened another. He was dropping off as the Russian called out for the Arabs to come unload their supplies.

Price moved back into the grass a few yards and examined his samples. Somewhere in the distance he could hear the drone of an approaching aircraft. The gomers must have graduated from bomb making 101 and were heading home, or wherever the fuck the rag heads wanted to kill people. Price decided not to let that happen.

The Arabs finished unloading the truck just as the plane began to make its approach. The Russians were making no effort at stealth. All the lights were on. Price rejoined Sharp as the plane, another AN-124, was pivoting at the end of the runway, it's engines still in full rev. Combat loading. They weren't planning on staying on the ground long. Price gave an 'assembly' hand signal and pointed towards the creek bed. Sharp understood and called over the radio for everyone to rally there. They took up a defensive position while Sharp went down the line, physically touching each soldier to make sure he had everyone. Once that was done, he hunkered down with Price to get a briefing.

Price told him that the group was entirely made up of Arabs. "It must have been the graduating class from bomb making U. I counted 35 of them lined up unloading the truck."

"What was it carrying?"

"Looked like a lot of Semtex and detonators." Semtex was a powerful class of plastic explosives. "From what I could hear, the

Russians seemed to be having a problem and decided to close the school and get everybody out of Dodge. They were happy to go."

"Any idea where they're heading?"

"Straight to hell, I hope!"

Sharp studied his friend's face. He had a twisted, pained expression.

"What did you put in the crates?"

"You saw that, huh?" Price looked towards the plane, which was starting its take off roll. He sat back down, leaning against one of the vehicles. "I grabbed a couple of bricks and a detonator."

"You rigged it to blow? You're the man!"

"Well, I hope I got it right in the dark. I was shooting for an hour delay, but it could be anywhere from ten minutes to a day."

The plane was off the ground and banking to the northeast. The vehicles that had provided illumination pulled onto the runway and reformed their little convoy around the explosives truck. Price was still watching the navigation lights of the AN-124 as it continued to climb. "I just hope the son of a bitch gets far enough away so we don't get blamed for anything."

"Wait'll Grant hears about this! He's gonna be one happy Sergeant Major!"

Price grabbed Sharps arm and squeezed it hard. "Don't say anything to him about this. If that plane blows in mid-air it'll be called a commercial bird somebody bombed. How much shit do you think it'll stir up if they find out it was us that did it?"

"Grant ain't gonna tell anybody!"

"Bullshit! He'll have to report it to somebody, even if it's only Morgan. We've got no control over the story once it gets past us two."

Elko crawled up to where they were huddled. "Hey, how long are we gonna wait here?"

Sharp looked at her, then stood up to look for the plane. It was almost out of sight. The trucks on the runway were heading off toward the south. Sharp knelt back down. "Pass the word. We'll wait until the Ivans are gone."

Sharp waited until the Russian vehicles were out of sight before he broke down his perimeter. For good measure, he had a quick sweep made of the area to make sure the Russians hadn't left any stay behind observers. Once he was satisfied they were alone, he had his group load up and they headed back towards the night firing range. Once they were on the road he turned to Elko to ask, "Was that exciting enough for you?"

She smiled at him. "That'll do for tonight, as long as you remember you always need a medic with you."


Back at the range, Sharp had them start breaking down just as the sun started to glow over the eastern horizon. Carstairs and Winder were still sleeping as the Moldovan troops pulled out. Sharp debated with himself about leaving them out here, then decided it would just give them a reason to think they had been used and abused. He had Elko get back in and slump down in the back, like she had been sleeping too. Then he woke Carstairs. The Major jumped up like he had been shocked. He looked at Sharp, then looked around at Winder. In the back seat, Elko shifted and groaned for effect. Carstairs looked at her, then turned back to Sharp and smiled. As he exited the vehicle. "It's a good thing at least one of us was able to stay awake, eh Sergeant Sharp?" Then he walked around to the passenger side and whacked the door with his helmet. Winder, and Elko playing along, jumped up. Winder was rubbing his eyes and reaching for the thermos. Sharp looked over to Elko with his eyes wide. She smiled and gave him a thumb up. She had swapped out the drugged coffee for some untainted stuff as soon as she had given them their shots. Carstairs missed the exchange as he berated Winder. "You lucky bastard. It's a good thing I'm a nice guy and I let you sleep all night!" Winder grumbled a thanks and got out to empty his bladder on a tire. On the other side of the Hummer, Sharp opened the back door and invited Elko to ride back with him. As they were walking away, Sharp could hear Winder ask Carstairs, "When did she put on the camo paint?" Sharp looked at Elko and realized neither of them had taken off the face paint before they had roused the patsys.

Lieutenant Stanley had been keeping an eye on Sergeant Price all day. He hadn't been his usual bouncy self, and she was worried that her platoon sergeant was burning the candle at both ends. She knew he was heavily involved in all of the clandestine operations the unit was conducting at night. It seemed that at one time or another most of the soldiers assigned to the heavy equipment platoon were, including the female soldiers. Stanley had even tried, on more than one occasion, to go out with them to see for herself what was going on, but Major Morgan had repeatedly shot down her requests. He was very blunt about it: there was a need for Indians, not chiefs. She was welcome to any of the night training they were conducting, but the ops were another story. She had taken her requests to the CO, but Perkins was of no help. He had told her that she did not have a 'need to know' what was going on, and in any event, was better off not knowing what was going on. The answer had made her angry, but once the answer was couched in terms that implied a classified mission, her hands were tied. Some of the details had filtered up to her from the members who had gone, and it seemed that most of them had just spent the night in the grass watching the Russians. Not very exciting, unless you realized there were some of them who had actually *entered* the compound. Still, she remembered that less than half of the unit had earned the Combat Action Badge in the Sudan, and she had not been one of them. She liked to think that, if she made a career out of the Guard, being an engineer officer *and* having the CAB would mean something on her military resume.

"Sergeant Price?"

"Yes, Ma'am?"

Even his answers weren't as sharp as they normally were. "You really look beat today. Wouldn't you rather go back to the rear and get some sleep?"

Price liked his Platoon Leader. He hadn't been sure at first, but he got used to having a female boss. It wasn't as much of a culture shock that an old infantryman would have expected. He smiled at her. She was almost young enough to be his daughter. "I'd like nothing more, but once we get the site cleaned up, the locals are going back for Sage's party. It'll probably be the last we see of them, and I kind of liked having them around." It was true. The locals had been industrious, and more than that, friendly with the Americans. They had shared their meals, their wines and their stories. Many of the Moldovans had picked up a smattering of English, and many of the GIs had picked up some Moldovan. There was hardly any need for a translator on the site.

"That what got you down today?"

Price was quiet for a moment. What he was down about was the Russian plane. He knew that the passengers were terrorists, pure and simple. The pilots and crew knew what they were getting into, transporting them and their cargo, so they had willingly accepted the risks that went into the job. What bothered him was what would happen when the plane came down from 10,000 or 15.000 feet. It was the innocents on the ground that he hadn't been thinking about when he rigged his explosives. He could only hope that nothing happened. "Yeah. I'm gonna miss these guys."

When quitting time rolled around, Price was in a little better mood. The work party was waiting by the trucks while Price and Stanley made their walk through. The Moldovans had done quality work. The reinforced concrete of the bridge structure had been completely clad in hand laid stone work. Once the road dust and the weather had a chance to do it's work, the entire bridge would look like it had been there for a century, exactly what they had intended. They were inspecting the underside when another soldier ran up with a radio.

"The check point says there's a lot of traffic coming from up north." Price scrambled back up to the road and took the radio. He used his binoculars to see what was coming as he asked the checkpoint what they had.

"Looks like a convoy, Sarge. I've got about 10 or so trucks kicking up dust and heading this way!"

"Have the Moldovan stop them and see what's going on."

"Will do!"

Price walked back to his vehicle. The radio buzzed again. "Sarge, they just blew through here like they owned the road. I think they're Russian!"

He could see the dust cloud getting closer. The checkpoint had only been set up half a mile up the road. Thinking quickly, he yelled at the bus driver to back his vehicle up and block the bridge. "Then open the hood! Make it look like you broke down!"

Stanley had a concerned look on her face. "What are you planning?"

"I want to know what's in those trucks. I can't look if they're moving."

As the convoy approached, the lead vehicle leaned on his horn as he came up on the bridge. Price walked around the bus and spoke to the driver. The man was surprised when he heard this American address him in Russian, but he quickly recovered. "Get that piece of shit out of my way or I'll push it off!"

Price stepped up on the running board and just stared at the man. He and his assistant driver were both armed. He leaned back and looked down the line. It looked like an officer was getting out of the second vehicle and heading his way. He waved for Lieutenant Stanley to join him. "I'm about to cause an incident. You might want to take notes in case they complain to Perkins later."

Price gave the Russian Lieutenant a salute and asked him where he was headed. The Russian launched into a flurry of insults and demanded to be allowed to pass. Price just saluted again and smiled, then walked around the officer and looked into the back of the truck.

It was empty. There were more shouts, and the Russian drew his side arm. He heard Stanley call out a warning. It was bluff time.

Price put his hands up about shoulder height, palms out. He had a smirk on his face that made the Russian uncomfortable. "Don't worry about this shit head. If he shoots, have the fifties take out his convoy!"

The Russian reacted to that. He yelled a few more orders, then holstered his weapon. Price walked back up to him. "So you do speak English, you little fuck!" There was a pause, "Johnson!"

The soldier with the radio ran up. "Have the bus move far enough over to let these barbarians pass." The Russian looked like he was going to boil over, but he remained silent. Price smiled again. "So, you've got orders not to let anything stop you, and not to call any attention to yourself. Run along, little man. The big kids are done playing now."

The Russian spoke as he walked backwards to his truck. "I hope we meet again, Sergeant. I may not be so understanding."

"Looking forward to it, pal."

Stanley joined him as he watched the trucks roll by. "What's in the trucks?"

"They're empty."

"You almost started a war over empty trucks?"

"I was looking for his level of dedication. If he had nothing to hide, I hadn't expected him to shoot once he pulled his gun. He probably would have if he didn't understand English."

"What would that have proved?"

"Other than my incredible stupidity, which is probably because I'm so fucking tired, I think it means that these trucks are more important than the *comrade's* dignity." He looked at her and smiled. "And learning that, Lieutenant, was well worth taking the risk of getting shot at."

"You're certain the trucks were empty?" Morgan was pacing the room as Price described what had happened.

"I don't know about all of them, but the ones I could look into were. Think they're getting ready to haul out their trash?"

"They're planning to do something. First the plane goes down, then the Arabs get the boot. Now trucks. It all means something when you put it together, and it's probably that they're getting ready for a move". He stopped by the window and looked out. "But I don't think 10 empty trucks is what they're waiting for, unless we're giving them credit for having more chemical stuff than they really have."

Grant interrupted. "Let's back up a bit and think about what we have here." All eyes turned to him. Sharp was the first to ask, "How far back do you want to go?"

"Let's start with this whole project. How we ended up with it, we may never know, but the Russians briefed it. They wanted us here."

"Yeah," Price interjected. "They wanted us to build this road for them."

Grant shook his head. "Too simple. They've got an airstrip. They didn't need the road. Other than one plane going down, they still don't. It's probably lucky for us it crashed in Albania, or we'd be taking the heat for it."

Morgan was shaking his head. "It still doesn't add up. Why fly the stuff here? An Antonov could have easily made it into Mother Russia.

There was no need to stop here, on a dirt strip. Why not just take it all the way home?"

"Because they don't want it home!" All eyes turned to Price. "What do you mean?"

"Forget politics for a minute. Let's look at it from a smuggling point of view. You have a load of dope you want to sell, but you don't want to get caught with it. What do you do?" Everybody just looked at him. "You hide it. Or better still, you have somebody else hide it where nobody's looking, and let you know where it is."

"You mean like keeping it next door to a police station?" Sharp asked.

"Exactly. And we're the cops."

Morgan was starting to put it together. "And what better camouflage than having us park our asses right next to it. You'd expect them to want to keep us as far away from it as possible. But the bomb school?"

Grant stepped in again. "I'll bet if somebody started to dig, there's an agreement with some Arab country to train 'engineers'. If there was some kind of an accident, the rag heads could be blamed. Even better, once they got us here, we'd be guilty just because we are here."

"That being the case, " Morgan asked. "what's with the trucks? Another deception plan?"

"No. I think that would be giving them too much credit. Having us build the road was one thing. Running convoys up and down it while we're sitting next to it is a little ballsy, even for them. Something else must have happened, something we don't know about yet."

Price got up and went over to the window. "Then I think this would be as good a time as any to tell you."

"Tell us what?"

"I think I know what might have happened."

# CHAPTER 11

Major Morgan walked into the room with a serious look on his face. The Sergeant Major took off his glasses and put them down on the desk. Morgan had gone to try to contact Colonel Schaeffer in CENTCOM headquarters. Schaeffer was the intelligence chief. There had been too many developments in the past few days, most of which they couldn't pass up the chain through Perkins. Schaeffer was supposed to be out of the loop, but they needed information. It was always a trade off.

"What did the head shed have to say?"

Morgan dropped heavily into a folding chair. It started to roll over backwards, but he caught himself. After all four legs were back on the floor, he answered.

"Schaeffer had some info on the Russian air fleet. Looks like they grounded all of their AN-124s."

"Because of us?"

"Hard to say. They had two more go down in the last 24 hours. One up in Siberia, the other in the Ukraine. They're calling it a 'potential structural fault' in the tail, pending further investigation. He didn't have tail numbers. I don't know if the Kiev plane was ours."

"Schaeffer ask why you wanted to know?"

"I told him about the Arabs hopping a flight out last night. He didn't ask for any details, and I didn't offer any."

Grant picked up his glasses and put them in his pocket. "This is only going to help us."

"How?"

"Russians won't let anyone start digging around the crash site if the plane was loaded with Arabs and Semtex. They can't afford the explanations. They'll close it off and look at it themselves. It was a bad cargo mix. They'll have to assume the rag heads were playing with the shit. Otherwise, they have to point fingers at somebody, open it up to Ukrainian inspection. Somebody's going to wonder why they were hauling all that Semtex around."

"I hope you're right, Sergeant Major."

"Let it go. There are too many variables now to trace it back to us. Three planes in a few days is more than a coincidence."

Grant picked up his beret and headed towards the door. "I'm going to chow. You going to join me?"

"It'll have to be later. Perkins wants to talk to me about last nights training."

"His watch dogs suspect something?" Carstairs and Winder were supposed to keep an eye on the night firing course. They had ended up sleeping through it, thanks to a little extra added to their coffee.

"No. He put them on the spot for a report. Instead of keeping it simple, Winder decided to tell him how they kept everybody on their toes and made sure there was nobody fucking off. Perkins thought that was wonderful news, and decided to allow some more night training, as long as Winder and Carstairs go along. He's going to explain his new plan to me."

Grant walked down the street to the Mess Hall, his mind on everything but food. He glanced at the workers who were queuing up for the supper meal. It was a practice he didn't like, but the S-5, Lieutenant Sage, in an effort to win the hearts and minds of the locals, had convinced the Colonel to allow the contract labor to have little celebration in the mess hall before they left for the last time. The argument had gone back and forth about where to hold a party. Price had already sprung for a feast at one of the farms in the project zone. This was going to be the 'official' celebration, complete with a speech.

The workers were lined up by a field expedient wash rack, rinsing off. The sun had been intense today, with a lack of cloud cover. He noticed most of the workers had a fine coating of dust on them. Most of them were talking in their usual animated fashion, joking with one another. Grant passed them, then stopped and looked back. It had been reflexive, and he didn't know why he had done it. He didn't even concentrate on what he was looking at. He stared for a moment, then went into the building.

There was nothing particularly appetizing about the meal, and he filled his tray and sat at his usual table, against the wall so he could watch the entire room. It was an old habit, one he found especially hard to break. Sharp and Price left the group they were sitting with and came over to join him. There was the usual exchange of pleasantries, then the three fell into silence and ate their meals. Grant looked over to the door and watched the Moldovan workers come in. This was the third time he had looked at them, and still didn't know why. Price saw him looking and made an idle comment. "It sure got dusty out there today. The damn water truck broke down again. If we've got to do much more work, I'm going to have the Motor Pool transfer the bladders to one of our trucks. That fucking Russian relic ain't cutting it."

Dust! That was it! All the workers weren't dusty.

Grant stood and looked towards the door. His hand went to the pistol he carried on his hip under his blouse. One of the workers was moving away from the others, moving towards a group of GIs enjoying their supper.

"Down! Everybody on the floor!" He heard his voice call out. The hall went silent as heads turned to look at him. One soldier saw the pistol come out and called to his friends, "Oh fuck! The Sergeant Major's lost it!" Others saw the gun and sat frozen.

Grant was fixated on the worker who had moved away from the group. It was the lack of dirt and dust on this one that must have caught his attention earlier, it just hadn't registered. He kept moving towards the group of GIs. Everyone was watching Grant. No one was paying attention to the lone worker. His eyes were shifting around, and then he saw Grant and the outstretched pistol. He was holding a cell phone to his ear, his other hand started to move to the front of his shirt.

Grant saw the movement and yelled at him, "Hands! Show me your hands!" The Moldovan looked blankly at him, his hands hesitating. Grant repeated the command, this time gesturing with his left hand, showing the Moldovan what he wanted.

The worker understood, and began to walk faster. His hands went to the center of his shirt.

Grant saw the movement. "Fuck me!" was all he said as he squeezed the first shot off. The bullet slammed into the bridge of the workers nose, throwing his head back. Grant brought the sights backed down, and they line up on the now wide-open mouth as the Moldovan fell backwards. He fired again, the bullet entering the roof of the mouth. The Moldovan went down, his arms now flung wide. There was a crash of trays, chairs and tables as the room finally came alive, soldiers diving for the floor to get out of the line of fire.

All except Price and Sharp. As soon as Grant's gun came out they were up and drawing theirs, moving to each side of him. They didn't know why at first, but they knew they had to give him backup. As soon as they saw the Moldovan worker, they understood, and swung around to cover the other workers.

Grant was standing over the dead man, his pistol still aimed at his face. He started giving commands. "Get everybody outside! Secure the workers and start searching them!"

Perkins had heard the shooting in the headquarters building and had run over to the source with Morgan and Carstairs in tow. Troops were moving out as ordered, and Price and Sharp had the workers in a group, putting them on their knees with their hands on their heads. They were the first Perkins spoke to.

"What the hell is going on here?"

"Don't know yet, Colonel," Sharp answered. "The CSM has one down on the floor in there."

Perkins entered the building and went to where Grant was bending over the body. He had opened the shirt, and Perkins could see the wires and the black plastic pouches. There was a cell phone connected to the array. The man had been a suicide bomber, intent on killing as many Americans as he could.

"How'd you know, Sergeant Major?"

"The dust."

Perkins looked down. This one seemed to be as dirty as the rest, and he said so.

"Yeah, they're all dirty. But everybody else was covered in that red dust. This one just rubbed in dirt to look like he was working all day He hadn't planned on the water truck breaking down."

"How did he get in?"

Grant was distracted by a ringing. He looked around, and spotted the phone the bomber had been carrying. Someone was trying to reach him. The ringing stopped. Grant turned to look at the body. Perkins and Carstairs were kneeling over it. He could hear Morgan giving them a warning. "I wouldn't be touching that, Colonel." Perkins was tugging on the cell phone. He started to shout at them to get back, just as the phone in Perkins hand started to ring. Grant dived to the floor away from the body. The blast was less than he had expected, but he still felt himself slammed against a pillar. He could feel something digging into his shoulder.

He lay face down for a minute, mentally taking inventory of his body. There must have been a couple of kilos of Semtex in the vest. He was surprised he was still conscious, and even more surprised he wasn't in worse pain. Shock? He tried to kneel up, and found that other than a pain in his left shoulder, everything seemed to be working fine. The dust was settling. He could see the bomber. He had been cut in half by the blast, but not splattered. The charge must have misfired. Perkins and Carstairs lay on their backs on either side of him. What had gone off must have caught them full in the faces. Morgan was beyond them, picking himself up. He must have jumped back as the phone started to ring. There was a medic kneeling over him. Then Grant felt an arm on his shoulder, telling him to lay back down.

"I'm fine." He waved towards the other bodies. "Check on them."

The medic did as she was told, but it appeared to Grant that Perkins and Carstairs were dead.

Sharp was at the bombers body, examining what was left of the vest. Grant joined him. "Who's got the rest of the workers?"

"Price is with them. I figured he speaks the language, he can get something out of them." Sharp gingerly disconnected what was left of the firing circuit and put it aside on a table. "It looks like somebody decided to rig this for both command and remote detonation." He held up the remains of a phone and a push button, still wired together. "Then they added something with ball bearings to the front of the vest, most likely for a bigger shrapnel effect." He gestured towards the two American bodies. "That's what must have gotten them." He turned back to the bomber. "All he managed to do was fuck up his firing circuits. The only thing that went off was the supplemental he put on the front. Fucking amateurs."

Grant put his hand on Sharps shoulder to steady himself as he stood up. The pain in his shoulder wasn't bad, but he knew it would be if they had to go digging out some ball bearings.

"You better thank God for amateurs, Dave. Can you imagine what this place would look like if he had been a pro?" He walked over to where Price had the workers on their knees. Armed Moldovan soldiers were starting to appear.

"Any of these guys know anything?"

"No, but there's one missing. They tell me he introduced that one," he pointed to the bomber, "as his nephew, and said he was sneaking him in for a free meal. The rest of them didn't think anything of it."

"Where is he now?"

"I don't know, but I'll check. I'll bet the guy couldn't have gotten very far."

Senior Sergeant Kosavich was on the scene. His guards had seen one of the workers running away just as the bomb went off. They had shot him when he refused to halt. That source of information was gone.

Grant was having his back worked on while he spoke to the Moldovan NCO. "Yevigny, you said something bad had happened. Did you know about this?"

The old soldier shook his head. "This is not what I spoke of. We had learned that one of my soldiers, a Muslim, had been following you. One of his bunkmates heard him speaking about it."

"Speaking? With who?"

"I don't know. He had a cell phone, which is why his bunkmate was suspicious. None of my soldiers can afford such a thing."

Grant winced as Elko probed for another ball. "Why had he been following me?"

"We turned him over to our intelligence service. He was very disrespectful when our officers questioned him. The others used different methods. All I was told was that he had orders to locate your quarters and plant a device. My commander would tell me no more."

"Why didn't you tell me?"

"I was ordered not to. My commander told me your colonel was getting a full briefing, and it would be up to him to inform you. It pained me to follow that order."

Major Carson came up behind them and examined Grants wounds. She gave Elko a few quick instructions, then addressed Grant. "You got lucky, Sergeant Major. Sergeant Elko has you cleaned up. I'll have her give you a tetanus booster and some antibiotics and wrap you up. Give that shoulder a break for a few days."

"The Colonel?"

"He looks like he caught the main blast in his chest and under his chin. His head was just about torn off. He was lucky. He was dead before he hit the floor. Carstairs should have been so lucky. He took a little longer. Not much, but I think he was aware that he was going."

"How's Major Morgan?"

"He's almost as lucky as you. He caught a bunch of junk in his legs, plural. He'll be limping for a bit. The Moldovans are sending an ambulance for Perkins and Carstairs. I'll get another one for you and him."

Grant shook his head. "Maybe him, but I'm not going. I got hit worse in Sudan."

Morgan came limping over to where they were talking. Kosavich excused himself. "I must make my report. I hope we can speak later. Perhaps there is something we can do to make this right."

Grant put out his hand. Kosavich took it and smiled. "We'll talk, Yevigny," Grant said. "I may want to borrow some of your equipment."

Morgan winced as he leaned against a table, then slid down to sit on the bench. "What kind of equipment?"

"I'll tell you later. How's the legs? The Major tells me you're getting sent to the local hospital."

Morgan looked at Carson. "Over my dead body. That would leave either Fisher or Menklin in charge." Fisher was the Assistant S-3. Menklin was the S-2. Morgan had little faith in either one. "Neither one of them has a clue about what's about to happen. Doc, I don't care what it takes. I need to stay."

Carson closed up her aid bag and shrugged. "You macho guys are all alike. You've got some deep shrapnel that needs to come out. You need a surgeon and a hospital for that. Can't you brief them and be done with it?"

"I'd rather tell you, but you won't be in charge. I just need a few days. Shoot me up with some antibiotics and I'll hope for the best."

"I don't suppose you want any pain killers?"

"If I can walk, I don't need them."

Carson shook her head and walked away. When she was out of earshot, Grant pulled some documents out of his pocket and passed them to Morgan. He looked them over and passed them back. "From the gomer?"

"Yeah. Sharp went through his pockets before the local cavalry arrived. We've got that and the other cell phone. If we had any intelligence assets we could recover the memory from it and see who was trying to call him, but from the papers, he's from the same neighborhood as the two we killed the other day."

"You sure?"

"The addresses are only a couple of doors apart. Looks like they went to the same mosque, too."

"What can we do about it?"

"Right now, Kosavich is feeling pretty bad about what happened. He caught one of his soldiers working with the bad guys. He was supposed to take me out."

Morgan just looked at him. "And you're only finding out now?"

"There was more to it. Supposedly, Perkins got the word on it and was supposed to tell me the night the plane crashed in Albania. Somehow, it must have slipped his mind."

"Can you use that to leverage Kosavich?"

"When some of the dust settles I'm hoping he feels bad enough to give us a guided tour of the Muslim quarter of Kipercheny."

"And then?"

"And then I hope I can convince him to get a cup of coffee around the corner."

Morgan nodded. "And what was the equipment you were talking about?"

Grant gave him a run down on what he had seen in the warehouse. "All German, and all clean. From what I understand, Kosavich is the only one who pays any attention to it, and he's the only guy who's ever done an inventory."

Morgan let that sink in for a while. The Moldovan Military Police had arrived. One of them, a short, rat faced looking fellow, was shouting at the civilian laborers and trying to slap them around. Price wasn't having any of that, and pulled the little guy back and sat him down, giving him an ass chewing in Moldovan that stunned him into silence. His fellow MPs, obviously used to his tactics, but not very fond of them, stood back and grinned as they listened to Price explain the little fellows genealogy, going back to the first rat in the garden of Eden copulating with the snake. It was impressive. Senior Sergeant Kosavich returned as he was wrapping up. The little MP started to protest, but Kosavich cut him off and launched into his own tirade. This time it was accompanied by a few slaps to the side of the head. Everyone looking could tell this guy had been warned about his heavy-handed approach before. It wasn't going to be tolerated any more.

Grant watched it with Morgan. A Moldovan officer joined Kosavich. Grant hadn't seen him before, and Morgan identified him as the local commander. The two men had a brief conversation, with a lot of gesturing. Kosavich pointed at Grant a couple of times, before the commander walked away. He apparently was asking American officers who was senior now. Most of the Captains and Lieutenants weren't sure, so they pointed out both Major Carson and Major Morgan. The commander, from the looks of his shoulder boards was at least a full Colonel, asked one of the junior officers to fetch Morgan. And the term he used had been 'fetch', as the Lieutenant who delivered the message told him.

"That's fucking great," Morgan said to Grant as he prepared to limp off. "The bastard knows he outranks me, so I'm the one who has to hobble over!"

"You should have taken the stretcher when it was offered."

"So you could watch Menklin or Fisher fall all over themselves for this guy? Not fucking likely this time around, Sergeant Major!"


Grant and Kosavich were sitting in a beat up Trabant parked a block away from the Kipercheny mosque. It had one of those glorious Arabic names, celebrating some dead guy or other, but it was still just a street front shit hole on a back street. Back in the US, this neighborhood would give urban blight a bad name.

Kosavich had been driving. He originally wanted Grant to sit in the back and try to stay out of sight, but ten minutes on the road in a space smaller than a VW bug had Grant cramped up and screaming to get out. The front seat wasn't much better, but at least the seat could be pushed back. There was no legroom, but it didn't feel like a tourniquet was twisted around his legs. A baseball cap advertising some Japanese copy place was pulled low over his face. It wasn't much of a disguise, but there weren't that many people in the neighborhood who could identify him. The one that could was the object of their attention.

Kosavich's colonel had been apologetic to Morgan. Correct, insufferable, overbearing and a few other egalitarian terms, but apologetic none the less. Morgan arranged an information swap with him in exchange for assistance in taking down Ali Alawa Sharif. There had been no negotiation, no hemming and hawing, no put offs until higher headquarters could be consulted. Morgan said he wanted help killing Sharif. In exchange, he would provide information about Russian chemical weapons in the Moldovans back yard. The colonel didn't bat an eye. He agreed. Morgan was suspicious, but laid out what he knew. He held nothing back, and it was a good thing. The Moldovans had a pretty good idea about the Russian stockpile. Morgan filled in a few gray areas for him, but not many. What had come as a big surprise was the fact that the Russians had grounded their transport fleet. This was a concern. As long as the chemical weapons had been flown in and out, with minimal exposure to the populace, the Moldovans were willing to turn a blind eye. They were not, however, about to allow road convoys to risk contamination of hundreds of square miles.

Colonel Ivanov was a pragmatic man. Initially the Russians had offered to use their influence with the European Union to get the road upgraded. It was now obvious that the Russians had two things in mind. The first was undoubtedly having an alternate route to evacuate their weapons. The second, and most sinister, was to have a scapegoat in place in case there was an accident. Ivanov disliked his country being used like this, but he still recognized the value of having someone else to blame if things went awry. Killing the Arab would send a message to other potential radicals in the country, but if the Americans did it and botched the job, no mud would splash on the Moldovan government.

The Americans could be ordered out of the country as bandits. And if the operation worked, there was no need to even mention the American participation. It was the best of both worlds.

Kosavich pointed out a small coffee shop several doors down. He suggested they go there as part of their cover. "We are strangers in this part of town, and we've already been noticed. If we are even more casual, they may not give us any thought." Grant agreed. Every one of those sappy detective movies had the hero staking out a suspect by parking in front of the house for days on end, as if no one would notice somebody living out of their car. He would also welcome the opportunity to stretch his legs. He knew it was a risk, but he was willing to take it.

The shop was open to the street, and surprisingly clean. Kosavich took a table halfway back, and both men sat with their backs to the wall. Kosavich carried on a running conversation in Moldovan with Grant, pausing every so often to give a little sign that Grant should respond with a grunt, a shrug, or a laugh. If they were being watched it wouldn't fool anyone, but the casual observer might buy it. By their second coffee the shop had thinned out, and Kosavich could address Grant in English. "There is a man who is out of place here." He pointed towards a man who was sitting on a stoop across from them. He was watching for someone, and he was agitated. "He is a Russian. He doesn't belong in this neighborhood."

"If he's Russian intelligence, he's not very good. He stands out worse than I do," Grant opined.

"He's probably an intermediary. He's waiting for someone who is late. Could he be waiting for the same one you are?"

Grant gave him another once over before he answered. "Let's hope so. Two men are easier to follow."

They were about to order a third drink when the Russian suddenly stood up and walked a few feet to his left to meet someone. The newcomer was agitated at being accosted in the street. A brief argument ensued, but Kosavich couldn't hear enough of it to make any sense. Grant waited for the newcomer to turn his head to get a better look at him. The man glanced his way. Grant put his head down, but there was no need to. The street was in bright sunlight, and the shop was dark. But he did see the face clearly. It was Sharif. Kosavich saw the recognition in his face. "So that is our prey." He saw Grant moving his shirttail to clear the butt of his weapon. Kosavich put his hand out to stop him. "That would be a bad idea out on the crowded street."

"I don't want to lose him!"

"And we won't, but haste would be foolish." He made a small gesture. "The left, a brown building.." Grant looked that way. "Second floor, corner window." Grant could make out a figure just inside. There was the curve of an AK magazine visible. Kosavich spoke again. "To the right, hanging back in the alley."

"I don't see anything." Grant strained to look without being obvious.

"What you are looking at is the man sitting behind the boxes."

Grant could see him now. "Our quarry, or someone in the neighborhood, sees it necessary to post guards. Let us not make his preparedness pay off for him. We can be patient."

He made a vague gesture, then returned to his drink. Grant looked out and could see two men approaching from opposite angles. They followed Sharif as he pulled his contact with him into the apartment house.

"Those are my men. Very good, and very trustworthy. The short one is the one who identified the man who had been following you. He is also my nephew. "

"Now what?"

"Now we wait. Come. Leave some money for the shop keeper." He watched Grant peel off a few bills. "No, no, my friend. You leave that much and they will be speaking of us for weeks." He picked up a bill and handed it back to Grant. "That's enough. The shopkeeper will be grateful, but not enough to advertise our patronage. He will be willing to allow us to sit here again, untroubled, if we should have a need to return."

They walked for several blocks. The buildings were in better condition here, and there were no Arabic signs. They had left the Arab quarter. There was a car horn behind them. Grant looked, and it was the Trabant, driven by one of Kosavich's men. The man got out and started to speak, but Kosavich cut him off. He sent him back to another Trabant, then motioned Grant to get in.

"He wanted me to debrief him here. I had a better thought. We will go to a safer place, and you will be able to question him." They drove to a gas station that had several service bays on the side. One bay was large enough for both Trabants to park in. Kosavich had one of his men close the doors, then he led the group to a small room off to one side. He switched on a radio and offered Grant a beer from a small refrigerator.

Grant looked around. The Moldovans were casual, but still alert. Outside, the mechanics continued to work, but other men had also appeared. They had taken up what only could be considered overwatch positions. Grant addressed his counterpart. "Very nice. Your men?" Kosavich nodded. Grant went on, "Soldiers or secret police?"

Kosavich laughed. "You Americans toss out that term like it leaves a bad taste in your mouth. You shouldn't be so judgmental. Your country has just as many 'secret policemen' as any other nation. You just give them different names and glamorize them on you television."

"You didn't answer my question."

"I didn't see a need to. Who they are is unimportant, but if it makes you feel better, they are soldiers, more of my men."

Grant didn't understand one word of what followed. The two men Kosavich had follow Sharif began drawing diagrams and alternated in their descriptions. Grant recognized the street they were on, and the positions of observers Kosavich had pointed out. They also indicated others that hadn't been so obvious. Kosavich asked questions, and got his answers, accompanied by more sketching. Now and again, one of the briefers would make a rapping motion on the chart, then smile at Grant as if he could understand him. Grant forced a grin in response, then leaned into the chart. Without understanding what they were saying, he could follow the course of events.

When the briefing was done the men took seats on the side of the room. Grant figured they were hanging around to answer any questions he might have. Kosavich began' "This is very interesting."

"Who are you?"

Kosavich just smiled. "I'm just like you. A senior sergeant in my army who is trying to do his job to protect his country and his soldiers." He waved to the men around them. "And these are my soldiers. Maybe not as experienced as yours, but well trained, dedicated to their cause, and, just as important, like yours they are very loyal."

"And all this?"

"I am a soldier. The rest of my brothers had their own lives to live. In hard times, I was able to support them. Now that they are successful, they share it with me."

The briefing was detailed, but Grant had the feeling he was missing something. Although there seemed to be a lot of security on the street, Kosavich was dismissive of it. "They are armed, and they are watching, but they don't know what they are looking for. That is one of their two major mistakes."

"What's the other one?"

Kosavich got closer to the chart. He tapped each sentry in turn, and pointed out that his or her entire focus was the front of the building. "One block down, and they could care less what is happening. And they have no one in back."

"How is that?"

"They are thinking like what they are. Students and unemployed laborers, amateurs playing at Jihad. They don't understand the stakes yet. They think the two men you killed on the road died by accident."

"You know about that?"

He smiled. "My men are good watchers, too. After you left the scene, they made certain the car was well burnt."

Grant let that pass. The Moldovans obviously knew more about the situation than they were letting on. He did have questions about how involved they were willing to get. He decided the best approach would be to just ask. Kosavich was delighted. "This is so much better that all that diplomatic talk. You come right to the point. "

He drained his beer and opened a fresh one, offering another to Grant. When they were both seated, Kosavich explained his position. "Except for the Russian and the Arab, these are my countrymen. Misguided as they may be, they are my problem. I cannot allow you to take any action against them. The Russian and the Arab, on the other hand, I give to you. Will they go to your Guantanamo camp?"

Grant shook his head. "No camp, no interrogation."

Kosavich just looked at him. Grant continued. "The Arab is a killer, pure and simple. He enjoys it. In Sudan, an entire refugee camp was gassed just so he could make a point. I'll kill him here. The Russian? I don't know his history, but he's playing with the big boys now, with big boy rules. He's dead too."

"What if I told you the French are interested in having him? My government has been considering it. That's why we've been watching him."

"I don't care about the French. They'd just fuck it up. When we're done, you can let them have his body."

Kosavich considered this for a while, sipping his beer. "I agree. The French would just try to use him for their own purposes. Then people like us would be experiencing this exercise again. His death will serve the greater good. I suggest we return to camp and make plans."

Dillinghouse looked at the copies of the E-mails his chief of staff had gotten from Winder. "Has any of this been reported yet?"

The chief of staff shook his head. "Not yet. They seem to be keeping this pretty quiet, but I'm certain the soldiers have probably contacted their families. They can't stop that."

"My God!" Dillinghouse had no love for these soldiers, they had caused him considerable embarrassment, but a suicide bomber in their mess hall? This was definitely a hard luck unit. "How long does the Army think they can keep this quiet? They're a National Guard unit, for God's sake! Those families keep pretty close track of their people." A thought occurred to Dillinghouse. "We can use this. Get me someone in the Pentagon. Anyone, as long as he is high up. These soldiers just became our pet project!"


"This fucking guy wants us to do what?"

Sharp was explaining to Price what had just come into the Operations Section and been passed on to Morgan. "Dillinghouse wants the Army to bring us home, right now. To quote him, we're 'a gallant band of brothers who have been thrown out as bait around the world, a magnet, unprotected, for any radical who hates America' and has a gun or a couple of spare pounds of dynamite."

"This is the guy who keeps trying to get us killed!"

"He's a politician, and people have short memories between elections."

Price was enraged. "We should have left that son of a bitch in Africa. He's a thief, and probably a traitor. I can't believe he weaseled his way out of going to jail. Wait'll Luke hears about this. When's he due back?"

Sharp shook his head. "I don't know. He went out with his Moldovan buddy in another one of those little Trabants."

"I still don't think we should have let him go on his own. One of us should be backing him up."

"Pricey, I tried. You know how he gets when he's pissed, and he is pissed, but I don't think Kosavich will let him do anything stupid."

"I don't think Kosavich will be able to stop him." He grabbed his hydration pack and headed for the door. "I gotta go. Morgan wants us to recover any equipment we don't need on the job site. We're almost done out there, and he's getting nervous about security. We're using too many of the locals and we already know one of them was dirty. He doesn't want any more surprises."

"I gotta go too. The Russians rolled in another bunch of trucks overnight. The Moldovans are planning on blocking the road out so they can't haul any of that chemical shit anywhere. They briefed Morgan about it, but they want us to butt out for now. That Ivanov guy says it's an internal matter, and they'll handle it their way," Sharp said.

Morgan had been on the phone with NATO for over an hour. They were on the verge of ordering the 289th out when word came down that they were being transferred back to Centcom control. This had caused a stir in the European Union. The anti-American elements were pushing for a quick removal of US troops from Moldova and introduction of EU observers. Russian elements were also pushing for an American withdrawal, but for different reasons. They had managed to embarrass the Americans in an unknown part of the world in a way they hadn't thought possible. It was a part of their plan that had worked very well.

It was developing into a classic cluster fuck, and he was happy when the connection was broken. Two things had become perfectly clear to him: first, nobody wanted him to do anything, and second, he wasn't going to get any support, no matter what happened. They were out at the end of that long limb again, and the beavers were hungry.

Before he could get very far from his desk, he was called to the phone again. This time it was Ramirez. "Didn't I ask you not to fuck up that part of the world?"

"I'm sorry, General. We were having a slow day."

"OK, smart ass. I've got Schaeffer here. I'm going to put you on speakerphone. Tell me everything."

Forty-five minutes later, Morgan had no better idea of where he stood than before, only now he was going to have a bunch of people looking over his shoulder while he did whatever he was going to. Ramirez promised that a plane would be in the next day to recover the bodies of Perkins and Carstairs, an intelligence team, and God help us all, some civilians who though they were entitled to 'oversight' of the situation.

He also had an additional assignment. He was to secure the airfield and deny its use to any other aircraft. Morgan could see this entire situation deteriorating in a hurry. It was time to recover all his assets and get them behind the wire. It wouldn't do to have a crew out on the road where they couldn't be supported if the Russians decided they wanted their chemicals and the airfield. He called his S-3, Captain Fisher, who was also acting as XO. "Fisher, shut down all your operations. I want every man, woman and piece of equipment back here before nightfall."

"Are we leaving?"

" I don't know yet, but get the staff together. We've got a lot to get ready for."

"That's not much of a plan, Luke. What if your buddy decides he'd rather keep the Frenchies happy?" Sharp was concerned the plan relied to heavily of Moldovan cooperation. "Every time we count on somebody else, we usually get left waiting at the altar."

"I know." Grant wasn't happy with the plan either, but Kosavich had him in a corner. "But as long as we have to rely on Kosavich's men to cover our move through the neighborhood, we're stuck with it. This isn't Darfur. We can't go in and shoot up the town."

Kosavich's plan was simple. His men would provide security out on the street. He had enough soldiers he could put in place to neutralize the "neighborhood watch" he had located. His idea of neutralizing was different from Grant's, but it was his country. They would be put out of commission 'temporarily' and released after they were advised of the error of their ways. While that was going on outside, his men would seal off the apartment house, and Grant would be given the 'honor' of taking down Sharif, his Russian and anyone else who happened to be with them. That was Kosavich's only exception to the 'no harming the locals' rule. Anyone that close to the Arab was probably too far-gone to rehabilitate into a productive Moldovan citizen.

"Why can't we go tonight?"

"Kosavich claims logistics problems. I think it's more likely he has to clear everything through his people first. He guaranteed me that he can keep Sharif under observation even if he tries to run."

Grant planned for his end to be as small as possible. He would enter with Sharp, and two soldiers as hallway security to isolate the floor. Price would stay on the street, with one man, while Harrison would take the back, also with one man, just in case Sharif got out of the building. From somewhere, Kosavich had gotten an old delivery truck, big enough to hold a half dozen more troops. This would be the reaction force, just in case the whole op went to shit in a hurry. There would be a medic with them, to handle any unexpected casualties. The medic had been added at Price's request. They had all been in situations where there was never a medic when you needed one. Having one along was almost a good luck charm to them now.

"How about the air strip?" Grant had been out of the loop when the plans were made to secure it. Price or Sharp had been the logical choice for NCOIC of that detail, but both had other plans. There were other NCOs who could fill the slot, and they could have close to 50 soldiers for the task. Kosavich would also provide a detail to cover it, in conjunction with the embargo that had been placed on convoy movement out of the Russian base. The Russians seemed content to let the Moldovans pen them in. There was something about the casual way they accepted the situation that made Grant uneasy.

Morgan wasn't satisfied with the plan either, but, as the new commander, he was up to his ass in details over the arrival of the plane in the morning. CENTCOM was being very tight lipped about how big the party would be, how long they would stay, or what their orders would be. He decided that his only rational alternative was to trust his Sergeant Major. The four NCOs running the show had over a century of experience between them. If they didn't know what they were doing, there was probably very little Morgan could do to improve on it.

The plane came in right on time. It looked to be the same C-27J that had brought Ramirez in, but it probably wasn't. Price watched it taxi to a stop and made a rude comment under his breath. Morgan, sitting next to him, looked at him with a quizzical look. "Sergeant Price, are you blaspheming our guests before you even see them?"

Price hawked up some phlegm and spit it out. "No, Sir. I'll have something worse to say when I see them. I was just commenting on the fact that these fuckers can fly that bird all over hell and gone, and we have to wait for a fucking train to bring our supplies in. It makes you wonder where you stand. The tourists get better service than the shooters."

"And the shot at," Morgan replied, shifting his still throbbing legs to try to ease the pain. Major Carson had been right. The deep shrapnel was painful as hell, and refusing to take any of the really good painkillers wasn't helping.

The ramp dropped and the crew chief hopped off. Price could see he was the same guy as the last time when he turned and waved. Price returned the gesture and trotted over to help him with the ramp extensions. They had folded the second one out before Price glanced into the belly of the plane.

"Son of a bitch!" was all he could say as he saw Dillinghouse standing there. Morgan hobbled over and joined him at the foot of the ramp. Price made a show of pointing at Dillinghouse and explaining to Morgan that this was the guy who had the diamonds. Dillinghouse heard the last of it, and walked up to Price. "I've been cleared of that,

Sergeant. You better watch your mouth before you start slandering a Member of Congress."

Price just leaned in close to the crooked congressman's ear. He smiled as he said, "Fuck you. I still have a couple of copies of that DVD. I ain't never going away."

Dillinghouse just gave him a scowl, then turned to Morgan. He pointed over his shoulder at a drawn up honor guard. "Is that for me?" Price turned away, laughing. Morgan ignored him. "No, Mr. Dillinghouse, that's for our casualties."

Dillinghouse turned to Colonel Schaeffer, who was coming down the ramp behind him. "I though I was clear about not having my plane turned into flying hospital! I will not be flying anywhere with those on board!"

Schaeffer just shrugged. "Suit yourself. The plane is leaving as soon as they're on board. You'll have to wait until it comes back in a day or two."

"We'll see about that. Get me to a secure phone!"

His aide looked around and saw a Hummer sitting off to the side. He recognized Winder leaning against it. He touched the congressman's elbow and directed him to it. "We can take that vehicle over there, Sir." Price looked over to where Winder was standing, a big grin on his face. "Birds of a feather," was all he said.

They exchanged introductions with Winder. Price was surprised to see Winder render a salute. They all got into the Hummer and drove off. Morgan saluted Schaeffer and looked up into the cargo bay. "I thought you were bringing a camera crew?"

Schaeffer laughed. "Yeah, so did Dillinghouse. Too bad they didn't make it in time. They were traveling with that asshole, but they got held up in customs at Ramstein."

"No problem," Price said. "I've got my own guy video taping all of this." He tapped his chest. "I'm wearing the remote mike. That fucker's dirty, and I'm going to get him. Him taking off instead of rendering honors will be a nice lead in. So will his comment to you."

"Sergeant Price, you're going to push that a little too far one of these days, and it's going to fry your ass."

"Maybe so, Colonel, as long as he's close enough to get burned too."

Morgan cut off the discussion and signaled to the honor guard. Lieutenant Stanley marched them up smartly to either side of the ramp. Two Moldovan ambulances, each with another honor guard, backed up to the ramp. The Moldovans took their positions with the Americans as the casket parties removed the flag draped coffins and carried them on board. As soon as they had disappeared inside, Stanley gave a series of commands and marched both groups off. Price again assisted the crew chief with the ramp extensions. The pilot came back and spoke to Schaeffer. After a brief conversation that neither Price nor Morgan could hear, they exchanged salutes and the pilot walked forward. The crew chief whipped off a Hollywood salute to the group on the ground as the ramp closed. As quickly as the plane had come in, it was gone again.

On the ride back to the base Schaeffer asked what was going on with Dillinghouse. "His boy seemed to know that Sergeant. Isn't he the one we had a problem with?"

Morgan told him not to worry about it. "He's been e-mailing information to Dillinghouse almost since you left. They've been carrying on quite a correspondence."

"And you aren't worried about that?"

"Hell, no." Price was trying to stifle his laughter, without much success. Morgan tried to maintain control, but he started laughing too. The driver even joined in, to the point where he had to stop the vehicle before he could regain self-control.

Schaeffer looked at all of them, and started to loose his temper. "Somebody want to tell me what the hell is going on?"

Morgan finally caught himself and was able to respond. "We've been reluctantly feeding Winder a load of bullshit, and he's been buying every word. We tell him just enough so he has to make an assumption, and the boy has always been wrong."

"How do you know he's been passing it on to Dillinghouse?"

"Sergeant Devers here, our faithful driver," Devers gave them a little smile, "as well as being a fine construction supervisor, is also an excellent web master and software engineer. We get a copy of everything Winder does, in real time, as well as anything Dillinghouse sends to him."

"Isn't that illegal?"

Price added his comment. "Yeah, and all the rest of the stuff we're doing is above board."

Schaeffer ignored him. Morgan filled in the blanks. "He's using a military server, so there's no problem with the monitoring. And Dillinghouse asking for information helps us know what to feed him.

If you want a legal definition, Winder is practicing espionage, and we're countering it."

"Can you prove it?"

Morgan nodded to Devers, who answered. "If we can't prove that, there's always the other stuff."

"What other stuff?"

"Master Sergeant Winder, or 'Sidewinder' as he likes to call himself on-line, has a serious problem with kiddy porn. He likes to download it onto his government owned laptop. That's almost as bad as the espionage. We own him. We even own his second mortgage."

Schaeffer wasn't convinced. "So what is Dillinghouse going to be doing here?"

"Hopefully, he's going to be out about a mile behind the Russian compound. There are some abandoned bunkers from the war back there. We suspect that's where the Russians have been stashing their looted Nazi gold."

"Really?"

"Well, it sounded good when we let it slip to Winder."


"You want to go to the commo section for a phone, Congressman?"

"Fuck the phone, Sergeant. Let's go!"

Dillinghouse's aide was more soft spoken. "Maybe we should wait here for a bit. It looks like the ambulances will be loading the wounded. It might make a nice photo op if you shook a few hands."

The congressman ignored him. "Are you certain about your information, Winder? This seems a little too simple to be true." Dillinghouse's aide was just as skeptical about the story of the find in abandoned bunkers behind the Russian compound as his boss was, but he felt they should be at least trying to put on a good face. Dillinghouse was too impatient. Just in case it was a wild goose chase he had already left an 'alibi' letter back in his office. If this turned out to be another set-up by the FBI, he had explained his true intent to recover any funds and return them to their rightful owners. He had Winder's e-mails to make it look like he suspected the Army was trying to cover up the gold. It still seemed far-fetched. The story had seemed too implausible to him at first. If there hadn't been the issue of the suicide bomber killing two American officers in this backwater little piece of nowhere, he wouldn't have bothered to come. There were too many ways he could deliver his revenge on the soldiers that had jeopardized his political career without inconveniencing himself like this.

Winder was adamant. "If they had come out and told me about this I would have been skeptical myself. But they seemed to be going to a lot of trouble to keep this bit of information from me. They were going as far as to photo-shop the satellite photos to hide this piece of terrain. I only found it when I happened to be comparing it to some old images they had forgotten about. I'm telling, you, Congressman, they plan to keep this stuff for themselves and get it back to the States. Look what they did with that B-17!"

Dillinghouse remembered that plane. It looked like a pile of junk. By the time he found out what all that 'junk' was actually worth, some Sergeant's wife had hired a lawyer and got the Air Force to give it to her for pennies on the pound in shipping costs. By then he was too wrapped up in his own legal problems to try to dispute her claim through one of his shell companies. He wasn't going to be kept out of this windfall.

His plan was simple, and it was already underway. Winder would take him on a quick inspection tour of the Russian compound, at a safe distance, of course, and then they would get conveniently lost on the return trip. Between Winder and his aide, blame would be easy to place. Stumbling across old bunkers would just be one of those serendipitous events, and an innocent desire to explore a piece of history shouldn't raise any suspicions. A quick check, a few samples, and he could make other arrangements to recover the loot. There had to be crooked politicians here. They would be easy to approach and convince that the gold could be easily shared. And if the samples were found, well, they would be in his aides baggage, not his. Even that could serve two purposes. Catch the aide with his hand in the cookie jar, and it would be easy to deflect blame on him for the Sudanese diamonds too. There wasn't a down side to this little adventure.

A sudden buzzing caught his attention. He looked out the window, searching for the sound. In the distance he could see a speck rising from the ground. As it came closer and grew larger, he could see it was the Air Force transport he had just gotten off.

"Son of a bitch!" he cried. "Those bastards weren't supposed to go anywhere without me!"

Winder pulled the Hummer over, not knowing whether he should continue or turn back. Dillinghouse looked at him, a blank expression on his face. Winder's was equally blank. "What do you want me to do, Sir?"

"Idiot! Is there anybody in this fucking military that knows how to follow an order?" He looked at his aide, then back at Winder. "Just drive! We're out here now. We might as well see if you fucked this story up too!" Winder put the vehicle back on the road and drove on. He noticed that neither Dillinghouse nor his aide as much as glanced at the compound as they drove past. Winder noted the Moldovan roadblocks, as well as the picket line that had been thrown around the perimeter. Everybody seemed to be just standing around, even the Russians, just waiting to see what would happen next. He glanced down at the map he had marked up with the location of the bunkers. It had been easy to transcribe the location to a map from the photos. He suddenly realized that he hadn't brought a compass or a GPS set with him. He found himself wishing he had taken part in some of the remedial land navigation courses that Sharp and Price had been giving over the past few months. It was a sad thing to have to admit, but Winder now had to face up to it: once he got off the road, he had a tendency to get lost. That's why he usually relied on a driver. His plan to take a roundabout route to the bunkers suddenly changed. There was a trail marked on the map leading out from the rear of the Russian compound. He decided to take that. If he traveled in a straight line, cross-country, he couldn't help but find it. He would just drive a little further on before he turned off road, far enough to miss the security cordon.

"This is it?" Dillinghouse was beside the vehicle, kicking dirt and looking around. "There's nothing here! No bunkers, no tracks, nothing!"

Winder didn't know what to do. This was the place. He had hit the trail, just like the map said he would, then followed the trail here.

This depression, it looked like an old gravel pit, was exactly what was marked on the map, and exactly what the photos had shown. He picked them up and walked around the Hummer, looking at the rising dirt banks. It was starting to dawn on him. Those bastards! They had been baiting him with this phony gold story to keep him from finding out what they were really doing. Then he caught himself. Could they have found out he was passing information to Dillinghouse? After the incident with Ramirez and his Colonel, if he got caught pulling a fast one with classified information could put him in jail. He was still trying to process this discovery when Dillinghouse started to upbraid him. To add to his problems, Winder would have to listen to this guy rant until the plane came back to pick him up, whenever that would be. Winder decided he would have to try to find someway to either give up Dillinghouse to protect himself, or try to get into good graces with Morgan. It was just his luck. That fucking Perkins, his old friend and protector, had to go and get himself blown up.

# CHAPTER 12

Schaeffer had gone off to meet with the Moldovan Colonel, Ivanov. Morgan had gone with him, more because he had nothing to do now that the plans to get Sharif were in place. His wounded legs precluded him having any part in the operation, and Grant had reminded him of a key command principle: If you're on the firing line pulling the trigger, the only thing you're in charge of is your weapon.

The briefing the NCO's had given on the plan was short. Not that they had been holding back, just that the plan was intended to have three brief phases. The approach phase involved being driven close to the site by the Moldovans in a couple of vans. They wouldn't unload until word had been received that Sharif was actually in the apartment and the Moldovans had neutralized the lookouts. The three teams would approach and take up positions, Price in the front, Harrison in the rear of the building, and Grant outside the apartment. The security team would wait in another van, close enough to provide immediate fire support.

The next phase would be the entry phase. On a signal, power to the building would be cut by one of Kosavich's' men. Two more, located on the roof opposite, would launch two flash-bang grenades through the window. As soon as they had detonated, Grant and Sharp would enter the apartment wearing NVGs and carrying suppressed weapons. Sharp had fabricated them in the Moldovan machine shop. They had been test fired and were found to be effective. Anybody in the apartment would be killed. There would be no finesse, no attempts to take prisoners. This was not part of the plan.

It was here that Schaeffer made his only recommendations, both of which were accepted. It involved adding Major Carson to the plan. Schaeffer wanted photos, fingerprints and DNA samples taken of anyone in the apartment. He also wanted a quick search made, and any identification papers, documents or photographs seized. He had brought a backpack kit with all the necessary equipment. Kosavich was present for the briefing. He quickly consulted some notes, and agreed that both would be possible, as long as they spent no more than five minutes. That was all the time he could guarantee he could hold off the local police. Major Carson had to be brought in and briefed on her part. Surprisingly, she agreed to handle the forensics without any questions. Schaeffer wanted her to wait on the street until the room was cleared. Grant and Kosavich discussed that. It would add time to the operation. Carson offered to go in with the entry team. She would wait in the hall with the security team until called. Schaeffer reluctantly agreed. When the briefing on the mission continued, she sat quietly to one side. Grant glanced over at her at one point. She met his gaze with a slight smile and a twinkle in her eyes. I'll be damned, Grant thought to himself. She's looking forward to this.

Loading up in the same vehicles and rallying at the Kosavich family garage would complete the last phase, the withdrawal. After all personnel and weapons were accounted for, they would transfer to smaller vehicles and leave the city. The vans would make it a point to find police check points and be stopped and searched. Then they would continue to another rally point, outside the city, then carry the raiders back to base. From arrival outside the apartment to recovery at the garage, they would be on the clock for a total of nineteen and a half minutes. Schaeffer thought they were cutting it close, but Grant assured him there was plenty of time. Price suggested a thermos of coffee while they were waiting for the entry team to come out. It was meant as a joke, and after a brief flash of concern, Schaeffer realized his leg was being pulled.

At the end of the briefing, Schaeffer wished everyone good luck and shook hands all around. "You know," he said, "this is exactly the kind of thing we didn't want to happen here."

Price interrupted before anyone else could speak. "This wasn't our idea, Colonel. That rag head could have left well enough alone. We weren't going out looking for him."

Sharp had a comment too. "At least he was dumb enough to make it easy to find him. He won't get away."

"Well, don't turn this into another 'Blackhawk Down.' Get in, get out. Don't turn the neighborhood into a shooting gallery."

Kosavich left to organize his men in town. Sharp and Price went off to conduct their pre-mission inspections, and Carson emptied the pack to familiarize herself with the equipment. Grant offered to help, but she declined. "I think I can handle this on my own. You just make sure I have time to do it." She smiled when she said it. "Besides, from what I heard in there, you'll have your hands full with everything else that'll be going on. I'll just count on you to keep me safe." She put her hand up and stroked his cheek. "You know, you could have warned me about this last night. It didn't have to be a surprise. I wouldn't have told anyone."

Carson had visited his room the night before to change the dressing on his shoulder. She had stayed for what she called 'physical therapy', which amounted to some very intense sex. Grant hadn't been thinking about that when she first came in, but the woman had a body that knew how to satisfy a man, and, once unleashed, expected to be repaid in kind.

"Last night I had no idea Schaeffer was going to involve you. And, even if I did, you didn't leave me in a state of mind to talk about it."

"I'll take that as a compliment, Sergeant Major." She finished repacking the gear. "Make sure you don't do any more damage to yourself tonight. You're going to owe me for this, and I'm pretty sure I'm going to be looking for regular payments!"

It was getting dark as Dillinghouse and Winder entered the compound. The congressman was in a foul mood, knowing he had been duped about the gold. He had been taking it out on Winder for the entire trip. In spite of his aide's best efforts, Dillinghouse was looking to tear strips off of Major Morgan's hide. There was no way this hadn't been a deliberate set-up, and he wasn't going to be trifled with by a bunch of low class soldiers. His aide was more pragmatic.

"Congressman, we need to cut our losses on this one. The last thing you need is another scandal over something like this. Pretend it never happened, and let people think you were just here honoring a couple of casualties from the people who saved your life in Africa."

Dillinghouse just stared at him for a minute. His mind was processing all the alternatives, and none of them looked good. If the Speaker found out about this, any support he might have counted on would be out the window. If his political opponents found out, there would be no way he could recover from two scandals so close to one another. As short as the memory of the voters might be, there are some things that stick in their mind. This would be one of them. He decided to give in to his aide's suggestion.

"OK, Freeman, we'll try it your way." Shifting around, he tried to adopt a conciliatory tone with Winder. "Tell me, Sergeant, what are the arrangements for the memorial service for your Colonel? I think I would like to make a few remarks."

Winder's eyes went wide. He looked around at the aide, then stammered out an answer. "Didn't you notice the honor guard when you got off the plane?"

"Honor guard? You mean those soldiers who were lined up? What were they there for?"

"They were the honor guard for Perkins and Carstairs. Their coffins were in the ambulances. They were getting loaded on the plane when we pulled out."

Dillinghouse's face went red. "Those weren't the wounded?"

"No, Sir. I thought you knew. The only wounded were Morgan and Grant, and they both refused evacuation. Those ambulances had the bodies in them."

Price and Sharp had finished securing the gear in one of the vans when Winder's Hummer entered the compound. Price called over to one of his soldiers who wasn't going on the raid. "Still got your video camera handy?"

"Yeah, Sarge, right here."

"Well, get it out. Looks like you're gonna have some more juicy stuff to write home about."

Dillinghouse and his aide went into the Headquarters building and came out in just over a minute. They had a few words with Winder, loud, profane words, from what Price could hear. Winder pointed over to where Grant was going over some sketches with Kosavich, and all three headed his way.

Price called out a warning. "Luke! Head's up!"

Grant looked over to where Price was pointing and folded up the papers in his hand. He spoke to Kosavich. "You better head on out and get things ready. We'll meet you at the garage."

"I'll be waiting, my friend. Tonight will solve many problems for both of us."

"I hope you're right."

Kosavich boarded an already loaded van and drove off as Dillinghouse approached. Winder was staring after the van, wondering what was going on. There were more civilian type vehicles here than he had ever seen in the compound before. There were also a lot of people, Moldovan and American, standing around in civilian clothes. He knew something was up, but he had been totally out of the loop on this. Dillinghouse planted himself in front of Grant and leaned into him.

"What the hell do you people think you're trying to pull with me?" He brought up his hand to poke his finger in Grant's chest. Grant blocked the move, and before Dillinghouse could react his aide grabbed his arm. "Congressman, slow down." Dillinghouse looked at him for a moment then followed his nod to the soldier who was operating a video camera. The warning registered and he took a deep breath and started over. His aide was right. This was no place to cause a scene. Grant was just looking at him, a faint smile on his lips. Dillinghouse knew that whatever had happened, this Sergeant knew about it. He could see the other son of a bitch, the one who had come to his office, the one that still said he had proof, walking over. They were all in on it.

"Where's your Major?"

"I believe you'll find him with the local commandant. They had a conference scheduled."

"Where would that be?"

"My guess would be their headquarters on the other side of the compound. I'm sure your boy here" he nodded towards Winder, "knows exactly where it is."

Actually, Winder didn't. He had no use for the local soldiers, and had made no effort to work with them. Any contact he had had was always in the American area. "Where are you all going?" he asked Grant. Sharp pulled him over. "Not that it's any of your fucking business, but we have a party to go to."

"A party?"

"Yeah. You know, one of those social gatherings between friends. If you had any, you might know what they were."

Winder looked around, and saw Major Carson putting a pack into one of the vehicles. She was in civilian clothes, too. "What's she doing with you?"

"It's a rough crowd. You must remember that. You weren't that drunk." Sharp was referring to an incident in Darfur. Winder had gotten into his face over some sniper rifles they had confiscated from the Janjaweed. Sharp had made short work of him.

"I'm still your superior, Sharp. You better watch how you talk to me."

Sharp laughed. He reached out and pulled the velcro'd rank insignia off the front of his chest. He looked at it for a moment, then handed it back. "Enjoy the feeling while you can, Sidewinder. You'd think a snake like you could cover his tracks better." He looked over at Dillinghouse, then back to Winder. "Your boss wants to go someplace. You better run along."

Winder, Dillinghouse and the aide got back into the Hummer. Winder drove around the corner, then pulled up against the back of the building. "Those bastards are up to something. I think we need to follow them!"

"What makes you say that?"

"They never wear civilian clothes, and they never take an officer with them, especially the doctor. Wherever they're going, there's going to be shooting, and they expect casualties."

Linda Bonneville was watching the activity from her upstairs room. Her relationship with Luke Grant was dead for all intents and purposes. He had made friendly overtures, even tried to get her to talk about what had happened between them, but she had cut off any of his efforts. Now, she was watching him load up with a bunch of his soldiers. From the preparations, the secrecy and the gear they had prepared, she knew wherever they were going, whatever they were doing, it was high risk. That was obvious. They had included both a medic and the doctor, and they were both armed. Bonneville felt an old twinge. She remembered how she used to worry when Grant was getting ready to go out into the darkness, and how relieved she would be when he returned. She had never been able to balance her own feelings with the reality of who he was and what he did. Even now, looking down on him, she could see he was in his element. There was a casual, yet reassuring way he moved among his soldiers, and she could see they responded to him.

She found herself hoping he would come back safely, remembering what their reunions were like, and angry that he had chosen danger ahead of her feelings. The tingling she felt in her body told her the good memories were winning out.

She felt a movement behind her. Sheila Gordon was in the room with her. The other girl came up behind her and slipped her hands under her blouse. "What are you looking at?" Gordon leaned over her and looked out into the compound. "They haven't left yet? I thought they'd be gone by now. I'm supposed to see Dave when they get back." Gordon giggled. "I can tell you're thinking about the Sergeant Major again!"

Bonneville could see another vehicle pull up. Master Sergeant Winder and that Congressman Dillinghouse got out. She closed the curtains and turned around. Gordon kissed her, and she returned it. Gordon led her to the bed and they lay down together. "I like it when you think about the CSM when we make love. It makes you so hot!"

"Sheila, doesn't it bother you to do this with me, knowing you're going to be doing it with Sharp in a few hours?"

The girl giggled as she was sliding down. "Nope! He does things to me you can't, and you do things he can't. I get the best of both worlds. You should get over being mad at the CSM. Let's face it. We both like sex with each other, but you still like to have a man, too. You can have the best of both worlds if you'll let yourself!" Then Bonneville felt the first waves of pleasure wash over her. Gordon was right. She did want Grant.

The assault teams and the security force waited at the garage with their drivers. Grant had a second radio tuned to the frequency Kosavich said he'd be using, but so far he had heard nothing on that channel. Either something was wrong with his set, or Kosavich was the best at communications security he had ever seen. One of the drivers was also monitoring the frequency, and through Price's translation he learned that Kosavich rarely came up on the net unless there was a problem.

Suddenly, there was some background noise on the set. Grant looked at his watch. They had been waiting for almost an hour while Kosavich's men got into position to neutralize the lookouts. Finally, there was some chatter. Grant couldn't understand any of it, so he looked over to the driver, who smiled and gave him a thumbs up. Then he heard Kosavich, first in Moldovan, then addressing him in English.

"All is ready. The target is in residence, and he appears to be alone. My men have the lookouts covered. I have given orders for the drivers to get you into position. Once you are set, give the word. We will all go."

Grant gave the orders, and the teams sorted themselves out into their transport vehicles. Harrison and his partner left first. Their route to the rear of the building was the most circuitous. He would need a few extra minutes. While they had been waiting he had sat by Grant. The First Sergeant had been quiet all evening, not saying much to anyone. Finally he spoke to Grant, thanking him for the opportunity. "Thanks for letting me tag along, Luke. You young guys have been carrying all the weight. It's about time I stepped up and did something."

Grant gave his friend's shoulder a squeeze. "You've been doing your share. You're the First Sergeant. Your job was to make sure we could do ours, and you always delivered." Grant was silent for a while. Harrison started to speak, but Grant cut him off. "And about us 'young guys' carrying all the weight, I seem to remember that I've got a couple of months on you, or did that escape your attention?" Harrison chuckled, then moved off to sit with his partner.

Grant waited for Harrison to hit his first checkpoint. Once he radioed in, he set the other teams in motion. As he was getting his team loaded, he pulled Major Carson aside for some last minute reminders. "You stay right next to Robinson when we enter the building. Don't even think about coming into the room until we call for you, no matter what you hear. Got it?"

Carson nodded her understanding. She had butterflies in her stomach, and felt like she was going to throw up. It wasn't the thought of handling the forensics on the dead Arab that was bothering her. It was everything else about going on a combat raid like this. When Colonel Schaeffer had first briefed her, she thought it would just be a simple in and out. Once the mission got rolling, and she listened to the detailed planning and the preparation for any contingencies, she realized that this wasn't a simple matter. There were a lot of things that could go wrong. The pistol she was wearing high on her hip didn't seem very reassuring anymore. She boarded the van and sat between the security element. Robinson on her left smiled at her. "Don't worry, Ma'am. You just stay close and you'll be fine. The Sergeant Major would have my ass if anything happened to you. He must have told us a dozen times how important the stuff you have to get is."

Carson smiled at him. Maybe Grant was telling them how important the forensics were, but she knew they were an after thought on the mission. Grant was concerned about her safety. That was reassuring.

The distance from the garage to the Arab quarter wasn't far, but there were a total of four vehicles in this element. The routes and the times were all staggered so they wouldn't give the appearance of a convoy arriving in the neighborhood, but they would all be on station within moments of one another. Traffic wasn't heavy, but even a fender bender could throw them all off.

Grant could see the apartment block ahead of them. In his earpiece he heard Harrison report he had reached his position and was standing by. Seconds later, Price radioed in. Grant could see his vehicle parked at the far corner of the block. His driver pulled to the curb, just past the front entrance. He clicked on both radios so his teams could hear everything that was going on. "Yvegniy, we are in position. Give the word!"

He heard a few short commands in Moldovan, followed by silence. Then, different voices could be heard, one after the other. Grant knew these were the lookouts being taken out.

Then he heard Kosavich again, this time in English. "There are no prying eyes. You may go!" Grant gave the command to execute and pulled his door open. As he entered the building he looked up and down the sidewalk. Price and his partner were casually walking towards the entrance. They would seal off the building from the front. In the other direction, he could see the security element van pull up. The side door was opened, but nobody came out. These men were all heavily armed. They would only make an appearance if the situation went sour and their firepower was needed. He was moving up the stairs, Sharp behind him, the security element, with Carson between them, bringing up the rear. Harrison reported in that the rear entrance was secure. They reached the floor that Sharif's apartment was on. Grant and Sharp took positions on either side. Robinson held his position by the stairs while the other man crept silently down to the far end of the corridor. Grant watched, and when he was in position, he gave the signal for them to don their NVGs, then Grant whispered one word into his microphone: "Contact!"

In his earpiece he heard Kosavich give a few quick commands. Suddenly, the hallway went dark. The green phosphorescence of the NVGs filled his eyes. He strained to hear some sound from the apartment. There was nothing. Across the street, two Moldovan soldiers hefted grenade launchers to their shoulders. Each loosed a flash-bang grenade through one of the windows facing them. They both hit their target, and they were rewarded with the bright flash and 'crump' of the grenades that would momentarily stun anybody in the room with it.

Kosavich was watching from down the street. He could hear the grenades explode, then he leaned into the Citroen sedan he was standing next to. He looked at the figures in the back seat. One was on his knees on the floor, his hands cuffed behind him. His legs were bound, and there was a sack taped over his head. The figure sitting next to him spoke in French. "My government will be grateful for this assistance."

Kosavich grunted. "As long as the Americans don't find out how they've been deceived."

"Don't worry, my friend. They won't be able to identify the Arab we left for them. As far as they know, Ali Alawa Sharif has gone to claim his virgins in paradise."

Kosavich looked back to the building. He put his hand to his ear, then spoke a few commands into his radio. He could see the lights come back on in some of the apartments. "All the same, you better wait here until everyone is gone. I wouldn't want you to get in the way of our escape." Then he straightened and turned toward the apartment building. He glance back down at the figure bundled up in the back seat, then walked back to where his Trabant was parked.

Grant crashed the door as soon as the second grenade exploded. Sharp was right behind him. They both had their pistols up and were sweeping the room for a target. There was a figure on a couch opposite the door. Grant put two quick rounds into it, then two more as he got closer. Sharp had spotted another figure sitting in a chair in the far corner of the room. He followed the same drill: two quick rounds, then two more as he got closer.

There was another door on Grant's side of the room. He kicked it open to find a small bedroom. He quickly checked around and under the bed, then announced it was clear. Sharp checked his end. There was a small water closet, the door wide open. It too was clear, and he reported it. Grant came back into the room. He called for Kosavich to restore power. He dangled his NVGs from his neck as the lights came back on, and called Robinson to bring in the doctor. Then he looked at the man he had shot. He could sense Carson at his side. He heard her gasp. The face was obliterated. Carson was asking him "Did you do that?"

Grant stepped forward. He could see his first two rounds in the targets forehead. His second two were centered on the chest. "I didn't do this."

Carson knelt beside the body and opened her pack. She drew out the camera and took a few quick photos. "Did he get hit by the flash-bangs?"

Grant looked around the room. The detonation points of both grenades were evident on the far walls. He called to Sharp, who was kneeling over his body. "What does yours look like?"

Sharp lifted the head and looked at the deep gash going across the throat. "Mine seems to have had his neck cut. He was dead before we got here."

"Yeah, this one too." There was a single barreled shotgun lying on the floor between the two bodies. A curve bladed knife was clamped in the hand of the Arab. "Falling out among friends?"

Sharp looked back and forth between them. "I don't know. Hell of a coincidence for them both to end up sitting like that. I smell a rat."

Carson was finished with the first body. "What about him?" she asked.

"Have you got enough stuff to get samples off him?"

She looked in her kit. "I think so. There are spares of everything."

"OK. Do him, then lets get out of here. Robinson!"

Robinson stuck his head in the door. "Give the good Doctor a hand, then get her out of here." He turned to watch Sharp stuffing documents in his bag. "Anything good?"

Sharp shrugged. "Hard to say. There isn't very much, though. It almost looks like somebody was here ahead of us, you know what I mean?"

Major Carson was done and had her bag packed. Robinson was shepherding her out the door. Grant gave the room one last look. Other than their shell casings, and those had Serbian head stamps, nothing would be left behind. Grant looked at his watch. They were running slightly ahead of schedule.

He was exiting the building, the last man out, giving the order to head for the rally point, when there was an explosion over his head. He looked up to see the front of the apartment they had just been in shoot fire and debris out the windows. Everybody froze for a moment and stared at the blast. Grant could hear Sharp cursing they had been set-up. Grant agreed, but there was nothing they could do about it now. He yelled out for everybody to get in the van.

As he was getting in, he looked back up the street, in the direction of sirens that could be heard. A couple of blocks back, he could see a Hummer. Who the fuck was that?

Winder had insisted on following Grant. He lagged far enough behind with his headlights off so he could see their taillights, but, hopefully, they wouldn't notice him. It worked until he got into the city, then he lost the convoy. He decided to drive up and down a few streets, hoping to spot them. Dillinghouse started to get impatient, and insisted they stop at what looked like an open-air bar for a drink.

One drink led to several, and when Winder tried to insist they leave, Dillinghouse grew abusive. The aide quieted him down and got him back to the Hummer. Winder didn't want to admit it, but he had no idea where he was. He decided to just stay on this street, and maybe he would either see a route sign he could recognize, or he would run across a major intersection. What the hell, Dillinghouse was too drunk to notice they were lost.

He had driven a couple of blocks when traffic started to back up, slowing him to a crawl. He resorted to the old trick of leaning on the horn, as if that ever worked to move traffic, when down the street he could see the front of a building suddenly explode, showering the street with debris. Under the explosion, he thought he could see Grant and Sharp getting into a van. One of the figures paused as he was getting in and looked in his direction. Winder was sure it was Grant.

Dillinghouse was staring out the windshield at the explosion. "What the hell is that?"

Winder smiled at him. "That was Grant. I just saw him getting into a van down there!"

Dillinghouse looked at him blankly, then it registered. "Well, don't just sit here! Catch up to him! Those bastards are blowing up the city!" Winder was trying to keep his eyes on the van as it sped away. It went around a corner, and he lost it. He was edging around traffic when another car pulled out in front of him. He slammed on the brakes, but not in time to avoid smashing into the rear. Dillinghouse was rocked by the impact, then stuck his head out the window and started swearing at the other vehicle. "You stupid son of a bitch! Don't you know how to look before you pull out?" Winder was getting out when both front doors of the other car opened. Two men got out. Winder faced the driver and smiled, then noticed the gun in his hand. He looked over to the other man. He was raising what looked like a submachine gun to his shoulder. Winder called out a warning, then tried to get back in the Hummer.

The occupants of the Citroen watched Kosavich walk away. The driver turned and asked, "What do you want to do?" The man in the back seat told him to wait for a few minutes. He was glancing between his watch and the building down the street when he saw the Americans coming out. He looked at his watch again. The Americans were ahead of schedule. Just then, the upper floor of the building exploded. "A pity" he said to no one in particular. "If they had been a little slower it would have made the entire exercise much more interesting." He leaned forward and tapped his driver on the shoulder. "As soon as the *Amis* have driven off you can go." The driver grunted his acknowledgement as the bound figure began to stir. The man in the back seat reached for a container holding a hypodermic needle. He drew it out and jabbed it into the upturned butt of the man on the floor as the car pulled away from the curb. He was depressing the plunger as the car was struck sharply from the rear. He turned around and saw the American Hummer. Somebody was yelling out the window, and the driver was getting out. "Deal with them" was all he said. The Americans were good, he thought. He never would have expected them to be watching behind them after they left the scene. He could hear the American driver shouting something. Then he heard his driver shoot him. His other man had his MP5 up, and was spraying the other occupants. There was a brief burst of fire, than silence. He watched his driver walk up to the Hummer and fire one shot into each of the bodies. The other man threw something into the cab, then both his men got back into the Citroen.

He reached down and withdrew the needle from his prisoner's backside. "That's how you deal with the unexpected, Ali Alawa. You would have done well to remember that." He twisted in his seat to look back at the Hummer. Just before they turned the corner, he saw it explode. He again spoke, this time to his companions in the front. "It has been a very good days work my friends. Let's see if we can get to the airport without any more interruptions."

Grant and Sharp were trying to piece together what happened at the apartment. The two bodies, their location at either end of the room, and the demolition charge left behind raised hackles on both their necks. Sharp was convinced they had been set up. Grant, remembering checking his watch just before they exited the building, had to agree. "We were running ahead of schedule. If we had spent another 30 seconds in that room, we would have gone up with it."

"Yeah, but why?" Sharp asked.

Grant could only shake his head. "One guy has his throat cut, the other has his face shot off. Can't be a coincidence. And that bomb going off when it did? That can't be a coincidence either. Somebody got there ahead of us and set us up."

"You thinking Kosavich?"

"I'm trying not to, but it's not looking good. Where the hell is he, anyway?"

The Moldovans didn't know, and Kosavich wasn't answering his radio. He was the only one who hadn't arrived at the rally point yet.

Price had been listening to the discussion. He added another piece of information. "Kosavich isn't the only one not here. I saw him up the street just as you were going in. He was talking to somebody in a car up there."

Sharp turned his head. "You sure?"

Price nodded. "He was leaning into the side window just before you gave the signal. He straightened up, looked back, then walked away. He didn't brief anything about another vehicle."

There was a burst of chatter on the radio. Grant looked at Price, but he had his headset off, and didn't hear it. One of the Moldovans came over and spoke to Price. There was a quick exchange, and Price stood up. He looked at Grant and Sharp. "Kosavich just called. He wants us to go with this guy."

"What's up?" Grant asked as he gathered his hear.

"He said we took some casualties. This guy doesn't know if they were ours or his."

Grant and Sharp exchanged glances. "I thought I saw a Hummer when we were coming out of the building."

"Who? The only people with a vehicle on line when we left were Winder and the politician. Think they might have followed us? Is Winder smart enough to figure out where we'd be?"

Grant shrugged, then started giving orders. "We'll worry about that later. Me and Dave with this guy and the Major." He looked around for Carson, who was sorting out her kit with Elko. She looked up with a puzzled look, and Grant repeated himself. Then he told Price to take Elko and the security detail and follow in the van.

"Gonna be cramped, Luke."

"I don't care. Sit in somebody's lap, and everybody stays off the net. Lets be alert for any more surprises."

"What about the rest of us?" Harrison had his gear on and was ready to go. "Do you think it's a good idea for us to split up now?"

Sharp agreed. "He's right Luke. If the apartment was a set-up we could be looking at more trouble here."

"All the more reason. If it's a trap, this place has already been compromised. The exfil routes are probably already under observation. Ralph, you take the rest out by a different route. Once we're out of here, take your driver's radio. Keep him off the air. If I'm wrong, I'll apologize later."

"What about your group?"

"We'll have most of the firepower. If there's a problem, we'll just have to try to shoot our way out."

When they arrived on the scene Grant had Price hold the security team back. The area seemed to be swarming with uniforms. None of them looked like local police. There was a fire truck blocking the street. They had to get out and walk around it. Grant recognized the bumper markings on the rear panel. It was the vehicle Winder had been driving. Three stretchers were off to the side, each covered by a bloody sheet. Grant motioned to Major Carson to go check them out. A uniform tried to stop here, but Kosavich intervened. The uniform started to salute Kosavich, but he caught his arm and held it down. Grant averted his gaze before Kosavich turned to see if he was watching. Sharp had seen the motion too, but he was out of Kosavich's line of sight when he turned. He was just behind Grant at the side of the Hummer when Grant looked over his shoulder and cocked his head. Sharp mouthed the words "I saw it", then looked into the back seat. He could see where something, probably a flash-bang, had exploded on the gunners platform between the seats. The soft-top had shredded, and the windshield had been blown out onto the sloped hood. Sharp could see a row of bullet holes. He started to speak, but Grant cut him off. "Get the camera from Carson and take as many pictures as you can. Don't make any comments or answer any questions. Have Price check his guys. If anybody has a camera, get them out in the crowd and shoot some more. Tell them to watch for anything out of the ordinary on the street."

Sharp nodded and went to where Carson was kneeling next to the bodies. She pulled an extra camera from her bag and handed it to Sharp. The uniform standing next to them looked at the camera, then at Sharp. He made no comment.

Grant felt a hand on his arm. It was Kosavich, leading him off to a sheltered spot by the fire truck. Both men were silent as Kosavich referred to some notes, then bade Grant to sit by him on the running board.

"What happened here, Yevigny?"

Kosavich made a sweeping motion with his hands. "I don't know my friend. All I can surmise is that we must have missed one of the sentries. Your vehicle must have stumbled in at an inopportune moment and caught the backlash." Grant looked down at his feet. Someone had kicked a nine-millimeter casing from the other side of the Hummer. Grant reached down and picked it up. Kosavich looked at it, then took it from Grant's hand and slipped it in his pocket. His whole demeanor changed.

"This can get very ugly here, very quickly. For all concerned, let me tell you what happened.

"Your congressman decided he wanted to see the city. His driver, without getting any authorization, complied with the request. While driving about, they were involved in an accident with a street vendor's cart. It had a stove and a gas tank. They exploded."

"That won't explain the gunshot wounds, Yvegniy."

"Your congressman's companion was armed, illegally, of course. He was carrying spare ammunition, which detonated in the blast."

"That won't stand up in an autopsy."

"Yes, it will, my friend. Our doctors will perform the autopsies on the bodies, which, incidentally, were burned beyond recognition. Once we return the remains, they will be consistent with the story." He looked around and saw both Sharp and Carson had cameras in their hands. "I will, of course, have to confiscate the cameras."

"What about the pictures of Sharif?"

"My people will process them and make them available. You will have your proof." He stood up. "Now, you must excuse me." He walked over to Sharp and held out his hand for the camera. Sharp balked and made a protest. Both men looked back at Grant. As Grant returned the look, he could see Sharp give a little grin and pat his pocket. He had already switched the memory card. Grant nodded, and he passed over the camera, accompanying it with a stream of curses. Kosavich walked over to where Carson was standing. She handed him the camera without comment. She too gave Grant a little smile. Sharp had anticipated a problem with the cameras. He had told Carson to swap memory cards and take what she needed, then put the original card back in and take more. Sharps camera was the one originally used in the apartment. He pulled the same switch after he had taken his shots. The card he substituted had nothing but random shots of the ground and vehicle.

Nobody noticed Elko in the crowd, moving freely and taking her shots. There would be a complete digital record. Grant called to her over the radio and told her to get out. He saw her nod, then disappear back into the crowd.

Kosavich rejoined him. "Your consulate has been notified. They are sending a representative. Your commander has been notified as well. This is now a matter for diplomats and officers, my friend. You must withdraw your soldiers now."

"You're fucking me, Yvegniy."

"It may appear that way, but I assure you it isn't. We will talk tomorrow."

"You're not a Senior Sergeant either, are you?"

"Again, we will talk tomorrow."

After Kosavich was gone, Sharp and Carson came over to where he was standing. Sharp held up his hand to show he had two small blue memory cards from the cameras. When he tried to hand them to Grant, he shook his head. "Get back to the van and give them to Elko. Have her take them back to the base. Tell her not to give them to anyone, not even Morgan. Just hold on to them until we get back."

"We aren't going back now?" Carson asked.

"We're going to try, Ma'am, but if Kosavich is half the operator I think he is, he'll be looking at those cameras he took from you right about now. A bright man like him will probably realize that those aren't the only pictures you took, and will come back looking for the memory cards."

"And?"

Grant smiled. "And, if he still likes us, we'll probably get stopped and searched pretty thoroughly."

"If he doesn't still like us?" she asked, almost sensing what the answer would be.

Sharp answered for Grant. "In that case, Ma'am, you better hope he has a couple of female agents with him!"

"Why?"

"We'll probably get stripped out naked by the side of the road and cavity searched."

"Can they do that?"

"Yeah. They don't seem to have the same Bill of Rights we do, and if he has to justify it, we seem to recently have been involved in a number of illegal actions in their country."


Kosavich wasn't the operator Grant thought he was. The driver brought them straight to the base. There was never a peep on the Moldovan radio frequency. Morgan and Schaeffer were waiting for them. Harrison was hovering in the background. Grant looked his way, and Harrison gave him a thumbs up. "Good head count, Sergeant Major. All our people are back in the nest." Grant gave a wave of acknowledgement. At least nobody had been grabbed by Moldovan intelligence, or whoever the hell else was working in the background.

Schaeffer launched right into his questioning. He wanted to know what went wrong. Grant started to answer, but Morgan cut him off and led everyone into the headquarters building. There was a tape recorder set up in the conference room. What Grant liked to refer to as the blame-placing phase of the exercise was about to begin. He laid out the mission from the briefing onwards. He was very careful to detail the arrival of Dillinghouse and Winder at the compound. Sharp recounted the conversation he had with Winder, including the directions to where they could find Morgan and Schaeffer. The intelligence officer asked a few questions for clarification then allowed them to continue. There were no more questions until Grant ended his tale.

"You had no idea Dillinghouse had followed you?" Schaeffer asked.

"None. Once we hit the city our little convoy broke up and took separate routes. Traffic was pretty thin. Nobody saw a Hummer until we were leaving the building."

"Sergeant Major, I want you to consider this very carefully. Was there anything out of the ordinary, anything you can think of, that hasn't been discussed yet?"

Grant thought a moment. He looked at Sharp, then at Carson. Then he remembered. "We need Price in here."

Price was summoned, as it were. The runner found him waiting with several of the raiding party in front of headquarters. The usual debriefing process had been for all the team members to be present so they could feed off one another's information and memories. Price knew it was only a matter of time before the rest of them were called in. He had kept them together, and warned them not to talk about the mission until they were debriefed, so not to pollute their memories with 'war stories'.

When he entered the room, he asked about the rest of the teams debriefing. Schaeffer told him it would keep. He started to protest, but Morgan cut him off. "We've got a few details to cover first. We'll get everybody else in here in a few minutes."

"Tell them about the car," Grant prodded.

Price looked puzzled, then remembered what he had started to tell Grant back in the garage. While he was speaking, Sharp sorted through a pile of diagrams until he found the one he wanted. It was a line drawing of the neighborhood around the apartment building. He held it up next to a flip chart and started copying it in a larger scale, marking all the positions as they were in the plan. Price looked at it and picked up a marker. He made a mark where he saw Kosavich and the car. Sharp checked his notes. He made another mark on the chart. "Kosavich was supposed to be waiting here," pointing to the mark he had just made, "almost half a block forward of where Price saw him." He paused for effect, then made another mark, just to the side of where Price had seen him. "This is where Winder got ambushed!"

Schaeffer asked a few more questions, then cut off further discussion. Any mention of the car, he told them, was to be avoided in front of the rest of the group during the debriefing. Grant asked why. "There were a lot of eyes out there. Somebody might have seen something else."

Schaeffer repeated his warning, but wouldn't give any more explanation. Morgan didn't press him either. Grant sensed something wasn't right, but he held his own counsel. It nagged at him during the rest of the debriefing.


They were gathered in Grant's room. Price, Sharp, Harrison, Elko and both of the Robinson brothers. Sylvia Carson was the only officer present. Her observations of the Arab's apartment and the ambush scene on the street were needed to help answer some of the questions that were lingering. In spite of a case of beer and a bottle of tequila, nobody was drunk, and they weren't much closer to coming up with any answers. They had decided that there were a few facts that could have some ugly explanations. The biggest fact was Kosavich and his involvement in everything. He had set up the raid, provided the security and arranged the exfiltration. He was also out of place for part of the raid, next to the strange vehicle. Whoever was in that car seemed to have some part, probably the major role, in ambushing Winder and Dillinghouse. Kosavich also provided the explanation, transparent as it was, of how they died. Then there was the problem of the explosive set in the apartment. If they hadn't been ahead of schedule, it would have caught them in the room. If it had been command detonated, it would have to be by someone who could observe them enter the building and time their mission. The early exit probably saved their lives. It all kept coming back to that car. Kosavich had set them up. That was the only answer they could find given the facts that they had. Price wrapped it up nicely. The whole thing sucked. He had looked at the pictures taken in the room. It was his opinion, as well as everyone else's, that the bodies had been staged. "I'll bet that isn't even our fucking rag head. Either he knew we were coming and set it up, or Kosavich warned him off and set it up. Either way, none of you were supposed to walk out of there."

Grant agreed, but there was nothing more they could do tonight. Kosavich said they'd be talking tomorrow. All he could do is wait and hope to get some answers. He sent everyone off to bed. "It's late. Get some sleep. Morgan said there's some European Union people coming in tomorrow to deal with the Russians. We're probably about to get fucked again."

Sharp drained his beer and put the bottle back in the case. "Yeah, I told Sheila I'd see her when we got back." He looked at his watch. It was almost 0230. "If she's not already asleep, she'll be pissed." He smiled. "Ain't nothing like angry sex!"

From the glances they were giving each other, Grant could guess that Price and Elko would be continuing the conversation in his room. Carson was the next to leave. "I really had planned on spending some time tonight, Luke, but I'm beat. You didn't warn me how draining these things can be." She wrapped her arms around him and gave him a kiss. She pressed her body against his and purred when she felt him respond. "Hmm. Hold that thought. Tomorrow night has got to be better." Then she let go of him and walked out, giving the First Sergeant a little smile. Harrison just sat there, sipping his beer. He wasn't going to judge his friend, and he wasn't a gossip. Whatever Grant had going on, well, God bless him. He deserved whatever good he could get out of life.

Grant rubbed his eyes and looked around the room. It was a mess. There were empty bottles on every piece of furniture. He gathered them up in the case and put it outside his door. Somebody would take care of it in the morning. He poured himself another shot of tequila and sat on his bed. He took off his shoes and tossed them in a corner. "What I need", he said to his long time friend, "is a nice long run, a good hot shower, or both."

"We're both getting too old for this shit, Luke. It's a young man's game."

"If you can still call it a game, we're young enough. Now, before I throw your goat smellin' ass out of my room, tell me about the bomber."

The bomber. The Wicked Witch. He hadn't thought about it for a while, but he knew that Harrisons' wife was moving ahead with trying to put it back together. Ralph would leave him copies of e-mails, and sometimes pictures, but Grant never paid much attention to them. Catching up on it would help him wind down.

"You'd be amazed at what's been happening with that old bird" he began. "Once Willa contacted a few people to find out what she could do, it was full speed ahead." Willa was his wife.

"Did you know that when the Air Force shipped the pieces, they didn't bother taking out the guns? You can't buy those things legally for under $20,000, and we ended up with ten of them."

"Kind of hard to hide ten heavy machine guns from the Feds, isn't it?"

"You'd think so, but Willa hooked up with a lawyer who specializes in 2nd Amendment cases. He's the one that had her set up the charitable corporation, or whatever the hell it is. He filed the license paperwork. You might remember, you're one of the officers. I had you sign the forms a while back. It cost us two hundred bucks each gun."

Grant thought back on it. There had been a bunch of legal shit passed in front of him after Harrison told him about the tax dodge on the plane. Willa Harrison had been handling his financial affairs for so long, he just signed where the 'X' was. "So I'm on the license?"

"Yep, my friend. Anytime you get bored and want to blow off ammo at a couple of bucks a round, you're legal."

"What about the carcass?"

Harrison popped another beer. "That was the beautiful part. There was a write-up about it in the paper, and a guy from the regional airport saw it and offered her use of an old hanger at the end of an abandoned taxiway. All she has to do is pay utilities. Another guy, a pilot type, turned her on to some government programs and historical society shit. She ended up getting a couple of grants to cover expenses for a while. Then the good stuff really started to happen."

"Such as?"

"Well, to begin with, people started sending her stuff, old parts, manuals, odds and ends. Then a couple of old guys from the local VFW showed up and asked if they could work on her."

"On Willa?"

"No, you asshole, the plane. They got more friends involved, did some fund raising, and hired an aircraft restoration consultant. He took one look at the Witch and offered to work on it for free, and get some professionals to help for expenses only. Seems like there's a bunch of rich guys out there who work on these things, find parts, in exchange for getting to fly around on it when it's done. They've already got three of the engines running, and the fourth one is in Florida getting a rebuild."

"Ralph, the fucking thing pancaked in the desert. There can't be much of the underside left. What are they going to do when they hoist it up and things start falling out the bottom?"

"Luke, the bottom skin was gone, but the frame was intact. They had raised the bottom turret, and that only lost a little Plexiglas. The wheels were up, so they're in good shape. It wasn't as bad as you would think."

"I'll believe it when I see it."

"And you will, my friend, you will. Now, where are you hiding the good stuff?"

Grant thought about it again, then decided the few hours of sleep he could still get would probably serve him better. "Amigo, its time for you to hit the road. My day has sucked, and tomorrow ain't gonna get any better." Harrison saluted him with his beer, drained it, and then walked out. Grant was still thinking about that shower. Fuck it. He'd get a quick one in the morning.

There was a knock on his door. He looked around the room to see if there was anything someone might have left.

Nothing.

Must be more bad news, he thought. "Come in!"

He turned to ask what had happened and saw Linda Bonneville standing there. She was wearing her running shorts and a too tight T-shirt. He caught himself staring at her breasts, mentally comparing them to Sylvia Carson. In a dark room he'd have trouble telling them apart. He felt himself responding to the thought.

"Luke, I know it's late. Can we talk for a minute?"

"Sure." He reached for his glass and filled it again. "Can I offer you a drink?"

"Please."

He handed her the glass and looked around for another one. He saw one on the small dresser. Sylvia Carson had been using it. Fuck it, he thought. I'm going to hell anyway, so what difference will it make. He picked it up and poured another shot. Bonneville had already drained hers. He held out the bottle, offering another. She shook her head, but didn't put the glass down. She held it with both hands and walked over to sit on the bed. She hesitated as she looked up at him, then with a sigh she started talking.

"Things haven't been good with us, have they?"

"You have trouble with my lifestyle. I get shot at. A lot."

She seemed to think about that statement. It was true, he did get shot at a lot. It seemed like everywhere he went somebody tried to kill him. "I do, and it's not fair to you. You were a soldier before I met you. Sometimes I forget I'm one too. It's something I need to get past."

He didn't respond. There was nothing he could think of to say, plus, he was tired, and the booze wasn't helping. He made a gesture with his empty glass. She reached out and caught his hand, taking the glass out of it. She put hers down too, then stood up and wrapped her arms around his waist, her head on his chest. He didn't know what else to do, so he put his arms around her. He could feel her tense as he clasped her to him, then felt her relax. She pulled herself in tighter, grinding against him. He felt himself growing against her. She felt it too, and pushed herself against him harder. He dropped his hands down to her butt and lifted her face up to his. Her feet came off the floor, and he felt her legs wrap around him. He could hear her moaning as they kissed. She pushed herself down and her hands went to his waist, undoing his belt and his trousers. She slid them down and grabbed him with both hands, squeezing. His hands went to her breasts, toying with her nipples. She pulled him down onto the bed, using one hand to slide her running shorts down. She kicked them off and guided Grant into her. Her eyes were closed and her head back. "Please" she kept repeating. Grant plunged in. Her orgasm was almost instantaneous, but she wouldn't let him go. She wrapped her legs around him again and held him inside her. She was pushing herself against him, squeezing with her muscles. They both exploded together.

They lay next to one another in silence. Grant looked at her face. Her eyes were closed, and she had a smile on her lips. Her hand was stroking him, getting him aroused again. When she felt he was ready, she slid down his body. He ran his hands through her hair. Yeah, he thought, I'm going to hell. Then another thought crossed his mind. Fuck it. There ain't nothing I can do to change that now, I might as well enjoy it. With that he slowly started to thrust his hips. Neither one of them got much sleep.

# CHAPTER 13

The early morning briefing about the EU visit had been loaded with surprises. The biggest one had been that the Americans had been excluded from any of the negotiations. They also learned that the Moldovan military had excluded them from any aspect of the security cordon or the inspection process if and when the Russians consented to any inspections. It appeared to be a slap in the face, but it also appeared that Schaeffer and Morgan didn't have any problems with the change. There was another matter of protocol, one that Grant was certain came from the French. The officers were to have their own dining facility, meals, waiters, and proper dinnerware. They would not lower themselves to eating with the common soldiers, using trays or paper plates and plastic cutlery, or subsisting on American MREs or tray packs. So much for the vaunted French attitude of *liberte, egalite, fraternite* that they were so fond of spouting. Harrison was quick to point out that his dining facility would be unable to meet those requirements, and regulations prohibited the use of enlisted men as servants. The EU would have to use the Moldovan officer's mess.

Schaeffer just shrugged and let the Moldovan liaison officer know the US would not be doing the catering. The lieutenant just shrugged and sent his enlisted aide off to inform Colonel Ivanov. The Moldovan had expected the Americans to provide food service. That would put a crimp in his starched shorts.

Outside, Harrison had a puzzled look on his face as he asked, "What just happened in there?"

Grant had no idea. Things had been changing, and he had been totally cut out of the loop. He knew there had been a lot of after hours chatter back and forth with Tampa. At breakfast the commo chief related his tale of being rousted out of bed to keep the lines open, but had been kept out of the room for any of the conversation. He still had his meeting with Kosavich before the EU people arrived, but he doubted he would learn any more.

When Kosavich arrived he was in a different uniform, Overnight, the Senior Sergeant of the Moldovan Army had been transformed into Major Kosavich of the Internal Security Service. Grant took it all in at a glance. This was something that Price and Sharp should be here for. They wouldn't believe an ex-commie intelligence officer had suckered them. Kosavich was accompanied by his own aide now, one who had his ear constantly fastened to a cell phone. Grant was less than pleasant in his greeting.

"If you expect any military courtesy out of me, you'll be disappointed."

"I understand. I would probably feel the same if our roles were reversed."

Grant started right in. "So what happened last night? Was that a set up?"

Kosavich pulled himself erect, "That was no 'set-up' as you call it. Everything proceeded exactly as I had anticipated, except for your congressman and you disturbing some explosives cache in the apartment." He handed Grant two blue memory cards. "These are useless. You even secreted the real ones from me, as if you didn't trust me from the start."

"Yeah, like I'm the one who tried to pull a fast one. Who killed my people?"

"I don't know."

"Kosavich, that's bullshit, and you know it." Then he tried a bluff. "I know all about the car. My people saw you with them."

The statement caught Kosavich off guard. He had only gone to speak to the Frenchman after the Americans were in the building. He was too far away to be seen by their security team. "Impossible!" was all he could say.

Grant knew he had hit a hot button. "You underestimate Sergeant Price. He saw you speaking to the occupants. It made him curious. You got careless."

Kosavich regained his composure and waved the issue off with his hand. "So you know about the Frenchman. No matter. I told you he was interested in the Arab. I was merely warning him off."

That explained it all to Grant. Kosavich had sold them out to the French. "More bullshit, Major. You delayed the start by almost 45 minutes so they could clean up loose ends. You gave him Sharif, didn't you?"

"Sharif is dead. You saw his body in the apartment. He had a falling out with his Russian handler and they killed each other. That must have been obvious to you."

Grant smiled. Time to try another bluff. "The dead Arab was a good six inches too short. We measured. I was as close to the Arab in Darfur as I am to you now. It wasn't the same man." Grant waited for that to sink in for a moment. Before Kosavich could respond, he continued, "You didn't get any pictures from the room, so how would you know what it looked like in there? The explosion destroyed everything as soon as we left. Your French friends thought they were taking care of us at the same time. Did you give them Dillinghouse as a consolation prize?"

Kosavich ended the discussion. "Sergeant Major. I have gone on record stating that you and your men were allowed to seek revenge on a foreign national in my country. In spite of our best efforts to help you, you conducted a cowboy operation that only succeeded in stirring up local Muslim sentiment, causing a great deal of property damage, which we anticipate your country will make reparations for, and you got your commander, several of your soldiers, a congressman and his aide killed for no purpose." He put on his hat and issued a sharp order to his aide. "I suggest you collect your equipment and hold it in readiness. Once the diplomats finish with the Russians, they will start on you. I expect you will be ordered to leave my country rather quickly."

Grant also stood and put on his beret, something he didn't normally wear in the field. "Just remember this, Major. We built you a first class road for nothing. You were the one to come to me with the plan to capture the Arab. We asked for nothing. It was your plan to fuck us over that ended up in the shitter." He walked up closer to the Moldovan.

"And if you want to try to embarrass us, go ahead. Just remember that we've got recordings, pictures, documents and videotape. I don't know what the game was, but I don't think we'll use those rules anymore. Have a nice fucking day!"

Kosavich paused, then said something to his aide. The man left and closed the door, leaving them alone. He took off his hat and sighed as he sat back down. Grant remained standing.

"I am sorry our time together has to end like this. I think it was very beneficial for both our countries."

"Then why is it ending like this?"

Kosavich reached into an inside pocket and pulled out a small notebook. He handed it to Grant. "This is my mission book. Everything I have been instructed to do, and everything I have done, is in there. My country is trapped between two behemoths. On one side, the former Soviets want to regain their mastery. On the other, the European Union wants to make client states out of us, an enlightened domination, but domination, no less.

"The United States would be a good ally for us, militarily, diplomatically and financially. But your country is on a series of four-year plans. Every four years your politicians sacrifice whatever they need to for votes. Being courted by the United States is like a virgin dating a married man: You make many promises, but after you have your way, you leave us in the lurch."

"And dealing with the EU will be different?" Why the hell is he giving me this line of crap? Grant asked himself.

"Different? No. Their aim is the same. But if we fall into disarray, stumble our way into anarchy, we are still on their doorstep. What happens here will go there."

He stood again and opened the door. "I did what I had to." Pointing to the notebook, he mouthed the words 'Read that.'


Price and Sharp sat at the end of the runway waiting for the EU transport to come in. They were part of a small security detachment/ honor guard supplementing the Moldovan detail. This was supposed to be as close to the Russian compound as they would get. The Moldovan commander, Colonel Ivanov, was resplendent in his dress uniform. His officers were similarly dressed. In comparison, the American officers, led by Colonel Schaeffer and Major Morgan, looked like poor relations in their drab Army Combat Uniform, or ACUs. Just to be ornery, Price had pulled his last clean set of woodland pattern Battle Dress Uniform out of his duffel bag. When he lined up with his detail, he looked out of place, as he intended. He knew Schaeffer would probably call on him to translate, so he also planned to use as much fractured French as he could, just to piss the Frogs off.

"Where do they want us to line up?" Sharp asked. The officer in charge of the Moldovans had been marching and counter marching his soldiers back and forth on the apron, seeking just the right spot. He was inexperienced at his task, and was reluctant to ask one of the sergeants, or worse, one of the Americans, where the best spot would be. Price could have told him that there wouldn't be a good spot until the plane stopped. It was a packed dirt strip. The pilot would taxi in, then do a braking turn to get back into position for a take-off roll. It wasn't like a permanent site with paved areas a plane could be guided into. Once the plane stopped he would be able to position his detail before the ramp dropped or a stairway was lowered.

Price pointed at the Moldovan Lieutenant. "You don't really think that little fucker has planned it out that far yet, do you?" He had his men side stepping now. Colonel Ivanov looked over and shouted at him. Price had to stifle a laugh. "His Colonel is starting to get pissed at him too. He just called him poor excuse for a cadet, or something like that."

He reached into his vehicle for a bottle of water. "Once I see the plane on the ground, I'll just line my guys up at the side of the runway. Wherever he stops, we'll get into position. I'm not getting my guys out of the shade until then. When's the CSM getting here?"

Sharp didn't know. He knew there was a meeting with Kosavich, but that was all. "He'll probably show up with the brass."

"He looked like shit at breakfast."

"You would to if you had his night."

Price snorted. "Yeah, like his night was worse than ours. At least I got laid. All he had to do was go to bed."

"Don't bet on it. When Gordon came over last night she said Bonneville was with Grant. She said she had been talking about making nice and getting the good stuff again."

Price screwed up his face and spat. "Go figure. Two hot officers and he's doing them both. I'm gonna ask him how he does it!"

Sharp pointed off in the distance. "There's your chance coming." There were two Hummers coming down the edge of the runway. "Are you ready to get your ass kicked?" They walked over to where the vehicles stopped.

Grant was in the first Hummer with Morgan and Schaeffer. Grant was driving. Schaeffer had decided, at Ramirez's urging, to brief Grant on what had been going on behind the scenes. When Schaeffer had finished, all Grant could do was mutter "Fucking politicians."

"It's a done deal, Sergeant Major" Schaeffer continued. Everybody wants those weapons back in Mother Russia. That was the whole point of the road. The crash in Albania proved it. It's too risky moving that stuff by air or rail. The Russians needed a good road net to move it, and we provided it."

Grant looked at Morgan. "And you knew about it all along?"

Morgan shook his head. "No. I was put with you because I was a pain in the ass about the chemical stocks in Albania. Nobody thought we'd be able to get this close to anything here. Once the cat was out of the bag, they let me in on it. You were just supposed to finish the road, then go away."

"Yeah, how'd that plan work out?"

Schaeffer cut in again. "Everything was working fine until the Arab showed up. We had tracked him from Khartoum to Algeria, then on to France. All our information said he died there. This was a surprise. At least he's out of the picture now."

Grant pulled the vehicle up by the other Americans and shut off the engine. Morgan and Schaeffer got out and walked over to where Sharp and Price were standing. Grant joined them. "There was one other thing I learned from Major Kosavich this morning. Sharif isn't dead, at least he wasn't last night."

Schaeffer's eyes went wide. "What do you mean?"

"I'm pretty sure he traded him off to the French. They were the guys in the car."

"Then they're the ones who killed Winder and company" Sharp offered.

Grant nodded. "That's a pretty good bet." He pulled out the notebook Kosavich gave him and handed it to Schaeffer. "Kosavich told me all his mission notes were in here. I don't know why he gave it to me. Probably a guilty conscience."

"More like he's trying to set you up again." Price said.

"That may be so, but I'm giving it to the Colonel here. We've gotta wrap this up and get outta this place. If you're going to get us shot at, get us to Iraq or Afghanistan where we were supposed to go. These side trips are killing me!"

Schaeffer took the notebook with a grunt, and pocketed it as he walked away. Morgan looked at Grant with sad eyes, then followed.

Price and Sharp came up on either side of him. In the distance they could hear the drone of an aircraft. As it got closer, they could make out the shape of a C-130 Hercules with French Air Force markings. Price got his detail together and held them ready to march out when the plane stopped.

"So all this," Sharp was pointing at the assembled dog and pony show, "is just a big fucking joke?" It was more of a statement than a question. There was a lot of time, effort and money being wasted on show, and everybody was getting what they wanted. The Russians were keeping their chemicals, the Moldovans got a road and they got the chemicals and the Americans out of their country, the French got Sharif, influence with the Moldovans, good publicity, and a chance to rub some American noses in the dirt.

"And what do we get out of it, Luke? Crapped on by a bunch of ass holes?"

Grant pulled a small sheaf of papers out of his sleeve pocket. Sharp could see they had been torn out of a notebook. "All that I gave to Schaeffer was written in Cyrillic. It's probably him yanking somebody's chain. The last few pages were in English. I don't think they were meant for Schaeffer or Morgan to see."

Sharp looked through them, pausing every few sentences to look at Grant. "Is this for real?"

"I don't know. We'll find out later. Just me, you, Pricey and maybe Elko. We'll meet at Kosavich's warehouse while the 'gentlemen' over there are having lunch."

"Quick and dirty?"

"Quick and dirty."


Kosavich was waiting for the Americans by a rack of Mauser K98 sniper rifles. Sharp ignored the officer and started picking through the racks, checking the actions, examining the bores and inspecting the optics. Kosavich watched him examine a few, then turned to the rest.

"I was wrong" was all he said. The Americans exchanged glances. Grant was the first to speak. "Your note said you had been betrayed by the French and wanted to take steps to" Grant looked at the papers for the correct word, "amend the situation. What are you planning, another sacrifice?"

"Yeah," Price added, "you want us to do some more of your dirty work? Your guys afraid of a little dirty work?"

"I can understand your skepticism. When it comes to deviousness, we seem to be badly outclassed by those we choose to fool. We trusted the French. We thought they would adhere to our agreement. We were wrong. They took advantage of us."

"Where's Sharif?" Sharp asked as he slammed the bolt closed on the rifle he was holding.

"My information has him out of the country. The French had a military transport waiting. I am sorry. We should have let you take him."

"We weren't going to 'take' him, Yvegniy. We were going to kill him. Just him, and maybe the Russian. Who was the kid that got dumped in his place?" Grant asked.

Before the Moldovan could answer, Sharp cut in. "You got any ammo for these?" he asked, holding up the Mauser. Kosavich gestured to a stack of crates at the far wall. Sharp wandered over that way.

"I don't know who the boy was. The French provided him for the tableau. He was probably a local boy they took off the streets."

Price laughed. "And we're the bad guys."

Kosavich waited for the chuckling to die down. "I cannot give you the Arab, but perhaps I can make amends." When there was no comment, he continued. "These are the passports of the men who were watching the street." Grant took them from his hand and flipped through them. It was an interesting mix, Iraqi, Moroccan, Saudi, Yemeni, Syrian and Egyptian. All young, all with student visas. "If it were possible, I would let you interrogate them, but once they were discovered to be foreigners, they were neutralized."

Price laughed again. "Like I said, we're the bad guys."

Grant cut him off. "Shut up, Price. Let him finish."

Kosavich led them to a large table and opened a portfolio that had been lying there. He drew out a large-scale map of the valley that encompassed the airstrip, the Russian compound, and the line of hills. There were military annotations on the map, and Grant identified them as heavy machine gun and mortar positions. There were also some that seemed to indicate RPGs. "Dave, you better come over and look at this."

"You recognize what this is?" Kosavich asked. Sharp joined them and examined the map in silence. "What are the red X's for?" he asked.

"Those will be the bodies of the men who died attacking the Russians tonight. They will be led by this man." He tossed out another identity card. It belonged to a Sergeant of the *Legion Etrangere Francais*, the French Foreign Legion. "We believe he was a deserter. He made the mistake of coming to my country and committing several rapes. He is due to be executed tonight. This will be a more useful end."

"Who are the other corpses? Us?"

"No, No. They are the men we took last night who were watching the street for the Arab. They are not my countrymen. They will be given their martyrdom."

324

"Why are you telling us this, Yvegniy? What do you think I'm going to do?" Grant asked.

"I'm hoping you will join me. We are going to destroy the chemicals tonight."

"Isn't that dangerous?" Elko asked.

"Perhaps. But it is going to storm tonight and tomorrow. The wind will be to the east and will blow the cloud into a harmless area."

"What she's asking, Yevigny, is what about the assault team? When that building goes up, whoever is close won't stand much of a chance. Then there's your security cordon. If you lift it before the attack, somebody will notice. I don't imagine you're going to risk your soldiers for the sake of a deception." Grant put in.

"And you would be absolutely correct. We have learned that the French plan to request the *cordon sanitaire*, as they call it, be removed as an act of good faith. My government is already disposed to agreeing to this. Our attack will be with stand off weapons, the 120mm mortars and the RPGs. It will be fast and accurate."

Sharp spoke again. "Even with all that, you can't guarantee a precision job. If the weather closes in and you have trouble with accuracy, you could leave a lot for salvage."

"Exactly! That's why my men have already treated the storage building to a liberal preparation of explosives. Once our attack has been underway long enough to seem determined, the job will be done." He looked at his watch. "I have to join the delegates at the mess. Stay, study the plans. My aide will answer any questions. I will see you tonight after dark." He walked to the door, then turned around. "And

Sergeant Sharp, my soldiers tell me you were quite the marksman in the Sudan. Keep that rifle, a gift for your efforts as an instructor."

The French Colonel who was leading the delegation was insufferable. Because of his rule of 'no enlisted other than waiters' in the officers' mess, there was no one to perform an adequate translation for most of the Moldovan and American officers. Major Carson had been fairly conversational in French a long time ago, but many of the nuances were escaping her. She tried her best to keep up for Schaeffer and Morgan, but it was a lost cause. The French officers, many of whom could undoubtedly speak English, were openly snickering at her difficulty. Morgan finally had enough. He wadded up his napkin and laid it on his plate. "Colonel" he said to Schaeffer, I've had enough of this. If you need me I'll be in my office. I've got too many things going on to sit here and be insulted." He turned to Carson. "Major, I'll leave it up to you. You can stay or come with me."

Schaeffer asked Carson to stay. "I really need you here, Major. I don't have a clue what's going on."

"You really want to know what's going on, Colonel? I'll tell you." Her voice had been raised a couple of decibels.

"Major, please, lower your voice."

"No, Colonel, there's no need. These gentlemen, and I use the word loosely, don't seem to speak any English, so it won't matter what I say." Schaeffer tried to stop her, but she just ignored him and continued. "That pimply faced one down there," she pointed to a young lieutenant, "has been taking great pains to try to describe my breasts to his friend. That one over there," she pointed to an aging captain, has been speculating to his friend whether or not you're gay, Colonel, and if he should ask you to join him for a drink later."

Schaeffer stood up, meaning to apologize to the French for her outburst, but she continued. "And their Colonel, in the true spirit of setting the example, when asked by his aide if he wanted him to translate for us, told him we can go fuck ourselves. So much for allied unity."

She walked up to another officer, who suddenly found his plate to be very interesting. She spoke to him in French so all could hear. *"Monsieur, I hope you do come by dispensary so I can examine the rash you caught from the Tunisian whore. I have a treatment, especially for you!"* With that she turned and stalked out. Schaeffer was stammering at Morgan, "You better do something about that outburst, Major. That was uncalled for!"

Morgan watched Carson walk out the door. "Yes Sir, I intend to. I think an Army Commendation Medal will do nicely."

A French Major stood and started to demand an apology. Colonel Ivanov stood and told him to sit down. He spoke in English. "You have come into my Mess and insulted my guests, and acted like barbarians when they defended themselves." He turned to Schaeffer and Morgan. "You have my apologies, gentlemen." Turning back to the French, "Any future meals will be served in the enlisted mess. I don't seem to have enough gentlemen to warrant keeping this one open." With that he dismissed his enlisted waiters and ordered his officers out of the room. Lunch was over.

Colonel Ivanov pressed his point when it came time to leave for the first meeting with the Russians. He insisted, as the host, to be the one to provide the transportation, since the French had insisted on excluding the Americans from the talks. That meant that the line of Hummers that had been standing by were dismissed. A bus was provided. The French protested, and Ivanov acknowledged it. "Perhaps tomorrow we can start fresh and the Americans can be mollified."

Grant and Sharp followed the bus from a discreet distance. The sky was beginning to darken, just as Kosavich had predicted. Grant looked at it without comment. Kosavich was right. Sharp pulled the vehicle onto the shoulder of the road running parallel to the compound. Both men used their binoculars to scan the area. They could see tarps, probably from the trucks in the motor pool, had been stretched between the buildings, blocking view into the interior. "This is interesting" Sharp commented.

"Yeah, now that they're letting people in, they're trying to hide what's going on. Makes you wonder why we were shut out of this deal."

"I don't wonder," Sharp said. "I'll bet if the people who are supposed to be letting us know what was happening actually did, we'd find out that antenna array is pointed right at France. This is almost too orchestrated for even the Frogs to be involved."

The security cordon was already being dismantled, not that it had been that tight to begin with. The Moldovans had concentrated on the main entrance. Grant and Sharp could see that there had been little, if any, security at the rear, where they had made their nocturnal entrances. "Dave, let's take a drive down back there. Something is starting to really bother me about this whole set-up."

Sharp got behind the wheel and pulled out. He has angling out to keep a good distance when Grant told him to pull in closer. "Let's see what happens. Keep driving up to the gate until someone tells us to stop." Sharp did as he was told. Both men kept looking for some sign of a sentry, or anyone paying attention to what was happening outside the perimeter. There was nothing. None of the towers seemed to be manned, there were no foot patrols, and the back gate stood wide open. There was sign of a lot of traffic on the dirt trail leading away from the compound. A Russian soldier appeared in the open gate as they stopped on the road just outside the gate. Grant was thinking Price would have been a useful addition to this trip, when the guard spoke, in English. Neither American was sure of what he had heard. They looked from one another, back to the Russian, who was smiling at them, calmly smoking a cigarette. "There is nothing for you to see here. Go away." He didn't even seem to be armed.

"Diplomacy couldn't have worked that fast."

"Drive over to the other side. Let's see what else is going on."

The drove to the far side of the compound then followed the fence line. There didn't seen to be any activity they could see in the compound. They were almost back to the front when Sharp suddenly stopped. He was looking out his window, towards the rear. Grant followed his gaze, trying to see what Sharp had spotted. Then it struck him.

Nothing.

There was nothing to see.

They had both missed it at first glance.

The Motor Pool was empty. All the Russian trucks were gone.

"That can't be a good sign. Where'd they go, Luke?"

Grant was as puzzled as Sharp. "I don't know. Could they be in between the barracks?"

"Why hide them? They know we got a count on them when they came in. It's not like they're fooling anybody."

"Maybe they've got them loaded and they don't want us to see?"

"Why load them without the tarps?" Grant asked, pointing at the canvas screens stretched between the buildings. "If they loaded the trucks and left the tarps on, we'd never know. There's got to be something else going on. Let's go back and check the trail. There seemed to be a lot of traffic back there lately."

Grant was right. There had been a lot of traffic on the trail, and there had been no effort to hide it. "We should have noticed this the first time." Sharp followed the trail away from the compound. Down in the ravine there were signs that this had been used as a marshalling area. There were tracks on both sides, showing where the vehicles had been parked, side by side, then more tracks as they pulled out, convoy fashion, heading for the bluffs.

"Got a chemical detector kit with you, Dave?"

"No, think I need one?"

"Let's find out. Follow the tracks."

The tracks led them down the ravine towards the bluffs, then up what appeared to be an old cart track that followed a fold in the terrain that would keep a vehicle hidden from the valley. From there, the trail angled back from the edge of the hills. They followed the tracks until they joined with the road just beyond where the two idiots who had tried to attack the plane had hidden their vehicle.

"We should have checked the area a little better. This would have been a better approach when we were scouting the compound," Sharp said.

Grant was scanning the valley with his binoculars. There was nothing to see.

"Luke, you want me to go up to that overlook by the bridge?"

"Don't bother. They're out of the valley already, probably across the river."

Sharp followed the line of hills with his gaze, then pointed out a smudge on the distant horizon. The skies were exceptionally clear in that direction. The storm clouds hadn't moved in that far yet. Whatever he was looking at was a long way off. "Something's burning out there."

"Probably a brush fire. If that storm moves in it'll take care of it."

There was a cloud of dust on the road heading toward their compound. Sharp picked it up with his glasses. "Looks like the Frogs are headed back to the barn already." Grant looked to see what he was talking about. Sharp pointed out the bus. "Whatever they had to say to the Russians didn't take much time." There was another movement down on the airfield. Grant looked and could see activity on the ramp of the C-130. It looked like they were loading up. A puff of black exhaust escaped from the near side engines as they began to turn over, then the same from the far side. The two NCOs looked at each other as the engines revved up to their take-off pitch, then the bird began to roll. The EU delegation was leaving already. Something didn't make sense.

"Dave, did you bring a radio with you?"

"I keep one in my bag." He rummaged around until he located it, then turned it on and handed it to the Sergeant Major. There was no traffic. Grant keyed the mike and called in to the commo section. The response was immediate.

"Is there anything going on back there?"

"The locals seem to be worked up about something, but nothing happening on our side."

"Where's the CO?"

"Probably in HQ. Want me to patch you over to him?"

"Negative. Just relay there's something going on with the Frogs. Their plane is leaving. I'll be back there in about fifteen."

"OK, Dave, let's head back."

Sharp didn't answer him. He was looking back over the trail they had followed. He put his hand up, one finger extended. "You better get back in the vehicle." Grant did as he was told. Keeping his voice low he asked, "What have you got?"

Sharp got behind the wheel and eased out his pistol. He was carrying a Russian model Tokarev, a lightweight caliber that was only good for close in work. He smiled sheepishly at Grant when he saw him looking at the pistol. "I didn't think I'd need anything heavier today." Grant eased out his Argentine copy government model. "Live and learn. What have you got?"

"Back about a hundred yards. You can probably see it in the mirror."

Grant leaned forward so he could see back along the road. There was something there, but he wasn't sure what. "What am I looking at?"

Sharp was looking off to the right front now. He started the Hummer and slipped it into gear. Once they were moving he answered. "There are two guys and a heavy MG under a camo net and some grass."

"Kosavich's guys?"

Sharp pointed down slope to the right. There were a number of small hills visible. Grant looked at them, and started to say something. Hen he realized what he was looking at. The small hills were trucks, badly hidden under camo nets. There were at least five, and maybe more. Sharp finally answered him. "I don't think your buddy is bringing that many people to the party tonight. Looks like somebody else wants to play." He found a sidetrack and turned down into the valley.

Rain was falling when they got back to the compound. In spite of it, the Moldovans seemed to be mobilizing for something. Several trucks full of troops were already rolling out the gate, and more were lined up in the motor pool, loading with soldiers and gear. Price was standing off to one side, watching them load. When he saw the Hummer come in he walked over to brief Grant and Sharp.

"There's been some trouble up to the north. Seems like some bandits decided to ambush a convoy on the road. These guys are going out hunting them."

A runner came over from headquarters. Morgan had seen the truck pull in and wanted to see the CSM, ASAP. Grant turned for the HQ, but the runner stopped him. "He's not over there, Sergeant Major. Him and that Colonel got called over to the other side. That's where he wants you." The other side referred to the Moldovan HQ. "They got called over there right after the bus came back from the Russian place. That's when all this started."

"Think something's up, Boss?"

"Yeah, bandits my ass. Dave, that's what that smoke was. The Russians got hit on the road."

"Russians? Where?"

"Sharp'll tell you. Who ever did it has some friends up on the heights overlooking the Russian compound. I want you to start getting people on their feet. Get them in full battle rattle and have them stand by. I think we have big problems coming."

Grant found Morgan and Schaeffer with the Moldovan staff. Morgan gave him a quick briefing about the situation, using a situation map tacked to a wall. The Russian convoy had been ambushed earlier that morning, but not as early as Grant would have guessed. They must have waited until after daylight before they left their assembly point in the ravine. There were still bits and pieces of information trickling in, so Grant took the time to tell Morgan everything he and Sharp had seen. "That group on the hill must have come down after the convoy passed. The way they're hunkered down and camo'ed, they're probably waiting for dark to hit the compound." Morgan passed that on to an English speaking Moldovan officer, who translated it for another officer who had a telephone jammed in his ear. They had a brief conversation, then the officer returned and gave Morgan an update.

"The Russians were stopped here," he pointed to a junction where the road they had constructed tied in with a main highway headed for the Dnestr River bridge. "By first count, there were forty five trucks destroyed, and much loss of life from the damaged cargo." There was an indication of a small built up area by the site of the ambush. The loss of life must have been civilians.

"Were the Russians able to tell you anything?"

"There were no Russian survivors. Witnesses told our soldiers that the attackers were all wearing some kind of masks and capes, probably chemical suits, and went from truck to truck executing any survivors. Then they placed explosives on all the trucks and destroyed them."

"They didn't try to recover any of the cargo?"

The Moldovan wasn't certain. "There is still heavy fighting going on in the area. The first troops to respond were not equipped for chemical weapons and suffered heavily. They are trying to contain the attackers. Our soldiers are better equipped to enter the area."

"What about the people on the hill?"

"They will have to wait until we can get some more troops. As long as they seem interested in the Russians, the chemical convoy has priority." A call from the other side of the room summoned him away. Schaeffer excused himself to go back and report what had happened so far to CENTCOM. Morgan initially wanted to remain, but Grant convinced him he would be better off at his own headquarters. "You have a staff. That's their job. Detail an officer here as liaison. Give him a radio and have commo run a landline. He can keep you advised."

Grant noticed Morgan was having trouble standing for any length of time. His wounds were bothering him. "And have the medics give you something for the pain."

"No, I don't want anything clouding my head."

"You've never been wounded before, have you?" Grant asked.

"No, and I hope I never am again. Why? You want to compare scars?"

"Major, I learned the hard way that pain will fuck you up just as bad or worse than the pain killers. Get the edge off. You'll think clearer."

"You sure?"

"Don't believe me. Ask Sharp. He's been shot and not evacuated often enough. He knows what it'll take to stay in it."

"He's that good?"

"No, he's that much of an asshole, but he functions. You'd be amazed at how much effort you have to put into ignoring pain. Take the pain killers."

Kosavich came in the room as they were leaving. He was in battle dress, with his face painted. "I fear our plans for tonight have been changed!"

Morgan looked at Grant. "What's he talking about?"

They both ignored him. "Yvegniy, we have other problems close at hand."

"Yes, I know. I have had men scouting the hills ever since I heard about the convoy leaving this morning. They were almost surprised by the arrival of the Chechens."

"Chechens? They're a long way from home." Morgan said.

"Yes, and they are probably part of the same group that destroyed the convoy."

"Did they get any of the chemicals?"

Kosavich shook his head. "They overplayed their hand, very badly. From what I have learned, every truck was destroyed. They were a little overeager when it came to killing the Russians." He paused long enough to read a message a soldier handed him. "At last, some good news." He helped Grant take Morgan out to the vehicle. He sketched out a plan to take on the second group of Chechens. He asked Morgan to consider it, flesh it out if he could, and he would join them in a few minutes.

Grant got Morgan into his vehicle and took him back to headquarters. He stopped the first soldier he saw and sent him for Major Carson. "Tell her to bring her bag!"

Inside the office, Grant sent another soldier to find Price and Sharp, then laid out his ideas for Morgan. The Major listened, then said he wanted to pass the plan by Schaeffer. Grant shook his head. "That's the pain talking. Schaeffer is intelligence, not tactical. You're the commander. It's your call. He'll just kick it up to Tampa. We might not have time for that."

"What was Kosavich talking about, the 'plans for tonight' he said?"

"We were going to take out the chemical shed before they could move them."

"Without telling me?"

"You seemed to have forgotten to tell me a few things the past few days. Call it even."

Before Morgan could consider it, Carson arrived with Lieutenant Robles, her nurse, in tow. When she saw the two men, neither with any apparent new injuries, she looked back and forth between them with her hands out to the side, as if to ask 'what'?

"The Major has decided to take advantage of your services, Doctor. What can you give him to dull the pain, but not the brain?"

Carson rummaged through her bag and took out a small case. "Drop your trousers."

"Can't you give it to me in the arm?"

She smiled. "A couple of days ago I could have used your arm."

Sharp and Price walked in as she was finishing the injection. Price saw the size of the needle and winced. After Morgan had his trousers up, he told Grant to lay out his plan. "You might as well stay, Doctor. You'll need to know what you have to get ready for."

Fortunately, Kosavich made his appearance before Grant could get too detailed. He indicated that he had a platoon of soldiers, the same ones who had helped in the city, available for the plan. Grant grunted his acceptance, then laid out his plan. Kosavich interrupted here and there to suggest a change or offer an alternative. He and Grant bickered back and forth over a few items, and Price and Sharp made their own suggestions. After some give and take, a plan was agreed to. Kosavich made notes on his map, then left to handle his side of the arrangements. "I better let the Russians know that their old friends are in the area." Morgan saw him pass Schaeffer by the flagpole. He nudged Grant.

"What should I tell him?"

"Nothing. If he asks, tell him you upped our alert status, and we'll be patrolling outside the perimeter. Anything else, and I guarantee he'll fuck it up."

"He's not stupid. He'll figure something's up."

"As long as he thinks we're defending this place, I don't care. We have a right to self-defense. Keep him in the dark for a couple of hours. By then, it'll be too late to do anything."

As soon as Grant was gone he sent for the Headquarters Company Commander and First Sergeant. His wounds might be slowing him down, but they would not keep him out of the fight.

# CHAPTER 14

Grant assembled his teams on the Moldovan side of the compound, away from any chance of being seen by Schaeffer. To keep his fiction of defending this compound alive, he had Price organize a couple of reaction teams at headquarters, and sent a couple of listening posts outside the wire with instructions to keep the alert frequency busy. Edwin Robinson was given the task of maintaining a radio watch on the circuits Grant would be using. If there was a need, he was to respond with a surprise Kosavich had arranged. His brother would secure a rally point.

The rain was both a help and a hindrance. It would mask their approach to the defensive positions they would assume, but it would also mask the Chechens. The American NVGs would have their effectiveness limited. Sharp brought up the subject of illumination. Kosavich had a limited number of High Explosive shells for his 120mm mortars. Once they were used up his crews would switch to illumination. The Moldovan troops were not well equipped with NVGs, and Morgan nixed issuing American gear to them. "That illumination will white out the goggles. We might be better off without them."

"Negative. Use the NVGs as long as you can, and keep them handy. If these guys decide to make a fight of it after we open up, it's gonna be a rat hunt, and those 120mm mortar rounds won't last all that long."

It was a pitifully small force going out against the Chechens. The Americans mustered little more than a reinforced platoon. The Moldovans couldn't do much better. Most of their forces had been sent north to deal with the convoy ambush, and there was still a need to defend this compound in case there was another force they hadn't seen yet. There would be very little left in reserve.

Grant and Kosavich had worked out a very simple defensive plan around the Russian compound. The Russians would defend the center, the compound itself. They admitted to having an under strength company left, armed only with light weapons. They would have the benefit of a chain link fence topped with barbed wire, but there was nothing in the way of prepared positions. They would have to start digging holes. Grant had planned a series of trip flares located about 200 meters out from the fence. That would be the Russian signal to fire. Either end of the compound would be held by a platoon of infantry, Moldovans on the south, the Americans to the north. These wings would be laid out in 'L' shaped positions, short leg coming off a corner of the compound, a machine gun sited at the bend. There was a slight advantage of terrain where they had chosen to set up. The Moldovans had the benefit of part of the ravine that snaked along the edge of the valley towards the hills. The end of their line crossed it. The banks could be used as a rampart, while a single automatic weapon could interdict travel down the ravine. If the Chechens had planned their attack well enough, this was the obvious point of entry.

The Americans had a slight rise running the long leg of their position. At its highest, it wasn't more than three feet, but the elevation gave them a commanding position with which to sweep the ground in front of them. As much as Grant would have preferred to coordinate the fire of both wings, he realized the 500 plus meter separation would only result in a lot of wasted fire on targets out of range. Each wing would be responsible for their own early warning system, either outposts or flares, and they would respond when their line was approached. Kosavich agreed to it. He was, after all, a security service member, and not an infantryman. A battle out in the open was a lot different than a raid on an apartment building. Grant was hoping that the independent response would be enough to confuse the Chechens and mask the fact that they were facing an overextended force. There would be an under strength squad, this under Price, working their way from the airfield up the heights to try to take the Chechens in the rear, and take out any vehicles. Kosavich had provided a Chechen speaker to go with them. Price was already on the move. He had asked for an earlier start time in order to get into position and observe before dark. He'd be able to locate the trucks, and hopefully, check out the Chechen assembly areas to give the friendlies an idea of their axis of approach. Price thought it would be a good idea to know if they moved out before the friendly forces were ready. "It wouldn't hurt to know if they're getting lazy and decide to ride down the hill. It would make it easier to take them out in bunches, instead of one by one." Grant doubted they would risk their trucks up close in the attack. They had too far to travel over open country to use them in an attack that could damage or destroy them. Price would isolate them and take them out.

The rain was starting to let up as they pulled out of the compound. Grant hoped it wouldn't stop completely. It would mask the vehicles approach and any on-site organization. They got lucky. The rain continued in spurts. Another break was realized when Price radioed that he was on the heights and approaching the Chechens. There had been no security on his avenue of approach, and he could make out the Chechens forming up. His rough count was about one hundred infantry. It also looked like they had two heavy mortars of their own. He had brought one of Sharps suppressed pistols with him. He would try to take out the crews before they started firing.

Each squad had a medic. Carson wasn't happy with 'her girls' being spread out and in the line of fire, but she knew that if there was a need for them, they would want to be close to the action. Elko had insisted on accompanying Price. Hers would be the most exposed position, and she packed accordingly. She had weighed herself down with an extra medical bag, as well as grabbing two bandoleers for the riflemen. Carson had personally supervised loading her section ambulance. As soon as it got dark she was going to stage it at the airfield, with an additional Hummer. That would be her evacuation hospital with the rest of her staff. She toyed with the idea of grabbing a moment or two with Grant before he headed out, but realized it would be a futile attempt. He had a lot to do, and there were always people looking for both of them.

Bonneville hadn't been so noble. Even if Grant wasn't going to tell her what was going on, Sharp told Sheila, who passed it on to her. She waited for her opportunity to waylay him on one of his infrequent trips to his quarters. He was distracted, distant. She was disappointed. She wanted him again, but there wasn't time. Gordon found her in her room after the trucks started to move out. They sat together in silence. Gordon was the first to speak. "Don't worry. They'll be OK. We can help each other get ready for when they come back." Bonneville knew exactly what the other girl meant.

Price closed in on the Chechen position. One of his soldiers pointed out some activity around the trucks. The ragheads were loading crates onto one that had markings for a Russian army vehicle. The work was being supervised by what appeared to be a Russian soldier. He tapped the translator on the shoulder and indicated he should follow. He expected some reluctance, but to his surprise the Moldovan soldier dumped his pack and crawled up to him. Once he explained what he was going to do, the soldier grunted and nodded his head.

The rain was on and off now, and visibility was improving. It was somewhat offset by the fading light. Price cut a wide swath to stay behind some natural folds in the ground, or cut through high grass. The dampness helped to muffle the sound of their movement. Price depended on one of his soldiers to be alert for any signs the Chechens had seen his approach. He and his Moldovan partner kept their heads down and moved towards the sound. The rag heads weren't practicing any kind of noise discipline. He felt a hand on his ankle. He stopped and looked back as the translator crawled even with him. "I can hear them now." Was all he said. A couple of slow minutes passed as the Moldovan cocked his ear and listened. Price was relieved when he finally signaled he had heard enough and started backing out. He clicked his radio to let his team know he was on his way back.

At his protected position, the Moldovan took a long drink from his canteen before he spoke. "They're loading the truck with explosives."

Price could have told him that from the markings on the crates. He impatiently asked, "Did you hear why?"

Another long drink. "They were praising one man, I couldn't tell which. He had been selected for martyrdom, and they were envious of his first night with the virgins."

One of Price's soldiers, the one who had been keeping an overwatch, said it looked like the Russian was getting all the attention. "What do you think it means, Sarge?"

Price took the field glasses and moved to where he could see the truck. The Russian had unrolled a prayer mat and was kneeling on it, facing what was probably the direction of Mecca. He was probably saying his farewells. Another Chechen came over and started to berate the group. He felt the Moldovan besides him. "That one is angry. He says the truck should already be on its way. He's holding up the entire attack." There was an exchange as the driver stood and rolled his prayer mat, yelling back. The Moldovan snickered, then translated. "The driver told him that if he was in a hurry, he could drive into the Russians and go to Allah. Then he wouldn't have to hide under his father's shadow. The rest of the men laughed, and I couldn't hear the rest." Price crawled back and laid out what he thought.

"OK, that truck is going to drive into the compound and blow itself up. He's probably a distraction and the start of the attack."

"I think you're right, Sarge. It looks like the rag heads are moving out."

Price looked over, and in the fading light he could see two separate groups moving into the valley. The son with the attitude wasn't with either group. He had taken up a position just behind the mortars. The Moldovan said he was ordering the crews to prepare more shells for firing. Now, the sound of the truck was heard, and Price could see it heading to the north. It would probably come back down by the airstrip, then drive towards the compound. It was time to let Grant know what was going on.

Grant took the report, then relayed the information to Sharp and the squad leaders. There was another sound in the valley. Sharp identified it as one of their M920 tractors, probably hauling a flat bed. "What the hell is that doing here?" Sharp asked.

"One of Kosavich's little surprises." There were more engine noises. These had a high pitch whine that Sharp couldn't identify. There was some clanging, rattling and thuds, then all was quiet again. Sharp looked back but couldn't see what had made the noise. Grant didn't seem concerned.

"What are we going to do abut the Russian truck, Luke? Want to warn the Russians?"

"That's already taken care of now. Pass the word. The bad guys are on the move. They'll probably move into position before the truck gets here and wait. Keep everybody on their toes. We're here to surprise them, not the other way around. The sequence they probably expect will be the truck going up, mortars coming down, then their assault moving in before the Russians know what's hitting them." He looked around into the faces of his NCOs. They all knew what was expected of them and their men.

Grant went on. "The truck won't be an issue, and Price said he'll take care of their mortars. That leaves their infantry. We have them in a three-sided box. Watch your fields of fire, and this should be over quick. Nobody moves forward unless I give the word. Got it?"

Everybody acknowledged. Once they were gone, Sharp asked "Think it'll work?"

"I think we'll do our part, and Price will do his. Just remember that no battle plan has ever survived first contact with the enemy. Stay flexible, listen up for changes, and make sure everybody knows the rally point and the countersign, just in case."

Grant moved up and down the line, stopping at each position to speak to the soldiers. There were no officers present, a development that wasn't unusual for this outfit, but troubling, none the less. The only platoon leader who had stepped forward was Lieutenant Stanley, but because of Morgan's prohibition on females in combat, he wouldn't permit her to come forward of the aid station set up at the airstrip. The medics weren't supposed to be forward either, but Grant ignored that fact because he wanted them where they would do the most good if they were needed. Stanley would get her chance at the combat she craved if there was a need for the reaction force that should be moving into position about now. As long as they were practicing good light discipline, the suicide bomber wouldn't even notice them assembled there. Even if he did, he probably wouldn't have a radio to alert his friends, and his mission dictated he start the attack on the compound, not engage targets of opportunity that he probably couldn't identify in the dark.

The soldiers were well placed and dug in. Sharp had positioned them well. Grant quizzed them on their fields of fire, the rally points, countersigns and any other details covered in their mission brief. All of them had been involved in the dirtier side of operations, going all the way back to Darfur. Grant was certain they would do their jobs as he expected. They were all well protected from the elements with their wet weather gear. Polypropylene and Gore-Tex were an effective combination.

His last stop was at Sharp's position, at the far end of the line. He had dug a semi-circular position to share with a SAW gunner. They would anchor the left end of the line and react to any attempts to turn the flank. The gunner had his ready ammunition laid out. Next to it, Sharp had placed a pair of open bandoleers with 40mm grenades for his M-203. Whatever happened at this end, they would handle it roughly. Grant stopped and passed his canteen. He had two liters of water in his hydration pack. The canteen contained coffee. It was cold now, but it had a caffeine boost.

"I don't know about you, Luke, but this waiting around in the rain gets old. I have to say I prefer the desert."

"I seem to remember that getting cold too. And I've been shot in every desert we've ever been in."

"Luke, you get shot everywhere we go. So do I, for that matter. At least in the desert I get to the hospital with a good base tan." He looked at his SAW gunner. "It impresses the nurses."

The gunner laughed. "I like winter better."

"Skier?"

"Nah. I snow board. It scares the hell out of the old folks on the slope." Then he remembered the Sergeant Major. "No offense, Sergeant Major. I didn't mean all old people."

"No offense taken, Son, but you have to spend the night with Sergeant Sharp here. He is an old man, and he's sensitive." Grant collected his canteen and moved off, back to his position at the angle of the 'L'.

Price watched the Chechens move off. He positioned his troops to take out the trucks on his signal, and then he took the translator with him and closed in on the mortars. The crews were only made up of two men each. The rest must have been pressed into the attack, which made sense. The heavy mortars would be stationary, and the ammo was stockpiled. Two men could service the tube adequately. Price looked for the unfortunate son, as he began to think of him. The Moldovan anticipated him and pointed to a shadow to the rear of the tubes. Price drew his silenced pistol, but the Moldovan put his hand out to stop him. He showed Price his fighting knife and crawled away. Price watched the shadow. Another form merged with it, then they both disappeared. Next thing he knew, the Moldovan was by his side again. "For a man with an attitude like his, you would think he would have struggled more."

The Moldovan laid out a quick plan for the mortars. He would engage the far crew in conversation while Price took out the other pair. When the first pair turned at the sound of the suppressed weapon, and Price knew they would hear something, you can't quiet a 9mm like they do in the movies, the Moldovan would take out one with his knife while Price shot the other one. It worked just as they planned. The Moldovan was getting ready to disable one of the tubes when Price stopped him. He searched the body of the unfortunate son and found a radio. He handed it to the translator. "When they don't open up when they're supposed to, there'll probably be a call for fire. Do you know how to hang rounds?" The Moldovan said he did.

"Good, I'll get you some help." He retrieved one of his soldiers and explained what he wanted. Then he took out his flashlight and looked at the settings on the tubes. He estimated about where the Chechens would be when they started their attack, and gave the handles a couple of spins. He showed them how to adjust laterally, then he went looking for the drivers. He found them clustered around a little gas stove, brewing tea. He placed his soldiers on line about ten yards away, then they all knelt and waited.

The bomb truck passed the airstrip without slowing. Stanley and Robinson had seen his headlights coming out of the hills, and they had prepared a welcome if he had turned towards them. Grants guess that he would be focused on his mission and would ignore anything else had been correct. He hit the main trail and turned in the direction of the Russian compound. Robinson radioed the information to Grant. The message was acknowledged, and Kosavich came up onto the net. "I see his lights. We will take care of him."

Price heard the blast and gave the command to fire. The Chechens had no time to react. They were all cut down before the sound of the blast had a chance to fade. "Wait for the firing in the valley, then put a grenade into each cab!" He headed back to the mortars.

The attackers and the Russians were startled by the blast outside of the compound. The Russians hadn't expected it, and the Chechens had expected it to be in the compound. And there was something about the explosion. It sounded like there were two, one after the other, very quickly. The Chechen leader couldn't figure out what was going on, but figured that the Russian attention must be drawn to the blast, just like theirs. It was time to start the attack. He radioed for the mortars to begin. In his excitement, he didn't realize that it was not the voice of his son.

The Moldovan acknowledged the transmission and gave the signal to his American assistant to start hanging rounds. Each tube was only stocked with ten rounds, and they would go quickly. The first rounds were away by the time Price returned He looked into the valley, looking for the impacts. They seemed too short. "Add 50 meters and give me another round!" Both gunners worked a dial, then hung another round. The firing was staggered this time. Price watched the impacts again. He thought he could see a body thrown up in the light of the explosion. "You're on target. Waste 'em!"

Grant watched the explosions from his position. So far, so good, he thought. Having the M-3 tanks along had been a good idea, but Kosavich was reporting that one of them had already thrown a tread. It would be of no further use. Grant told Kosavich to abandon it and have the crew join his men on the south side. It was also time for his heavy mortars to start firing illumination rounds. The Russians in the compound were firing wildly at the mortar burst, a waste of their fire. Grant wanted to give them some real targets.

The night lit up under the burning magnesium. Grant could see figures in the grass milling around. The unexpected mortar barrage confused and shocked them. The illumination added to the confusion. He could see them start moving away from the explosions, into his kill zones. He got on the radio to remind his troops. "Watch your lanes of fire. Let them hit our flare line before you open up!" Sharp reported the Chechens were moving quickly. The illumination hadn't affected the Russian fire. Their tracers were all still heading into the mortar barrage, where there weren't any more targets. Five hundred yards away, Sharp could see the flares in front of the Moldovan positions ignite. There were a series of small explosions, probably grenades.

Grant was monitoring his and the Moldovan frequency, just in case. Right after the flares went off in front of their position, the Moldovans started passing a lot of chatter. He couldn't understand what was being said, but some of it sounded panicky. He heard Kosavich's voice come on and issue some harsh orders, and then he came up on the American channel. "I have a problem at my position. My men say someone is grenading them from the rear. I think I have a traitor."

The Moldovans did have a problem. The Chechens had slipped a squad down the ravine without being detected. They managed to get into the rear of the Moldovan position with the help of a turncoat. They were now working their way down the line, taking out Moldovan positions one at a time from the rear. The attackers in the center noticed the fire slackening from their left and started shifting that way. The Moldovans were getting caught in a vice.

"Yvegniy, take the tank and any spare men you have at your mortars. Reduce the illumination to one tube and shift the others to high explosive in front of your position. I'll get my ready squad moving over to you."

He gave his front a quick scan. The flares in front of Sharp's position were starting to ignite. He got back on his radio as a SAW gunner opened up. "Robinson, come in!"

"Robinson, roger."

"Did you copy the Moldovan transmission?"

"I copied. We're loading up now. You want me to drop anyone off at your position?"

"Negative. Back up the other guys. Be alert, and don't get mixed in their lines. They have a bad guy working on them."

"Roger that." There was a brief pause. "The medics want to know if you need anything."

More flares were going off, and his entire line was firing now. He could see muzzle flashes from the Chechens, returning fire. "Negative at this time. I don't want any more people moving around in the dark!" A whoosh from an RPG went over his head and exploded to the rear of his position, too far away to do any harm. The back blast from the launcher dried and ignited enough of the grass to give him an idea where the position was. He pointed it out to a grenadier next to him, who put a round in the approximate location. He was rewarded with a secondary explosion.

The illumination had stopped, as well as the mortar rounds from the hills. All the tubes were out of ammunition. There were several small fires burning out in the field, but the damp grass was resisting. Grant noticed that the rain had stopped as well. The firing to his front had ended for the most part, except for one persistent gunner to his immediate front. He would fire a burst, change positions, and then fire again, going back and forth. Grant pointed out the pattern to the grenadier, then moved down the line. He had the feeling the Chechens were trying to sidestep and run around his flank. He let Sharp know what he thought.

"I'm on it, Boss. I had the same idea. I'm rolling back to extend the line north."

"OK. I'm on my way to you." Grant looked up to the hills and could see the glow of fires behind them. Price had accomplished his part.

Price gathered his team up. There were no live Chechens on the heights, and the trucks were all in flames. The only thing left was to police up the weapons and destroy the tubes, and that would have to wait. He looked into the valley to try to get a sense of how the battle was going down there. The firing had died down along the line. The only spot that still looked hot was to the south, in the Moldovan sector. He had heard the radio calls from Kosavich and knew they had a problem, but the tank and the reaction force should stabilize it soon. His first concern was about the Chechens side slipping and flanking the American line. Sharp seemed to be taking action to prevent that.

"This is Price. We're done up here, where do you want us?"

"Price, stay where you're at. I don't need any more bodies moving around in the dark!"

"But we can help!"

"Stay put! The rag heads will be heading back your way as soon as they figure out they're getting their asses whacked. Establish a blocking position and don't let them back on the hills!"

The arrival of the M-3 stabilized the Moldovan sector, but there was still heavy pressure from the Chechens who had infiltrated the position. The 37mm gun in the tank turret jammed after four rounds, but the fire had been enough to put a damper on any Chechen bravado. There was a distinct lack of volunteers for martyrdom. There were also three .30 caliber Browning machine guns mounted on the tank. The crew proceeded to fire up every available round before they withdrew.

The distractions from the flanks had given the Russians the impression they had repelled the main attack. The poorly trained conscripts started to come out of their firing positions to watch the action to either flank. The tracers flying across the ground made them believe all the action was directed away from them. It was a severe shock when the Chechens managed to mass their RPGs at the center of the fence line and renew their attack. The unprotected Russians were cut down like dry hay, and the survivors went to ground, their only instinct now being for self-protection.

The concentrated blast drew attention from all across the field. Surviving Chechen sub-commanders rallied their fighters and started moving them to the breach in the wire, leaving small groups to hold the attention of the flank positions. Their primary mission was to capture the chemical building. They had detailed plans of the compound and knew exactly where to go.

The first indication that the Russians weren't fighting anymore came when vehicles started coming out of the compound. The machine gun crew set up at the apex was the first to notice. They heard the vehicles behind them and saw the trucks, beds full of panicked soldiers heading out to the north. One of the squad leaders, Grant couldn't tell which, called and reported what he had seen. Pressure in front of the American position suddenly eased, and he asked if he should take his team into the compound. Grant gauged the situation and told him to stay put. As far as he knew, only a couple of the senior people were aware that the chemical shed had been rigged with explosives. He didn't want his men wandering too close to it when it was touched off.

"Put a fire team on the gate and stop anybody coming through who doesn't look like a Russian."

"What if we can't tell the difference?"

"Then they aren't Russians!"

There was another distraction. Someone was on the radio, asking where he should place his troops. There was a lot of static, but it sounded like the First Sergeant. Grant responded with a quick question. "Who the fuck is this?"

"First Sergeant here. I have another platoon en route. Where do you want them?"

Reinforcements are nice when you need them, but not if you have to leave something else undefended. Another platoon out here seriously weakened their compound. If the Chechens had plans in that direction, this would be their opportunity. Grant didn't want them wandering around in the dark, especially now that the Russians were wandering around in a panic. He made a quick decision and told him to hold at the airstrip. "The Ivans broke. I don't know where they are. Support the aid station. Give yourself a 360* perimeter and be prepared to respond in any direction." Harrison acknowledged. Grant heard Sharp call him. "What genius sent you out here?"

"Morgan" was the one word reply. Grant should have known. Morgan went from pain addled to drug confident. He was trying to influence events he had no information about. "Ralph, this is Grant. Do not, I say again, do not leave that position unless you hear from me, is that clear?"

"I copy. The boss is anxious."

There was only sporadic firing to the American front now. The Chechens had left a few men to occupy the line while they invested the Russian compound. Kosavich reported that, except for a large group that was trying to force its way up the ravine, most of the pressure was off his front also. He asked if this would be a good time to spring his surprise. 'Light the candle' as he put it. Grant said it would be. He passed the word down the line for everyone to get into their chemical masks and gloves. They were already wearing their suits, just in case. The rain had stopped, and there was a breeze coming from the west. He had the chemical detector set deployed.

The blast was larger than he had expected. It looked like the roof came off intact and went straight up in the air. The shock waves ripped out the canvas strung between the buildings, and the ball of fire reached out and involved the neighboring buildings. He could hear the muffled "Holy shit" come from the mask of the soldier next to him. The fire lit the compound like someone had turned on the sun. There wasn't any movement. Grant hadn't expected any. It would take the survivors a bit to gather their wits and begin to stir. He started to move up the line, warning his soldiers to be alert for movement in the compound, and to shoot any they saw. The mask was frustrating, and hard to talk through. He ripped it off and stuffed it into his jacket. The Chechens who had been keeping them occupied had resumed their firing by the time he reached Sharp at the far end. Sharp had his mask off too, as well as his SAW gunner. "If there's a problem, we'll hear the chemical alarm."

The grenadiers were engaging the Chechens with good results. The last of them decided he had had enough and raced back to rejoin his comrades. Several M-16s tracked him and hurried him along to paradise. The firing line went quiet.

"What do you think, Boss?" Sharp asked.

"I think we better stay on our toes. There's probably still a bunch of them out there. As soon as they get the ringing out of their ears, they'll be doing something."

"Think they'll throw in the towel?"

Grant shook his head. "Not these guys. They came a long way for this. I doubt they expected to go home." He paused and looked out at the compound. "No, they'll probably head back for the hills and go out shooting."

"We gonna go in and clean out the compound?"

"No. We'll wait until first light and watch the Moldovans do it. I don't want any of our people getting involved in going house to house in there or fucking with booby traps. We did our part."

Grant had been right. The Chechens started their retreat shortly after he had spoken with Sharp. His gunners did their best to kill them, but some still managed to get to the end of the valley and start to scale the heights. The biggest group came from the ravine, finally giving up their attempt to get through the Moldovans. They followed the road, unaware of the automatic weapons sited on it. They still believed their trucks were waiting for them, and they weren't prepared for Price and his blocking position. It was like shooting ducks in a barrel. The Chechens recoiled and went back into the valley. There was no more firing for the rest of the night.

The sky was getting light in the east when Kosavich informed Grant he was beginning his mop-up sweep through the compound. The Sergeant Major had Sharp reposition his men to close off the northern end, and had Price start moving down from the heights to clear the ground between him and the compound. He put his men on line and started off slowly. They paused at each body they passed, checking for life and removing weapons and documents. They didn't find any live Chechens in their path.

There was occasional firing in the compound as Kosavich and his men came across wounded Chechens. They made no effort to take prisoners. The chemical shed had been completely destroyed, with many of the remaining buildings heavily damaged. The Russians had done a thorough job of removing any weapons they had stockpiled. There were trace readings on the chemical detector kits, but no dangerous levels. Everything had been removed and was in the ambushed convoy.

The heaviest friendly casualties had been with the Moldovans. Kosavich reported he had six dead and eleven wounded, three seriously. He requested medical assistance. Grants casualties were three wounded, none seriously. One of them had been with Price. His attached medics were able to handle the load, and then he dispatched them over to the Moldovan side to do what they could. He also called for the aid station to send up the ambulance, under escort, just in case. There was a possibility some of the rag heads had survived and had so far evaded the mop up. Harrison came up with the escort. He sent the ambulance and the other vehicles on south while he joined Sharp and Grant.

"I've got a chow truck coming up with coffee and sandwiches. I thought you could use something." He looked around. "You just about done here?"

"Yeah. Just mop up all of that's left, and that'll be for the locals."

"What do you want to do with the Russians I've got?"

"Where have you got Russians?"

Harrison waved over his shoulder. "Hell, a couple of hours ago they showed up at the airfield, about sixty of them. No officers, just a bunch of privates. Most of them didn't even have weapons. The medics are patching up their wounded. I thought you might have sent them back to me."

Grant shook his head. "The Chechens opened up with a bunch of RPGs, and they decided they didn't want to serve Mother Russia any more. When you get back, round them up and put them on the east side of the runway. Keep them out of the way of our coming and goings until the Moldovans can figure out what to do with them."

Kosavich chose that moment to come walking out the gate. He had removed his helmet. His face was smeared with camouflage paint and his hair was sweaty and matted. His left arm hung at his side, the sleeve discolored from blood. Sharp reached out and pulled the material away. He shook some betadine solution onto the wound and covered it with his combat bandaged. Kosavich was smiling. "That was exhilarating, my friends, but I think I prefer the life of Internal Security!" He gave Grant a quick after action report, then announced there was a battalion of Moldovan infantry enroute to secure the area and search for any Chechen survivors. Harrison offered him a flask from one of his cargo pockets. Kosavich accepted and took a long swallow. There was a radio call. Another of his men had died. He looked at the Americans. "Regrettable, but this action has been good for my country."

"How do you mean?" Grant asked.

"We have been blooded, for the first time since 1945. And my soldiers stood and fought," his grin got wider, "while the Russians broke and ran." He bobbed his head up and down. "We can build on this."

Sharp asked about the tank. "How come I didn't hear more cannon fire?"

"I'm afraid the breech mechanism jammed, and my soldiers didn't know what to do." Kosavich answered. "The machine guns were effective until a rocket hit the drivers hatch. The blast killed the occupants."

"Damn, I wanted to take one home," Grant said.

"I still have two more. I will see what I can do for you."

Harrison hitched up his gear and headed back to the airstrip. He was on the radio giving instructions for the Russians to be rounded up when he got a surprise. "They're gone already" He turned to look at Grant and shrugged. It was one less problem to deal with. "Make sure the main compound knows they're wandering around in case they show up there." As an after thought he asked, "Why'd they leave?"

There were a few moments of silence, then the response came back, "Some of them were wandering around when they started jabbering at each other, Top. I guess they were scared by what they saw in the valley. Anyway, they all spooked and grabbed some of their walking wounded and left. They didn't even stop for the chow truck!"

Grant was up now, and so was Sharp. Grant keyed his radio. "This is the Sergeant Major. What did they see in the valley?"

"Nothing much, Sergeant Major. They just spotted Price and his troops heading in."

That didn't sound right. Sharp scanned the valley with his field glasses. There was a small group of men approaching through the high grass. "If Price is over at the airfield, who's that coming over there?"

Grant and Harrison both looked. Harrison had a better set of glasses. He was able to identify the men in the field. "That's Price! Who's at the airstrip? More Russians?"

Grant didn't like what was developing. He had Sharp overload Harrisons Hummer with a squad and sent them back to the airfield. Then he called back and told the NCO to get out security and send out patrols to the east and south. "Don't let those people get close until you identify them." He waited for an answer. There was nothing but silence on the radio. He repeated his instructions. There was a faint rattle in the distance. His radio came alive. There was an unknown voice shouting into it. He couldn't identify what was being said, but he could hear firing in the background. The airfield was being attacked. He called a warning to Sharp, but it was unnecessary. Sharp had been monitoring the frequency.

The Chechens had not been expecting anyone at the airfield. The activity surprised them, but when there was no reaction to their approach they went to ground and made plans to try to take one of the trucks they could see parked there. As they were deploying to attack they could see several of the vehicles speed away, but there was another large truck approaching. It was the mess truck Harrison had arranged. The Chechens decided that it, and any of the smaller vehicles, would make an adequate prize and continued their approach.

There were less than twenty Chechens left, but they still had two RPG launchers with a couple of rockets each. The first rocket was high, and passed over the heads of the assembled soldiers. While they were looking at the impact on the far side of the runway, the second rocket detonated on the front end of a Hummer, destroying the vehicle and bowling over a half a dozen Americans, wounding some seriously. Before they could react, the Chechens poured AK fire into them, driving the rest to ground. An alert machine gunner, standing off to the side of the group, was able to react by dropping into an exposed firing position on the open runway and lay down some suppressing fire. He was able to drive the attackers to cover before he was targeted by another RPG round. He escaped serious injury, thanks to his body armor and helmet, but the gun was wrecked. His quick response did give the remainder of the reaction team time to shake off their surprise and start returning fire.

The rag heads were maneuvering to flank them. They were extending their lines and closing in on both ends of the American position. Some of the wounded had recovered their weapons and joined the firing line. The chow truck had pulled into the center of the position just as the firing started. Sergeant Moura, the mess sergeant, was stepping down from the cab when he was hit by a piece of shrapnel in the shoulder. The cook he had brought with him hadn't bothered to bring a weapon. Instead of trying to reach Moura, he hunkered down behind a tire on his side of the truck.

More firing broke out from the south. Lieutenant Stanley was trying to shift fire to cover it, when she heard Sharps voice calling for anyone at the strip. She located the radio under the body of a wounded soldier and answered. Sharp had dismounted his squad at a low spot in the road and had made a rapid foot approach. His men were deployed on the rear of the Chechens, and it was their firing she was hearing. Sharp gave her directions to shift her firing to his left flank, away from the reinforcements. Stanley acknowledged, then high crawled around her position passing the word.

The volume of fire from outside his little perimeter continued to grow. The Chechens, caught off guard, again, responded by breaking off and attempting to flee to the east. Sharp called out orders to keep firing at the retreating figures. He was not going to deal with these people a third time today. When he couldn't see any more targets running away, he gave the order to cease-fire. He advanced his line to the position on the airstrip and started to reorganize. Harrison joined him, and called in his vehicle. In spite of the attack and the amount of fire they had taken, they were lucky. There had been no fatalities, and, even luckier, none of the medics had been hit. They were quick in responding to treat the wounded. Harrison got down to the task of detailing men to fan out in the grass, in fire teams, to police up any weapons and documents they could find.

"What about wounded, Top?"

"Secure any weapons first. We'll get to them after we make sure nobody else is going to shoot at us. And watch for booby traps. Some of those assholes might still be looking for a free ticket to martyrdom." He got on his radio and gave the all clear for the ambulance, which had followed him back with the collected wounded, to pull into the area. He could protect it better here than on the road. It pulled in and the medics began unloading the wounded for more treatment. Carson's uniform was stained with the blood of the casualties, as were most of the medics. She gave some quick directions and turned to work on the new casualties. Fortunately, they looked worse than they were. Once she had them stripped out of their body armor, she could see most of the wounds were confined to the arms and legs, and none of them appeared life threatening.

There was more traffic coming down the road. The lead vehicle pulled up to him and a Moldovan officer in combat garb got out. The man could speak English. He was the commander of the Moldovan troops sent to reinforce the area. Harrison gave him a quick briefing. They exchanged salutes, and the Moldovan detailed one of his platoons to drop off and secure the area and police up the Chechen dead. "You understand" the Moldovan officer said, "it would be better if you and your men were not involved in the clean up." Harrison knew what he meant. There would be no prisoners.

The Moldovan also told him that there would be another group trailing him. He had intercepted the Russians further up the road. His men had disarmed them and taken away their vehicles. They would be walking back to the airstrip, under guard. The Russians were sending a plane to collect them. "My men will deal with the plane. The Russians will not be allowed to leave this area. It would also be best if you gathered up your men and returned to your barracks."

"And your wounded?" Harrison asked.

The Moldovan walked to the treatment area. He spoke to several of the wounded men, then called back to his driver. There was a brief conversation, then he asked to speak to the doctor. He thanked her for the care she was giving his soldiers. He indicated a marked ambulance that was passing his stopped vehicles. He had a medical team that would be joining her to assist. He hesitated, thinking, then turned and returned to his vehicle. The convoy pushed on.

Grant was collecting his troops from around the Russian compound. Their blood was up and they were eager for some more action, but Grant didn't want his soldiers involved with any mopping up or dealing with any surviving Chechens. That was going to be solely a Moldovan responsibility. Their blood was up too. The massacre of the Russian convoy had also caused hundreds of Moldovan civilian and military casualties. The Moldovans, who had previously held themselves aloof from terrorist problems in the world, had been drawn into it kicking and screaming. It would be best to let them sort things out with the Chechens and the Russians.

He was having his squad leaders do another head count. Once Sharp had taken off to reinforce the airstrip, there had been some mixing of the squads. There was a lot of radio traffic sorting out who was where, but Grant wasn't going to let up until every man had been physically located.

The Moldovans were efficient. They had swept the compound, the fields and the heights and gathered up every piece of equipment and body they could find. Even the damaged gear, like the Chechen trucks and mortars that had been destroyed were being dragged down and lined up on the parade ground of the Russian compound. To the extent they could, the dead were separated by nationality. When there was doubt, as in the bodies that had been mangled by the explosion, they were placed apart. If the Russians wanted them, they could send a grave registration team to identify them later.

He had his men formed up once they headcount was done. The First Sergeant had sent trucks to pick them up. Colonel Schaeffer and Major Morgan had come with them. Schaeffer had worked himself up over being kept in the dark about the American involvement. He had been reassuring Centcom all night that the situation was not affecting the Americans, and all the shooting was taking place miles away. It was only when the commo sergeant had brought a fresh set of batteries for the radio he had been monitoring that he learned the truth. A

Specialist had brought his hand held unit with him, and didn't turn it off, or even down, like he was supposed to around the operations section. Schaeffer heard the calls for help at the airfield when the Chechens attacked. That pretty much destroyed the myth of American neutrality. The report that there had been casualties, fortunately none serious, did nothing to calm him down. He had been trying to get out to the site ever since, but the Moldovan reinforcements had arrived, and their commander had locked down the compound and wouldn't let any more Americans leave until he was satisfied the affair had been settled.

The Moldovan commander intercepted Schaeffer before he could get to Grant. Schaeffer had been working over Morgan for a couple of hours, but he knew that Grant had been the architect of anything that had happened in the field. He was going to place the Sergeant Major under arrest and have him flown out of the country in irons to face charges that would put him away for the rest of his life. Schaeffer had been savoring the thought when the Moldovan asked for a moment of his time. Diplomatically, Schaeffer had no choice but to agree.

He was barely listening as the Moldovan expressed his concern for the American wounded, his mind on Grant, standing just yards away with Morgan. It took him a few moments to realize that the Moldovan officer was thanking him for Grant's participation, and describing how, without American help, the situation could have been radically different. Schaeffer cut off the Moldovan. "He's disobeyed orders and broken the law. I plan to see him arrested and thrown out of the Army for what he's done!"

The Commander took a step back. He asked Schaeffer to repeat what he had just said. Schaeffer did. The Moldovan shook his head. "I don't think you understand. I plan to see all your men, especially your

Sergeant Major, are decorated by my government. They were responsible for helping to stop a chemical nightmare of global proportions. I'm afraid I can't permit you to interfere with that."

Schaeffer took a step back and glared. The Moldovan continued. "If this is going to be a problem, I'll settle it right now." He looked around and saw Kosavich, who had joined Grant and Morgan and seemed to be sharing a funny story with them. He motioned to Kosavich, who excused himself and joined his commander. They had a brief conversation. The two Moldovans exchanged salutes and the commander walked away. Schaeffer started to leave too, but Kosavich grabbed his arm. "I'm afraid, Colonel Schaeffer, that we have already spoken to your government. There was an agreement put into effect at 1700 hours local time last night, authorizing your soldiers to provide, and I quote, 'whatever assistance is considered necessary' in helping us with our little problem."

"I was on the horn with Centcom all last night. They didn't tell me anything about this!"

Kosavich smiled. "Centcom? No, we didn't bother with them. There was no time. We did, however, find your Consulate and State Department very accommodating." He signaled more soldiers who were standing by. "Your Military Attaché has requested your presence so that he can brief you on the situation. These men will take you to him now."

Morgan and Grant watched as the two soldiers each took an arm and took the protesting Schaeffer to a waiting vehicle. Kosavich joined them. "That should take care of the problems with your government."

Morgan wasn't so sure. "All that's going to do is piss off Schaeffer and anyone he gets to talk to. It might make matters worse."

"I doubt it. As we speak, a note is being presented to your Consulate. It seems Colonel Schaeffer attempted to interfere with operations here. When my commander declined his advice, he became verbally aggressive and insulted my commander, his soldiers and my country. He has been declared *persona non grata* and is being directed to leave the country immediately. It will take him a long time to straighten this out."

"Major, do you really think that story is going to work? Seems like a lot of people will have to be involved to keep things straight." Morgan said.

"That's where you confuse your system with ours. Where you come from, everybody and anybody can ask questions and poke around in places they don't belong. It's not like that here. The official story is the only one that will be discussed. If there are more questions, they will be directed to people who are authorized to answer."

"That won't work in the U.S." Grant added.

"Please remember, we are less than a generation away from being under the communist system. Old habits die hard. Perhaps in a few years a fantasy such as we are going to spin won't be possible. But for now, if I may quote something I heard in an American movie, that's my story and I'm sticking to it. Since only you two know the entire story on the American side, I hope you two can remember it."

With that last piece of advice Kosavich said goodbye and waved for his vehicle. It bounced across the grass, and Kosavich hauled himself into it. He gave a salute, and he was gone. Grant looked at Morgan. "I didn't have any contact with Schaeffer last night after around 1800. Anything that he may or may not have heard all came from you. If this all heads south, the monkey'll be on your back."

370

"Don't worry about me, Sergeant Major. Remember that I'm the guy who had to get juiced up last night just to function. There's a lot I don't recall."

Grant looked at him with one eyebrow lifted. "Don't worry, Sergeant Major. That's my story and I'm sticking to it."

# CHAPTER 15

It had been three weeks since the action around the Russian compound and the airstrip. All the vehicles and equipment had been loaded. There had been a sudden rush to get the Americans out of the country, so two trains had been provided. They would leave an hour apart to avoid any rail tie-ups. Security, all of it provided by the Moldovan army, was tight. The last official act in the country would be the ceremony at which the Moldovan government presented its awards to the Americans who had been involved in the fighting. They would make nice souvenirs for the soldiers, but until they had been approved by their own government, they couldn't be displayed on their uniforms. It was a pity. The Moldovans had some colorful decorations.

Morgan was already gone. Centcom had recalled him as soon as they figured out they had been snookered by the Moldovans and the State Department. General Ramirez was especially eager to get him back so that he could be 'debriefed' properly. Major Carson, by necessity brought into the part of the cover story about him being too medicated to remember everything, doctored his medical records to make it appear that he had been heavily medicated and was only functioning against medical advice. The medical records would be her cover if there was a discrepancy between her and Morgan. He was, after all, too doped up to know what was going on.

In the meanwhile, Captain Fisher had been named acting Commander. He had been kept in the dark about most of what was going on, so Centcom, NATO and USAREUR (US Army Europe) pretty much left him alone after the first round of debriefings. That made him very happy.

Sharp and Price had been subject to some scrutiny, but in spite of Ramirez' insistence, the debriefers had difficulty believing that two retreads, one functioning as a platoon sergeant and the other the subordinate of Fisher and Winder, could have any knowledge of the planning beyond following orders.

Harrison had been largely ignored. He played the part of the First Sergeant, deferring to his Company Commander on any questions outside his normal realm. Since Lieutenant Fuller, the Company Commander, knew absolutely nothing beyond what he had heard as rumors, that line of investigation was quickly dropped.

That left Grant. He had stuck to the basic story during the first several sessions. His Medal of Honor kept the debriefers from accusing him of lying, but they were determined to find a chink in his armor. That was when their investigation made its fatal flaw. They requested an interview with the Moldovan military. It was granted, in the person of Internal Security Service Lieutenant Colonel (he had been promoted in the aftermath) Yvegniy Kosavich. The debriefers never stood a chance.

Kosavich began the interview, actually, took control of the interview, and never paused. He described the events leading up to the last battle, sticking to the prepared story of his government, and omitting his role as a Senior Sergeant. When he finished his version, he was asked about the role of Sergeant Major Grant in the planning.

"What? A sergeant involved in the planning? Is your opinion of the Moldovan Army so low that you think we need to rely on your enlisted men for assistance?"

"We mean no disrespect, Colonel Kosavich. We were led to believe his role was greater than had been stated."

Kosavich continued with his show of indignation. "I did not even want your soldiers involved! This was purely an internal matter. My government requested your support only to provide a fall back position. It was never intended for them to get so involved. They were in the wrong place as far as I'm concerned, and the arrival of the relief battalion probably saved them from worse harm."

"Then it's your claim that he was not involved beyond providing ground support?"

"My claim? Why do you insist on insulting my government and me? I have given you the facts. This interview is concluded!"

The investigation ended without Grant being subject to a follow-up interview.


Grant was walking down the line of railcars with Captain Bonneville. Their relationship had settled in to a routine. It wasn't quite what it had been in the past, but Grant couldn't figure out what the difference was. It was almost as though she was expecting something else from him. Still, he figured he shouldn't complain. Major Carson was still in the picture. He couldn't figure her out either. After the battle of the airstrip she had walked in on him and Bonneville in *flagrante delecto*. She had smiled and excused herself. Bonneville had been all flustered at being caught like that. She grabbed her clothes and dressed quickly, and fled the room. Carson had waited a few minutes to be sure she was gone, then she came in and took Bonneville's place. There were no recriminations, no accusations. Her only comment had been "Just remember, I'm always available." He didn't know why, but he decided it was probably for the best if he didn't try to figure it out.

On the train, the senior officers, what was left of them, would have private compartments in a separate car. Bonneville planned to use that to her advantage during the time it took to return to Germany. After that, she didn't know. The 289th still had months to go on their activation, and they were probably going to finally get to Iraq, as originally planned. For now, she would just enjoy whatever time she could spend with Grant. And when he was gone, there was always Gordon.

They came across Price and Sharp, doing their own inspection of the loads. Price was checking chain binders on the heavy equipment, making certain nothing would work itself loose. Tumbling a bulldozer off a flat car in some out of the way little village was sure to generate some more bad press for them, and they already had plenty of that. Schaeffer may have been contained by the Moldovan government complaints about him, but there were enough politicians who were eager for anything that would discredit the military, and they embraced Schaeffer's' version of events. There would probably be some kind of hearing again, only this time, Price didn't have a CD of one of them taking a bribe. It was too bad Dillinghouse was dead. That moron could have been leveraged.

Grant and Bonneville joined them. They exchanged some small talk, and then Sharp wanted to know if there was any news on their next destination. "I'm getting sick of this small time shit. I signed on to go to Iraq."

Bonneville could only answer no. If there were any plans made for the 289th, the Army was keeping them quiet, and for good reason. Muslim sentiments were a bit hot over so many Chechens finding Martyrdom with the Americans so close. The massacre of the Russians, the death of the civilians around the convoy site, the invasion of a sovereign nation, or the attempt to seize chemical weapons didn't seem to bother them one little bit. All they were concerned about was some rag-headed jihadists getting to claim their virgins. Logic and rational thinking did not seem to be part of their mantra.

Price jumped down from the car he was checking. "Captain, I don't care where we go next. People don't seem to like us wherever we go. How about someplace where I know I won't be liked, so it won't come as a shock when they start shooting at my ass?"

"Pricey, they wouldn't like you in New Mexico!"

"Maybe so, but at least the beer will be cold."

"They'd find a reason not to let you have any."

There was a whistle blowing towards the front of this train. Grant checked his watch. It was time for the formation Harrison was going to hold to give the movement instructions. He could see the soldiers forming up by the loading platform. The remaining battalion staff was on one side, the company on the other, facing inward.

"Looks like it's time to go," Grant said to everyone and no one in particular. He looked past the formation, out into the valley. "Yeah," he repeated, "it's time to go."

Price and Sharp looked at him. Price was the first to speak. "I guess it's time to see how the rest of the Army lives again."

"I've seen it, Pricey," Sharp answered. "It don't get better than this."

# On The Mexican Border

"Hey, Matt! There's that Mexican again."

"What's he doing now?" Matt asked.

"You better look at this. I think he's carrying a rifle!"

The Sergeant rolled out of his seat and tossed his magazine on a dash. They had been in this location long enough to know there wasn't much going on, and this Mexican had captured their interest. It was almost as if he was trying to attract attention to himself. The senior agent leaned over the hood and picked up another pair of field glasses. There was nothing to be seen, and asked his partner where he had seen the Mexican.

"He was just a couple of yards over the border, Matt. I lost track of him when I called you."

Matt scanned the area one more time. There was still nothing to be seen. He turned to his partner just as a shot rang out. The other agent's head snapped back and he sprawled backwards on to the hood.. What was happening didn't register with the Senior agent at first. He stared blankly at the figure on the hood in front of him, watching the dark stain spread out from under the head, running down the front of the engine compartment. Suddenly, what was happening dawned on him. He turned to look back out at the border again.

He had the brief image of a flash in the distance. Then everything went dark.